INDISCRETION

Also by Jude Morgan and available from Review

THE KING'S TOUCH
PASSION

INDISCRETION

Jude Morgan

review

First published in 2005 by Review
An imprint of HEADLINE BOOK PUBLISHING

10 9 8 7 6 5 4 3 2 1

Cataloguing in Publication Data is available from the British Library

ISBN 0 7553 0764 X (hardback)
ISBN 0 7553 2643 1 (trade paperback)

Typeset in Bembo by Palimpsest Book Production Limited,
Polmont, Stirlingshire

Printed and bound in Great Britain by
Clays Ltd, St Ives plc

Headline's policy is to use papers that are natural, renewable and recyclable products and made from wood grown in sustainable forests. The logging and manufacturing processes are expected to conform to the environmental regulations of the country of origin.

HEADLINE BOOK PUBLISHING
A division of Hodder Headline
338 Euston Road
London NW1 3BH

www.reviewbooks.co.uk
www.hodderheadline.com

For Steve Webb

Chapter I

The well-travelled trunks stood on the dusty floorboards of their new lodgings. The porter was grumbling away down the stairs with his unsatisfying sixpence. Now it was Caroline's familiar task to make their accommodation as comfortable as possible, whilst soothing her father's mind, made gloomy and fretful by the necessity of the removal.

He had liked living where they were before. But their landlord had not liked them. The man had adopted an attitude towards rent arrears that Captain Fortune, sorrowfully, could only call irrational.

Caroline was so accustomed to this situation, and to making the best of it, that at first she did not notice something more than usually depressed in her father's demeanour. She busied herself with the unpacking, and with making such tactful improvements to the furnished rooms as could be managed. She covered the holes in the sofa's upholstery with cushions. She threw a cloth across the stained and scratched table. With artful swags and bunches she made the curtains look as if they actually fitted the windows. Meanwhile she kept up a cheerful commentary on the conveniences of their new home – one that, however, taxed her considerable powers of invention to the utmost. For these were the shabbiest lodgings yet, and her own spirits were more cast down than she cared to show.

Still, she was unprepared for the lingering groan that her father gave, just as she was hanging her mother's miniature portrait above the parlour mantelshelf; and for his booming cry of: 'It is all over, Caro – the die is cast – our revels now are ended – we are ruined!'

Caroline turned to find that he had sunk into a chair, and with another groan had buried his face in his hands. 'Come, Papa, don't take on so. It's not so very bad,' she urged, putting an arm about his shaking shoulders. 'Perhaps we aren't as pleasantly situated as we were at Frith Street, but we might do worse. Now let me mix you a glass of hock-and-soda-water. It's not like you to be long in the dismals, and I suspicion you may have drunk bad port-wine last night – at the Cocoa-Tree, was it? You know that always—'

'We might do worse, indeed,' her father said hollowly, through his hands. 'And I fear we will. Oh, yes. The debtors' prison, Caro – that will be next for me.'

'Oh, nonsense,' said Caroline, who had heard this before; but as her father still groaned, and would not look at her, she was constrained to add: 'It *is* nonsense – isn't it, Papa?'

'You would be better off, my dear, if I dropped myself in the river directly.'

'No, I wouldn't. For one, I would be no better off materially, because you've nothing to leave me. And more than that, I should be horribly grieved and miss you sorely. So no more watery talk, I beg you.' Caroline went to the side-table on which stood their small hoard of glassware and made him a drink, taking a little genteel tipple for herself. When she turned back to her father, he was regarding her with tragic, bleary, agelessly blue eyes.

'Oh,' she said; and, an octave lower: 'Oh.'

'I had hoped,' Captain Fortune said, reaching out for her hand, 'to be giving you news of a very different kind at this time, my dear – news of a wonderful turn-about in our fortunes. I had it all planned – a turtle dinner from the King's Head, or supper at Grillon's – and you were to have a new gown for it, of course, my love, made by a modiste of the very first stare; and then we were to talk about what manner of carriage to set up, whether a curricle or barouche – for our Town residence only, naturally – for myself I have a fancy for a rather smart little high-perch phaeton I saw at the coachmaker's in Long Acre, just being varnished—'

'Well, but, Papa, that's the different news,' Caroline interrupted him, gently yet firmly, 'the news you can't give me. The real news, I fear, is very bad, is it not?'

'I dare say,' the Captain said, with a disgruntled look, as if it were rather churlish of her not to want to hear about the carriage they couldn't have. 'Yes. It could hardly be worse, indeed. But it was *meant* to be good, my dear, truly it was! I very nearly, you know, pulled off the most remarkable stroke! And instead we are – we are most damnably high and dry, Caro. In short, we have no money.'

'We never do. But this, I collect, is a different sort of having-no-money.' She sat down by him. 'Be frank with me, Papa.'

The Captain drained his glass. 'It's all gone,' he said simply, as if referring to the wine. 'You recall that run of luck I had just lately, at Brooks's? And how I resolved I wouldn't let the money slip through my fingers this time, but set it to work? Well, so I did. Now, I considered at first paying off some of my creditors; but on reflection that seemed a stupid idea.'

'Did it?' said Caroline, feeling her face fall.

'Aye, aye – you may stop the dog's mouth, but the teeth are still there,' her father said, with grand obscurity. 'What was needed, I saw, was to put our finances on an entirely new footing. You'll agree, my dear, that there can positively be nothing worse than this eternal *getting by*.'

Caroline could think of something worse; and she was afraid it was coming. But she held her peace.

'So, I took advice. And not from Bennett – oh, I know the fellow has handled my affairs well enough in his time. But he is still a cautious pettifogging old lawyer after all. No, my informant was a smart young fellow I ran into at Tattersall's. Now everyone knew him for a lodger in Queer Street, on account of being disappointed in his expectations of a rich uncle, who on his deathbed took against him and left his fortune to the Society for the Suppression of Vice. He had been living high, and was generally expected to crash before the season was out. And instead there was the young sprig with diamonds in his tiepin, laying out a mint on new bloodstock! What was his secret? One word. Speculation.'

Caroline made a creditable try at looking delighted, but plainly it did not come off.

'My dear, you frown. You need not. Why, half the mansions of Russell Square were built from speculation on the Exchange. And what one must remember is there's no arcane mystery about it, even though the cits like to pretend so. Five per cents, and Consols, and what-naught. As my young friend told me, any man of sense and spirit, especially if he knows what it is to chance all at the dice-box, can turn his hand to the Funds.' From being cheerfully informative, the Captain's tone took a sudden plunge into desolation. 'And curse my bones that I ever listened to him, because it has ruined us!'

With another groan, he hid his face in his hands again, and for some while could give only muffled and disjointed replies to Caroline's questions. The facts of the matter did not, however, require much elucidation. Her father, she soon gathered, had lost everything by speculating in the Funds: he had added to the number of his creditors, many of whom were at the end of their patience; and the rent even on this unprepossessing set of rooms in unfashionable Henrietta Street was paid only for a month, beyond which he saw no means of satisfying their new landlord.

Caroline sat for some moments mechanically patting her father's hand, and taking the news in. It would have been doing it too brown, as he would say, to call herself shocked. She was used to dwelling with her father on the shady margins of insolvency. But hitherto he had always found another well of credit to dip into; now came sudden realisation, like nasty breath on the face, that that old life was at an end. The ground on which she had stood, however insecurely, had crumbled away altogether.

An observer might not have guessed how shaken she was. But where Captain Fortune shouted aloud when he was happy, just as he wailed when brought low, his daughter was less prodigal with her feelings, or at least with the expression of them. This was not reserve: more the prudence of someone who keeps still in a wildly pitching boat. So Caroline maintained an appearance of soothing cheerfulness, while she wrestled inwardly with this new knowledge.

One conclusion she came to swiftly. If she had had no direct hand in the fall, she had surely been guilty of averting her eyes from the true facts of their situation. Well, no more of that.

'Papa, listen now,' she said, having mixed him the last of the hock-and-soda, lit the candles against the encroaching evening, and drawn up a seat by the sofa where her father had sunk prostrated, like a man literally crushed by circumstance. 'This is all most alarming and distressing, and it cuts me quite to see you so brought down. And believe me, I'm very far from making light of matters when I say this, but – is there not opportunity here also?'

'No!' her father intoned sepulchrally, his eyes closed; and then, opening them: 'Where?'

'Well, at the very least, in our being forced to sit down together and be honest, and look certain hard questions in the face. Which we have scarcely done, Papa – have we? Yet I can't pretend to have had no notion. And indeed it has set me to thinking of late.' She drew a deep breath and went on: 'Do you recollect I mentioned – a little while ago, when we had to leave the house before last – the idea of governessing?'

'I certainly do.' Her father rose slowly and dramatically to a sitting position. 'And *you* will recollect, Caro, how utterly damnable I found it. No, no. The river before that. Before that, my dear, the rivers of *hell*—'

'I don't imagine there are any – wouldn't they be cool and refreshing and defeat the purpose? Oh, there's the Styx, I suppose. But truly, I don't think we need to talk in these hellish terms. Not about something that is the lot of many a young woman without . . .'

'Ah.' He nodded in fierce gloomy encouragement. 'Go on. Out with it. Without *prospects*.'

'Well, there is no use in mincing words. And there – now it's out, and it's not so very terrible, is it? Consider. If I were to take a post as a governess, I would be provided for, and that burden would be lifted from you—'

'Burden?' cried Captain Fortune, with a woeful shake of his head. 'I must have been a wretched father indeed – worse even than I can suppose – if I have been complaining of you as a burden, my dear.'

'Oh, Papa – say responsibility, then. Suppose me placed with an agreeable family, or even a half-way agreeable one. I will be comfortably accommodated and secure, and I will have a stipend, and you will have the satisfaction of knowing—'

'Of knowing how I have failed you. To be sure,' said her father, breathing hard. 'You do well, my dear, to reproach me with it. Oh, but is it not so? Look at these rooms. A man can barely even make a show as a bachelor in such a place. Poor Marriner will be sleeping in what amounts to a boot-cupboard, when his loyalty has already been put to the severe test of living on board-wages. I smell damp in the hall. And that wallpaper is beyond anything.' He pointed a majestically disdainful finger. 'Indeed, it is my one request that you take a sample of that wallpaper, Caro, and paste it upon my gravestone when I am gone, as an emblem of my failure. Your promise, now!'

'Nonsense, Papa,' she murmured, between pain and laughter; but the Captain sprang up, flushed with self-punishing energy.

'This is not what I wanted for you,' he went on, ruffling his hair savagely. 'When I saw you growing up so pretty and accomplished – oh, yes,' he added, as she made a face, 'and accomplished – remember what that music master said of you? What was his name? Signor – Signor—'

'Higginbottom.'

'That's the man. And then your drawing – and the most elegant way of carrying yourself, just like your poor mother – well, I thought that when I brought you into society, you'd surely conquer. Conquer! It's not long since I ran into Stanton of my old regiment at Limmer's, and he said he'd seen you and me walking in Hyde Park, and demanded to know when that delicious daughter of mine – his words, my dear! – was going to make her début at Almack's. Heyo! I can think of nothing that would please me better. But without money and without connections . . . Even a season at Bath is beyond us now, Caro: do you know why? Because I have creditors there who would pounce on me the moment I crossed Pulteney Bridge. Now, Caro, admit it –' he hung his head with dogmatic gloom '– admit that I have failed you!'

'Well, but you don't want me to, Papa – you want me to say the opposite. And that I gladly do. I never did expect a début at Almack's, you know, and I never supposed we were well connected—'

'Ah! but there's the bitter kernel. The connections *are* there, or should be. In Devonshire my name stands as high as any, but my side have all died out. And then there's your poor mother's family, very comfortably situated. They could undoubtedly do something for you, if they *would*. But they're a damned hard-faced unforgiving set . . .' He sighed and looked perplexed: here was a genuine unhappiness that could not be dramatized. 'As for me, I live in a man's world, and there's precious little for you there.'

'Why, I've learnt how to play faro, and macao, and hazard, and billiards, and how to judge a good cravat, and how to make a bowl of rack-punch—'

'Hush, hush – you make me blush for shame. Not that you don't play a devilish hand at cards, and I fancy you'd have the coat off the back of the hardest gamester at Brooks's . . . but that is not as it should be, Caro, as well you know. I speak of society. When did you last enjoy a genteel social evening, in mixed company?'

'Well . . . when I went to stay with Miss Willis last year.' Caroline spoke reluctantly, for she did not want to confirm his pessimistic opinion; but neither did she wish, for her own sake, to revive that happy memory.

Miss Willis was a friend made at her last school, who had had Caroline to her family home in Hertfordshire for the vacation. There, Caroline had enjoyed all the commonplace amusements of gossip, of shopping, of charades and dinners and picnics, from which her father's raffish life had debarred her. They were not great things, of course – but she would willingly have sampled more of them. And Miss Willis had not been a great friend – but she would rather have drifted naturally away from her than had their association severed. For Caroline had made an abrupt and premature departure from that Seminary for Young Ladies in Chelsea. The proprietress had fetched her early one morning to her private parlour, and told her she must pack her things: six months' fees were owing, and her father's bankers would not honour his last draft. So she had left the school secretly, with none of the customary farewells and exchanges, and had been obliged to borrow five shillings from the kindly, brandy-tippling French-mistress to get her and her luggage by hackney to her father's then lodging in Frith Street.

'Ah, yes, Hertfordshire,' her father said sorrowfully. 'And there, I dare swear, the young men were mightily impressed with you.'

'Well, there was Miss Willis's brother. But he was only sixteen and quite the puppy. The fact of my being called Miss Fortune he could not get over. He even kept going out of his way to stumble and have accidents so he could say it was a *misfortune*. In the end he quite hurt himself—'

'Caroline, Caroline. You know well what I mean. This – this is where I feel most the lack of a mother's care. For she would know how to put you in the way of a good marriage.'

'Put me in the way? You make it sound like a speeding coach that would flatten me!'

'Well, so it is, in some sort. A happy marriage – and by that I mean a love-match – is something overwhelming, and overpowering. It is the end of choices, but happily, most happily so . . .' His eyes grew misty. 'That was how it was with your poor mother and me, at any rate.'

'But, Papa, you spoke of a *good* marriage. And that is something entirely different, is it not? No, don't pout. You know what I mean. A girl should set her sights on a man who has money; or if not, who can expect to come into money; or if not, who has moneyed connections. That's the order, is it not? But you know I'm not sure I want to marry on those terms. Or indeed marry at all. So you must not reproach yourself because I am not forever being crushed by eligible young men at carpet-dances. That I don't hanker for in the least.'

'Hm. But not to marry? That's as much to say, to grow old alone,

Caro. Think of that. For you know the rest of me will catch up with this damned leg soon enough.'

'Isn't it better to be alone than tied to a man you don't love or care for?'

'I don't know. I have had love, and so for me everything is coloured by that. But I know that there are many women and men grown old and solitary who spoke as you do when they were young, and now regret it.'

'To be sure; but is it a sufficient reason to do something, that if you do not, the opportunity may be lost? There are some workmen getting ready to demolish an old brick wall across the street – but I'm not about to run out there and beat my head against it, just because soon I shall not be able to.'

'Well, well,' he said, smiling sadly, 'I would not have you do aught against your will. But, Caro, don't, I pray you, be caught in narrow notions of love and marriage. Your mother and I made a love-match, yes. But it would also have been a good, sound, prosperous match, if her family had not been so damnably determined to disoblige us. Love and prudence *can* go together. And that, you know, is what I see for you. No old-maidish solitude, no, no: a good man who loves you, and a comfortable situation – the sort of soil that makes love flourish, and not grow crooked. That's what I see for you, my darling, and always have!'

Her father beamed at her: he had cheered himself up considerably; and he appeared as proud of this golden vision of her future as if he had ever done anything to secure or foster it for her. But this was not untypical of Captain Fortune, who in his cups would often talk in vivid detail of what he would do when he was rich, and how much he would bestow and where; to the extent that Caroline even found herself once profusely thanking him for a notional fifty thousand, while he wagged his head in bashful modesty. But then she supposed he was not the first to establish himself in the character of a generous man on such easy terms.

It was a relief, at any rate, to find him no longer desponding. Indeed only someone less used to the Captain's quixotic ways would have been surprised to see him now fairly bouncing off the sofa, and calling lustily to his manservant, Marriner, to send out for a bottle of brandy. Marriner, a bald long-faced dry Yorkshireman, only asked where they might apply, for they had no credit left at any place he knew of; but the Captain breezily told him to use his imagination. 'That's the blessing of shifting to new quarters, man – we're not known hereabouts!'

'Yet,' grunted Marriner, stumping out.

'Well, Papa,' Caroline said, taking advantage of his altered mood to press her point, 'the governess notion – it is not so very terrible, is it? And there is nothing against my beginning to make enquiries to that end, at least?'

'Nothing,' Captain Fortune said, 'except this: it will not be needed. Because I have an idea.' He began to pace the narrow width of their parlour, his lame leg thumping on the floor. 'It has come to me in a flash – an inspiration – I don't know from where – unless it was talking of the old days. But I cannot conceive why I did not think of it before. Indeed it is so simple it is absurd. The remedy has lain beneath my hand the whole time. My dear, you recollect when we were thrown – that is, asked to leave our old lodging t'other day? And I gave that impudent clod of a landlord a thorough set-down in the street, where he had so unwarrantably placed my possessions, with the result that an urchin made off with my boot-trees? Did you observe? Did you not notice how people congregated as I ripped him up, and gaped and cheered?'

'Yes, Papa,' she answered, not without constraint. 'I noticed.'

'Then you will smoke my meaning at once, Caro – you have me, I am sure – and will concur that there was never a better notion. I *have* a resource. The man who was unanimously declared the finest Romeo ever seen in Bristol – to say nothing of Gloucester – need not fear pecuniary embarrassment. I shall tread the boards again!'

He struck a flourishing pose, and seemed to invite her applause. There was no denying that, at nearly fifty, her father remained a handsome man. He was upright and broad-shouldered: his complexion had survived soldiering and port-wine remarkably well;

and he had eyes of a singularly bright, fresh, beguiling blue, which he often reminded Caroline she had inherited from him, as complacently as if they were ten thousand pounds. And yet, a man of nearly fifty he remained; and as for treading the boards, the phrase threw into relief the principal objection, which still she hesitated to name.

'You doubt me,' he said.

'No, no,' she said hastily. 'I was only wondering, Papa – it has been so long, and perhaps you have grown rusty—'

'Ah, not I. Before Talavera, you know, I gave my brother officers recitations from *Henry V*, taking all the parts. One fellow said after that he couldn't wait to throw himself at the French guns. To be sure, there is the question of gentility. I believe it may be got over. For my part, I see myself as a devoted amateur of the thespian art, who will accept, with good grace, a fee.' He came and sat by her. 'You won't find your sense of decorum offended, I hope, Caro, seeing me perform in the theatre? I'd drop myself in the river before that.'

'Of course not, Papa.' She looked helplessly at him. It was the regrettable consequence of being the more realistic of a pair, that one of you must always be appearing a carper and a spoiler. It was not a character particularly wanted by Caroline, who had a strong fanciful vein of her own. Indeed if she resented anything about her father, it was that he was so reliably silly it left her no scope. So with hesitation she poured her trickling of cold water, saying: 'But if it does not answer – if by some chance this excellent idea does not bear the fruit you hope – then we must consider something else. And that means me doing something for my living, like becoming a governess. Which is a prospect I truly do not fear, Papa. Is that agreed?'

Her father gave the eager, smiling, attentive nod that meant he was not listening at all; then limped over to the little store of books she had lovingly arranged on the alcove-shelf, took down his Shakespeare and began excitedly thumbing. 'The fruit, my dear,' he said, with an expressive gesture, 'will be plump, and juicy, and delicious – trust me for that! By heaven, I really cannot conceive why I did not think of this idea before!'

The answer to that was, that it was not a very good idea. But Captain Fortune began the pursuing of it the next day, with all the energy and address at his command.

For it was no lack of these qualities that had brought him to the condition of a near-bankrupt. When he had an end in view, he fairly drove himself at it; but his judgement as to whether an end was attainable, or worthwhile, was less to be relied upon.

Caroline's father had come from a genteel Devon family, but had alienated their affections by a flamboyantly rebellious youth, which had culminated in his engaging as a strolling actor with a touring theatre company. This was where eccentricity had descended into disgrace. Becoming a tapster at a gin-shop could hardly have made a worse impression on the sensibilities of his elderly and conventional parents. The names of Garrick and Sheridan might have rendered the stage illustrious: they could not make it respectable; and James Fortune's parents took their hostility to the grave. At last he had recovered his credit with one of his surviving relatives, an uncle, by joining the militia, then embodied against the new-risen threat of Bonaparte. The uncle, an old military man, had smiled upon his errant nephew, and settled on him sufficient money to buy a commission in the regulars. It was in a line regiment only; but the young James Fortune had a dash and brilliancy that would have suited the Prince of Wales' Own Hussars – and a spending habit to go with it. It was thus, as a handsome young officer, that he had met Caroline's mother.

She was then a very young woman of gentle upbringing and untried character, making her first sortie from Huntingdonshire, where her father had a good property, to London. No amount of parental protectiveness could overcome the fact that she was very ready to be dazzled; and much worse might have befallen her than the passion for young Captain Fortune, which swiftly led to their elopement and marriage by the Gretna blacksmith. For he loved his bride as steadily as his volatile temperament would allow: nor could he be fairly said to want her for her money, for that was at the disposal of her outraged parents, who withheld it, and still he stood by her.

But she was not cut out to be a soldier's wife, at least not one of those who followed the drum. Her health and spirits were alike unequal to the hardships of campaign, and when Captain Fortune went with the army to the Peninsula she remained in England, living upon very little, and perpetually in fear that her grass-widowhood might at any moment become the real thing. She was by now the mother of the infant Caroline, but her parents remained unreconciled to her marriage: the estrangement was lasting and complete. The portion she might have expected was bestowed on her more dutiful sister: and only the fondness, or senility as some called it, of a grandparent secured her a legacy at last, and soothed her anxiety as to the future of herself and her child, should the worst happen.

The worst did not happen – apparently so, at any rate. Captain Fortune returned from the Peninsula alive, though wounded, his right knee shot away so that he limped, as he said, like Jago's donkey. The restored family were not rich, but with the price of his commission, and Mrs Fortune's inheritance, they had a competence. But the Captain, with his expansive schemes and expensive tastes, soon brought them into difficulty. Caroline's mother, never strong, had died when her daughter was twelve, in the unhappy knowledge that there was not much money left, nor much prospect of any more.

Captain Fortune's elastic temper recognized neither of these things, just as he recovered swiftly from the loss of the woman he genuinely loved. Reality was not to him oppressive: it was a garment he could shrug on and off at will. Caroline spent her youth in a succession of London boarding-schools, whilst her father kept up a semi-regimental life of clubs, gaming, and running up debts, in between infallible plans for making money. He bought and sold horses, of which he was a tolerable judge, for friends and acquaintances: he invested in commercial enterprises, of which he was no judge at all. And except when talking of putting an end to his existence, he remained cheerful.

To some, this was an affront. The Captain had been a shockingly bad father to his daughter: everyone must think so. Her education had been fitful, her mode of life unsettled: she had no large circle of acquaintance, and her wardrobe was sadly inadequate to set off such beauty as nature had blessed her with; and from long mixing in male company, and that not of the best, she knew far too many curse-words. This at any rate was the opinion of such respectable people as came into their orbit – Miss Willis's mother, for one, had voiced these very sentiments, not quite out of Caroline's earshot. And now her father had expressed them himself, in the extremity of gloom.

But Caroline was less severe. She could regret her father's delinquencies without hate or blame. Besides, life with him had been an interesting experience, and that counted for much. In her father the colourful worlds of the soldier, the dandy, and the artist met, and she had glimpsed all of them. As a girl she had sat on the weighing-scales at Gentleman Jackson's boxing-rooms in Bond Street watching the young bloods sparring with the great pugilist. At school she had shocked her teachers by singing an Italian song learnt from the lips of a buxom opera-singer with whom she had shared a backstage supper, and which was not, as she had supposed, about anything so innocent as nightingales. In her nearly twenty years she had been nourished by a very rich diet of experience compared with the bland fare served to most young ladies; and excepting the loss of her mother, she had known no enduring pain.

Thus there was no bitterness in her, even as she regarded her father with the last veil of illusion stripped, saw him as incorrigible, and realized she must make her own way. As for his scheme of relaunching himself as an actor, she gave it a tolerant attention, listening to him read Romeo, and even accompanying him to auditions, where she took charge of the flannel with which he protected his throat and the scented gargle with which he lubricated it. 'The voice,' he instructed her, 'the voice is all.' Their new lodgings were certainly well situated for his purpose, being so close to Covent Garden and Drury Lane, and much of the neighbourhood inhabited by theatre people. But the time of year was unpropitious. It was June, when the season ended, the town emptied, and the Patent Theatres closed until September. The Haymarket stayed open for the summer, but the manager there – as Captain Fortune was informed with a firmness he judged excessive – had already contracted all the performers he could require. It was in the touring companies, preparing to sally to the provinces, the spas and the seaside watering-places, that the Captain's best hope lay; and it was to their auditions, in fair-tents and inn club-rooms, that he repaired, with the supplementary hope that he would find people who remembered him from his first career thirty years ago.

Here was a sorrow, however. Those members of the theatrical fraternity who would have helped him had all died. Unaccountably, the only survivors were those who had always been dead set against him.

'I was popular, you see, my dear. I was a great draw, in my day. The votaries of Thespis, alas, have always been sadly prone to envy and jealousy. And they have long memories. They will never forgive you a triumph!'

But even Captain Fortune's sanguine temper was unequal to the series of rebuffs he met with at these auditions. Nor could the voice, which was undeniably resonant, efface the impression made as soon as he stepped on to the makeshift stage.

'Can't you disguise that limp?' the manager called out, at the last audition.

'What do you suggest, sir?' answered her father with breezy exasperation. 'I put a wig and moustache on it?'

'Next!'

Caroline was diverted, but she felt his humiliation – more, perhaps, than he did. And it spurred her on to making enquiries on her own account for a governess's position.

She had thought the matter round, and concluded that, town-bred as she was, a post in London would best suit her: that she would prefer older to younger children; and that if there were a fascinating elder son with the looks and wit of Byron ready to fall in love with her, she would have no strenuous objection. In other words, she would take what she could get.

When her father was out of the way, she went to consult with her old nurse, a sensible woman and a valuable source of advice for a motherless girl. She was now settled at Marylebone as a poultry-keeper, Captain Fortune having sorrowfully dismissed her a few years since, when financial difficulties made it an impossible extravagance to keep a permanent female servant. (Marriner, of course, was a necessity, the Captain being particular about his coats.) Directed by her to the Petty Register Office where prospective governesses and employers were matched, and counselled not to tell *too* many fibs about her accomplishments – so that was the end of the fluent Russian and clarinet – Caroline was excited about her new undertaking, and only a little knocked back by the Office's request for references.

This was problematic. Her father's circle of acquaintance, though it included a number of well-born swells and pinks of the *ton*, was more racy than respectable. The natural person was the proprietress of the Seminary in Chelsea, but the fact that that lady was among her father's creditors cast an unpromising shadow over any application. However, Caroline concluded that the sooner she was helped to a remunerated position, the more chance there was of her father's finances improving, and hence of the proprietress some day getting her money. Admittedly it was not a great chance even then. But she set herself at once to composing the most artful letter within her power, and had just despatched Marriner to the post-office with it when her father came home with news that changed everything.

She could not read his face at first. By now he had accepted that there was no opening for him in the companies based in London, and he had spoken of trying the provinces, or even Dublin. But he had not done anything about it: he had begun to look chop-fallen again, and Caroline suspected his thoughts of turning riverward. He had taken in the last couple of days to lingering about his old haunts, Tattersall's and Jackson's and the Burlington Arcade, as if in wistful farewell. When he came in that afternoon, breathing hard from negotiating the steep, narrow stairs, and with a pained, wondering look about his brow, she supposed at first that he was sunk back into melancholy reflections, and that she would soon be called upon to perform her usual office of cheering him up. But he surprised her by refusing any liquor, by disdaining a wish for any particular delicacy for dinner, and by not wailing or declaring the world a vale of ashes and clinker.

Instead he called her to sit down by him and, after studying her in the most dreamy and perplexing way for some minutes, said: 'Caro, how would you like to be a rich woman?'

Chapter II

Mrs Catling: such was the name of the person who was to be the agent of this spectacular change in Caroline's fortunes. 'Miss-is *Cat*-ling!' as the Captain impressively pronounced it, with such a mingling of respect, admiration, warmth, and sheer wonderment that Caroline felt almost shamed by her admission that she had never heard of her.

'Mrs Catling,' her father said, 'is a splendid woman. Mrs Catling is all that is estimable. There is not, I think, a more excellent woman to be found in London – in the whole kingdom. I do not base this judgement upon personal acquaintance,' he added, with a faintly superior look, as if that would be mere crudity. 'I have never met her. But she is very familiar to me nonetheless. Her late husband was colonel of my regiment. You've heard me talk of old Devil's-Eye Catling, perhaps? Magnificent fellow. Everyone was terrified of him. At Torres Vedras he would turn out of a morning and go hunting poisonous snakes with nothing but a soda-bottle. Fierce as a yard-goose. But there was one thing, and one thing only, that he was afraid of.'

'Mrs Catling?'

'Aye! "The commander-in-chief" he used to call her,' Captain Fortune said, with a reminiscent chuckle. 'They used to say Devil's-Eye Catling could stare down old Douro himself, but to his wife he always deferred. Well, he's been dead above a year now: the gout did what the Frenchies couldn't; and there's Mrs Catling a rich widow without any children, past sixty, quite alone. She lives mainly at Brighton, for the air, but she's been staying in London for the past month, seeing to some legal business. It was Stanton of Ours who told me this. I ran into him again, at Tattersall's. And it was he who very thoughtfully put the notion in my head.'

'What notion, Papa?' Rackety as he was, he had always remained faithful to the memory of her mother, and disdained any thought of marrying again; but perhaps his desperate straits had brought him to the point. 'Do you mean – do you mean Mrs Catling as a wife?'

'A wife – dear God, whatever made you think of that? She is above sixty, I tell you – and besides, that is not it at all.' The Captain sniffed: he had felt the insult to his vanity rather than his fidelity, and had made it too plain. 'Hearken to me, my dear – you girls *will* be talking – listen, I say, to what Stanton told me. Mrs Catling was a true army wife, as loyal to the colours as the Colonel. Now as a widow it's her way always to look kindly on anyone connected with the regiment, in his memory, and help them where she can. There's an old corporal of Ours that she lately found a job in the Excise, through a word in the right ear, so I hear; for she's pretty well connected. Old Devil's-Eye was cousin to Lord Dereham, and a rich man in his own right, besides what he raked off: so all in all she's comfortably situated. Except in one regard, my dear – she's solitary. She's in need of a companion.'

Caroline, feeling from her father's benignly smiling pause that she was expected to make a remark, asked if the widow had no relations.

'She does! And here, as Stanton pointed out to me, is the most interesting circumstance of all – she has quarrelled with them! There are, I understand, a nephew and a niece, who presume on their expectations from the old lady. But she and they do not agree. It is not a congenial family. Mrs Catling is now minded to look elsewhere for company to cheer her solitude, to comfort her infirmity, and to be perhaps – who knows? – what she cannot find in her ungrateful kin: a worthy heir.' The Captain took Caroline's hand in both of his, patted it, and appeared momentarily preoccupied with the shape of one of her nails as he added: 'Or heiress.'

'Papa,' she said, staring at the top of his lowered head, 'I can hardly mistake your meaning. But what can we have to do with this lady, and why—?'

'Her business in Town is not only legal. She has been seeking a companion also – but has not found one to suit. Now you cannot fail to follow me, my dear.'

Indeed she could not; but it was with perplexity, and some heart-sinking, that she contemplated the path her father was throwing open. Besides governessing, acting as a paid companion was one of the few occupations open to the unprovided woman; and it was true that she had thought of it. But instructing children was at least making herself truly useful; whereas the profession of toad-eating, as it was unflatteringly called, often amounted to nothing more than placating the capricious temper of a rich old woman who could not purchase companionship at any lower rate. The dependence she must face in any event: the sacrifice of dignity she could face if need be; but what Caroline doubted she could manage was the self-control demanded by a situation in which you could never, ever answer back.

'I know what you are thinking, Caro,' said her father, who so very seldom did. 'You are thinking, what is this turn-about? Did not my wretch of a papa set himself against my taking up any post whatsoever, and engage to secure my future by means of a triumphant and lucrative return to the stage? Is he not a lying, stinking, contemptible varlet?'

'Now, I draw the line at varlet. And you know, Papa, as to my taking a post—'

'It is an abomination. Yes. But there are two provisos. One, my triumph is not yet achieved. Were you not so admirably loyal, you might voice a doubt that it ever will be. It will: the day will come; but I must accept the fact that it will be a little time yet. You know I am nothing, my dear, if not a realist. Two, though I could not with equanimity see you enter a situation of a demeaning or degrading character – and indeed could only erase the reproach of such a sight by a swift descent from Westminster Bridge – there are other situations, very few, very rare, that may be considered golden opportunities. This is one such. And it may be –' for an instant there was a dimming in his eyes, of sadness and self-knowledge '– it may be the last thing I can do for you, my dear.' He shook himself. 'Now, what do you say? I have assumed your consent. I may be wrong. The notion may not appeal: it may appal. If so, say the word, and I am silent on the subject for ever more.'

'Well – I hardly know what to say. This comes as a great surprise . . . You said you have never met this Mrs Catling?'

'Not beyond giving her a bow from a distance – but I shall soon repair the omission. I took the liberty of sending a little note in to her house at Dover Street, asking if I might wait on her tomorrow, and I received a favourable answer. Now, this commits us to nothing, Caro. Mrs Catling's is an acquaintance I would cultivate in any event, in tribute to my old colonel. But you see the advantage. There's she, disposed to favour the families of the old regiment: there's she, seeking a young lady companion to solace her twilight years of widowhood: there's she, with a great deal of money, and no one to lay it out on. And here – well, damn me for a dunce if I've added the sum wrong, but here's you!'

Caroline, wanting space to think, went to the window and looked out. It was a lively enough scene: more perhaps to entertain than to please the eye. Carts and wagons coming away from the market at Covent Garden jostled with carriages heading for the fashionable milliners, glovers and button-makers in its purlieus: piemen and sausage-vendors wailed out their wares; whilst directly across the way the linen-draper stood out on his doorstep and gossiped gravely with the apothecary next door, each with his hands tucked in the pockets of his tight white waistcoat. But a down-at-heel young drab, far gone in gin and supported on the arm of a very young and idiotic-looking buck, served as a sharp reminder that this was a harsh world for the unlucky and unprotected. And what was more, Caroline realized after a moment that she was, all unconsciously, lurking behind the curtain, and running a practised glance over the men in the street in case any of them were duns come to demand a debt.

Revealing.

She turned back to her father. 'Here am I, as you say, Papa. And I am very willing to consider anything that may – well, in short, I will consider anything. But tell me – is Mrs Catling amiable, do you suppose?'

'Amiable isn't in it!' her father exclaimed. This meant, of course, that he did not know, but his choice of words was discouraging. 'My dear, I am delighted with you. Not because you have fallen in with my notion – nothing like that: if you told me to go to the devil I would happily surrender; no, I am delighted because you have embraced your golden opportunity!'

'Well, but, Papa, I'm not going to think of it as such – the golden part, I mean. That's my one condition. If I am to put myself up for this position, it must only be on the same terms as if I were applying for a governess post – that is, employment, and no other expectations. Do you see? I can be as shameless as the next girl, heaven knows, but I cannot step into such a place and begin angling for legacies.'

'My dear, I said nothing of angling,' her father said solemnly. 'Nothing could be further from my intention. I speak only of probabilities. And what could be more probable than that an elderly widow, estranged from her relatives, but supported by a deserving young companion, should choose to bestow on that companion her wordly wealth and—'

'No, no! That is precisely what I cannot entertain. I think I could be very fond of worldly wealth, believe me, if I got it. But I won't be a vulture, Papa. Don't ask it.'

'Very well!' He sighed, with shining melancholy eyes. 'I expressed myself poorly perhaps. I only thought of you getting your deserts at last, my dear – all the good things of life you should have had, but for your futile old father!'

'In any case,' she said, ignoring that, 'Mrs Catling may not take to *me*.'

'Oh, pooh, how could she not? There is nothing to take against. You have only to be yourself, my dear Caro, no more nor less! Of course when you do meet her there is absolutely no need for you to mention how your education ended, or to use any slang-words, or give your opinions. Marriner! I'll have my coat brushed – I think

I'll step across to Offley's. Well, my love, don't wait up. I shall put your case before Mrs Catling, when I call on her tomorrow – and you know, I really have the strongest presentiment of success!'

Mrs Catling would, of course, be a Gorgon. It was so very much in the nature of things that an elderly widow seeking a companion would be a tyrannical monster that Caroline, turning the matter over in bed that night, took this as an unalterable given. It was the other aspects of the case that exercised her mind: what would it be like to live at Brighton? Could she learn to counterfeit an interest in the spiteful prosings of old invalid tabbies? And what would it be like to be parted, at last, from her father?

From this she anticipated some tears; but the pangs of the parting must be softened by the apprehension of its mutual benefits. No longer would her father have to struggle to provide for her. And no longer would she have to witness the struggles – a selfish consideration, perhaps. But they tell.

The morning brought a letter that, short as it was, weighed heavily in the balance of decision. The proprietress of the Chelsea seminary, in a few violet-inked lines, declined altogether to furnish a testimonial to Miss Caroline Fortune. Her former pupil's unpaid fees had produced a shortfall in her accounts, as a result of which she had been obliged to put herself into the hands of moneylenders, with such painful sensations that merely to pen her former pupil's name was to invite an apoplexy.

Perhaps, then, it was fate: so Caroline thought, as she watched her father, a little seedy from his late night, set off for his appointment at Dover Street. He was very soon back: when she heard his limping foot on the stair, she supposed he must have been shown the door, and felt a disappointment that surprised her.

But no: he was jaunty.

'Ah, she wastes no time, Mrs Catling! Estimable woman! She knew my name at once – she remembers the name of every officer who served under her husband. She said she was glad to see me, and no doubt I wanted something from her, so out with it and she would see if she could oblige. *Very* plain speaking! I was struck all of a heap; but I got it out somehow. I started to describe you, my dear, and how well I thought you'd suit, but she cut me off and said she would judge for herself. When she said she'd see you at the earliest opportunity, I suggested this afternoon – like a fool! She soon put me in my place with that one. She does *not* receive visitors in the afternoon, says she, very high – which, of course, she don't! I should have known that. She's a true stickler, that's what: and I admire her for it!'

Caroline could not entirely share his admiration. That mental picture of a Gorgon was growing more complete by the minute. But it was no use pressing her father for a more detailed portrait of her prospective employer. Captain Fortune, in his gallant way, liked all women, classing them as fine, damned fine, splendid or estimable. She must cultivate a fatalistic patience until the next morning, when she was to present herself to Mrs Catling.

A hag-ridden night, in which various dimly seen but terrifying creatures pursued her down corridors with gaping jaws, drove her to an early waking; and before breakfast she spent a rather disconsolate time laying out her clothes, and wishing that she had a mother or sister to counsel her on what to choose from the modest array. The task was made more difficult by the small foxed mirror that was all she had to dress by. It was apt that Caroline was used to seeing only a dim, cramped, and partial reflection of herself; for while she did not lack a sense of her own merits, and had too much spirit ever to submit to being walked over, still she thought herself no more than tolerable-looking, and nurtured abysmal doubts about her ability ever to shine in company. She had a quick tongue, an active fancy, and a turn for wit, but these she employed, in truth, somewhat as a shield behind which she could shelter.

As for the figure in the mirror, which any observer must approve as tall, slender, and flexuous, she thought it gawky. To be sure, men paid it the tribute of glances, but she knew that went for any woman short of senility and lacking an absolute hump. Her hair, which was of a dark chestnut, coiled at the crown and fringed on the brow with a few curls around the ears, she could just contemplate without bitterness. As to her face, the strongly arched eyebrows that had been the secret envy of her schoolfellows at the Chelsea seminary gave her, she thought, a ridiculously surprised look. The thinness of her nose displeased her: 'cut cheese with it,' was her murmur. And the waxy fairness of skin that her contemporaries sought in vain with buttermilk washes and powder of pearl-of-India she hardly noticed, except to mutter that she looked like a ghost as usual.

Frugality at least simplified her choices. If Mrs Catling was a stickler for correctness, then a morning-dress it must be, and of those Caroline had precisely two. They were the same two, in fact, that served her as afternoon-dresses, walking-dresses and carriage-dresses.

'How much more simple could it be!' she said to herself, with a laugh; and all at once passed from despondency to a peculiar light-heartedness. She was young, the June sun was streaming through the window and turning the dust to powdered gold, and her cream figured muslin, with the green spencer, would do very well.

This euphoria accompanied her all the way to Dover Street – as did her father: equally cheerful, yet somewhat nibbled by anxiety as they approached the house, and inclined to wonder whether the whole idea was a bad one after all. But this was no more than characteristic of Captain Fortune, the type of man who would jump gaily off a cliff and then experience second thoughts when he neared the bottom.

'You need go no further,' he said, at the area steps. 'We may turn round, Caro, and go home, and forget all about it: the choice is yours.' But she would not hear of that, having come so far. A curious truth about Caroline, whose whole chaotic life had been subject to the wayward vagaries of her father: she disliked uncertainty.

The house was imposing and, as Caroline saw when the footman admitted them, elegantly fitted out. Mrs Catling's purse must be long indeed for her to be able to afford such a place as a mere lodging for a Town-visit. So her father proclaimed, in what could only be called a stage whisper, as they were conducted upstairs; and whatever the old lady's infirmities might be, they plainly did not include deafness, for her voice came sharply from the drawing room: 'Yes,

Fortune, I'm rich enough, as no doubt you knew very well when you sought me out.'

The Captain composed himself into an apologetic attitude, and went into the room bowing if not quite scraping; but the lady seated there in solitary state gave a snort of amusement when she saw him, and waved at him to desist.

'Stop that mopping and mowing, man, you look ridiculous. Yes, very large and splendid the place is, for one old woman, and that is just how I like it. This is your daughter, I dare say.' Mrs Catling gave Caroline a short, hard, thorough look – it made her feel like a cushion briskly plumped up – and then extended a hand to her father. 'Well, Fortune, I'll say how d'you do again, and I may as well add that she's as handsome as I'd expect from a pretty bandbox fellow like yourself.'

'Mrs Catling –' he bowed enthusiastically over her hand – 'you are all goodness.'

No, she was not, as anyone less chivalrous than the Captain would have perceived at once on beholding Mrs Sophia Catling. The relict of the late Colonel 'Devil's-Eye' Catling had herself a penetrating glance and a carrying voice that would have suited the parade-ground; nor was hers a face that promised a charitable disposition or pleasant temper. And yet she was not the Gorgon for whom Caroline had been preparing herself. She was a solid and large-boned but by no means heavy woman: her Circassian turban and dove-grey crêpe, single band of pearls and silver gauze mantle spoke not only of fashion but of style. A dark, hawkish sort of handsomeness, heightened more than obscured by her sixty-five years, was offset by something shrewd and pawky lurking about her eyelids and lips – something strongly suggestive of a sense of humour. And for that, Caroline was always prepared to forgive much.

'Allow me to present, my dear madam, Caroline. My daughter – as you so justly observe. You're like your late husband, Mrs Catling, nothing escaped him: I remember him saying to me, "Fortune" he said, "you must learn to take notice. Learn—"'

'If you behaved like such a fool with Colonel Catling, he would never have spoken a word to you. What is all this nonsense? You're nervous, I think. You probably need drink to settle you – you have that look. There's a tavern in Dover Yard. My coachman goes there, though he doesn't know I know it. He's sweet on the landlord's daughter. He supposes her buxom: she is actually *enceinte* by the potman. I do indeed, as you may collect, take notice. Go there, man, go. We cannot talk with you standing by. I shall send her to you in thirty minutes: that's all I will need.'

Captain Fortune, a great lingerer and ditherer, had never been so smartly got rid of. There was time only for a glance of mutual reassurance, and then Caroline was left alone with Mrs Catling in her lofty drawing room.

'Well, he didn't introduce me,' her hostess went on, motioning Caroline to a seat on the other side of a great cold, swept, scrubbed marble fireplace, like a funerary monument domesticated. 'But then you know who I am, of course. So, the chief question is, why do you want to be my companion?'

Mrs Catling put up her chin as she spoke, and stared Caroline down in a manner that had surely excoriated numerous drapers and ostlers. Caroline merely returned her look. She was anxious, certainly: conscious of a fateful moment presenting itself; but as for fear – well, the old lady was only *like* a dragon. She had, besides, a flash of intuition, telling her that Mrs Catling was actually rather shy. 'I am in need of a position, ma'am. My father told me of this one, and I agreed that I would try for it. I know of you only what he has told me—'

'Which I doubt can be relied on.'

'Just so – as you can know of me only what he has told you. So we are in like case, ma'am, and may both be wrong.'

Mrs Catling put her head on one side, studying her: a reluctant smile dawned. 'I dare say. Oh, he has represented you to me as a prodigy, of course. All the virtues. But then he needs to find a place for you, does he not? I have made enquiries, and it's common knowledge that he hasn't a bean. Your late mother was a Perrymount, I find, from Huntingdon? A good family. Of course they won't own you: it's an old story – your precious father stole her away and spent all her money. And now he's stuck with a grown girl, and no provision for her! Lord, what fools these mortals be. Men most of all; and of all men, soldiers. Dice, wine, and trollops is all they are good for.'

'You would know them, of course, from your late husband.'

'Colonel Catling was the exception that proves the rule,' the widow said, her chin going up again. 'I will show him to you.'

Having known a gentleman who kept his favourite spaniel, after its decease, stuffed and uncased on his dining-table, Caroline experienced a momentary alarm at this proposed introduction. But Mrs Catling went to a bureau and took from a drawer a miniature portrait.

'That is Colonel Catling,' she said, placing the picture in Caroline's hand. 'What do you think of him?'

Caroline couldn't be sure, but she didn't think she had ever seen a man quite so red, fierce, cross-eyed, and mad-looking. 'I wonder if the painter—' she began.

'It is an excellent likeness.'

'A face of much decision,' Caroline said, after a short struggle, offering the miniature back.

Mrs Catling did not take it. 'But not handsome?'

'I wouldn't presume, Mrs Catling, to pass judgement on such a matter; I would be trespassing on sacred feelings—'

'Suppose I insisted? What then?'

'Then – then I should think you were testing me out.'

Favouring her with the reluctant smile again, Mrs Catling took the miniature back. 'Quite right. The fact of the matter is I have a horror of flatterers. On the other hand, I am a difficult woman and must have my whims pandered to. So you see, pleasing me will not be an easy task. However. At least you did not go into raptures over the late Colonel. Who was certainly not handsome, nor indeed charming. I emphasize this for another reason. I am not a sentimental or romantic woman, Miss Fortune: I was not so when I became a bride, nor when I became a widow. Thus I am not a *lonely* woman either, and it would be a very great mistake in you to suppose it. I seek a companion to make my life easier. Society is more a chaise than a sedan: it is built for two. A solitary woman cannot go about freely, or accept invitations or receive company, without a lot of fussing about her solitary state. Yes, society: that will be our sphere. You will not be required to sit doing poker-work in a wainscoted parlour, singing Dr Watts's hymns. At least, if such is your desire, don't ask me to join you.'

'I confess that is far from my desire, ma'am,' Caroline said, relaxing into a smile herself.

'Hm: that's no surprise. You don't have *that* look about you. Well, what I do require is correctness. Form is my foible. You must know how to conduct yourself upon every social occasion: I will have no hoydens. Really that is why I considered your father's application. He is a sad rake, but he has lived in the world, and so I imagine have you. I observe you know how to walk – and how few girls learn that nowadays! – and to deport yourself, and I dare swear you could dress well enough too, if there were any money. Plainly *that* is an old friend of yours,' Mrs Catling said, with a sniff, indicating the figured muslin. 'Well, on top of the stipend, there would be an allowance for dress, if I were to take you. This is not generosity: I simply could not bear to have a dowd about me. Do you read novels, verse, or improving literature?'

'I read whatever I can get my hands on,' Caroline answered honestly, 'but I would choose for preference Lord Byron's Eastern tales or—'

'Not a bluestocking, then – that's a mercy. Nothing more vulgar than an over-cultivated taste. And you play, I hear, a little – which is meaningless. All young ladies play a little.'

'In my case it truly is a little. If I play a lot, people begin throwing things.'

'Hm. And you draw, no doubt.'

'I do. I know that is traditionally the other accomplishment, but I actually do it for pleasure.'

'Well, that I can approve. The good thing about a picture is that one can admire it for a few seconds, and then justice is done and all is over with. To pay the proper attention to some wretched sonata one must give up a quarter-hour of one's life. Now, let's see: suppose you were to be introduced, at some rout or drum, to the Honourable Mr Jenkins, how would you address him?'

'As Mr Jenkins. And I would think the Honourable rather strange, as it is not a title used socially.'

'Good enough. Now let us fancy Mr Jenkins is young, and handsome, and makes a great fuss of you, and is forever holding your shawl and declaring you an angel. What then?'

'Mr Jenkins is dreadfully mistaken, because I am assuredly not an angel.'

'That won't stop him. If anything, the reverse. You take my meaning, I feel sure, but I will state it unequivocally: I will not countenance your throwing yourself at men. Call it my other foible. I was fortunate enough to contract a rational marriage. The Colonel was not, thank heaven, a *pressing* man. I would commend such a sensible attitude to attachments to the whole world: a great deal of trouble would be saved by it. I know the world will not listen, but I can make sure my writ runs in my own household. I am no friend to that overprized imp Cupid. Look at what he did to your mother. You don't resemble *her*, I hope.'

'You'll forgive me if I can't join you in that hope, ma'am,' Caroline said, colouring, 'as I have tender memories of my mother, and would be very pleased to be like her.'

'Hey, well, that's loyal of you, I suppose, and not to be reproved,' Mrs Catling said, with a shrug. 'But my conditions, Miss Fortune, remain. You may be foolish, vain, and acquisitive, and no doubt you are. But what I will not tolerate is if you are flighty. I may as well add that the same conditions would surely apply if you went to be governess to some merchant's brats, which is your only other recourse. But there your world would consist of sticky stubborn faces, spiteful lies tattled to Mama, and solitary suppers in some draughty schoolroom. With me, there would be elegance, society, and rational conversation. The choice is yours.'

'Do you mean – the post is mine?'

'Let me put it this way: I have seen three other young women, and each was on her way home by this time. One had a squint, which I could not look at: one kept talking of her duty to God, which is such a vulgar subject for polite intercourse: and as for the third, she breathed altogether too loudly.' Mrs Catling made a gruff sound, which Caroline recognized after a moment as laughter. 'I jest about the last, of course.' But there was a cockerel beadiness about her eye, which hinted that she could be quite as capricious in earnest, if she chose. 'Well, I suppose you hardly know what to say, and all the rest of it?'

'That would be affectation, as I came here to apply for the post. No, I will say a very heartfelt thank-you, and beg leave to ask a question.'

'About your remuneration, no doubt.'

'That I shall be happy to learn about; but my question is really to myself. That is, you are so good as to suggest I will suit for the position – but do I think the position will suit me?'

Mrs Catling gave her the narrow sideways look again. 'You are fencing with me, Miss Fortune. I don't mind it, in moderation.'

'I dare say it is my habit. But I am quite serious also. It's true that I need the post, ma'am, and I suspect a certain well-worn phrase about beggars and choosers may have crossed your mind. But still it will mean going away from my father, perhaps finally, and though I hope I'm not over-sentimental myself, I can't help but feel deeply about that, and wonder if I'm doing the right thing.'

'Wonder? Nonsense. A moment's reflection will convince you there can hardly be a doubt of *that*. I have known a good many men like your father, Miss Fortune, and I will engage for it that your presence does not make him any better or worse. Well, is it not so? He is a sad rake now, and will be a sad rake left to his own devices, and the only difference will be in your situation. Which will be safer and steadier,' Mrs Catling pitilessly concluded, 'and free of the pretence that *he* looks after *you*, when of course it is the other way around.'

This was a shrewd hit. Plainly not much was lost on Mrs Catling:

just as plainly, she was more clever than kind. But Caroline found she did not at all dislike the old lady. Indeed, even as she posed herself the question of whether this was to be her new life, she answered it: yes.

'You know, of course, that I live principally at Brighton,' Mrs Catling went on. 'So you must make a removal from London. I come up to Town only once a year, for a small part of the season. But you have no family or connections hereabouts, at least not such as will acknowledge you, I'm sure; so there can be no loss there. And unless I have much misread you, you are no Evangelical, to disapprove Brighton's reputation.'

'Quite the reverse, Mrs Catling – I've always wanted to go there. I have been at Bath, and Margate—'

'Not the same thing at all,' Mrs Catling said, with a fastidious shudder. 'The Colonel, on his deathbed, urged me to retire to Bath when he was gone. I informed him that as I was neither decayed spinster, ambitious tradesman nor disreputable fortune-hunter, I could not fall in with his wishes. He was not in a condition to laugh, but I flatter myself there was amusement in his respiration. As for Margate, it has its votaries, and I dare say there are people there I could, at a pinch, speak to. But for fashion of the first water, Brighton is the place. To be sure, there is a fast set there. The moral influence of the Prince, making it his favoured resort, is not entirely salubrious. But there is no denying that where he goes, fashion attends. I am not of his inner circle, of course; but the Colonel knew him, and I have been invited to the Pavilion a few times.'

In her heart Caroline deplored the Regent as the gluttonous buffoon of the public prints, but that did not affect the fascination of that fabulous palace by the sea, which he was continually improving, and spending vaster sums on, and – reputedly – holding orgiastic parties in. 'Oh, ma'am, what is it like? Is it true that they burn two hundred pounds' worth of wax candles a night, and that everything is in an Oriental shape, even down to the close-stools?'

'Let us just say that reports of the Prince's style of living are seldom exaggerated. I might tell you a tale or two, on another occasion. But come! Is there to be another occasion, Miss Fortune? I am making you the offer, and I am not at all used to being turned down. I leave for Brighton the day after tomorrow. Will you come?'

'I will be very glad to come. I – well, thank you, Mrs Catling.'

The widow waved a hand with a repressive look, as if even this degree of warmth unsettled her. 'Very well. Now, I suppose the rest of your wardrobe is like that? Dear me. You had better come here tomorrow, and we will go to my modiste at Bond Street and begin fitting you out. Aside from clothes, I do not anticipate you will have much luggage. If there are some books and other small effects, those may travel with us: anything larger will have to be sent to Brighton separately. You will, of course, have your own room there, and the servants will wait on you in the ordinary way. I may send my maid to help dress your hair when we go out. And now there is one last test. My passion, Miss Fortune, is cards. I must have cards every night. I know every card game. I look on a careless lay at cards as a sin. I will play for hours and never get tired. Now I am watching your face carefully.'

As this was one area of her education that had not been neglected, Caroline had no fear of what her face might betray.

'So, you do not quail at the prospect of partnering an old woman at whist for years upon years? For I should add, Miss Fortune, that I fully intend to live for ever.' Mrs Catling's eyes took on a hooded look as she said this. 'I hope that does not disappoint you. Does it?'

'I can't fairly answer that, Mrs Catling,' Caroline said candidly, 'so I wonder if it's perhaps not a fair question.'

'Of course it isn't. I have often heard people make the most sickening brag that they are *hard* but *fair*. Not I. I am nearly always unfair. Like the world. You might say thus I harmonize with Nature, as those dreary poets of the Lakes would have it. Uff!'

Caroline was already coming to recognize this gruff exclamation as Mrs Catling's version of laughter. It was wry but also scornful.

'Never mind. You have evaded the question neatly enough. In truth I acquit you of any conscious designs on my wealth: I think you are probably too naïve for that, and still thrive on the blissful belief that a rich and handsome man will descend from the skies and marry you. Your father, on the other hand, is most assuredly hoping that I will *do something* for you. He could hardly have made it plainer if he had said so. Hey, well, I am used to that, God knows, with my family.' Mrs Catling made a face of distaste, her eyes hard and absent; then stirred, and looked up at the clock on the mantel. 'There – less than thirty minutes, just as I said. Come – shake hands upon the arrangement, Miss Caroline Fortune: and now ring the bell and go and find that father of yours, and tell him the news. By the by, he has debts, I suppose? Well, I am not a charitable foundation; but I did promise the Colonel to stick by the colours. Tell him that if he supplies me with the names of his principal creditors, I *may* be able to relieve him of his most pressing difficulties. As for you, return here at noon tomorrow, for the shopping – without him: he will only be fawning.' The footman came. Mrs Catling rose and, as Caroline did likewise, ran an unrelenting eye over her figure. 'As tall as me: dreadful to be so stalky, is it not?'

A little dazed, Caroline found herself following the footman to the drawing-room door; where he coughed apologetically, and stepped back to Mrs Catling. 'Ma'am,' he murmured, bending and seeming to wince, 'I should say – Mr Downey is here. I wasn't sure – he would insist—'

'Again? I made it quite clear to him. Tell him to be gone,' Mrs Catling snapped; and the footman bowed out of the room precipitately, propelling Caroline before him, so that she was half-way down the stairs before she knew it.

Below, in the hall, a young gentleman was waiting in peculiar agitation – pacing about and swishing his cane as if he were in a field of dandelions. He looked up sharply when Caroline appeared: the disappointment on his face swiftly thinned into a narrow glance of suspicion; but then he turned bodily from her, and demanded of the footman, 'Well?'

'Mrs Catling is not at home, sir,' the footman said, with a suffering look.

'I see.' The young gentleman breathed hard, and clapped his hat on his head. 'And *she*, I suppose –' with a twitch of his cane in Caroline's direction – 'has just been here to clean the chimneys.'

'Quite so – and shockingly dirty they were,' Caroline said, moving past him to the front door. Glancing into his face, she fancied a resemblance to the old lady upstairs, for though he was rather of the middle height, and square-cut, there was the same dark colouring, and the same wilful hitch of the chin as he returned her look. This, and his hostility, disposed her to think him Mrs Catling's relative; but having no particular desire to be introduced, she advanced to the door, telling the footman with a smile that he need not trouble.

Before she could open it, however, Mr Downey made a lunge at it, muttering, 'Oh – here, allow me.' He flung it open and stood frowning ungraciously a moment, and then with another grumble of 'Oh – but I should go first – I mean, as it is I who am not *wanted* here,' squeezed ahead of her, and went with an angry drumming of hessian boots down the steps, and off along the street.

There was more in this to amuse than to quell Caroline's spirits – for had she not succeeded where others had failed? – and by prospects that offered, at the very least, the excitement of novelty. Bursting with her news, she sought out her father at the tavern in Dover Yard. The sight of him in the tap-room should have dispelled any lingering doubts about how he would get on without her. Within half an hour he had acquired three new bosom-friends, all standing about with one leather-breeched leg up on the fender in the sporting manner, deferring to his views on horseflesh, and had moreover charmed them into standing him drinks; so that it was a vague, swaying, benevolent, open-armed Captain Fortune who received her news, and whom she just restrained from offering to treat the whole tavern on the strength of it.

'It will be,' he cried, kissing her heartily, 'the making of you, Caro!' His speech was a little foxed, of course, and it was noisy in the tap-room – which accounted for her mishearing *making*, for an alarming moment, as *breaking*.

Chapter III

Now, two days later, a travelling-carriage stands before the house in Dover Street, ready to depart. A neat equipage, but substantial enough to bear the trunks, boxes, and dressing-cases strapped up behind: the four well-matched bays, the shining harness, the coachman's blue livery with silk facings and gold-laced buttonholes, all produce a smart and spanking appearance in the high June morning; and they have attracted a rag-taggle of boys who stand watching with intense interest the last preparations, commenting knowingly on 'how she will go', and calling up unwarranted speculations on the private life of his mother to the postilion – who, the same age as they but liveried, waged, placed, blushes and cringes across the little gulf of class.

The carriage belongs, of course, to Mrs Sophia Catling, and offers ample evidence of her wealth, her taste for the best, and her insistence on privacy. Not for her the hire of a post-chaise, with its attendant exposure to the independent ways of post-boys employed by a livery-stable and not under her own strict control. Indeed if money could buy such a thing, she would have her own private road all the way from London to Brighton.

Caroline Fortune has certainly never travelled in such style, and while her new employer makes some last uncomplimentary remarks to the lawyer's clerk who has come to collect the house-keys, she too stands regarding the turn-out with admiration. Melancholy, very faintly, tinges her view. She has parted with her father at his Henrietta Street lodging early that morning – Mrs Catling laying a strict injunction on his coming to see them off, for fear of what she called 'theatrics' – and the occasion brought out the blue devils in him.

'Well, my dear, I hope your poor mother's shade looks kindly on me today. It *is* an opportunity for you; but I could have wished for a better. I should, in truth, have done better. I know it: I feel it. No more of that. Just remember, Caro, who you are. Keep hold of your pride – for I venture that Mrs Catling, splendid woman though she is, may come it a little high now and then – keep hold of it, and remember that your father's family were well settled in Devonshire when Wellington's were trotting the bogs; and that there's good family on your mother's side likewise, for all they've got vinegar in their veins. You are a young woman of quality, my dear, and never forget it. Of course, that need not stand in the way of your being *obliging*.'

As to what he will do when she has gone, he has airily assured her that he has various irons in the fire, and still has hopes of a return to the stage, perhaps back in the West Country – he will write and tell her all about it. She can only suppose that he will hang about his old Town haunts, and pursue his old Town dissipations; and though she dearly wished to beg him to keep clear of the debtors' prison, she concluded that such an appeal was equally unfitting for a leave-taking, and unlikely to be heeded; and so she held her peace, promised to come away if she had a moment's unhappiness with Mrs Catling, and kissed him goodbye.

Caroline loves her father as much as any daughter should, and probably a little better than he deserves. The wrench is felt, without threatening to kill her; and the simple burst of tears shed at their parting, whilst it might dissatisfy a sentimentalist, is all that nature demands.

Now the coachman, deciding that the gang of boys has peered and crowed enough, steps down and sends them away with a shake of his whip; and ambling near to Caroline quietly comments: 'I thought we might see the danglers today, before she gets off – but no sign of 'em.'

'Danglers?'

'That's what I call 'em. On account of their dangling after her money, you see, which is on account of her having nobody to leave it to but them. That's what they reckon, anyways.'

'This is Mrs Catling's family?' Caroline asks, finding she has adopted the coachman's hoarse whisper. 'There's a nephew and niece, I understand?'

'That's them.'

'Is one a Mr Downey?'

'One *is* a Mr Downey. And the other's a Miss Downey. But you know what I call 'em?'

'Danglers.'

'Just so. Oh, she likes to keep 'em dangling, you may be sure. It's nuts to her. Why, she loves it better than a rubber of whist. Well, it doesn't look as if they're coming today: I thought they might turn up, and make a great fuss of her. You'll meet them sooner or later, no doubt, miss. Of course, they won't like *you*.'

'Won't they?'

'They won't. On account of seeing you as another dangler.' The coachman gives a shrill chuckle, whilst keeping his face absolutely straight – to very peculiar effect; then adds, 'I never said any of this, mind,' before sauntering back to the carriage.

No danglers appear, however; and soon all is ready, and Caroline takes her seat in the carriage along with Mrs Catling, and Mrs Catling's personal maid – a little pinched comfit-chewer with a look of settled, not to say lifelong discontent.

'Well, Shrewmouse?' Mrs Catling accosts her. 'You are sorry to be leaving Town, no doubt, just as you were sorry to come here. That's about what I'd expect of you.' Caroline was at first surprised that a woman of Mrs Catling's *ton* should be attended by a servant so very drab and dour, and so undeniably moustached; but remarks such as this point to the heart of the matter. The Shrewmouse – whose name is Miss Lott, but who mostly comes in for this and other unloving nicknames – is of that useful class of people, whose function in the social sphere corresponds to that of the boot-scraper and the slop-basin in the domestic.

Caroline is sorry for her; but, Mrs Catling shall not make a boot-scraper out of *me*, is her own silent resolution as the carriage begins to move. It is taking her into a new life, which she is entering without doubts or reservations: she sincerely wishes its success, and intends that no failure of effort, temper, or spirits on her part will jeopardize it. But she has made very sure to bring her self-respect in the top of her luggage.

'Hm – I knew it. The milk-seller has left her chalk-mark by the door, and now there is a chimney smoking,' Mrs Catling says, peering out at a house on the other side of the street. 'They *are* home. But they have put up their shutters, and are hiding, so that no one will suppose they are so unfashionable as to stay in Town for the summer. What nonsense!'

'Unless they have just left some servants there,' Caroline suggests.

'Oh, not they. The woman is a perfect nipcheese, and would never leave servants to burn coal and drink milk at her expense. No, no: I have found them out.' This fact alone seems to put Mrs Catling in high good humour. 'Well, Miss Fortune, I am pleased to observe your father heeded my instruction, and did not pursue you to the end. I am no friend to protracted farewells. My own goodbyes have been said, at the expense of very little time or trouble. I have a large circle of acquaintance, but I admit few intimates. Now what, your romantic girlish imagination wonders, can have happened to Mrs Catling to make her so chary of intimacy? Nothing. I simply do not like most people, and those I like I do not like very much. Now you think me a cold, unnatural woman: but you are also thinking rather well of yourself, for after all *you* are being let in. Isn't it so?'

'Oh! I beg your pardon, Mrs Catling,' Caroline says after a moment. 'You seemed so confident of reading my thoughts to your own satisfaction that I supposed my assent irrelevant.'

'Very good! You mean me to understand, right from the beginning, that you will not be tyrannized. Very well, miss, I have read the signal, and you have asserted your independence of mind, and now there's an end of it. Tell me, what was my coachman talking to you about? Oh, don't fear, you won't get him into trouble. I know anyway. My family. My precious nephew and niece. He thought they might come to see me off. As did I. But even they must have baulked at such a naked display of interested hypocrisy. You will suppose me deficient in family feeling also – but in truth I am not. I am very fond of my nephew and niece, certainly fonder than their conduct towards me warrants. You are sure to hear a deal of gossip about the matter, so you may as well know the facts now. I have one sister living. Her return for being the pretty, blessed, and indulged one of the family was to make a thoroughly bad marriage. When the man died, and left her with two children and very little else, she considered herself ill-used rather than the author of her misfortunes. She has cultivated sickliness more or less continually since then, and scarcely stirs from her house – which is in no better an address than Golden Square, if you please. The one effort to which she will rouse herself is to remind her offspring, who are now grown, that they have a rich old aunt. Oh, when their booby of a father was alive, Matthew and Maria paid me no attentions at all; and you may be sure that if they were to find a fortune in a cave, fairy-tale-like, I would see no more of them. But for now the precious pair are most devoted to me. They are forever seeking reassurance as to the state of my *health*.' Mrs Catling utters her scornful laugh. 'And for all that, they are creatures of dreadful caprice – let them fancy that I have slighted them, or in some way been *unfair*, and they get upon the high ropes at once. Dear, dear!'

Caroline sees that a game is being played here, between Mrs Catling and her young nephew and niece – not a pleasant one: she senses resentment, power, and greed as only some of its elements. But what chiefly troubles her is the prospect, which the coachman seemed to hint at, of her being dragged into it.

Well, she thinks, if I meet them, I shall tell this Matthew and Maria at once that I have no designs on their aunt's fortune, that they are not to consider me a rival or enemy, and that I do not wish to be involved in the matter at all.

And they, of course, will then see me as the most cunning designing mercenary minx that ever schemed for a fortune.

This thought, like breath on glass, a little smudges her vision of the future. But for now there is the excitement of bowling out of London on the Brighton coach road – probably the fastest, smoothest, and smartest in the kingdom. Mrs Catling's carriage cannot make the pace set by the post-chaises, the sleek curricles, tilburies, chariots and chair-back gigs that pass them with a whirl of red-rimmed wheels, but still they get along at a great rate, the postilion blowing a horn to alert the turnpike-keepers on the road ahead. The strong sun throws shifting cloud-shadows on the Downs, and adds to the exciting sensation of the whole world being in swift motion.

Exciting in a different way is the glance of frank admiration bestowed on Caroline by one of the speeding curricle-drivers – a fashionable young buck with a sparky eye, making great play with his skill at the ribbons, and casually transferring the straining reins of his mettlesome pair to one hand so as to raise his hat with the other.

'We shall see him in the ditch later on, I dare say,' remarks Mrs Catling. 'A pretty fellow, eh? I saw those sheep's eyes. No doubt you would believe everything he told you, even after he had ruined you.' Before Caroline can protest, the old lady chuckles and turns to give a prodigious poke in the ribs of her maid, who had taken out her Bible. 'And as for you, Shrewmouse, you put all your trust in the promises of that volume, don't you? So I have a fool on either side of me – what fun!'

Caroline quickly concludes that it would be as useless to continue replying to these asperities, as it would be imprudent, given that subservience must be her lot. It is plainly Mrs Catling's pleasure to pin her acquaintance like so many butterflies, and there is nothing to be gained by wriggling.

They stop to water the horses and refresh themselves at Reigate, and then at Cuckfield, where they dine. And here Caroline has an opportunity of observing Mrs Catling's conduct towards the waiting-people at the inn. They all know her; and all, from landlord to chambermaid to waterman, attend her with a sort of stiff-jointed promptness that looks very much like smothered terror. And yet Mrs Catling is all affability. The one fleeting indication of another side to her character is when the waiter in their private dining room lays a dish of cream on the table, and is sharply addressed by the old lady with the words: 'Not there. *There*.' As she does not even look up from her plate as she says this, and makes no accompanying gesture whatsoever, the poor man is thrown into confusion, from which Caroline feels she must rescue him at last, by asking for the cream herself. She thinks he lets out a stifled sob, whether of anguish or relief, as he leaves the room: but she cannot be sure.

Even with stops they make such good speed that it is still afternoon when they come to Brighton; and the resort, seen for the first time in coppery sunlight that softens the edges of newness, answers all Caroline's expectations.

It was Brighthelmstone, fifty years ago when it was a plain little fishing-port. Now there is aptness in the contracted name for the expanded resort. You can even find the appropriate words *bright* and *ton* in it: *ton* meaning fashion, stylishness: *bright* just right for its new stuccoed and whitewashed terraces and squares and crescents adorned with wrought-iron, the colourful tents and pennants of Brighton Camp, the painted bathing-machines – like gypsy caravans trying to drown themselves – that are drawn up all along the beach.

Not too fanciful also to pursue the sound of that name, and remark that Brighton is also brisk, breezy, brilliant – and, for those of a more conservative disposition, a little brash. You can put that down to the Prince Regent, whose patronage has made the town, and whose principal creation rises above it all, strange and splendid and gargantuan like an architectural expression of his own fabulous bulk: the Royal Pavilion, still unfinished, a cheese-dream of domes and minarets.

You may detect that near-presence of absurdity in the great concourse of carriages, riders and walkers parading along the Steyne. Fashion flaps and flares in the briny air. Here, parasols are hoisted over bandeaux and coiled curls, bosoms thrust up above the high waistlines and the filmy and shimmering silks with their flickering glimpses of slender sandal shoes. Last year Waterloo closed the twenty-year account of war that temporarily turned the nation of shopkeepers into a warrior race, but the military imprint is still to be seen in male modes, not just in the swagger of uniforms, scarlet and blue, but in braided and frogged and Prussian-collared coats, worn by gentlemen who have only ever gone into battle against pheasants. High-perch carriages bowl along, phaetons and barouches and landaus – and it is right that their names are a little fantastical, for these vehicles are only for going from one end of the town to the other in, whilst being looked at.

And yet absurdity is just held at bay: if these people, this place are not all they think they are, still they are not contemptibly far off their ideal of elegance; and any shortfall is made up for by an abundance of life. Which is greeted with a shudder by Mrs Catling, when Caroline remarks on the number of people.

'Aye – the town is most shockingly full of company,' the widow sniffs; revealing herself to be one of that not uncommon class of people who choose to live in attractive places, and then deplore anyone else doing so.

Mrs Catling's house in West Street has this in common with its owner, that it is substantial, handsome in a severe way, and dominates those around it. Old compared with many of Brighton's gingerbread villas: but within, all convenience and cleanness. This latter is confirmed by its mistress, whose first action on entering the hall is to sweep a white-gloved finger along the surfaces of a table, a Chinese bowl, and a picture-frame. The platoon of servants drawn up at rigid attention evince no surprise at this; but Caroline sees twitches of alarm at Mrs Catling's next proceeding. She takes a straight-backed chair, places it next to the door to the dining room, and instructs Caroline to step up on to it.

'Run your finger along the top of the lintel. Stay – let me see your glove first. Good. Now, up you go.'

Caroline does as she is bid. With dismay, she finds the finger of her glove coming away black, but there is no hiding it or wiping it with Mrs Catling below watching intently. She steps down: Mrs Catling's eyes sparkle at the sight of her glove. 'Dear, dear,' she intones, and taking Caroline by the other hand as if they are beginning a dance, leads her ceremoniously over to the servants, and urges her to display the offending finger.

'I cannot suppose you were not expecting me, as I wrote you with every detail,' Mrs Catling says, addressing her household as her late husband might have addressed a regimental parade. 'Nor can I suppose you unaware of my strong objections to living in a sink-hole or cess-pit. The only supposition remaining is that you care neither for my opinion nor for your situation, and would gladly forfeit both. Do speak, if so: allow me only to add that with the character I shall give you, your prospects of alternative employment in Brighton at least will be slender to the point of emaciation.' Mrs Catling smiles blandly at the pained silence that ensues. 'Well, well. I am in indulgent mood, for I have been fortunate enough as you know to find a companion – she is Miss Caroline Fortune, and here she is, and you are to answer to her as you would to me; and so I am pretty well contented, and will overlook the dereliction – this *once*.' She turns to Caroline and adds, 'You had better put the glove aside to be laundered, my dear. You are thinking that next time you will simply make a pass with your finger without touching the surface, but believe me I will *know*.'

As this is precisely what Caroline is thinking, she can only gape in a vanquished manner, just like the servants. But Mrs Catling is all of a sudden in genial spirits, and ordering a maid to show Caroline to her room, cordially hopes she will like it, and urges her to mention anything that is missing for her comfort.

Nothing is: the room is admirably fitted out, if more formal than homely. Caroline turns to the maid, thanks her, and assures her she isn't going to investigate the lintel for dust; but she gets no answering smile from the girl, who scuttles away as if Caroline has offered her some terrible temptation.

'Well,' breathes Caroline, facing the room and her future, 'I wonder how I shall get used to this.'

A domestic tyrant – that her new employer was, to be sure; and Caroline's first days at West Street offered many further evidences of it. But she found, to her slightly guilty relief, that her own duties were light, and her own treatment by Mrs Catling fair and even generous. She would not have blamed the servants for resenting her over this, but they seemed too cowed even for that much independence of mind; and if anything unspeakable was done to her soup or her coffee, she never detected it.

Eating and drinking, indeed, was a signal pleasure at Mrs Catling's house, for she kept a good table, and had no finicking notions of continence. This again was a relief to Caroline, who had long striven without success to cultivate the dislike of sustenance proper to young ladies. Probably her appetite had been quickened by the habits of her father's household, where lobster-salad and champagne one day would be followed by a week of bread and cheese. So she dined well, and slept well also – Mrs Catling being no friend to early rising, nor exercise of any kind.

'You may try it if you choose,' she remarked one afternoon on the sea-front, of the bathers issuing into the surf from the bathing-machines in their voluminous capes. 'It is wet and cold and salty, and that is all there is to be said about it.'

Caroline, who thought the sea a very fine thing in its place, which was a long way from her body, was happy to decline. Nothing more strenuous was required of her than taking her employer's arm on these daily airings along the Marine Parade, and even they were liable to culminate in jellies and tarts at Dutton's, the celebrated confectioner's. There might be a look-in at the circulating-library, or the fashionable shops in Poplar Place; but Mrs Catling's chief amusement consisted in observing and satirically commenting upon the people they passed. She knew everybody, resident or visitor; and there was no one of whom she did not know something discreditable.

'Now *she* has just turned down an offer for her daughter's hand,' Mrs Catling told Caroline, in reference to a lady with whom she had just exchanged the most cordial of greetings, 'from a highly eligible man. She says she cannot approve his morals, as he has an acknowledged by-blow with an actress. And yet her own husband has done the same half a dozen times. In truth she is holding out for old Lord Lissard, who is waiting for his current wife to die, of the malady he gave her. Uff! Such hypocrisy! But then the girl is a minx, whom no one could care for, so we may save our tears. And now over there is a gentleman who *should not* wear tight pantaloons. You will see when he turns around. There. *That* is why . . .'

Caroline had prepared herself to be bored: she had not prepared herself to be amused and entertained, even so disgracefully. Indeed, in writing her first letter to her father – which she anxiously hoped he would have the eightpence to pay for – she could find very little to complain of in her new position. Her time, beyond one half-day a week, was not her own, but it passed agreeably enough even indoors. Mrs Catling was grown short-sighted, and Caroline took charge of her correspondence, as well as reading out loud to her from light novels and verse. It was true that these had to be very light to retain Mrs Catling's attention: any hint of abstruse thought or, worse, deep feeling, and she would snort and demand the book be closed.

'Take up *La Belle Assemblée*,' she would say, 'or the *Lady's Monthly Museum*,' directing Caroline to the periodicals with their engraved fashion-plates, which showed ladies in morning-dress looking at engravings of ladies in morning-dress – and so on *ad infinitum*, Caroline thought, with a queasy feeling. So she would read out these undemanding texts instead, with their diligent accounts of the latest Parisian headdresses, and Mrs Catling would murmur her surprise that Provence roses were in fashion as an ornament again. And this was when Caroline did feel a little discontent, and wonder whether there wasn't more to life; and often she would smuggle the offending book to her own room, and finish it by candlelight.

Mrs Catling relished society and cards, as she had told Caroline on their first meeting; and these between them disposed of most evenings. Piquet and vingt-et-un filled the hours between dinner – which Mrs Catling took fashionably late – and supper, whenever they were alone at home; but that was not frequent. At least once a week Mrs Catling had company to dine, entertaining her guests politely, feeding them royally, and after they were gone satirizing them comprehensively. Then there were the assemblies – a ball at the Old Ship every Thursday, and card-parties on Wednesdays and Fridays – besides concerts, promenades, and the theatre. Mrs Catling's appetite for all these amusements was indefatigable.

So was her attention to Caroline's conduct.

'You are a young woman alone, and I as your employer am in some degree responsible for you. What this does *not* mean, my dear, is that I stand *in loco parentis* to you. You'll agree that I am the least motherly person that ever breathed: don't even for a moment allow yourself to forget that useful fact, and begin supposing that there can be latitude on your side or indulgence on mine. I take a very particular interest in how you look and how you behave, because these things reflect on me. For instance that coquelicot shawl is quite the thing for walking-dress, but it will not do for this evening: you must have the black gauze. Now, as to this evening, there will be dancing, and I expect that pink-faced ensign will be after you again. You are not to give him any encouragement, or to stand up with him unless expressly desired to by the Master of Ceremonies.'

'As I cannot remember any pink-faced ensign, ma'am, I do not fear giving encouragement.'

'Pooh, you won't catch me with such a bare hook as that. You danced the third and fifth with him last week.'

'I remember dancing – but only with your leave.' Caroline was permitted a ration of dances, rather like her dress allowance, for the look of the thing. 'And I'm sure I gave no encouragement, or any kind of sign whatsoever, beyond the blankest indifference.'

'Ah, I'm glad you make the admission. Well? Don't you know that blank indifference is the most unequivocal signal you can make to a man, short of throwing yourself at his feet? Of course you do. Oh, you can't give me the bob, my dear – I have you!'

Though Caroline truly could not remember any pink-faced ensign, and certainly did not like the sound of him, there was nothing to be done but bow to Mrs Catling's injunction. The old lady had entrenched herself in the position of being *undeceivable*; and like most dogmas, this one exacted absurdity as the price of assurance. Caroline had more than once seen her turn down a genuine bargain in a shop, through attributing all sorts of cunning subtleties to the innocent shopkeeper's mind.

As for the dances themselves, the assemblies and card-parties, she liked them very well. If her status as Mrs Catling's dependant, whose first concern must always be her employer's comfort, her mantle or her iced-water or her fire-screen, meant that she was always more looker-on than participant, she was not dissatisfied with this, for she had always taken pleasure in observing people. Indeed nothing could have suited such a habit of mind better than the position of a lady's companion, who was often treated as some insensible object like a hat-stand or dumb-waiter, and in consequence often witnessed the instructive spectacle of how people behaved when they supposed no one was watching them. Which, she found, was seldom well.

But Caroline was twenty years old, and could have been forgiven more sighs than she allowed herself, at the prospect of forever creeping along in the craggy shadow of Mrs Catling: of never standing up to dance with a man because she liked the look of him, or accepting a glass of wine without first looking to her employer for approval, or even going into a giggling huddle with other twenty year olds and making solemn appointments to meet at the milliner's tomorrow and tell all.

She tried not to repine: mostly she succeeded; but still there were nights when she threw open her bedroom window to gasp the fresh air that was never allowed to circulate in Mrs Catling's house, and to hear the near murmur of the sea, which to her young mind, fretted by endless rubbers of whist, seemed the very sound of life going on tantalizingly without her.

Mrs Catling's ill-humours were not unbearably frequent, and when they did come the storm was soon ridden out. More unpredictable, and more troubling, were the tremendous fits of gloom to which she was subject.

These were referable to no object or event: the widow did not fall to thinking on her husband or her lone state, and there was no question of chivvying her out of them – Caroline made the attempt once, and retreated scorched. It was rather as if some alteration came over her vision: the wry satire fell away, and the greedy relish, and instead there was only the world and her vast, bleak contempt for it. At such times Mrs Catling's hard black eyes seemed to be looking out, not over the liveliness of Brighton, but over a lunar terrain, rocky, blasted, and hopeless.

Caroline tried not to be infected by this, even though it had a peculiarly pervasive effect on the household: at such times even the carriage-horses seemed to hang their heads in depression. The best of all remedies was a letter from her father. These came irregularly, and were full of nonsense, chaos, self-glorification, thumping fibs, and fondness. She could almost physically warm herself at them.

But it was a letter from another source that finally broke through the most forbidding of Mrs Catling's moods, a spell of cold brooding that seemed set to turn into everlasting winter. Caroline, reading out her correspondence to her one morning when the brilliant sun streaming into the breakfast-parlour seemed to chill and fade as it touched the old lady's bombazine skirts, had despaired of any communication raising anything but a scowl – and then she came to a letter that changed everything.

'From Mr and Miss Downey, ma'am.' Ah, the danglers. 'Shall I read it?'

'Oh, yes.' All at once there was a light in Mrs Catling's eyes – a very feline, if not kindly light; like a bored cat that hears a mouse in the wainscot. 'Oh, yes, read it. Let us hear what they have to say.'

'"My dear aunt,"' Caroline began. '"It is in no spirit of trifling formality, but with the greatest earnestness, that Maria and I enquire after your health. That we were not able to satisfy ourselves upon that score, before your removal from London, was owing to our not being informed of the exact date of your departure. I called at Dover Street, and found you gone two days since. The disagreement there had been between you and me on my last visit, I take to account for your leaving without affording us the opportunity of goodbyes. I am as far from reprehending this omission, as I am from welcoming it; I fear it was a too natural consequence of our late quarrel – which, I hasten to add, was not of my seeking; but the share of blame that is portionable to my impetuosity of temper I willingly accept. You must know, Aunt, that to hear my late father abused is a thing I can never endure – however no more of that. If you have any doubt of the strong love and duty that both Maria and I bear to you, then I know not what may suffice to convince you: if I tell you that I have had not a moment's easiness since our unhappy parting, you will deplore my language as insincere and over-dramatic. Well, you may be in the right of it. We hear, by the by, through mutual acquaintance, that you have found a companion to your satisfaction: it is a satisfaction that finds a willing echo here in Golden Square. We are pleased to think of you no longer solitary – I would not say lonely, which, knowing your resources of mind, temper and character, could only be an impudence. I hope the connection prospers, and that the young woman is properly sensible of her good fortune. My dear aunt, Maria and I hope that we will see you very soon. We intend coming to Brighton the day after tomorrow, that is Wednesday, on purpose to do so. You would reprove I am sure the extravagance of travelling post, and so we shall come on the Eclipse coach, which I hear can complete the journey, most remarkably, in under six hours. We shall wait upon you as soon as we arrive, if we may; and I look forward with the eagerest anticipation to the final repairing of the breach, of which this letter is the first attempt. How long we shall stay must wait upon the issue of that meeting – until which happy time I sign myself, your most dutiful and affectionate nephew, Matthew Downey."'

'Well! There is a study for you, my dear,' said Mrs Catling, who throughout the reading of the letter had made faces as if she were sipping an unthinkably dry yet refreshing champagne. 'Did you ever read such a letter? One hardly knows where to begin. You may know more of these things than I, being fresh from the seminary and all, but one would surely not recommend *portionable* or *eagerest* to the connoisseur of style. But there, my nephew would no doubt put the inelegancies down to his overflowing feelings. He is a great one for his feelings. Notice how even such small blame as he will accept he turns to his own account – showing how honest and frank and loyal to his father he is. Oh, excellent! And a most friendly and disinterested reference to *you*, my dear. They are pleased I have you! Oh, of course they are! And they are not coming to Brighton to make sure that I am not growing *too* fond of you, of course they are not!'

'Mrs Catling, you know I don't want to be a bone of contention between you and your family. It is fair to no one.'

'I know that, my dear, of course I do. Why, you are all innocence and sweetness, and you absolutely shudder at the thought of replacing my family in my favour!'

'I disclaim the innocence and sweetness, ma'am, but as for the rest – yes. If you think I have such designs—'

'But this is delicious! Now *everyone* is protesting their sincerity,' Mrs Catling cried, with her sharp jangling laugh. 'You might add, my dear, that you would be just as fond of me if I hadn't a penny – that's one of my nephew's old favourites, though he hasn't used it in this letter. Saving it for our meeting, no doubt.'

'Ma'am,' Caroline said, studying her acidly smiling employer with some pain, 'you truly do not believe I am sincere? And nothing I can do can convince you of it?'

'My dear Miss Fortune, you must not suppose yourself singled out. I trust your sincerity quite as much as anyone else's. And I am not in the least displeased with you. I greatly look forward to introducing you to that precious pair. Uff! Indeed I *look forward with anticipation*, as my inimitably redundant nephew would say. Well, so they will be upon us tomorrow! I dare say I should ask them to dine. Friday will do: we have no one else coming.'

'Won't they be staying here, ma'am?'

'Here? Why so?' Mrs Catling's eyes narrowed. 'They do not ask if they can come and stay, and neither were they invited. They merely announce their intention of coming to Brighton. I am not a hotel-keeper. They must do as they please. I have a great deal more to think of than their whims and fancies.'

This was of course not true. Nothing else was to be thought of at West Street from the moment of the letter's arrival, which the Downeys must surely know; and Mrs Catling surely knew that they knew – and so on. Such was the game into which Caroline found herself unwillingly drawn.

For her part the letter aroused various emotions. There was eager curiosity, for she sorely felt the need of new company: something like sympathetic interest too. Reading out Mr Matthew Downey's words had given her a sense of him as a flatterer, to be sure; but then perhaps being on close terms with a rich aunt made you so. Caroline knew that her own late mother had a sister somewhere still in Huntingdonshire, the one who had retained parental approval, and had the family money settled on her; and perhaps if she herself had been dancing attendance on that mysterious lady for years, now in favour and now out, she would have developed just such a blandishing habit.

However, if there had been only servility, she must have been repulsed. It was the hint of something tindery and spirited in the letter that engaged her attention – even perhaps simply the accents of youth, which though she had been with Mrs Catling for only a month, seemed not to have reached her ears in an age. The danglers would not like Caroline, of course; but Caroline was quite prepared to like the danglers.

Chapter IV

The Downeys being due to arrive in Brighton on Wednesday afternoon and promising a call as soon as they did, Mrs Catling made sure that her carriage was ready by noon on Wednesday – so that she could be out all day.

'I need an airing,' she said to Caroline, 'and so, I have decided, do you. A *long* one.'

So they went on a drive. They trundled about the Downs. They drew up above Brighton Camp, and watched some decidedly unspectacular horse-exercise: they went on to Rottingdean and Saltdean, and looked at churches and views while the shadows lengthened. As Caroline, if asked to name half a dozen things that Mrs Catling did not like, would have placed churches and views high amongst them, she soon gathered the purpose of the jaunt, and resigned herself to a weary day. It was evening when the coachman was allowed at last to turn the horses' heads towards home. There, Mrs Catling had the satisfaction of finding that her relatives had called, and called again, and gone away to their inn much perplexed.

If this was her purpose, then why the old lady could not have simply stayed at home, and had the servants say she was not, Caroline could not fathom. But that was to apply reason to the question – and about these relations of hers, Mrs Catling was not reasonable: she was, in fact, mad. From her observation of life, Caroline was coming to the conclusion that every individual, however sane and sensible, had one aspect in which they were to all intents and purposes mad. In her father, for instance, it was his belief that he was a shrewd man of affairs. In Miss Willis, it had been a fixed delusion that if she threw back her head and laughed at the ceiling with her eyes closed she rendered herself instantly more attractive to the opposite sex. Plainly Mrs Catling, who questioned the footman for twenty minutes on *exactly* how the callers had looked on being told she was not at home, when it came to her nephew and niece, was as mad as Ajax.

Caroline herself was, of course, the exception that proved this interesting rule, being all rationality.

The meeting came at last – the next morning, when Caroline was accompanying Mrs Catling on her usual promenade along the Steyne, and being treated to the usual scurrilous information on every passer-by. A man's voice cried, 'Aunt! Aunt Sophia!' from some distance behind them.

'And now this woman on our left, with the crown of curls, is actually as bald as an egg—'

'Ma'am,' Caroline interrupted her, 'someone is calling you – surely Mr Downey.' She turned to look back, but was steered firmly round by Mrs Catling, who could hear perfectly well, and was determined on a last triumph of making her relatives run after her, and get out of breath, and be generally at a disadvantage.

So they were: Mr Matthew Downey, and Miss Maria Downey, stood panting before them, he that same dark and stocky young man Caroline had encountered in the hall at Dover Street, she a golden-fair, long-limbed, languorous sylph of a girl, who looked as if she strongly disliked running, now or ever.

'Matthew – Maria – how d'you do, my dears? We are blessed by the weather again, are we not? Though I do smell a shower in the wind,' Mrs Catling said, with provoking blandness; and gathering Caroline's arm tightly to her, 'This is Miss Caroline Fortune, my new companion – I say *new*, though we are so wonderfully used to each other, and so entirely in each other's confidence, that I feel as if I have known her all my life! My dear, what are you thinking? Pray put up your parasol – you'll spoil that beautiful skin.'

This mark of affectionate attention was so utterly unlike Mrs Catling that Caroline could not have been more surprised if her employer had got down upon all fours and invited her to a game of Gee-Up Dobbin. But it succeeded in its chief aim. Mr Matthew

Downey, at least, looked thoroughly put out: he could manage only stiff civility as the introductions were made.

'But, Aunt,' he went on impatiently, 'you must know we have tried to call upon you. And you never at home – we were quite concerned—'

'Were you?' Mrs Catling said, smiling, with a tremendous question mark. 'Why? Did you suppose the servants had murdered me, and were concealing the fact? But, my dear Matthew, you forget yourself – here is a gentleman unintroduced.'

This was a tall, fine-figured man who had been accompanying the Downeys, and who, having declined altogether to break into a run, only now came up with them. He was dressed with negligent elegance, his coat fashionably tight across his broad shoulders, but not so that it would require two strong men and a winch to get him out of it: his cravat tied with careful carelessness, seals at his waist, his patent boots dazzling. He was about thirty, and in his aquiline good looks the best qualities of youth and maturity stood in such striking balance that Caroline turned a little dry-mouthed at the sight. His smile, though, completed him: it had the right dash of self-mockery in it, and seemed to contradict Caroline's inward proviso that a man so handsome must be very stupid.

'This is Mr Leabrook,' Matthew said, impatient as before. 'We met on the coach, and came down to Brighton together, and so we became a sort of friends. Oh, hang it –' as Mrs Catling's satirical eyebrows rose '– I don't mean it to sound so – only it was *you* we came to see, Aunt, as you well know.'

'I am flattered,' Mrs Catling said, 'and now you see me, and you might, my dear Matthew, be a little more gracious. I shall be very glad to have Mr Leabrook's acquaintance also. Your name, sir, suggests a Northampton connection . . . ?'

'My family have long been settled in Northamptonshire, yes, ma'am,' said Mr Leabrook, in an agreeable surprisingly light-toned voice. 'Your own name is familiar to me from the splendid reputation of the late Colonel – also from your young relatives here, who have spoken much of you, and with the warmest admiration, this last couple of days. I confess it is I who have stuck to them rather, as I have found them such pleasant company, and me an idle fellow without resources. However, here is a family reunion, and I am *de trop*; so I'll wish you good day.'

But Mrs Catling would not hear of that. Mr Leabrook, fashionable and well connected, was just the sort of gentleman to recommend himself to her taste in any event: he was doubly welcome as another stick with which to beat her relatives, for by giving him a deal of attention she still withheld it from them. While she plied him with questions about how he liked Brighton, and had he seen the latest improvements to the Pavilion, and did he know Lord Fitzwilliam up in Northamptonshire, she retained Caroline's arm with every appearance of possessive fondness.

Meanwhile Mr and Miss Downey stood by: she had a pretty sulky mouth and looked simply bored, but he was cross and heated, and Caroline felt that the charade had gone on long enough. She disengaged herself from Mrs Catling with the excuse that her bootlace was undone, and hung back, making a long pretence of fixing it. At last she had the satisfaction of seeing her employer walking on with her nephew and niece on each arm, questioning them minutely about the standard of service at the Old Ship, where they were staying. Danglers they might be, she thought, but they had come a long way to see her after all.

'It was well done,' quietly said Mr Leabrook, falling into step with her. 'Whether appreciated, who can say? I caught your name, Miss Fortune, and I have gathered from my new friends the position you have taken up. I do not suppose it to be an easy one. But where do you hail from?'

'I have lived mostly in London. I suppose that is where I hail from – which is a curious expression, isn't it? Hailing sounds rather strong and decided for me. I fear I drizzle if anything. Or mizzle. They are the same, I dare say, though I always fancy mizzle as that little bit wetter – not that you can have rain that *isn't* wet.' Caroline listened to herself with rising mortification: if it were possible to blabber worse nonsense, she could not see how.

'I thought you must be London,' Mr Leabrook said, looking at her with great attention, only delicately laced with amusement. 'There is an air.'

'Why are you at Brighton?' She meant a polite enquiry: it came out grossly forensic. 'I wonder,' she added limply.

'I am here on a family errand also. I have a younger sister – all of thirteen years younger than me, which means that we are just about on a level – and she has been at a boarding-school at Hove, and I have come to bring her home. That *was* the plan. It has all gone rather awry. First the pole of my carriage broke while I was in London, the very day before I was due to come here and fetch her away in it. Hence my taking the public coach instead – which, of course, was one of those lucky accidents, as it introduced me to our friends here. And now I find that Georgiana, my sister, does not wish to come home. She is invited to Weymouth for the summer by a schoolfellow, whose father has a pleasure-yacht, and Georgiana has a great fancy for sailing. Our place in Northamptonshire is about as far from the sea as it is possible to be in England, so perhaps that accounts for it. So here I am in Brighton with nothing to do. Are they reconciled now, do you suppose?' he added in a lower tone, nodding at Mrs Catling and her supporters. 'Downey has been most anxious about it all. What is the substance of this quarrel, do you know? Of course I realize you must be discreet.'

'I suspect it is one of those quarrels that will always be breaking out, from the pride of either party. But you are right – I must be discreet.'

'Else they will be making *you* the subject of a quarrel, eh? Never fear me, I shall say no more. So, do you go to the Thursday assemblies, Miss Fortune? And do you find them tolerably well attended?'

'I think those are polite form questions,' she said, observing his faint smile.

'Just so. I thought it time we had a couple. Like bread with your ragout.'

'Then yes and yes are your answers. It might be easier if one could just hold up a little flag for those social interchanges, don't you think? Up for "Yes, quite," half-cock for "Shocking weather", and down for "I am bored to death". Why do you say that you and your sister are on a level?'

'I mean in mental development – women being so forward of us in that regard that we men need twelve or thirteen years' head start to put us on an equality.'

'That is very flattering, and surely meant to be.'

'Certainly. But surely you would not have it otherwise?'

'You mean, being a woman I must like to hear complimentary things said about women? Perhaps. But then each of us always makes an exception for ourselves in such generalizations. Hence that other class of men, who seek to win the favour of the female sex by roundly abusing them. Many a woman sees that as a challenge: "I'll convert him," thinks she. And if she can get the man to esteem *her*, whilst despising all her sisterhood, then all the better. Where's the merit in fascinating a man who admires all women anyway?'

'Well, I am of the admiring class: I freely admit it – and my side has at least the virtue of honesty.'

'Ah, but isn't a virtue something exercised for its own sake? Whereas flattery has always an *aim*.'

'Not always. There are some men, I believe, who cannot help themselves, and will keep it up with no notion of anything coming of it.'

And are *you* of that sort? Caroline wondered, studying askance his gracefully strolling figure, his clear-cut profile with the grey eye sparked by humour. There were elegant gentlemen aplenty walking that promenade, but beside Mr Leabrook they showed all sorts of awkwardness, asymmetry, affection. Here was such ease and naturalness, combined with polish and civility, that she had been at first a little knocked back by him. Now she suspected he was an accomplished flirt; though even so she remained, if not knocked back, at least half horizontal.

'You are wanted, I think,' he said, gently pressing her arm and nodding ahead. Mrs Catling, obviously feeling she had indulged her relatives enough, was turning herself about, and demanding: 'Where is my Caroline? I am quite lost, you know, without my Caroline – quite lost.' Caroline, who had never even heard her employer use her first name, let alone decorate it with that fond possessive, tried to keep the surprise from her face. But Mr Leabrook missed nothing: he repeated the pressure, and said quietly, 'My feeling is that if someone tries to use you as a tool, you shouldn't mind it, because it is their choice and folly, not yours.'

'My dear,' Mrs Catling cried, as Caroline rejoined her, 'we must go home soon, and this mantle is all in a twist from the wind, and I must have your delicate fingers. No one can set it right just as you do – here is Matthew making it ten times worse with his fumbling.'

'I can't see much amiss with it, ma'am,' Caroline said, primping, 'and Mr Downey has made a much better job than I would of a man's riding-coat.'

'Well, upon my word, I tried my best,' Matthew Downey said, fuming and frowning as if she had said something against him instead of for him: whilst Maria only yawned.

I shall not try any more, Caroline thought, if they are so resolved upon enmity: I shall just not try. Still, it was disheartening. When Mrs Catling, on parting, invited the Downeys to come later and dine at West Street, Caroline greeted the prospect with inward dismay. She felt she had been hated enough for one day; nor could she relish the thought of being unnaturally made much of by her employer all evening, no matter what Mr Leabrook said about not minding it.

What made her feel differently was when Mrs Catling turned to Mr Leabrook, and cordially invited him too.

'That is an invitation I would gladly accept,' he answered, 'if I did not fear that I would be intruding on a family party.'

'Oh, my dear sir, we are not that sort of family, believe me – you see us in one of our rare intervals of not quarrelling – is it not so, Matthew?' Mrs Catling chuckled, to her nephew's obvious discomfiture.

'That I cannot credit, for there is too much amiability on either side. But I shall certainly come if you will have me – it will be a great pleasure,' Mr Leabrook said. His glance rested on Caroline as he said it.

If she was a chief part of that pleasure, Caroline was far from proof against feeling gratified by the compliment; but she hoped she was in no danger of overestimating it either. Mr Leabrook was after all a single gentleman at a loose end, and a good dinner offered him with an unattached young woman to flirt with. However, the evening brought further demonstrations of his regard, of a kind to weigh more heavily with Caroline than any amount of pretty flattery. Mr Richard Leabrook understood her position; and it was a relief to be understood.

If there was a general feeling about her being companion to Mrs Catling, it was that she had fallen on her feet. Even her father supposed that attending a rich widow and waiting for her to die was a comfortable berth. Mr Leabrook, through numerous instances of tact and delicacy, showed his perception of the other side: that though Caroline might eat the best turbot and truffles, she had no freedom to say she did not like them; that though Mrs Catling might reprove a snub to her companion, as wanting in respect for herself, Caroline could never take any offence on her own account. And the strongest proof of his understanding was that he did not make it too obvious. He was not about to get her into trouble with her employer by attentions that were too marked and particular.

To Mr Leabrook's presence also she felt she owed such ease as was established between herself and Mrs Catling's devoted nephew. For while Mr Leabrook set an example of unstinting civility to her, Matthew Downey could hardly refuse to follow it without declaring himself an irredeemable boor; and it was plain that the young man looked up to his new friend, and set some store by his opinion. Matthew's softened manner towards Caroline at dinner was the less surprising, however, after her encounter with Maria, which took place before they even went in.

Maria, on arrival, declared that she wanted the use of a mirror, and slipping her arm through Caroline's, and saying that the one in her room would do very well, impelled her upstairs; where, once alone, she gave Caroline's cheek a kiss, and sat down with a yawn and a sigh on her bed.

'And so you are the terrible creature who is to cut us out of the will!' she said. 'And yet you have but the one head, and no horns that I can see. And I shall take it on trust that those pretty kid shoes contain no cloven hoofs – or hooves – or can it even be hooven? They must be from Bond Street, by the by. Well, you wicked minx, turning the feeble mind of our frail old aunt, what have you to say for yourself?'

'I must confess,' Caroline said, laughing, 'that I have been fearing you believe these things in earnest.'

'Lord! Well, *I* don't. And the kiss is meant to say so – and also, if they do force us into falling out in the end, as a sort of making-up in advance. Because I know them: *she* is a shocking make-mischief, and my poor brother is so easily caught in her toils. He's so susceptible, and so rash-headed, and he *will* work himself up into a pother, though that's the very thing she relishes. So it's no wonder there's always a quarrel at the end of it. Dear, dear – you must think us a sad set!'

There is no beautifier like sympathy, and under its influence Caroline perceived that Maria Downey's mouth was not sulky at all, but rather charmingly indolent. Her whole demeanour indeed was that of someone just awoken from a refreshing sleep but wondering whether to doze for another half-hour.

'I thought you must hate me,' Caroline said. 'And all I want is to keep my position – and, oh, Lord, how soapy *that* sounds! You see? There is no winning with such a hand!'

They laughed, which felt like an enormous relief to Caroline: laughter in Mrs Catling's company tending only to be a pungent extract of malice.

'Then the best thing, my dear, is to forget all about it. My brother suspects *everyone* of coming between him and his aunt, while I do not give a hang, so it doesn't signify how you behave. But how *do* you come to want such a position? You are neither pruny old maid nor country vicar's clumsy daughter. Though I fancy I can make a guess. Esteemed parents somehow omitted to set you up as esteemed parents are supposed to? Ah, I have smoked it, because I am – well, not in the same boat, but in a vessel very like it. Poky and leaky and liable to sink at the first wave. You've heard Aunt Sophia speak of my papa and mama, no doubt?'

'I – yes, just incidentally.'

'Ah, is that a new word for "with scathing contempt"? She despises 'em. Mama, who's her sister, went and married Papa for love, which Aunt Sophia can never approve to begin with. Then Papa, who was a lawyer and a middling successful one, set himself to changing the world instead of feathering his nest. He wanted to get into Parliament and reform it, and when that didn't answer, he devoted himself to getting other men in, which all cost him a deal of effort and money. So when he sank into the grave, as the poets have it, there wasn't much left for us. But what vexes Aunt Sophia about my mama is that she obstinately refuses to regret marrying Papa, ever: still wears a lock of his hair at her breast, if you please. And yet where Mama, who's pretty much an invalid, will always rouse herself to energy is in calling on Aunt Sophia to *do something* for us. Poor Mama! I don't *think* she means any harm; but when she pens a letter to her sister, brazenly remarking that Sophia has far more money than she can ever know what to do with, and no children to consider, which she thank heaven *has* to gladden her autumn years – well, let us just say Mama doesn't help matters.'

'I begin to see a little more clearly now. It is all a sad pity – and really, would it not be better if Mrs Catling would simply say what she intends, instead of keeping you –' Caroline nearly said *dangling* '– forever in suspense?'

'It certainly would be better. But then she would not have the enjoyment of power. Oh, she has taken Matthew under her wing to some degree. He is studying for the Bar like Papa, and she has contributed an allowance until he is qualified, and I think he is as close to her heart as anyone. I use the word "heart",' Maria added, with a droll glance, 'in the very loosest sense possible.'

'But surely,' Caroline faltered, 'to favour one and not the other—'

'Not me, you mean? Well, you have probably observed, my dear, that Aunt Sophia likes *men* best. But as for favour, I am not shut out – dear me, no: when she is displeased with Matthew, *I* am the one who is going to get everything, *I* am the one who has always been more sensible, deserving, et cetera and so on.' Maria chuckled and lifted her willowy limbs from the bed. 'I was meant to be using the mirror, wasn't I? I had better look. Ugh. I see a freckle. That tedious sun – always shine, shine. No, my dear, if I were to found all my hopes of felicity on *her*, I would be – well, just such a desperate high-strung creature as poor Matthew is turning into. Luckily I have another resource. I think this face of mine as bland as butter – but I have found that it *can* captivate. This is all very unofficial and in a way secret, but there is a gentleman I met at the beginning of the season, who intends making me what he quaintly terms *his own*, just as soon as he is able.'

'Oh, I'm so very pleased for you! That is – if he is a *nice* gentleman.'

'He has the requisite number of eyes and teeth,' Maria said, laughing, 'and is good-natured and pleasant, and if he is six-and-thirty I don't mind it. Best of all, he is very comfortably off; and so what my aunt chooses to do with her fortune is up to her – I am thankful to be spared the fatigue of caring any more about it. All I must do is wait: he is gone to the West Indies, where he has property from an uncle that must be seen to before he can settle his affairs, and I cannot look for his return at least until the beginning of next year.'

'So long – that must be a sore trial of patience for you.'

'I dare say it would, if I were very much in love,' answered Maria, smiling at her in the mirror, 'but my regard for him is quite manageable, believe me, and hence so is the anxiety.'

This was said with the lightness that Caroline already recognized as characteristic of Miss Downey, and that did not necessarily preclude true feeling: it was Caroline's own habit to speak lightly of what touched her most deeply. Still, she found herself wondering for a moment whether the years of being played on their wealthy aunt's hook had not had a more demoralizing effect on both the young Downeys than they realized.

But she for her own part was simply happy to have made a friend where she had feared an enemy. And with Matthew managing to be polite to her, and Mr Leabrook being rather more than that, Caroline found nothing but enjoyment in the dinner. Her employer too was in mellowest mood: on moving to the drawing room, while the men sat on, she did not seize the cards as was usual and order Caroline to an immediate hand of piquet, but let her do as she would, and even mentioned that if Caroline chose to open the pianoforte later, she would have no objection. This was certainly out of the common: for on previous evenings when there had been guests, Mrs Catling had forewarned her with some such remark as, 'Mrs Smith fancies herself musical, and will no doubt want you to play – give her two short pieces and then if she croaks for more plead indisposition, for I can't endure to hear you jangling away all night.'

The gentlemen were not long over their wine, but long enough, it seemed, for Mr Matthew Downey to take a good deal of it. His colour, always high, was quite fiery, and his gait was a little unsteady, which misled Caroline for a moment. He could not surely be coming to sit by her.

But he was; and between mastering her disappointment that he was not Mr Leabrook, who had joined his hostess, and her apprehension that Matthew was going to be unpleasant to her, Caroline was so discomposed as not to be able to say anything at first. He seemed tongue-tied, and so they stared at one another. There was much intelligence in those dark eyes, she decided, for all his dogged clenched look; and he was one of the few men she had seen who suited the fashionable Windswept style that his thick black hair was dressed in – perhaps because he seemed always caught in a gust of emotion.

'Miss Fortune, I must apologize to you,' he said abruptly: then went no further.

'Is it for something specific,' she gently asked, 'or are you meaning to be apologetic generally? No need for either. Though I can see where the second might be useful. I'm sure in the future I shall say and do many things I shall be sorry for, and it would be agreeable if one could do the apologizing for them all now. A sort of wash-day of regrets. But I interrupt you.'

Matthew, after some lip-biting and staring, gave a gasp. 'Why, yes – it would be – a wash-day of regrets – an excellent notion—' and he laughed loud, even excessively. He was, she saw, one of those people who must first make sure a joke is not against them, before they will consent to be amused. 'But no – it is for something very specific. We have met before, in London – you remember it, of course – at Dover Street. And I fear on that occasion I was deficient in courtesy. Indeed, I believe I was thoroughly rude.'

'I hardly remember it, Mr Downey, and I would be glad if you would think no more of it.'

'You are very good – but that I can hardly do. The only excuse I can offer is that my mind – my heart also – were much occupied – and that any failure of civility came less from intention than sheer distraction.'

'Truly, it is forgotten.'

'By you perhaps – I cannot so easily efface the painful impression. But then it was so horribly like me – when I am overmastered by some great feeling, I become quite blind and insensible in that way. I wish I would not – but I am made so.'

Well, he had gone rather swiftly from apology to talking about his feelings, a subject in which she could hardly be expected to share his lively interest. But of course it was much better than hostility; and when she offered to make him tea, and was rapturously thanked, she concluded that he was surely after making friends, and that any reserve on her part would be churlish.

'I cannot make a fuller explanation,' he said, returning to the point. 'Discretion forbids – and I could not burden you with confidences.'

He looked, though, in his inflammable way, as if he might be going to; and so she said hastily, to divert him, 'Well, and so you met Mr Leabrook on the road, I believe, and were not previously acquainted?'

'Oh! yes, to be sure – a piece of great good luck, was it not? I have made a capital friend in Leabrook. But you must not suppose there to be something flimsy in a friendship so quickly made. Indeed, there is nothing like a day's coaching for enabling people to get to know one another. We were perfectly easy together before the first stage was reached. Where there is true cordiality and sympathy, an hour can do as much as a lifetime: *more*, I would say.'

She had meant only a commonplace enquiry: it was rather fatiguing to be taken up like this; but at that moment Mr Leabrook, catching her eye, demonstrated his talent for understanding once more, and drew Matthew into a general conversation. Presently Caroline, at Mrs Catling's urging, went to the piano. Mr Leabrook got up to do the offices of unlocking it, and sorting the music-sheets, and while so occupied murmured to her: 'Matthew is an excellent fellow – the warmest heart – but he does make a meal of the *bread*.'

She subdued her smiles, and played. No one was ever likely to call her performance brilliant, and she was grateful that Richard Leabrook did not imperil her good opinion of him by doing so. Still, she found herself concentrating on the music more intensely than usual, and his attention was unforced. She would tax no one's patience beyond three pieces, and asked Maria if she would replace her; but that serene young lady's instrument was the harp, as she reported with satisfaction, for it spared her the trouble of walking over to the pianoforte. Maria herself soon transferred the attention back to Caroline, however, for she had found on a table within reach of her sinuous arm Caroline's sketchbook, and now the contents must be admired.

'How provoking – your people truly look like people, instead of dolls in very foldy dresses like mine,' Maria said. 'And hands – how does one draw hands? Mine always seem to have *one* finger too many, though I keep on counting them.'

'Figures I can manage, but they must float in limbo,' Caroline said. 'You see how few are the landscapes, and decidedly not good. There is no telling my trees from my clouds.'

'I fancy the ability to draw landscape is uncommoner than generally supposed,' Mr Leabrook said, bending over the book. 'I mean to have some views of my estate made, when I find an artist equal to them. My late father engaged a fellow who had been highly praised, but produced the most fearful scribbles – we were perplexed which way up to hang them, and hid them away at last.'

'Your property in Northamptonshire is large, Mr Leabrook?' Mrs Catling asked.

'It is large enough to content me – and my father took pains to improve it. I am perhaps less fond of country living than he, or my mother, who is very content to remain there all the year, rearing doves and making cures for the work-folk. But I shall grow more attached to it, I don't doubt; and the curious thing is, I begin thinking wistfully of it as soon as I come away from it. A wise friend told me that is the height of felicity: when you wish yourself elsewhere to *have* an elsewhere to go to.'

'There can be no sounder basis for happiness than such a property,' Mrs Catling said, with stern approval. 'I have never understood people who come to prosperity and do not so invest, thus providing for the future. It is stupid irresponsibility, and worse; for having frittered away their substance, these people then expect others to support their offspring; and I fear the children of such will contract the same habits.'

Even someone less prickly than Matthew would have felt this hit: and full of wine as he was, his face flamed up in a moment. A thorough quarrel would surely have begun, had Matthew not been so very choked up he could not find his tongue for some moments – time that allowed his sister to put in with: 'Rearing doves, you say, Mr Leabrook? I find that enchanting. Everyone used to have a dovecote, didn't they, in the old days? So pretty and medieval, like mead – which I always fancy as very refreshing but was probably quite odious and sticky – what do you think, Caroline?'

'I think it was probably horrible, and I do not think I could have worn one of those pointed hats with a handkerchief on it, and kept my countenance.'

'True – but you ladies would have been in better case than us men,' Mr Leabrook said. 'Just think – Matthew and I would be in tabards and hose, and that I am sure I could not carry off.'

Caroline, running her eye over his tall lean figure, thought that he would probably look very well in it. She suspected that he knew it too – though this diminished only slightly her good opinion of him. A man should know his own worth, she felt. Besides, it was of no account, because she was *not* falling in love with Richard Leabrook.

This admonition, which rang like a chime in her head even as she kept up the conversation, was partly simple prudence. In worldly terms there was much against it: a portionless girl should not set her sights so high, and so on; and if she were to make a fool of herself over him, she could not imagine Mrs Catling being very tolerant. He had much more freedom than her, of course. Indeed he could surely do just what he liked. And if it were Caroline that he liked . . .

But here the chime rang again. She was *not* falling in love with Richard Leabrook. She thought him all that was handsome and amiable, and no doubt her head would be full of him after he had gone. 'But that does not mean falling in love with him,' she said to herself – so distinctly, that for a moment of real alarm she thought she had spoken the words out loud.

Chapter V

The dinner-party had ended peaceably, in spite of its hostess's best efforts. Caroline's view of the Downeys had already begun to alter, but this revelation of Mrs Catling's wilfully trouble-making temper completed the process. Without regarding either Matthew or Maria as plaster saints, she saw in them two well-disposed young people who had been as much ill-used as spoiled, and whose defects, so acidly dwelled upon by their aunt, had been fostered if not created by her caprice.

As to why Mrs Catling should play this unpleasant game, perhaps no further reason needed to be sought than that it gave her pleasure to meddle, mar, and hurt: this human propensity not being so uncommon as ever to excite surprise when detected. In her case, however, there seemed an extra element. Mrs Catling scoffed at love, and made it plain that in her life she had kept the blind god firmly in his place. Yet it was the intensity of a lover that she brought to her tangled relation with the young Downeys. No coquette ever put her hapless suitors so thoroughly through the mill, or priced her wooing at the cost of so many pets, teazes and tantrums. The whole tormenting business was, in the truest sense, close to her heart.

But to perceive this was not to approve it. Caroline's sympathies were now firmly with the Downeys, and over the next week they ripened, for they were much together. Having made her point, Mrs Catling now invited her relatives to socialize every day. With Maria, Caroline continued on excellent terms – no less, and no more: it was hard to imagine so self-contained a nature admitting any deep friendship. With Matthew there was a startling change.

'I wish I knew what you really thought of me!' he burst out one afternoon. They had all gone in Mrs Catling's carriage to picnic at Rottingdean: Mr Leabrook was one of the party. Matthew had asked Caroline to take a turn along the cliff-path with him, and she was just glancing regretfully back at Mr Leabrook when he spoke – so it was with a sort of guilty start that she replied, 'Oh – why – why, I think very well of you, Mr Downey.'

'I would be glad to believe it!' he said, shaking his head with a great sigh.

'You alarm me. Have I been making faces at you? If so, I assure you it is only the egg I had at nuncheon, which I fear was *not* very fresh.'

'Oh! to be sure, you are joking,' he said – wincing as at some regrettable infirmity. 'Making faces, no – quite otherwise. After our unfortunate beginning you have turned utterly polite and closed-up, and I can't tell what may lie behind your expression. It may conceal hatred. For myself, I can never conceal anything – that is not my nature – I am terribly open.' He paused but, as she declined the opportunity of congratulating him on his lack of duplicity, went on with a frown, 'I will be honest – indeed I can be no other – and confess that I suspected you, at first, a schemer. But you will be happy to know that I no longer think that: you will be happy to know, in fact, that I am very well affected to you now.'

Caroline signified that her happiness was so great she was practically paralysed with it.

'It was unjust of me,' he pursued, 'a piece of shocking injustice and prejudice. *Now* I realize that we are pretty much in the same boat. You have no doubt heard my aunt abusing my late father. The other day she was talking to me of *your* father, Miss Fortune, and characterizing him as a shabby sort of reprobate, who could not provide for his daughter, and so had foisted the little chit on to her in hopes of a legacy. Her exact words. I could not help but feel goodwill to you after them.'

Caroline felt that the exactness might have been omitted, but was prepared to accept the goodwill. 'Well, as to a legacy, or anything of that kind, Mr Downey,' she said, 'if I could sign something – some document – renouncing any claim on Mrs Catling's fortune, ever, I would do it – here and now! Failing that, I do not see how I can convince you.'

He hesitated, and then with a look of genuine frankness said in appeal: 'You must think me very mercenary! Looking only to what my aunt can do for me – hanging on my expectations – indeed it has a very bad appearance, and I for my part don't see how I can convince *you* otherwise, unless – unless I take you into my confidence.'

'Oh, you don't have to do that!'

'No – but I shall, because there is something about you, Miss Fortune, that invites it. I have peculiar instincts about people. I feel I can trust you.' He had drunk several glasses of champagne at nuncheon, and she wondered whether she ought to remind him of it; but already he was plunging on – unexpectedly – with the demand, 'Tell me, have you ever been in love?'

'I ought to giggle and blush at such a question,' she said, 'and though I do not, I am still not sure how to answer it.'

'Oh, I don't mean any trifling, silly, here-today-gone-tomorrow attachment. I mean truly in love – so that you are half ecstatic and half tormented, and your heart drums wildly and your mind wanders, and you cannot sleep at night.'

Caroline did not answer. She was ruefully admitting to herself that, for all her thoughts about Mr Leabrook, her heart kept a steady beat and she had not the slightest trouble in sleeping. Was she lacking in sensibility?

'Well,' went on Matthew, 'such a love is mine. Dear God! it is tremendous, and wonderful, to let this out at last – for I can confide in no one. Maria is a dear sister, but she and I are cut from different cloth. I think she could never understand – she is so dreadfully practical. That day at Dover Street, Miss Fortune – when I was rude to you – I had just come from seeing my love. A most agitating interview. I offer this as some explanation for my conduct. I offer you her name also: it is Perdita.'

'Oh, like the mist . . .' The Prince Regent had had a notorious mistress named Perdita Robinson: Caroline realized, just too late, that this would not be a tasteful comparison. 'Like the mist on the sea,' she improvised desperately, 'in beauty, I mean – I imagine her – so your tender expression suggests – isn't she?'

'I was not mistaken in you, Miss Fortune – you have described her exactly!' cried Matthew. 'You do have a feeling heart – and you embolden me to unveil the secret. Oh, a sacred secret, I mean – nothing dishonourable. Between Perdita and me burns the purest of flames. It is only my unfortunate situation that renders secrecy necessary. For, you know, I am not meant to be attached in this way. I am but two-and-twenty, and not yet qualified, and I have no money, and no expectations beyond Aunt Sophia. As for Perdita, she is quite without fortune. Her father is a doctor, and their circumstances are modest. Shall I lie? He is not a physician or a surgeon. He is a mere apothecary, and he lives at Snow Hill. Contemptible! Such must be society's cry. Never mind his moral worth – the nobility of spirit that has led him to ply his healing arts amongst the sick and needy, though he is of gentle birth himself. A bad match it must remain – and for me, who must shun all attachments, it is unthinkable. My aunt has explicitly told me that if I go rushing after a petticoat, as she terms it, then I can expect no more help from her.'

'Good Lord – how long is such a prohibition to last?'

'I have heard her say that no man should marry till he is at least thirty,' Matthew said, with a grimace, 'and then only from motives of the most careful prudence. The fact of the matter is, if she knew about Perdita, my credit with her would be lost for ever. But what about my dear girl? It is intolerably hard on her to be turned into a secret, as if she were something shameful. And though she has the mildest of tempers, the strain of it has told on her. That day when I saw you at Dover Street, she had spoken most passionately of our wretched situation – of her fears that she might be deceived in me – that her reputation might be lost by degrees, whilst she fasted on a meagre diet of hope.' Matthew tugged out his handkerchief and mopped his brow. 'It was a painful meeting – even though it concluded with the happiest thing that can ever come to pass. What *should* be the happiest, under different . . . No. I still say, the happiest. We became engaged, Miss Fortune: secret the bond must be, but solemn it is, and indivisible.'

'Oh . . . I can see how very hard it is for you, Mr Downey. I want to congratulate you on your engagement, and yet one can hardly properly do so!'

'No – but I take the thought kindly,' he said, with warmth. 'And so – when you saw me that day, I was in an excessively *raw* state, after such a buffeting of emotions. I mean explanation not excuse. I dare say love has run rougher courses than this; but still it is an out-and-out facer, to think that our future depends upon a woman who would never allow us a future at all!'

'It is a shocking pity. And yet you are plainly devoted to this young lady – and if she is amiable and true, then surely . . .' She stopped, and exchanged a wry glance with her companion. She had been going to say that surely Mrs Catling might be brought round to a more sympathetic view of the couple's plight; but as even a moment's reflection established that there was an equal likelihood of her launching herself off this cliff and flying all the way to Calais, she curbed her tongue.

'There is nothing to be done,' he said, briskly enough. 'I must wait: I *can* wait. The last thing I am, I hope, is weak-spirited. And I am relieved to have spoken out, you know. I hardly intended to go so far – but then I never plan – I loathe all such cold dead preparation – and you have shown yourself so friendly, Miss Fortune. It has been preying on me, how rude I was to you at the beginning; one thing I cannot endure is to feel I have caused pain. I must always repair it, or I have no rest. Now you know all, and I am content.'

And so he really seemed. She found in him none of that inclination to regret a confidence, which made the receiving of them too often a burden. He looked indeed as if a weight had lifted from him. Perhaps as a consequence, all the pleasanter aspects of Matthew Downey's character remained uppermost for the rest of that day; and Caroline felt she had misjudged him. He still tended to speak too partially of his own feelings, and to suppose that his idiosyncrasies were of necessity interesting; whereas she could not be convinced, even by ever so emphatic a manner, that a violent dislike of onion-sauce called for any special comment, still less admiration. But he was sincere and well-meaning, of that she was sure; and she felt for his difficult situation. Indeed, it was this that made Caroline his partisan.

It would not do to be too obvious about it, and start at once pleading his cause with her employer. But she flattered herself that Mrs Catling did set some store by her opinion, and was less inclined to look for calculation in what she said than most others. So when the card-table was set out for the two of them that night, and Mrs Catling, snapping the seal from a new pack as if she were mercifully despatching some small creature, asked her how she had liked the picnic today, Caroline was prompt with her answer.

'Oh, I never enjoyed a day more, ma'am. Not just the beauty of the spot – there was true ease and cordiality on all sides, and that is very comfortable to my spirits.'

'Is it now? Well, I noticed Matthew paying you a deal of attention. He was giving you his life-history, no doubt, in minute detail, with him as a saintly hero, and with *my* cruel misdeeds painted in glowing colours. You hid your yawns creditably, my dear, I will say that.'

'Well, we had a great talk; and I must confess I have come to know him better, and find much in him that is estimable.'

'Piquet,' Mrs Catling pronounced, handing Caroline the pack for preparation. 'Matthew estimable, eh? That must have been *very* good champagne.'

'Oh, I know you are satirical, ma'am,' Caroline said, removing all the lower cards and putting them aside. 'But I also know – well, I had thought he was a little of a favourite of yours. I think there can be no doubting that he is warmly attached to you, in spite of quarrels; and indeed he does not speak ill of you, Mrs Catling – only with a proper measure of respect and affection.'

'Uff! A proper fiddlestick!' Mrs Catling grunted; yet Caroline, glancing up at her from lowered lids, thought she did not look displeased. 'Hey, well, there are worse fellows about, I dare say. Cut. So: your deal. But he's unsteady – that's his failing.'

'Perhaps. And yet I think he might be less unsteady, if he were securer. I think anything in the nature of uncertainty is bad for him. If he were sure of your regard, ma'am, he would surely be more settled in his temper.'

'Hm! So I am to follow *your* recommendations now, am I?'

Caroline shrugged casually, her eyes on her cards. 'I am merely remarking how it strikes me: it's of no moment.' And soon she turned the conversation as if it really were, congratulating herself on an adroit move; and had the satisfaction of hearing Mrs Catling speak of her nephew almost indulgently before they retired.

But there was an unlucky sequel. The next day, in place of their usual call, came a note of apology from Matthew and Maria. It was Mr Leabrook who brought it to West Street: he had parted with them at the Old Ship that morning, and remarked pleasantly that Matthew was going to get that haystack hair of his cut, and Maria to shop for some small necessaries. 'So, I said I was happy, idle fellow that I am, to be their envoy,' he concluded, with a genial smile – which faded as he saw the mask of Mrs Catling's black fury descend.

Caroline was used to this, and registered only a weary regret at the hours of ill-temper to come. For Mr Leabrook it was a new and disconcerting experience to witness his hostess apparently petrifying before his eyes into a graven image of some implacable pagan deity whose department dealt with blood, death, revenge, and despair.

Terrible stillness and silence characterized this apparition, laced with a brooding menace that Caroline had seen reduce strong men to milksops, and cleave the tongues of the most urbane talkers to their mouths. But it did speak occasionally.

'I want my hussif,' it pronounced, after allowing Mr Leabrook to talk himself to a perplexed standstill on every subject under the sun without the slightest response. The shadowed eyes turned to Caroline, and there was a twitch in the stony cheek. 'Why you should be so slow to oblige me in this matter I cannot think. It is not simply that your remuneration is ample and your duties light: it is the reflection that any well-disposed person would surely be prompt in such little civilities to an elderly lady that confirms my reluctant opinion of your increasingly *spoilt, saucy* disposition.'

Mrs Catling's voice rose on the last words to a soft snarl, which Caroline, jumping up to do her bidding, saw Mr Leabrook's handsome face react to first with amazement, then with distaste. Sheer bafflement had made her slow to move; for if her employer possessed one of those tidy needle-cases known as hussifs, she had certainly never seen it; and the idea of Mrs Catling *sewing* was strange as a dream. Nor did she know where to look for it – but she was not about to stir Mrs Catling's wrath by asking. She proceeded by trial and error, moving towards the bureau whilst keeping an eye on the old lady's expression. It darkened, so she hived off towards the window-chest, where the faintest of growls informed her she was on the wrong track. There remained a little japanned table with a single drawer – could it be? The fearful goddess was still. Caroline looked in, steeling herself for a roar. But she was in luck: there was the hussif, a little case of shagreen, looking as if it had never been touched. She handed it over. A lesser tyrant would have felt the need to do something with it: not Mrs Catling, who glanced at it, then deliberately tossed it aside.

It was to Mr Leabrook's credit that he hung on for a good half-hour, during which Mrs Catling maintained her mulish ill-humour as diligently as if it were something worth doing. Caroline came in for some more reproof. The sunlight was hurting Mrs Catling's eyes and setting off one of those headaches to which anyone who had the slightest care for her would know she was prone; but it apparently did not occur to her companion, who might be supposed at least to pretend such a care even if only for the look of the thing, to draw the curtain across, this being too much like effort for her pert and missish nature; and so on. Caroline's spirits did not quite sink under it. There was the blessed consideration that today was her half-day: this afternoon she would be free. And there was some relief in the mere presence of Mr Leabrook, who had sense enough to realize that any attempts to intercede on Caroline's behalf would only make her situation worse. His cool grey eyes missed nothing, however.

Mrs Catling's mood did not sweeten after his departure. For long it seemed she might even deny Caroline her half-day; but as granting it allowed her to appear neglected and ill-used, she let her companion go at last. It was Caroline's habit on these afternoons to take a dawdling walk about the town, finishing up at Crawford's circulating-library. Today she varied her exercise by descending to the beach and striding its length very vigorously, the sea-breeze blowing in her face and carrying safely away what a lip-reader might have discerned as a string of rich and heartfelt curse-words.

When she came up to the town again, she was refreshed and all in a glow. The brilliancy of her complexion caught the eye of more than one visitor to the circulating-library, which with its coffee-room, reading-room, and even music was the resort of much company: a starched and creaking dandy who was conning the satirical prints, perhaps in hope of finding himself caricatured there, lifted his quizzing-glass to her, and an officer of the Hussars gave her such a glance as quite infuriated the well-bosomed young mistress on his arm, who recalled his attention to the trinket-cabinets with some savagery, and made him at once buy her something she did not want. Caroline's attention was all for the books: the means of escape furnished by reading was grown more vital to her; and she was just exulting at having procured the first volume of Lady Caroline Lamb's *Glenarvon*, which everyone was talking of, when her eye fell upon Mr Richard Leabrook.

He was outside, looking idly in at the bow-window. He appeared bored, but that expression lifted, flatteringly, on catching sight of her; and when she came out, he was waiting. 'Miss Fortune. If we are going the same way, may I walk with you? I should add that I am not going anywhere in particular.'

'No more am I, sir. So it will be curious to see how we go on!'

'Indeed – but to be serious – I would not impose. You may have compelling reasons for seeking the relief of solitude this afternoon:

reasons I will no further allude to than to say I entirely understand them, and to add that I admire your patience and forbearance.'

'Thank you – but I have had enough solitude now, and would be glad of your company. You allude very delicately, sir, and yet you need not. Mrs Catling was fierce upon me today, and will be again, no doubt, some other day: that's her way. I put up with it because that is what I am there for; and as the man said when he fell off the cliff for the third time, use is everything.' Caroline was the more breezy, perhaps, because she did not want to be pitied.

'Well, I had a notion she was formidable, from my friends the Downeys. Whom I saw not long ago, by the by, at Dutton's. I dropped a hint that their absence today from their aunt's had caused a certain acrimony in that quarter. Matthew despaired. It had seemed that the one thing sure to displease his aunt was to call *every* day: he had been reproved for it before on Brighton visits – it looked like taking her time for granted, and so on. Poor fellow: now he will have to work at making up lost ground again. You do not, I think, share this inflammable temper, Miss Fortune – and yet you are related to the lady by some connection?'

'No – not by family. The late Colonel Catling was officer of my father's regiment; and so my father besought Mrs Catling's interest on my behalf, having no other means to establish me.'

'Ah – he was in the Peninsula?'

'Yes – he was made captain before Talavera, and was wounded. I long ago lost my mother, and my father has had to do his best for me, without other resources.' Again with a strong resistance to being pitied, she added: 'He might have done a great deal worse, for my situation is quite eligible – I do not complain of it.'

'To be sure – and there are no terms short of the utmost respect and honour that may be accorded a hero of the war,' Mr Leabrook said, with a brief bow. 'It is curious and regrettable that, just a year after we were all thrilling to the news of Waterloo, the scarlet coat should come to be so little regarded. For myself I have always held the soldier's profession in high esteem: I could have liked to follow the drum, indeed – but, heyo, there is no military tradition in my family. We are squireish. Dare I say, a little too much so? To you, I dare. Because I believe that you, Miss Fortune, are as much attached to the pleasures of the town as I am.'

'Oh, you make me sound like a toper, or gambler, or worse!' Caroline said, laughing. 'How do you know that I am not fond of butter-making, and dogs, and tea and spillikins before an early bed?'

'From your lips, it all sounds charming,' said he readily, 'but I know that you would prefer the din of the Strand – the hugger-mugger of Vauxhall – the parade of Rotten Row. How?' he added at her look. 'How do we know the cat will like the hearth-rug and the cream?'

'And so now I am a tabby,' Caroline said, with a sigh. 'These are a very moral sort of compliments, Mr Leabrook, for there is not the least danger of my growing conceited from them.'

'Still,' he said amused, 'you do not deny it. But then I only spend a part of my time in London, and if I spent more no doubt it would fatigue me. Brighton is very well in its way; but now my carriage is mended, and has arrived here today, and that has set me wondering whether I should not be leaving. The luxury of choice, I know,' he added, with a sharp glance at her. 'I did not intend lingering, and yet part of me is disinclined to go: all very odd and vexing, is it not? What do you think I should do?'

'You can best determine, sir, whether there is anything to hold you here,' Caroline replied. She spoke a little more calmly than she felt – but only a little. While he was a most attractive man, and it seemed that this flirtation must shade at some point either into indifference or seriousness, still there was no high excitation or suspense in her. Strolling and talking in this way did very well; and so they might have gone on much longer, comparing places they knew in London, and gently disputing about books and plays, had not the weather intervened. It had been a fitful summer, liable at any time to drenching rain, and now down it came. They took shelter in a draper's shop, and when the rain slackened temporarily, whilst showing every sign of being a fixture for the day, Caroline decided she had better run for home.

'May I ask if I will see you at the Castle ball on Monday night?' he asked, before she darted off.

'That depends on whether your terrible *ennui* has taken you away by then,' she said, glinting a smile at him, 'but I will certainly be there.'

Chapter VI

If there were ever any doubt of Richard Leabrook's attending the ball at the Castle, it was resolved by Mrs Catling, who invited him to be one of her party for the evening. The others, of course, were the Downeys, on whom she had inflicted a new refinement of torment by an extravagant and even supernatural sweetness of manner the day after their mistake, complete with such an airy puzzlement as to why Matthew should possibly feel he had anything to apologize for that that unfortunate young gentleman could only gape like a trout: Caroline, whom she was treating quite normally again; and a rather staggery vague old crony of the late Colonel's, blue-faced from wine, who was newly arrived at Brighton, and inclined to profess himself Mrs Catling's Vassal and Slave with a gallantry somewhat debased by repetition, and quite vitiated by drooling lips. But Mrs Catling received these compliments very complacently; observing, as she sat in state having her stone-coloured locks dressed by the Shrewmouse, that he was related to half the best families in the kingdom.

It was now the height of the Brighton season: every lodging was taken, and every species of carriage was to be seen bowling along the Royal Crescent, the Marine Parade, and the Steyne; and the Monday evening ball at the Castle Assembly Rooms was so well subscribed that there was quite a crush going in at the inn-passage, made worse by the determination of everyone who aimed at fashion not to be early.

'A sad squeeze,' Maria remarked to Caroline, fastidiously gathering up her train where it had touched on the gritty flagstones, 'and I'll lay odds that half the people here have been ready for hours, and just peeping out of their windows waiting for their neighbours to leave. Well! this is something more like.'

The ballroom was magnificent in size, with a ceiling forty foot high, and stately in its mouldings, columns and frieze, all brilliantly lit by great chandeliers each as big as a barrel. Filled with company, it was however very noisy, the violins only a thin filigree of sound around the solid babble of talk, and very stuffy and hot: many older gentlemen were already looking cross, and fidgeting to be off to the card-room; and generally there was that degree of discomfort and inconvenience inseparable from social pleasures, and which in normal circumstances would be judged unendurable.

Caroline came here with a light heart and a willingness to enjoy herself that was not fretted by any conditions. Mr Leabrook had been much in her mind, and as Mrs Catling had given her permission to dance with any of her party, she looked forward to taking the floor with him. She had no doubt of his dancing as elegantly as he did everything else, and the prospect of standing up with a man whose good looks and distinguished manners must draw the eye even in such company was one her vanity could not resist. Splendid he certainly looked this evening, in a coat of superfine corbeau-grey, white marcella waistcoat, and cream breeches and stockings revealing a length and shape of leg to make stubbier gentlemen despair.

But she had decided that she was not going to make herself unhappy over him. The sum of his handsomeness, charm, and flattering attention was a substantial one; but the very fact that she found herself coolly adding these up suggested that she was not so captivated as to place her heart in any peril. He engaged her for the first pair of dances, and the third, and was every bit as graceful a partner as she had supposed; and she did not at all dislike the envious glances she received from young ladies who were ten times more fashionable, and a hundred times richer than herself. Still, there could be no monopolizing her in such a place; and whilst having to dance a quadrille with the drooling old soldier was something of a trial, she was quite happy to stand up with Matthew for the fifth.

He was in good spirits; and, on her remarking so, said with a smile, 'Aye – a letter has done that. Such a small thing as a letter is, and such worlds of happiness it can open up! I need not tell you, Miss Fortune, who it is from. The confidences you extracted from me the other day will supply the sacred name, which I hesitate to pronounce in so public a place.'

'To be sure,' said Caroline, feeling too cheerful to protest that the confidences he had poured out to her had hardly been *extracted*, 'very wise. I hope that person is well, Mr Downey.'

'She is,' he said eagerly, 'she is wonderfully well, I thank you – that is, she says so in the letter – I speak from that evidence only, of course – but then if she were not well, she would hardly be able to dissemble it even in writing, for she is like myself, quite incapable of disguise. And it is a communication so full of warmth and tenderness and patience that it has truly kindled my spirits. Affairs such as these I usually chafe at – their irksome formality oppresses me – but tonight I do not at all mind it. Strange effect from a square of paper!'

'So it is,' she agreed cordially, 'and I found the same effect myself this very morning.' Her father had written one of his rare letters – to her surprise, from Bath. He had fallen in with an old bachelor comrade who was going to try the waters, and had offered him a share of his board and lodging for the price of his company; and Captain Fortune, considering himself safe there now from creditors, had accepted; and he was obviously having the time of his life, for he could hardly take a turn through Sydney Gardens without hailing half a dozen familiar faces. But Caroline had a chance only of saying a little of this: Matthew smilingly told her that he was very glad, and then reverted to the subject of his own letter, thereby signalling that he shared the common preference for talking over listening.

Soon after this she would gladly have sat down a while, so overheated did she feel; and Maria was in worse case, having adopted the fashion of long sleeves, which she protested made her feel as if she were baking like a closed pie, though in truth she looked as coolly composed as ever. But Caroline had not been fanning herself long before the Master of Ceremonies approached her, and offered an introduction to a mild young man with a long chin and a feeble whisker, who said that he really did not dance, and proceeded to prove it through an excruciating cotillion. But he was, she gathered, very eligible; and this attention from the lordly M.C. was an indication that, if not quite the belle, she was making an impression. So Mr Leabrook murmured in her ear, as she took her seat again.

'I suppose I should be honoured – but now we have been introduced, that man can ask me again! And what if they have waltzing? I do not think I could bear it!'

'From that I shall be your preserver,' Mr Leabrook said, laughing, 'and as for waltzing, I believe the M.C. is old-fashioned, and still disapproves it. My wish, Miss Fortune, is to claim you again, but that uncanny perception of mine tells me you are fagged for the moment. Come – that chair is narrow – I see a sofa over there by the wall, and I can navigate you to it.'

He led her skilfully through the press, saw her comfortably seated on the sofa, then melted away, to return shortly with a glass of claret-cup that was very welcome. While she drank it he sat on the edge of the sofa, watching her in an attentive silence, which at last she taxed him with.

'Are you out of spirits, Mr Leabrook? You are rather abstracted. Unless you have forgotten my name and are desperately trying to think of it – that has happened to me – I find mentally going through the alphabet helps to jog the memory, though of course if the name is Young or Yates it takes an unconscionable time to get there—'

'I was never in better spirits,' he said, gently but distinctly, 'and I very well know your name, Miss Caroline Fortune. I have been thinking of it a good deal.'

'Have you indeed? You decidedly must lack things to occupy your mind, sir. A course of improving literature is needed. What would you say to Fordyce's *Sermons*?'

'Nothing I can repeat to a lady. You were right upon the mark the other day, you know, when you spoke of my *ennui*. In truth I am half dead from it!'

'Dear me. And which half do I have the honour of addressing now, Mr Leabrook?'

'It is only in the present company that the tedium is banished. And that has set me thinking, and wondering. About you, Miss Fortune.'

'Has it?' Caroline said – an answer that failed sadly of wit, but had at least the virtue of being intelligible, unlike the strangled gurgle that was all she had feared she could produce. Feared – for something seemed to have changed: Mr Leabrook lounged beside her as composedly as ever, but she felt his attention upon her tightening. And she knew now, if she had not known before, that if he were about to become serious with her, she must deeply regret the alteration: that it was not what she wanted.

Mr Leabrook seemed to find nothing in her silence or awkward looks to disconcert him, however; and proceeded in his soft yet precise voice, like the purposeful padding of cat's feet. 'I fancy myself an indifferent good judge of people. Dull sticks and prigs and prudes above all I can spot a good way off, because they bore me so. Likewise, I know when I meet their opposite. You, I imagine, would waltz very well, Miss Fortune: you would find nothing shocking about it, nor suppose that the pressure of a man's arm about your waist would kill you.'

'I had no idea I was so transparent,' she said, regarding him doubtfully.

'It depends who is looking. And you and I have the measure of each other, do we not?' Without waiting for an answer, his eyes still fixed on hers, he pursued: 'Brighton is very well: I like it for a time – but it is not the whole of life, as you know. I have had pleasant company here with Matthew and Maria, but they will be leaving soon enough: Matthew must return to the dreary law for the Michaelmas term, and their mother will surely want Maria. So I shall not linger once they go. And it occurs to me to wonder – my dear Miss Fortune, why should you be left behind? I have mentioned my carriage. It is fast, and well-upholstered, and you will find it comfortable. Let me take you away in it.'

'Take me away, sir? Where do you mean I am to go?'

'Away from here – from Mrs Catling – from grinding dreariness and mean subordination!'

'Well: I hardly know whether to be flattered or perturbed that you see me as so desperately in need of rescuing, Mr Leabrook. Do you suppose me so fragile that, if I wished to flee Brighton, I could not find the coach fare myself, and make my own way?'

'Of course I do not suppose you fragile in the least,' he said, chuckling, 'but you do right to reprove me for not speaking plainer, even though you know well what I mean. The carriage, Miss Fortune, is to contain the two of us – you and I, together. There is a moon. We might even go tonight.'

Caroline found her breath quite stopped in her throat, and when she struggled to speak, there came a gasp that she did not like: it sounded girlish and overwhelmed; and she was neither.

'Do you mean a Gretna elopement, sir? A romantic fancy – I would say even fantastical – for you well know I have no stern guardian reserving my hand for another suitor.' She looked levelly at him. 'But I think you do not mean that.'

'Nothing so conventional,' he said, renewing his smile after a bare moment. 'Conventional – and trite and narrowly respectable – the exact qualities that I do *not* find in you, Miss Fortune. We go – where, who knows? London, to be sure. There is the greatest felicity coupled with the least observation. We may do as we please: taste all that the town has to offer. To say no more, I find this a delicious prospect; and so, I flatter myself, do you.'

'"Come live with me and be my love, And we will all the pleasures prove . . .",' she recited flatly. 'I cannot remember the poet's name, but the sentiment is apt, I think.'

'It is very apt,' he said, with warmth, 'and my confidence was not misplaced – you *do* understand me.'

'Oh, yes, I do, sir. I understand very well. Forgive me – I am just trying to recollect how the verses continue. After all the pleasures have been proved, I mean: what then? I am almost sure they do not say. Poetry is often very vague like that. Life is more inclined to go on.'

'Yes – curse it. And that is why I truly believe one must always seize the day.'

'And gather ye rosebuds, and come kiss me sweet and twenty, and all the rest of it. I am afraid I must have a prosaic mind, Mr Leabrook: it will keep asking *what then*?'

He shrugged. 'What then? I protest against the dull phrase. Think how much happiness has been lost by a timid preoccupation with consequences!'

She was now so very disgusted with him that she feared she could not moderate her tone. But she mastered herself, for it was important that he understand in what the disgust consisted: that she took no prim, missish offence, but could not submit to be treated as if her life was of no account.

This was the nub of it. Richard Leabrook was well able to dismiss the question *what then*? He was a man, and rich, and independent: the consequences of any such affair must be slight. For her, they must be profound.

'I am not sure how to answer you, Mr Leabrook: there is so little precedent. When a man asks a woman to marry him, it is I believe usual to begin with an expression of gratitude for the offer, whether she means to accept or decline. When a man simply declares that he is in love with a woman, there is similarly I imagine some formula of acknowledgement that may cover the confusion of the moment, whether she returns his sentiments or not. But when a man asks a woman to go off with him and become his mistress for some unspecified time on some unspecified terms, there is as far as I can see no ready response – certainly none that could do justice to her indignation, or his conceit.'

'Very well,' he said, blinking rapidly, though his posture was unchanged. 'Very well, you have placed the matter in the worst light possible. But consider the better. Consider what you would be leaving behind. Servitude, no less; and servitude without hope of a prosperous release. For you have told me you have no other hopes or connections.'

Their conversation the other day, in which he had asked with such apparent sympathy about her father and her situation, came back to her with new understanding. Yes, he had made sure of her.

'I have nothing, in fact – that is what you are saying.'

'No indeed: you have charm – wit – taste – beauty – these have engaged my attention from our first meeting; and there was, I thought, something else also – spirit, daring. Without that, I would not have ventured thus. But above all, I did not suppose *you* indifferent to *me*.'

'Certainly there is, or was, a degree of regard, even partiality,' Caroline stated. 'I was always glad to see you: we agreed very well. But that is not enough to throw myself away for. I would have to set a very low value upon myself to do it. And though you represent Mrs Catling as treating me like a servant, in truth you esteem me at even less value than she does. For I am, as you say, without hopes or connections: consider then what my prospects would be once our little adventure was over.'

'So: I am mistaken in you, Miss Fortune.' His tone was dispassionate, even bored; but his look was much altered: he resembled a handsome boy denied a treat. 'You are a deal more conventional than I supposed: I am sorry for it.'

'Not wholly mistaken, perhaps, Mr Leabrook. I do not say that I could never be persuaded to sacrifice my reputation to passion – only that it would take a great deal more than I feel for *you* to make me do it.'

She got up and walked away from him. Absently she noticed that he was sufficiently discomfited to forget his manners, for he did not rise with her; but she was chiefly occupied with balancing the emotions of astonishment, anger, and hurt pride, which she bore just like heavy, awkward objects, requiring grim concentration.

The crowds of people around her were a blur, but she did catch sight of the sunflower-like head of Maria Downey, and turned instinctively away from it. She needed a space of solitude: she was unequal to enquiries about her agitated state. Worst of all, this evening's work appeared to her as something she could not tell anyone about.

Much as she might revile Mr Leabrook for his arrogance and

presumption, still she felt a sharp humiliation that he should suppose her a likely prey. Swiftly she reviewed her own conduct, pained lest it expose her to the reproach of having encouraged him. She could not imagine it had: her mind grasped an essential truth about the man, that he was a mere opportunist; and it further asserted that if to flirt was to declare oneself fair game, then half the women in the room were compromised. But this did not draw the sting of her feeling. She could not confide to Maria, for example, something so utterly mortifying to her sense of self. And from Mrs Catling, whose stony bosom one would not fall on in any event, she could imagine no response better than acid satire, whilst the worst – and most likely – would involve her own motives being suspected, and a cold conclusion drawn that she had thrown herself at him.

Bitterest of all, perhaps, was her reflection on her own misjudgement; for if her affections had never been wholly engaged, still she had liked Richard Leabrook very well. Silence, then, must be her portion, hard as it was; and cheerful composure must mark her outward appearance, difficult though it was to command – for she did not want him, above all, to perceive her trouble. She lingered in the card-room, on pretence of looking over a game, for as long as she dared, whilst summoning her normal looks and manner.

Mrs Catling was snappish with her on her return: the old lady had put on kid shoes for the two sedate dances she allowed herself, but now wanted them changing back for her overshoes, and only Caroline would do. This was usual enough to be reassuring. And then Mr Leabrook sauntered over, and declared to Mrs Catling, with a great yawn, that he was tired to death – he had been on a long walk today, which must account for it – and he craved her pardon for breaking up the party, but he simply must return to his lodging, or sleep where he stood.

He was uncomfortable, and would meet no one's eye. Here at least was a satisfaction to Caroline; but it was the only one she could draw from an evening that seemed to drag interminably to its close, and which to her own shame she rounded off, once she was alone in her room at West Street, by sitting down and crying for a good half-hour. Sleep would not be summoned; and the only help, at last, was to creep down when all the household was abed, and take a little of Mrs Catling's restorative brandy from the sideboard. She might have felt a renewed shame at this: but Caroline's sense of humour feebly rallied. 'I have been taken for a hussy tonight,' she quavered, to the small hours' silence, as the tot went soothingly down, 'what does it matter if I am a toper as well?'

Chapter VII

Mr Leabrook was leaving Brighton at once: he came to West Street to announce it, coolly and pleasantly, the very next morning. The Downeys were calling at the same time, and Matthew indignantly protested that this was the first he had heard of it.

'It is the first anyone has heard of it,' Mr Leabrook said, smiling, 'because I have only just made up my mind to it. My dear Matthew, don't look so surprised. I told you I can never endure to be in one place for very long; and now that my carriage is ready, I have the itch to be moving again. Deplorable, I know.'

'But why? We have all been getting along so famously.'

'That is always the best moment to part – before indifference and aversion set in. Not that I can imagine feeling either towards such excellent company, but you take my point.'

But Matthew was more inclined to labour a point than to take it. He went on declaring himself baffled and disappointed. Mr Leabrook laughed and appeared perfectly easy – but Caroline knew better now than to trust to appearances with that gentleman. And if there were any consolation to be found on this most unpleasant of mornings, it lay in the suspicion that she had wounded his pride more than he cared to show, and that he was hastily quitting the scene of a defeat.

Consolation – but not much. Caroline had woken with the unhappy recollections of last night aggravated by the after-effects of brandy, and was feeling thoroughly miserable. At breakfast her shaking hands had made such a clatter with the coffee-pot and the sugar-bowl that Mrs Catling had amiably remarked that she was more stupid than usual today. Of the secret that oppressed her, she still could not say a word; and between the twin stones of inner loneliness, and the obligation to be companionable, she felt herself ground to a very powder of perplexity.

And now here was Mr Leabrook calling, and as elegant and civil as ever, and actually sitting a yard or so from her in his rangy, lounging way, chatting on as if nothing had happened. Yet there was a change. He did not address a single word to Caroline.

The smooth surface of his manner was unruffled, which made the omission less noticeable – not that anyone there was inclined to take very much notice of her in any event. But Caroline felt, acutely, the intended sensation: he was turning her invisible.

For a few moments she contended with a fierce desire to pick up the nearest candlestick, and launch it at his handsome head along with the cordial enquiry, 'How was *that* for invisible?' But she overcame it, reflecting that such a demonstration might convey to his vanity a strength of emotion she certainly did not feel. The wretchedness and awkwardness must be borne: they would soon be over, since he was going away; and time would reduce the whole thing to a cautionary episode, even perhaps to be recalled with wry thankfulness as a lucky escape.

Such was her hope: but if only Matthew would let the matter lie!

'This is so very sudden,' he grumbled. 'Really, Leabrook, I cannot think why you must be so sudden about it. I had thought of your staying another week at least – I had thought, you know, of making up a party to Shoreham, or—'

'That you may still do without me, my dear fellow. And then, consider – how long before you and Miss Downey must return to London? A fortnight at most? You see, we are all impermanencies here, except your estimable aunt.'

'Who is beginning to wonder at you, Matthew,' said Mrs Catling, with relish. 'For it would seem that when Mr Leabrook is gone, there will be nothing in Brighton you care for. Not a flattering reflection on me, though not surprising.'

Oh, Matthew, don't rise to it, Caroline thought – even as Matthew did so.

'Really, Aunt Sophia, you could not suppose I meant – I only meant that Leabrook's company is, you know, an addition – and that without him—'

'It will not be the same!' put in Mrs Catling, sighing. 'Yes, I see, Nephew – I see very well!'

'No, no, it will be the same – that is, there is always pleasure in *your* society, Aunt – but the difference I mean . . .' Matthew toiled on: the effect was rather like watching a bound man trying to untie his ropes with his teeth.

It was Mr Leabrook who put an end to it. 'Downey, enough: your sentiments do you credit on both sides. Now here's my proposal: you and Miss Downey shall come and stay with me in Northamptonshire, just as soon as you are able, and as soon as it can be reconciled with your aunt's prior claim. What do you say to that?'

'Prior claim? Dear me, you make me sound quite the tyrant,' chuckled Mrs Catling. 'I would not dream of standing in the way of such an invitation: indeed I shall think quite the worse of you, you two, if you do not take it up. But I am not without regret on my own part for your going, Mr Leabrook: for who will we have now to compose our quarrels?'

'There, Matthew,' Maria said yawning prettily, 'it is all handsomely arranged, and I think you may leave off hammering at that same nail now.'

'True – to be sure, yes,' Matthew said, 'though I still think you might have said something, Leabrook, instead of being so sudden.' His eye fell for the first time on Caroline. 'Miss Fortune, don't you think so?'

Caroline said, looking at no one: 'I'm sure Mr Leabrook has excellent reasons for his departure.'

'On the contrary, only foolish trivial ones,' Leabrook said – but addressing Matthew, as if he had spoken. 'Still, they suffice. So, Mrs Catling, do you hear when the Prince will be next in residence . . . ?'

'Well, I never saw a better-bred man,' was Mrs Catling's conclusion, after Mr Leabrook had taken his final leave. 'You might do worse, Matthew, than look to him as your model. There is still time to erase your father's unfortunate influence, and make something of you.' And to Caroline: 'Hm, you're mighty quiet, miss: if going to balls puts you into a mopish mood, I shan't take you to any more.' Altogether Mrs Catling was in high good humour, and only needed to discover some negligence on the part of the servants for her day to be complete.

Caroline did not much care if she ever attended a ball again. When Mr Leabrook left West Street, he made such a cold, correct, and silent bow over her hand, accompanied by such a fleeting, inward twist of a smile – as if he drily laughed at himself for ever thinking of her – that she suffered a renewed gush of misery, sufficient quite to put out the spark of philosophical hope she had lit.

It was not that she sorrowed to see him go. Indeed there was the rub and rasp of it: she had been put in such a position that no usual emotions seemed appropriate. There was anger, indignation, humiliation – yet none in a strong enough measure to be purgative. Her sense of self had been dealt the severest blow. If Richard Leabrook had seen her as fair game, then was that how she habitually appeared? Did she bear some Cain-like mark that incited the adventurer, that roused the rake? Nonsense, said Reason: as well say the fox invites the hounds. But Reason's voice could not always be heard above the clamour of self-doubt, especially when she fell to a melancholy wondering whether this kind of offer – the kind that was hardly distinguishable from an insult – was the best she could ever hope for.

In this depression of spirits, it might be expected that Caroline would have little energy to devote to pleading Matthew's cause, especially as he had been, if unwittingly, the means of bringing Richard Leabrook into her life. But it was not so. During the ten days that remained of the Downeys' visit to Brighton, she took every opportunity of acting as his advocate with Mrs Catling. Simply, it was refreshing to think of this rather than of herself; and notwithstanding his occasional absurdities, Caroline remained well affected towards the young man, whose sincere attachment to the worthy apothecary's daughter appeared the more honourable in contrast to the grubby experience she had just undergone.

How much of this she could take credit for she could not tell, but by the time of the Downeys' departure Matthew stood well in his aunt's favour. Not only had they scarcely quarrelled for a week, but Mrs Catling had decided to increase his allowance, and unbent so far as to say she would miss his nonsensical ways when he returned to London.

'This harmony is almost sinister,' Maria confided to Caroline, as they took their farewell promenade along the Steyne, pointing her parasol at the figures of aunt and nephew walking arm in arm ahead. 'I hope it's not the calm before the storm.'

'Perhaps the storms are over.'

'Aunt Sophia and Matthew at peace – what a thought! It makes a sort of revolution in my brain – like when Galileo, or was it the other one, stood up and said the earth goes round the sun and not the other way, or does it? For my part I don't know how they can *tell*, anyhow. One has quite enough to do to get up in the mornings, without thinking about the universe. Mama will not be best pleased.'

'About the universe?'

'Lord, she don't know there's any such thing. A woman of limited views. I remember Papa patiently trying to explain to her where oysters come from. "But they come," says she, "from the fishmonger's, and that is all there is about it." No, she won't be pleased about Matthew and Aunt Sophia being friends.'

'Oh? I had thought – that is, I had supposed—'

'That Mama's forever angling for Aunt to untie her purse-strings for us? So she is. But still it wouldn't suit her for her sister to seem anything but an ogre. That way she shows up in the best light. Poor as a church mouse but warm-hearted. Oh, we are a sad set, aren't we? You're lucky you're not really connected to us.' Maria aimed a prod with the parasol at the fat bottom of a bad-tempered little boy who ran across their path, and feigned innocence when he glared round. 'I shall be so glad when my tropical gentleman comes home and changes my name.'

On the way back it was Matthew who claimed Caroline's arm, and began at once to speak warmly of her efforts on his behalf. 'I confess,' he said, 'to some misgivings at first – after you so very deftly got my secret out of me. I did wonder whether it would be safe – whether you might not let something slip, in the very act of trying to assist me.'

'Well,' Caroline said, after a speechless moment, 'you may rest assured, Mr Downey, I have used the utmost discretion.'

'Oh, to be sure, that is quite plain. There could hardly have been this cordiality otherwise. By the by, Leabrook writes me the pleasantest letter: he is back at his place in Northamptonshire now, and looks forward to welcoming Maria and me there as soon as may be. I'm so glad, you know, that it was not one of those invitations simply thrown out with no intention of their ever being made good. I dislike that sort of superficial dealing extremely. But then as soon as I met Leabrook I knew that here was a man after my own heart – plain, open, honest – it's odd how one can tell these things at once, is it not?'

There was nothing to be said to this except yes, unless she were to take it upon herself to warn Matthew about his friend's capacity for duplicity: which would mean making her own embarrassing disclosure. Having no intention of doing that, and considering she had already been officious enough on Matthew's behalf, Caroline contented herself with a murmured agreement that it was, indeed, odd.

'I knew you would think so!' he said, fairly beaming on her. 'You know, I was never more pleased by anything than the capital way we two have got along, Miss Fortune. I shall be very happy to think of Aunt Sophia's having your company when I am back in London – indeed, I shall be heartily glad to see you again when we next visit. I'm not sure when it may be – before Christmas perhaps; but no matter, because you will still be here.'

'I will still be here,' Caroline echoed; and could not quite prevent the plunge of her heart at those words, and the grey picture they conjured up.

* * *

The Downeys returned to London, and soon, though the resort remained lively enough, a more general exodus was noticeable from the villas and lodging-houses of Brighton as the summer came to a close. The tints of September were little to be observed, as it had long been remarked that a man who wanted to hang himself at Brighton would be thwarted for lack of a tree to do it from; but the lessening bustle of wheels and hoofs about the streets, the appearance of shutters above the wrought-iron balconies, and the chill mists that stole in from seaward once the sun was down told their autumnal tale. And Mrs Catling revealed a new aspect to her character. Caroline would have credited her with the constitution of a grenadier, and had often heard her speak scathingly of displays of sickliness: but the first sniffle of a cold transformed her into a tremendous invalid.

'My colds,' she informed Caroline, 'are worse than anyone's.' Having made a morbid achievement out of her indisposition, she retired to the drawing-room sofa and devoted herself to it. Her physician, a spruce, obliging little man who knew the value of his fee, agreed that he had never seen a worse case, and prescribed any number of powders and possets, as well as complete rest, and a lowering diet – though at a look from his patient, he hastily altered this to a strengthening diet, with as much beef, chicken, lobster, and so on as she could manage to force down. Nursing, tender selfless nursing, she must have also: fortunately there was her young companion to provide that. He further prescribed the regular indulgence of bad temper – or he might as well have, from the way Mrs Catling went at it. Recumbent before a blazing fire – and requiring the screen to be moved no more than six or seven times an hour – surrounded by jars and dropping-bottles and foot-warmers, Mrs Catling settled herself in for a good long bout of demanding illness. And Caroline was the one satisfying the demands.

This was her most testing time so far. Besides the constant attendance of a nurse, Mrs Catling wanted almost as constant amusement – reading, cards, backgammon and, when those failed, talk; and even a moment's distracted silence on Caroline's part was liable to call forth from her employer a growl of self-pity and abuse, to the effect that the selfish chit plainly did not give a hang for her sufferings, but no doubt would consider herself ill-used if she were turned out on the street for an ungrateful hussy. This truly was what it meant not to have a minute to yourself: exhausted sleep was Caroline's only respite. (And she was made to feel guilty about that, Mrs Catling being unable, as she mournfully declared, to get so much as a wink – which made a minor curiosity of the heroic snores that issued from her bedchamber as soon as the candle was out.)

And then there was the mood of gloom to contend with. Being poorly made Mrs Catling depressed and, above all, inclined to fancy herself neglected.

'I suppose they have not a thought to spare for me,' was her lament, when a whole week passed without a letter from either of the Downeys in London. 'I might be on my deathbed for all they care. Mind – *then* they would care, oh, yes. Care for what they might get. And come to that so would you. Are you quite sure there were no letters this morning?'

Not that morning, or the next, dearly as Caroline wished there were. The desperate idea came to her, as Mrs Catling's despondency grew daily more savage, of forging a letter from Matthew, just to cheer her up. The handwriting would not matter, as Mrs Catling only gave such letters a glance, and passed them over for Caroline to read out; and she thought she could make a fair stab at counterfeiting Matthew's style, by frequent references to his feelings, and as many repetitions of the words *I* and *me* as possible. (Weariness had made her rather satirical.) She was on the point of trying the experiment when a letter arrived at West Street that altered everything at a stroke; and the letter was not for Mrs Catling, but for her.

She was permitted to open her letters after breakfast, and she broke the seal of this one in a sheer blank of puzzled inexpectancy. The hand on the cover was quite unknown to her. She never got letters at all except from her father – and it occurred to her, as the paper crackled open, that she had not received one lately: not that he was a regular correspondent, but still . . .

Mrs Catling, steeped in coddled eggs, devilled kidneys, and self-pity, waited for a rheumily breathing minute or so, and then demanded impatiently: 'Well, what have you there? You might tell me, since I never receive any letters of my own. It would be *something*.'

Caroline heard herself saying, as if from far off: 'It is a letter from my aunt.'

'Aunt? I wasn't aware you had one.'

'No . . . I knew of her. We have never met,' said the far-away voice. 'This – this is my first letter from her.'

'Aunt on the mother's side?' Mrs Catling enquired, morosely sniffing into a handkerchief.

'Yes. My mother's sister. Her name is – her name is Selina—' and then the far-off voice became her own again, and Caroline burst into helpless tears.

'Oh, come,' Mrs Catling said, after an open-mouthed moment, 'come, what's this? I never supposed you so sentimental. What, this aunt wants to be friends with you at last, hey? Probably she's heard you're well placed with me, and now all of a sudden she wants to develop the acquaintance. I know their ways. You should tell her—'

'It isn't that,' Caroline got out through her sobs. She did not want to pronounce the direful word; and, at any other time, what she came up with instead would have seemed absurd. 'My father,' she said, 'is no more.'

'No more what?' croaked Mrs Catling above her handkerchief: then meeting Caroline's swimming eyes, said: 'Ah! Ah, dear me. Dear me indeed. Well, that is a great – a great nuisance for you.' She composed her expression – with obvious difficulty, with a rusty grinding of long unused cogs and wheels – into an approximation of sympathy. 'You'll want to go off somewhere and cry, I should think.'

Caroline did. To cry on someone's shoulder would have been better, but here that was out of the question.

In the solitude of her room she could give full vent to her grief, which shock rendered more overwhelming. Even a lifetime of jolts and reversals had not prepared her for the suddenness of this loss: nor could the unquestionable fact that her father had more often been encumbrance than support to her prevent the doleful cry into her pillow that she was all alone in the world. At last the storm had quieted enough for her to sit up and read over again the fateful letter. Yet it was precious too – in a way it was the last of her father, and thus a relic to be touched tenderly. And strange, formal, and remote as were the accents of its writer, they did not lack a sort of tenderness, which made Caroline dwell droopingly on the letter in spite of its painful matter.

Gay-street, Bath – September 10th

My dear Caroline,

I pray you will forgive my addressing you thus, when I am scarcely known to you. I am your late mother's sister, and hence your aunt, Selina Langland: I dare swear even the name may not be familiar to you, the family breach having been so complete. It is not the least of my regrets at this long estrangement, that it should only be ended by the sad event I must tell you of. – My dear Caroline, your father died here at Bath last night after a short illness – so very short, and mercifully so I think, that there was no time to alert you to its progress.

How I come to be the bearer of this melancholy intelligence I may briefly state. It is simply this: my husband Dr Langland and I have been spending a part of this season at Bath as a result of a slight indisposition on his part, for which the physicians recommended the waters. This is a rarity for us, who go about very little – we are very far from being people of fashion – howsomever, we make our daily visit to the Pump Room, and it was there, not a fortnight since, that I turned and beheld your father.

We recognized one another at once, though we had not met for many years: not since my poor sister's marriage. Your father appeared to me little changed from the young captain whom our family once considered – wrongly, I see now – as the destroyer of my sister's happiness; and he was good enough to pronounce me unaltered by the years, which I know well was more kind than truthful. In short, you will see from this that we met cordially. The door to reconciliation stood open. I must confess that of late I have been a prey to sensations of shame and regret, whenever I have thought of the relatives lost to me through an old bitterness; yet always I lacked the courage to act upon such feelings, until I was as it were surprised into it, by the meeting with your father; whose openness, geniality, and readiness to be friends was a further reproach to me. He invited us to drink tea with him the next day: I accepted: so simply was the breach of years repaired. Or rather, a beginning was made: of course there was much to talk of yet, and much misunderstanding to be resolved, before there could be perfect ease between us.

Yet achieved it was: we met each succeeding day, with increasing friendliness – to the great satisfaction of Dr Langland, who as a man of the cloth has always deplored such familial disharmony. It was your father's greatest delight to give us his account of you, my dear, such was his pride in you; and we looked forward to completing the reconciliation, by meeting you, our unknown niece, at the earliest opportunity. Indeed your father had declared his intention of writing you with the cheerful news, the very night before he was taken ill.

This malady at first appeared a mere ague, which your father supposed he had got as a result of trying out the immersion-bath, the friend with whom he was staying having recommended it as a treatment for his lame leg. But he was rapidly prostrated, beyond any ordinary fever: there was evidence, according to the surgeon who attended him, of a severe heart-stroke; and though Dr Langland and I waited upon him as soon as we heard the news, he never recovered the power of speech, nor I think did he know us. Yet he left the world, at ten o'clock this morning, with no appearance of suffering: rather I would say he looked pleased.

My dear Caroline, I can only repeat how sorry I am to be the bearer of this news. I knew that the intercourse with you, which I hoped soon to have begun, must have commenced with apologies, but I did not imagine they would be of this sort. I do not like to prate of Providence, as that is too often the easy recourse of the lazy mind. Yet I remain grateful that I was permitted this opportunity of reconciliation before your father's passing, and hope you may find some comfort in the knowledge that your aunt and uncle await you in Bath, to help you in any way we can through the matter of your father's funeral, and the disposal of his effects. Dr Langland has such acquaintance among the clergy here, as make it certain we may procure your father a respectable burial at St Swithin's Walcot, unless you have some strong wishes to the contrary. If so, I expect to hear them from your lips very soon. I am aware of your situation, your father having told us all, and understand its dependence: nevertheless I know you will be released for such an event as this for as long as is necessary, and my only concern is how soon you may get here. Dr Langland agrees that travelling post would be best, and if as I suspect you are not able to bear the expense yourself, do pray assure your employer that if she will arrange it, we will refund the cost to her directly. As for lodging, there is ample room for you here – should you wish it: for it occurs to me that I am rather assuming a disposal to forgiveness and cordiality on your part, which may not exist. I should be sorry for it, but would not blame you.

Your affectionate aunt
SELINA LANGLAND

Caroline had just bathed her red eyes, and sat down to read this letter a third time, when there was a tap at the door and to her surprise, in tittuped the Shrewmouse, Mrs Catling's maid.

'The mistress thought you might care to use this,' she announced, thrusting into Caroline's hand a bottle of sal-volatile. 'And she wishes to know how long you're going to be, as she wants the newspaper read to her. *I* can't do that, you know: it's not my job.' And with a short but comprehensive look of disgust around her at the room, as if it were an abode of flagrant, perfumed, harem-like luxury, she minced out.

Caroline stared at the little bottle a moment, then set it down. She folded her letter carefully and placed it in the bureau, tidied herself in front of the mirror, and then went down to read the newspaper to Mrs Catling.

'Well! You've collected yourself, I see,' Mrs Catling said. 'Very good. You'll find it best: no amount of moping will help, you know. Now, there's the newspaper. Reading will take your mind off it. Oh! This wretched cold: you've no conception how I suffer.' She looked narrowly at Caroline over her trumpeting handkerchief. 'There was something you wanted to say, perhaps?'

'Oh – yes, Mrs Catling – thank you for the smelling-salts.'

Mrs Catling nodded, eyes modestly closed. 'You can return them to me later.'

In truth the mechanical exercise of reading out *The Times* to her employer suited Caroline as well as any activity just then: there was just enough occupation to keep her from being swallowed up by her grief, while a part of her mind could remain separate from her task, and pursue its own reflections.

In the midst of these, which were naturally melancholy, she remained Caroline enough to find a strand of loving humour in Captain Fortune's characteristically meeting his end in the very activity that was meant to do you good. No one would have laughed more heartily at that than the Captain himself; and feeble comfort as this was, it might have set Caroline in a fair way to consolation at last. But not while she was under Mrs Sophia Catling's eye. No one could make less allowance for the quiet nursing of emotional bruises than her employer – a woman so greedy of attention that she plainly resented and envied even the consideration that was due to bereavement. She expressed this at first by a niggling dissatisfaction with Caroline's manner of reading.

'What's that? Read that again. You mumbled through it. No, don't go on with that part – why on earth do you think a sick woman would be interested in a subject like that? I'm not talking about what I usually like. I'm talking about *now*. And hold your head up.'

But soon this was not enough: she snapped at Caroline to leave off reading, sighed windily, and said, with an ostentatious gathering of effort, 'Well, well, it's plain you're still brooding on your father, so you had better speak of it. Come, what's your concern? Did he suffer?'

'I believe he did not.'

'Very well. Are you troubling yourself about what he may have left you?'

'I know quite well he had nothing to leave,' Caroline said.

'Likely enough. Well, that simplifies matters, at any rate. Are you afraid his creditors will come after you for his debts? You won't be liable. Or d'you fear for your position here? It's true I took you on partly to oblige him, but I'm not about to go changing for that reason. Come, I can't think what else there can be to make you so untoward.'

'Only that I have lost my father, ma'am,' Caroline said, after an open-mouthed moment, 'and I can't help being sorry for it.'

'You might help it, if you exerted yourself. That is, by bearing up. Why, when Colonel Catling died, don't you think I bore up against my sorrow?'

Caroline murmured that she had not a doubt of it.

'Wait, what a fool I'm being – this cold has quite clouded my head – you'll want *mourning*, of course. Well, I dare say I can bear the expense. See my dressmaker tomorrow. I won't wear any myself, it would be affectation, but I daresay the coachman might have a hat-band when we go out, for a week or two. Now, I do believe that is all your little fusses dealt with, and all that remains to say is, be a credit to him, my dear, such as he was, and you can begin by mixing my sherry posset, as my throat is like sandpaper from all this talking.'

'There is one thing, Mrs Catling,' Caroline said, doing as she was bid, 'if you don't mind my mentioning it now. My aunt is arranging for my father's funeral in Bath, and wants to know how soon I may get there.'

Mrs Catling, applying herself to her handkerchief again, directed at Caroline such a grey, fishy, unresponsive look that her companion supposed for a moment she had not heard her.

'The funeral, ma'am. In Bath. I might go by the public coach, and willingly will do so, but my aunt says that if I go post, she will meet—'

'Go?' Mrs Catling repeated the word with as much force of amazement as if she had found it painted in large letters on her Chinese wallpaper. 'Go?' She ignored the steaming glass Caroline held out to her. 'I do not understand. Why on earth should you go?'

'Because he was my father,' Caroline found herself saying. Was this a trick question? Her fingers were burning: she turned to put the glass down.

'What are you doing?'

'I'm going to put this down to cool, Mrs—'

'I mean,' her employer barked, 'what are you doing, proposing this absolutely unwarranted absence from your duties to me, above all when I am in such particular need of attendance? My dear Miss Fortune, you have very much mistaken your position here, if you suppose you may gallivant off whenever the fancy takes you: and as for a time like *this*—'

'But it is an exceptional occasion, ma'am. I didn't suppose – that is, I assumed . . .' This was a dangerous word, she realized as soon as she had pronounced it.

'To assume is to presume,' Mrs Catling said. 'I will overlook the presumption in this one case, as you are something out of sorts on account of your loss. But you must know that your going to Bath is quite out of the question. I am surprised at you for even thinking it; and this aunt of yours must be a nonsensical woman to propose it. Does she not understand your position?'

'She assumes – that is, she thought I would certainly be permitted to go,' Caroline said.

'Pretty in her, to high-hand it with my private affairs! I'm afraid I cannot suppose her well bred: certainly it was not the custom in my day for women to attend funerals at all, let alone those in a dependent position. The whole thing is sentimental and ridiculous, and I would find it so even if I could spare you, which I cannot. You must write this woman and tell her so directly, if you please, and then no more of it. Well, didn't I tell you I wanted my sherry posset? Where is it?'

It was so very nearly all over Mrs Catling's head that for long afterwards Caroline could only wonder at her own self-control. But though she restrained her hand, she could not curb her tongue.

'Mrs Catling, I want very much to say goodbye to my father by attending his funeral, and I may as well say that I too assumed that I would be freely allowed to do so. I never intended a long absence from my duties, but an absence, yes, and one that I'm convinced most people would see as reasonable.'

'I am not most people,' Mrs Catling said, in a grinding tone, 'and you had better stop now.'

'I can't, ma'am, not without telling you my intention, which is that I shall go to Bath whether I have your permission or not. I do not think you can physically deny me, short of locking me up, and I assure you that nothing *but* that will prevent me. I do you the courtesy of telling you this, rather than simply going, because I do feel beholden to you for some kindnesses, above all to my father; but I emphatically refer to past events, and not your present conduct, which is nothing less than that of a selfish, unfeeling old tyrant.'

Caroline felt she was keeping commendably calm under the circumstances; and Mrs Catling – though she went from white to crimson to white again with a swiftness that was, viewed as an objective phenomenon, rather sensational – also maintained such command over herself that she sounded only capable of manslaughter rather than outright murder as she hissed at Caroline: 'Never – never have I been spoken to like that. I believe this grief of which you are making such a parade has turned your wits. I will allow you a few seconds to recover them, and then I will hear your full apology, and then I may consider – only consider – not dismissing you from your post at once.'

'You need not trouble with the consideration, ma'am, nor do I want your bounty of a few seconds. I am going to see my father laid to rest, and I am going today.'

'Then you will not be returning, Miss Fortune, ever. Pack all your bags, and consider our association at an end from the moment you step out of my door. You will not get a character from me, and I will acknowledge no communications. Is this your choice?'

'That's rather like the executioner asking the felon if he chooses to be hanged,' Caroline snapped. 'If you will see fit to give me my wage for this month, Mrs Catling, then I undertake to be out of your house by noon.'

'Apply to my steward: I'll have nothing more to do with you.' Mrs Catling waved her away curtly; but added with, it seemed, real bafflement: 'You are a fool – a fool against your own interests!'

It was in Caroline's mind to say that her father was too, but at least he would have one sincere mourner at his graveside, and this was one more than Mrs Catling could ever count upon. But that was not a thing to be said to an old woman, even in the heat of battle. So she walked to the drawing-room door with her head high, in silence, surrendering the last word.

Which Mrs Catling had still not spoken. 'And just you make sure,' she said to Caroline's back, 'you return my smelling-salts.'

Chapter VIII

Bath: finally it rose, a soft grey cluster of spires and hilltop crescents, before Caroline's weary eyes. She was in the public coach, aching comprehensively from a journey on roads churned up by autumn rain, and broken overnight at a very indifferent inn where her manifold bruises had proved no impairment to the appetite of the fleas. As a young woman travelling alone she had met with scant courtesy, the prevailing opinion being that she was either a harlot, or wished to be made into one: the scowls of matrons, and the winks of fat old men, conveying to her severally this disagreeable intelligence. Normally Caroline would have shrugged it off without a thought, having led a far from sheltered life, and being accustomed to self-reliance. But she had taken such a battering – the latest blow being the manner of her silent exit from Mrs Catling's house, with the very servants forbidden to speak to her, and only a hired porter to carry her baggage to the Ship, and not a single word or look of farewell to mark the end of this passage in her life – that her spirits were almost crushed.

So were her toes, from the clumsiness of the dozing attorney sitting opposite, who seemed to be stamping on a plague of beetles in his sleep. By stretching, she landed a sharp and almost accidental kick on his shin, but he only snorted and blew winy bubbles. Thank heaven, here was Pulteney Bridge like a graceful porch admitting them to Bath at last.

The Abbey bells did not ring for their arrival, of course, as they did for distinguished visitors in their own carriages, and Caroline was not here to write her name in the subscription books or parade the Pump Room. It was with a feeling not unlike the low light of autumn gold declining across the squares that she viewed this place, where her poor father had come to the end of his own eventful journey. But it was proof that her spirits were not quite as crushed as her toes that she was still curious to meet her unknown Aunt Selina, even so sorrowful as the occasion was. Nor had grief obscured the sight of the future, which must soon be faced in all its dizzying uncertainty.

Having been silently handed her outstanding wage before leaving Brighton, she was now in a position to calculate her worldly wealth, and to reckon up how she would manage with the ten pounds, eight shillings and some odd pence that she had tucked into a place, more secure than comfortable, under the bodice of her gown. Above all it must suffice to get her to London, where her best chances of employment lay – such as they were now, with no one to give her a character. She would have to apply to the Petty Register Office, and take absolutely what she could get, if it meant nursemaid or washerwoman. Well, turning a mangle could be no worse than pandering to the faradiddles of Mrs Catling – a situation she had no regrets about leaving, even though it was the one in which her father had placed his last hopes.

'He would not want me to be unhappy,' she told herself, as the coach swung to a halt. The thought made the tears start to her eyes again: she wiped them briskly away, and relieved her feelings by trampling all over the attorney's feet as she climbed out into the yard of the White Hart.

As a letter could scarcely have got here faster than herself, Caroline had not written her aunt of her coming, and it was with some nervousness that she directed her bags to be sent to Gay Street and, equipped with directions given her by a civil ostler, set out to walk there; for in spite of her aunt's invitation, there seemed to her a certain presumption in this. She had thought briefly of writing a note from the inn announcing her arrival, but that might give the even more presumptuous idea that she expected to be fetched.

Though it was the close of the season, Bath was busy yet, and there was no scarcity of strollers, of jogging sedan-chairs, of high-perch carriages negotiating the steep inclines. It was years since she had been here, and Caroline's mind was divided between recollecting familiar landmarks, noticing the sedater atmosphere after racy Brighton, and wistfully reflecting that these had been the last sights seen by her father's eyes; so that in no time at all she found herself at Gay Street, north of Queen's Square. On the subtle social index represented by Bath's various addresses, this stood high in solid respectability, without the glitter of fashion. The townhouse where her aunt and uncle lodged was tall, quiet, neat, a little gaunt, and wintry – all epithets that might have been applied to the lady who, to Caroline's amazement, flung open the front door when she was only half-way up the steps and, pushing aside an equally amazed maidservant, hurried down to meet her.

Not only to meet her, but to throw her arms about her, crying: 'My dear girl, I saw you from the parlour window – oh, my dear Caroline, I am so very thankful that you came.'

'But how could – how did you know who I was?'

'How? Because you are the image, the living image of my poor sister. I never saw such a likeness. You simply could not be anyone else.' Having embraced her, Caroline's aunt now withdrew to arm's length with an abrupt stiffness which suggested that such demonstrations were far more the exception than the rule with her. 'Forgive me, this conduct must seem quite extravagant. I haven't even introduced myself.'

'You're surely my aunt Selina,' Caroline said, moved by her reception, 'and I could have wanted no better introduction.'

'That's her again!' the other sighed. 'She would have said the same. I could never – well, what am I thinking? Walk up, my dear, please – you're surely tired after such a journey. You must have set off as soon as you got my letter.'

'Pretty much so,' Caroline said awkwardly.

'And you came post, I hope? Dr Langland will reimburse your employer just as soon as—'

'No – no, Aunt, I came by the coach.'

'Dear me. But she'll have sent someone with you, no doubt. Do they go straight back to Brighton? If they want refreshment, or a gratuity, we can surely—'

'I came alone.'

'Alone? By public coach? I never heard of such a thing.' And from the expression on Aunt Selina's long, honest face, it was plain that this was no mere figure of speech. 'What can she have been thinking? And you having suffered such a loss.'

This simple kindness nearly undid Caroline, in spite of her resolution not to begin the acquaintance by blubbering. Seeing this, her aunt changed the subject, saying her uncle was longing to meet her, and pressing her to walk in. Soon, without quite knowing how, she was in a comfortable parlour having her hand powerfully shaken by a lean, gangling, fresh-faced gentleman in clerical black with bright, boyish eyes under a profusion of grizzled-fair hair.

'My dear, I was never more glad in my life – but you must be tired. Hungry and thirsty too no doubt – we'll ring the bell directly. Only I was never more glad of anything in my life, you know, than this opportunity. John Langland. Your uncle John no less – I hope you'll call me so – I never knew Selina's sister, of course – not that that signifies – and in short I was never more glad – really this is quite delightful. Hard to see how it could be better.'

'Perhaps, my dear, it *could* be better,' suggested his wife, tentatively, with a pained look, 'as, happy though we are to see Caroline, it is not a happy occasion that brings her here.'

'Oh, to be sure, that's true – entirely true. Dear me, did I speak out of turn? I fear I must have, now you point it out, Selina. This is rather dreadful. My dear Caroline, I hope you don't think – really I'm quite floored now – and what I did not mean to suggest, and yet I fear I have suggested . . .'

Dr Langland's attempts to extricate himself reminded Caroline so forcibly of a carthorse backing out of the shafts that she was as near to laughter as the occasion allowed; and there was such an innocent good nature about him that she was very far from taking offence, and hastened to assure him so, whilst gently reclaiming the nerveless lump that used to be her hand.

'Refreshment you must certainly have, my dear,' her aunt said, pulling the bell-cord by the fireplace. 'Will you have – well, shall I suggest tea? You don't object to taking it at this time of day, I hope?'

'Not at all,' Caroline assured her aunt, who seemed really anxious on the point; indeed she would not have objected to something much stronger, but had an instant intuition that these were not people to whom one could say such a thing. There was much kindness and decency imprinted on their features, but everything – from her aunt's low, precise voice to her plain, untrimmed cap to the penitentially hard chairs where a heap of earnest sewing and a stack of devotional volumes, crowned with a magnifying-glass, attested the twin pursuits of their leisure – was serious: intensely serious.

'And now, you will be staying here with us until after the funeral?' Aunt Selina went on.

'If you will have me, I will, with many thanks. I'm sorry I couldn't write you before my coming – but things fell out rather awkwardly . . .' All at once a tremendous weariness overcame Caroline. It must have shown, for Dr Langland sprang forward and, with a great deal of hard breathing and banging, placed a chair for her close to the fire.

'Such a journey,' he fussed, 'and yet you didn't post it, my dear? Do I have you right? This is most odd – for when you wrote, Selina, you urged her to travel post, did you not? I could swear I remember you saying so – I was sitting by you when you wrote the letter, you recall, and we talked of it. I was looking into the fifth volume of Hooker's *Ecclesiastical Polity* – not the most cogent of the five, you'll agree, my dear,' he added, with a glance of humorous confidence at Caroline. 'And I distinctly remember marking my place with your pen-wiper, Selina, while we talked of the matter, and how we would settle the cost with Caroline's employer. Do I have that right? I could swear to it. Let me fetch the volume, and you'll see the pen-wiper still in it, I dare say—'

'I don't think you need do that, my dear,' said Aunt Selina, whose look of worn, fine-boned patience seemed at least partly attributable to dealing with her husband, like the ground-out hollow in a whetstone. 'I don't doubt you, but it really wouldn't prove anything, you know. I certainly did urge Caroline to travel post, but she did not, no doubt for very good reasons of her own.' A maid who, from her look of wholesome scrubbed seriousness might have been immediately identified as the Langlands' maid from a parade of a hundred, appeared noiselessly at the door. 'Jane, will you bring tea and bread-and-butter, if you please, and – is there a good kitchen fire?'

'There is a good kitchen fire, ma'am.'

'Then perhaps coddled eggs – if you consider our eggs are fresh enough to serve so. I am always in some doubt of Bath eggs. It is not like the country, where one may be sure – what do you feel, Jane? Would you advise the eggs?'

The maid, with due reflection, pronounced the eggs satisfactory, if no more. The question was now referred to Caroline, whether coddled eggs might not disagree with her; and Caroline, who from girlhood had freely eaten devilled kidneys, peppered steaks, mustard-patties, and other such spicy and soldierly fare, could only answer with proper solemnity that she was sure they would not.

'But these reasons,' went on Dr Langland, who plainly was not to be moved on from a subject, 'what can they be, my dear? Surely your employer cannot have refused to advance you the funds. Your late father, during our short acquaintance, constantly spoke of her as a sterling woman. Unless, dear me, she entertained a doubt of *us*, as guarantors for the sum? To be sure we are personally unknown to her, but our *bona fides* can be easily established. Selina is of course of unimpeachable family, and as for me a rectorship is surely recommendation enough, though one could add that my late sister was the first Lady Milner. Not that such worldly testimonials have any bearing upon virtue or honesty – they do not. One should never forget that humble poverty was often seen in the early Church as a positive aid towards virtue. You might easily find, my dear,' he said, with a benevolent nod at Caroline, 'a score of passages to that effect, in the writings of the Early Fathers.'

Caroline could not think of anything she could do *less* easily; but any hope that this diversion might lead her uncle away from the point was quickly crushed by his insisting: 'But tell us these reasons, my dear, pray – for my part I cannot at all guess them. I am at a loss. I am baffled. I really have not a notion—'

'Very well, sir,' Caroline burst out – partly to silence him, as he seemed prepared to go on finding different ways of saying he did not know more or less for ever; but also because she saw it must come out. She had not wanted to begin by telling her new-found relations that she had lost her position, and had hoped she might somehow avoid telling them at all. Caroline had not an atom of regret about leaving Mrs Catling, but she was human enough not to relish appearing a failure, especially as her father had obviously boasted to the Langlands about her late situation. 'The fact is, I have parted with my employer, and so it was scarcely to be expected she would pay for my carriage. She settled my wages up, but of course I will need to be careful of my funds, against my next situation; and so I came by coach. Really it wasn't so bad. I have gone about on the public coach before. A good stout umbrella protects you against most perils, believe me.'

Her aunt stared. 'You don't mean you rode *outside*?'

'Oh, no – I mean the umbrella is for fighting off the unwanted attentions of gentlemen. A good jab under the ribs usually does it – though with the fleshier sort of gentleman, whose ribs have long disappeared, you may have to go for the shin, or the kneecap.'

There was such a silence, such a stricken air of consternation, that Caroline swiftly made a mental review of what she had said, in case fatigue had made her pronounce some shocking indiscretion, or even one of her father's barrack-room curses. But no: and as her uncle and aunt continued to stare, she could only blunder on: 'Well, that is how it happened, at any rate. It was all rather absurd and unfortunate, but the main thing is I am here now, and so very relieved to meet you both at last. And yes, I am glad too, very glad, that Fate brought you and my father together before the end, Aunt: for my part I know and think nothing of the breach between our families except that it was a great pity, and now it's over and we can be friends at last, and that's something to be thankful for, and I still think so though I miss poor Papa sorely, and know I always will.' She had talked herself close to tears again, but successfully held them back. Still the silent gaze of her uncle and aunt was insupportable, and she said unsteadily, 'Lord, I'm afraid I've said something wrong, and I wish you would tell me what!'

'My poor child,' Aunt Selina said, stirring, 'oh, you poor child. The thought – the very thought, of what you have been through! I hesitate to pain you any more by alluding to it; but this parting with your employer – a Mrs Catling, I think – was it really absurd, as you call it? It was obviously not amicable. And though your father was at pains to praise her, I gained the impression of a strong-minded woman, to say the least. I fear this is uncharitable, but I have always entertained doubts about the temper of rich ladies who cannot secure themselves a companion unless they pay for one.' Something like a smile briefly lit the sombre face of Aunt Selina, who for all the plain-sewing and coddled eggs was clearly no fool. 'Am I on the right road, my dear?'

Caroline could not reply beyond a rueful smile in return, as the Reverend Dr Langland, who had been studying his wife in open-mouthed amazement as if she had just begun to talk in Aramaic, or even to quack like a duck, burst out: 'What? My dear Selina, what – what are we talking of? I really cannot understand you. The road you are talking of must be metaphorical, no doubt, but it might as well be in Samarkand for all I can set my feet on it.' He chuckled distractedly at his own joke, then cried: 'What?' again in such a fashion that, if he were not a transparently nice, kind man, it would have tempted you to brain him with his own magnifying-glass.

'I mean, my dear, that young women in such positions are often treated unfairly,' Aunt Selina said.

'*Are* they?' cried Dr Langland, with an inquisitive goggle at Caroline. 'Did you find that, my dear?'

'Well – yes,' Caroline said; and told them how she had come to lose her position with Mrs Catling, as briefly and coolly as she could, for she was not fond of people who made a great deal of their wrongs, and she certainly did not wish to seem continually angling after sympathy.

But even the bare account she gave of yesterday's events produced such gasps, such looks of dismay, and at last such another stricken silence that the wildest exaggeration could not have done more.

'This is shocking – shocking,' her aunt got out at last, shaking her head and going over to her husband to squeeze his hand. After a moment Caroline understood, with pleased surprise, what this gesture meant: it was true spontaneous affection: being moved, they reached out for each other. 'To dismiss you because you wished to attend your own father's funeral! It is absolutely inhuman.'

'Shocking,' echoed Dr Langland. 'I never knew there were people so lost to common feeling and decency. Dear, dear me! My eyes are opened.' Which they certainly were: to the extent that they were rather painful to look upon.

Caroline felt, in fact, altogether uncomfortable, so generous was the pity that enfolded her. Even from the maid, who presently brought the tea-tray, she received a degree of solicitous consideration that embarrassed her, being whisperingly entreated to try the eggs, and assured that if they were not just to her liking, they would be whisked away and replaced with something that was. Caroline found herself indeed in a similar case to Dr Langland, for she too had never known there were such people – such people as this, that is. She had moved amongst many circles in her life, some clever, some stupid, some moneyed, some threadbare, but all more or less sophisticated, and not inclined to expect much virtue in others, or to cultivate it in themselves. It came as a revelation, not quite commensurate with the proven existence of the fairies, but almost as charming and bewildering, that all the time there had been this other race of beings: kind, gentle, reliable, unworldly. It struck to her heart all the more after her recent experience with Richard Leabrook; and when her aunt wondered again at what she had been through, Caroline inwardly commented that she didn't know the half of it.

The coddled eggs were very good: they might have been even better as the *entrée* to a dish of roast mutton and capers and a pint of champagne, but Caroline was not about to quibble with any kindness extended her by the Langlands, whose transparent good nature was such that it set her wondering about something. How did this happen? How could the estrangement between the sisters, Selina and Caroline's mother, have been so lasting?

There were indications that Aunt Selina was, at least, conscious of the question. Several times Caroline caught her aunt gazing at her with a brimming look, as if she were on the verge of unburdening something; and when she showed Caroline up to her bedroom, urging her to rest, she seemed almost to choke on her parting words: 'I can't get over the likeness. Too long – really, it's been too long.'

Caroline was touched again to find the room all prepared for her. Nothing had been omitted for her comfort. Tired as she was, she did not think she could actually sleep, and was still thinking so when she opened bleary eyes on a room almost dark but for the firelight. She sprang up and hurried downstairs, realizing only when the drawing-room pier-glass told her so that she had all her hair dramatically on one side like a woman standing in a gale, and a sleep-crease not much deeper than a duelling-scar all the way down her cheek.

Her uncle, however, cried: 'There's a pleasant sight! Now, my dear, are you rested? And hungry? We waited dinner so you would not be disturbed – late hours are not our usual style. Mind, we dine later than in my youth – such is the irresistible pull of fashion – soon dinner will run into bed-time, and we shall all eat reclining like the ancient Romans – about whose digestion, you know, I have often wondered. Whether a dose of rhubarb might have made a difference to Nero or Caligula is a question you might ponder, my dear, next time you go through your Tacitus.'

Caroline promised she would, with a very indistinct idea of what she was promising; and hoped she had not put them out by sleeping so long.

'Not at all,' her uncle said, 'for we have been talking about you, my dear!'

'We have been discussing whether an appeal from us to this lady – this Mrs Catling,' Aunt Selina said, with barely concealed distaste, 'might help you: whether we could persuade her to change her mind, and reinstate you—'

'No,' said Caroline sharply. 'No – I'm sorry, I don't mean that I'm not grateful for the thought. But even if it were possible to alter Mrs Catling's decision, which is most unlikely, I would not go back to her on any account. What she said, you see, cannot be unsaid.'

'I see,' Aunt Selina said, with approval overtaking her surprise. 'Yes, I do see. But, my dear, this is a difficult situation for you. Are not such posts obtained by recommendation?'

'Oh, there is the Petty Register Office in Town – in London, that is. I mean to make that my first port of call.'

But Aunt Selina was unsure what that was; and when Caroline had explained it to her, she did not abate her expression of dubious regret. 'These things you know about,' she said, shaking her head. 'It does seem a pity!'

'Oh, not at all. The fact is, I am very well used to looking out for myself. That was how Papa –' she suffered a flinch of loyalty '– well, that is how I liked to live.'

'Ah – your poor papa. We have hardly spoken of him, have we? You'll want to know all, of course—'

'My dear aunt, I don't think I can bear *all*. It is very chicken-hearted of me I dare say – but I just want you to tell me he was happy to the end, and went off as if he were going to spend the evening at his club.'

'Happy? I do believe he was,' Aunt Selina said seriously. 'Most of all, that the families were reconciled at last. I never saw a man more unaffectedly glad of anything. Well, my dear, he lies yet at his friend's lodging in Westgate Buildings. I don't know whether you generally like to view . . .'

She soon did know, from Caroline's beseeching expression, that Caroline did not generally like to view at all.

'Well. Dr Langland has arranged, through his clerical acquaintance, that your father's funeral take place the day after tomorrow, and he will be pleased to officiate himself – if, that is, you are in agreement, my dear? And then there is the matter of your father's effects – his estate, as it were.' Aunt Selina looked exquisitely pained. 'It is, I'm afraid, rather a *small* matter.'

'Oh dear, it always was!' burst out Caroline, between laughing and crying; and it seemed the most natural thing in the world to bury her head on her aunt's neck while she decided the point.

The funeral was all it should have been – not an event to be dwelled upon, still less pronounced beautiful; but there was the satisfaction of a proper and dignified farewell: there was rightness, even in the parting tears; and there was besides abundant evidence of the sheer liking Captain Fortune had inspired in life, independently of his merits (or, in the jaundiced view, in spite of his not having any). His short stay in Bath had produced a long tally of acquaintance – mostly gentlemen of a military, sporting, or lounging type – and they all came to St Swithin's, filling the church with a potent presence of pomade, rum, tobacco, hessian-leather, and profanity. There was a characteristic flavour of eccentricity about them also – from the blue-nosed old commodore who swore he had seen a premonition of death in the bottom of his parrot's cage, to the starched dandy who declared, against all the evidence to the contrary, that he was Captain Fortune's long-lost brother and hence Caroline's guardian – the evidence being that he was Irish, red-haired, and all of seventeen years old. The young sprig's notions of guardianship consisting of a degree of physical consolation scarcely appropriate even in a true relative, Caroline was obliged to be firm with him.

'Oh dear,' Aunt Selina kept helplessly saying, in spite of Caroline's assurances that this was second nature to her. Caroline was quickly becoming aware how many things in her experience would call forth that 'Oh dear,' from her aunt: and that as her own life could hardly have been less sheltered, her aunt's could hardly have been more. Yet it was Aunt Selina's presence that got her through the day. She told her so, frankly, when in a sort of peeled rawness of feeling she faced the next morning – the first, it seemed to her, of her true orphaning – and was gently pressed to accompany her aunt on her morning walk to Sydney Gardens.

'My dear, I'm glad I could help,' Aunt Selina at last said, after one of her long meditative pauses, which Caroline was now beginning to find restful. Having long lived amongst people who must always be talking, she had been quite bewildered by these at first: had she offended? Was royalty present? 'All the same, I feel rather a fraud. It's late in the day for me to be a help to my one true niece – my one blood relative, in fact. Blood being thicker than water, as the proverb has it.'

'Well, but aren't those old proverbs nonsensical sometimes? As if one had ever supposed that blood was *not* thicker than water. And as for teaching my grandmother to suck eggs, I can think of nothing more grotesque.'

'Your grandmother would have thought the same,' Aunt Selina said, with a rueful look. 'My mother was a very *decided* woman in all ways, and the idea of her submitting to be taught anything . . . Not that I am so very different, I'm afraid, when it comes to stubbornness. I would go so far as to say, my dear, that I am a donkey and pig-head.'

She spoke in such gloomy earnest, that Caroline felt constrained to suppress the smile this image called up. 'My dear aunt,' she said, squeezing her arm, 'when I was at school once, the mistress having read my exercise asked me if I could really believe that Paris was in Spain, and I answered brightly that I could certainly believe it if I tried. But what you have just said, you know, I cannot believe.'

'Ah, you don't know me, Caroline.' Her aunt sighed. 'Indeed there is the point precisely! You don't know me, because you have not had the opportunity to do so, because of that stubbornness of mine. My quarrel with my poor sister was bad enough, but to transfer it to you—'

'Well, we haven't quarrelled, Aunt – we've just been apart.'

'Oh, in my heart I have kept up the bitterest quarrel, I'm afraid. Because of what Margaret did to me. There! That sounds thoroughly dramatic, does it not? What can your poor mother have done? Well, she didn't mean it, certainly: there was no malice in Margaret. Still, the result was the same. When she ran off with your father, you see, that left me: just me, at home with parents who were very fond but very severe and very, very disappointed in their elder daughter – the pretty graceful one from whom so much had been expected. Now, Caroline, you begin to see what a truly disagreeable person I am.'

'Do I?'

'Jealous and resentful – those are disagreeable qualities, surely. I resented the burden Margaret had placed on me – the burden of being the *good* one. Dear, dear, I'm shocked to hear myself saying this,' Aunt Selina went on, with a tremulous laugh, and a twitch in her sallow cheek. 'As if I did not wish to be good. When I have always been, from a girl, of the firmest Christian principles. And as for our family's way of living in Huntingdonshire – healthfully situated, retired and quiet, with very little society – why, that suited me too. And so did the prospect of a respectable marriage in due time to a gentleman of the neighbourhood. Why then the discontent? Perhaps because one would be pleased to have the *choice* – and after Margaret was gone from us, I felt I had none: only duty. Dear, dear,' she said again shakily. 'I have never spoken of this to anyone – not even John . . .' A look of alarm came over her, which was not difficult for Caroline to read: for what did this seem to say about her marriage to Uncle John? 'Don't mistake me, my dear. It could not have turned out better: that gentleman of the neighbourhood who came along in due course was the one man I could have loved: I have been wonderfully fortunate.'

'That I can believe. I never saw so well disposed a couple.'

Aunt Selina's look conveyed subtle thanks. 'Well! Stubbornness has a logic of its own. These bitter feelings can persist long after the occasion for them has gone. I became a most unpleasant people-watcher, observing and drawing conclusions. I can do it yet. Over there, you see that pretty girl in the blue pelisse, who seems to be fascinating the two young officers? I am monster enough to frown over that scene, and to hope that she hasn't got a plainer sister who will have to pay for her indiscretions. Delightful behaviour in a woman past forty who calls herself a Christian!'

'Well, Aunt, you have now been donkey, pig, and monster: but the word that occurs to me is human – that's all.'

'Does it?' Aunt Selina rejoined, with a sort of anxious hope; but then, shaking her head: 'Ah, you haven't heard the worst of it. I said how fortunate I had been in marriage: we were blessed in all but one regard – we never had a child. And will you believe I envied your poor mother there too? Not only had she been the daring one, she had got a child from it – and there was I . . .'

'Oh, Aunt, don't think of it.'

'No, no, I'm glad to.' Aunt Selina came out of one of her abstractions with a refreshed look. 'Severe self-examination, even when painful, is one of the best exercises for the soul.'

Caroline was not sure about that – looking into her own self seemed to her like rooting in an untidy long-neglected drawer, with no knowing what you might find at the bottom – but she was happy to see her aunt embarked on a more cheerful path of thought, and held her peace. The confession certainly seemed to have done Aunt Selina good; and when they got back to Gay Street, and Uncle John benignly asked if they had had a good walk, his wife surprised him by saying they had had the best of walks that ever was, and kissing him heartily.

The funeral being over, the Captain's clothes and effects being charitably made over to the poor, except for a few personal mementoes that Caroline divided with his manservant, dry, unimpressible old Marriner (who mopped his eyes at the graveside, but was canny enough to strike a bargain with a new employer amongst the mourners), the question of how long she was to stay at Gay Street was much in Caroline's mind. She had a lively aversion to trespassing on the Langlands' good nature; and when she went to bed, that night and the night after, was strongly conscious of significant looks between her aunt and uncle, and of being talked about after she had retired. Yet at each succeeding breakfast, when she gently raised the matter of her departure, they would put her off with some remarks about there being time enough to talk of that, or by producing some reason why she should stay a little longer. One of these, and not the most convincing, was the imminent arrival in Bath of someone called Stephen.

'My young kinsman,' Uncle John said, laying down the letter. 'He writes me from Beckhampton, where he is investigating a new find of antiquities – quite a hobby-horse of his – a Roman pavement no less – and if I know Stephen he will be down in the hole digging himself, regardless of propriety – even of danger. His poor mother used to get into fearful fidgets about it – wondered why he couldn't just run up tailors' bills like other young men. That was my late sister, my dear,' he explained to Caroline, 'Lady Milner. She married Sir Henry Milner of Wythorpe – my own parish, our dear, dear home ground – and Stephen Milner is their son. He says he will come and call on us while he is down this way – precisely *when* he does not say, which is just like him – but you must certainly stay, my dear, and meet him.'

'Not that you may find that a great enticement, as Stephen is not the most sociable of creatures, and you will be lucky to get a word out of him,' Aunt Selina said, smiling; and then, as if recollecting herself, 'But you must, indeed, stay until then, my dear, of course.'

Knowing their good nature, Caroline began to wonder if the Langlands simply could not bring themselves to tell her to go; and entertained herself with a vision of a guest less tactful than herself, staying to supper and bed and then simply never leaving. She did love being with her hosts, enjoying ever more warm and confidential talks with Aunt Selina during the daily visit to Sydney Gardens, and cementing her cordiality with her uncle by reading out to him of an evening from a very mildly comic novel (which caused him to laugh, hoot, shout in surprise, and stamp about, to a degree almost as alarming as gratifying to the reader), but for her own part she had a dread of imposing. After surreptitiously consulting the London newspapers in Duffield's circulating-library in Milsom Street – where, such was the elegant tone, one did not like to be seen drawing rings round the advertisements for situations – she began to have one set aside for her daily at a shop across the street, and pored its columns by the light of her bedtime candle.

And she found something that might suit. A lady at Highgate of independent means and infirm health wanted a respectable young person to fulfil the roles of companion, nurse, and general attendant. 'N.B. No Misses with Airs' was the advertisement's uncompromising conclusion; but as no references were required, Caroline felt that this was as good as could be hoped for, and wrote off at once. It was when she came back from posting this letter that she found her aunt waiting for her in the parlour, with the self-same newspaper in her hand, folded back at the marked advertisement.

'My dear, you'll think me intrusive. I was in your room to put fresh lavender in the chest. And then I saw this and – unforgivably perhaps – I grew inquisitive and looked. And read, and thought.' Aunt Selina, always sombre, was now so very sombre she seemed to be standing in her own pool of shadow. 'Caroline, may I ask you – are these your hope?' She pointed gingerly at the advertisements. 'Or rather – are they your desire? Because – oh, dear, I really shouldn't say it without John here—'

'But I *am* here, my love!' Uncle John leapt bodily into the room. 'I was listening at the door!'

Caroline had been unable to repress a small scream at this apparition, but Aunt Selina only clucked her tongue and said with mild reproof, 'My dear, really, this is almost as bad as the time you jumped out of the apple-cupboard.'

'I couldn't help it – I approached, I heard, and I knew what you were going to say.'

Aunt Selina reached for his hand. 'Did you?'

'To be sure – one doesn't, you know, after twenty blissful years, lose that ability. You were going to put to our niece the very question that we have been discussing.'

'Too soon, though, I fear,' Aunt Selina said, shaking her head. 'I'm afraid we may offend—'

'Come, we must grasp the nettle – and pray don't, my dear,' he added, with his glance of confidence at Caroline, 'be put out by that rather unflattering botanical proverb – it refers not to you but to the question – which is this: my dear Caroline, won't you come home with us?'

It had happened before, and she hoped it would not happen again, but with Caroline it seemed there was no help for it: she answered important questions absurdly. So now, weak-legged and groping blindly for a chair, she gasped out: 'For a visit?'

'To stay!' boomed her uncle exultantly. 'To live! To be – why, a daughter to us!'

'Not a daughter,' Aunt Selina put in, wincing. 'Whatever our own wishes, I think we offend against Caroline's recent loss to speak in quite that way, my dear.'

'True – true – dear me, how shocking, I am quite a fool,' said Uncle John, sagging and then rallying again all in one moment. 'Still, still – you do know what I mean – don't you, my dear?'

'Yes, I do. And you are too kind. And my heart is quite full,' Caroline wailed, and was taken into her aunt's arms.

'No, we're not, and so is mine!' cried Uncle John, embracing them both, skipping and laughing; so that they played a sort of tearful ring-a-rosie for a moment.

'My dear girl,' Aunt Selina whispered in her ear, 'I hope you will take to us! We are very, very different from what you have been used to!'

Chapter IX

The Langlands had thought it all through. They were able to meet every objection that Caroline raised over the next bewildering day or two.

Not that she did so out of any feeling against their proposal: for her heart had kindled to that at once, and not only in thankfulness at being rescued from insecurity and servitude. She considered her aunt and uncle, quite simply, the sweetest people she had ever known, and had already grieved at the thought of leaving them behind when she went to London. No, she raised objections because she fancied that this good fortune was somehow not deserved: that they must have made some mistake about her, which a very little reflection would reveal. Above all she wanted to be sure they knew what they were doing. Caroline thought herself no worse than any young woman of twenty years – but still, to take any of that species into a quiet, childless household was a great step.

The Langlands, however, were plainly in the habit of thinking round all sides of a question – witness a debate over whether the breakfast bacon was sufficiently salted so long, earnest, and exhaustive that it lasted till luncheon – and so there was nothing she could say that they had not anticipated. There was no rashness in this decision; and they were animated besides by a peculiar and rare brand of Christianity that consisted in deeds rather than words.

Even the details had been thought of. 'Your room,' Aunt Selina told her as they walked down Milsom Street, 'has lately been papered – a light olive stripe – I hope you will like it. It is at the front of the house, with a pleasant view of the main road through the village, which passes quite close to the Rectory. We have a wall and a little screen of box and holly – no more – and no carriage-drive, though Dr Langland did set up a carriage last year, to spare me from the damps as he said. I must confess we have hardly used it. You will spur us, perhaps – ginger us up, as the saying goes.' Aunt Selina wore a pleased little flush at having used a racy expression. 'We are lucky to have ample room at the Rectory, and a very healthful situation. The garden and shrubbery are well laid out for walks when the weather fails – not that Wythorpe is often muddy, as we are on the higher ground of the county – you don't know Huntingdonshire, my dear?'

Caroline hardly knew shires at all, except as the names of regiments. But she found the idea of them delightful: likewise the village, the house, the shrubbery, the olive-striped wallpaper, all of which she had begun to picture vividly, without ever quite being able to picture *herself* in the midst of them.

'Well, it is a quiet sort of district, though there is society to be had. Dr Langland and I do not go about much, but even so there are five or six families we dine with. Then there are assemblies at Huntingdon – not that we have attended those in years, but there again you will make all the difference, my dear. Now that reminds me –' they were passing a fashionable milliner's shop, and Aunt Selina cast a dubious eye over the flamboyantly trimmed bonnets in the window '– there is the matter of your dress. Would you rather have an allowance in your own hand for clothes, or leave it to us to settle? I don't mind which – only you'll forgive me observing that you're surely in need of winter dresses, and things like fichus.'

Caroline had thought what she had on was a winter dress, but realized after a moment that Aunt Selina was misinterpreting her taste for bare arms and low bosom, and mistaking fashion for lack. This caused her a moment of anxious self-questioning whether she was not really rather a strumpet; though she could recall ladies in her father's circles wearing gowns that were scarcely more than nudity, a little smudged.

This whole matter of money was an embarrassment, to her at least. It was plain that her aunt and uncle were comfortably situated, and well able to support her, but that did not mean she could contemplate her dependence without discomfort: nor could she bear their suggestions, that evening, of settling something on her, 'when the time came'. She did not want to think of any such thing or any such time, and so her aunt obligingly dropped it: adding only, 'But you are my niece, my dear, and it is as such that you shall live with us: family, you know: as simple as that.'

'Oh, but you're too good,' Caroline moaned.

'Well, if we are, you needn't weep for it,' her aunt said, with one of her rare laughs. 'What, would you prefer to bed down in the stable?'

In a curious way, she would have, at least for a while: at least until they had had time to accommodate any regrets at their decision. In fact Caroline had less anxiety on the question of how she would take to a country village than how a country village would take to her. Dark, proverbial mutterings about cuckoos and nests kept flitting around her mind.

But she did her best to stifle them. If her aunt and uncle were confident, then so should she be. Soon they were deep in preparations for their return to Huntingdonshire; reflection was banished by the agreeable cares of sorting and packing: and Aunt Selina pronounced herself very thankful to be going, for 'This frenzied pace of life,' she said as they returned from the usual sedate stroll to the Pump Room, 'it quite wears me out.' Before their departure, however, there came the promised visit from Dr Langland's nephew. A scribbled note arrived one evening from Mr Stephen Milner at the Bear Inn. 'Fagged to death – berthing here for the night – wait upon you in the morning if you'd care to see me – if not run a nightgown up the flagpole as a sign and token – what ye've no flagpole ye rascally dogs – a firework then – love and what you will,' was the substance, in what Caroline gathered was his characteristic style.

She wished she could share her aunt and uncle's pleasure in the prospect: but for some reason Caroline acutely wished this Mr Stephen Milner were not coming. She knew she must be introduced to the Langlands' circle of friends and relatives soon enough: in a way this was just getting one of them over with early; and after all did she really care so very much what they thought of her? Thus the voice of Reason: but it was faint beside her misgivings. She did not expect to find a man who got excited over Roman pavements sympathetic, and rose the next morning ready to be thoroughly scrutinized by a whimsical antiquary whom she had pictured right down to the *pince-nez* on his long, disdainful nose.

Or rather, not quite ready. There was one thing that she knew, to her shame, would help her: just a small glass of canary wine, such as was kept in the silver-topped decanter on the table in the front parlour. The door to the front parlour was the first you came to at the foot of the stairs. Going very softly, she slipped in: she would do the fortifying business, then join her aunt and uncle in the back parlour where they breakfasted. Caroline congratulated herself as she took the first sip. On the second sip, the voice spoke.

'True – it is rather early for it. Still, I'll join you in one of those.'

Choking, Caroline turned to meet the blearily blinking but observant eyes of a man who had just risen to a sitting position on the parlour sofa.

'Good God! What the devil—?'

'Swearing by both of them,' he commented, with a gaping yawn, ruffling a thick crown of much dishevelled fairish hair, 'has, I'll admit, an agreeable sort of comprehensiveness.'

'You startled me!' she cried defensively. 'And what the – what on earth are you doing here?' She cast a confused glance at the window, grasping at a fleeting notion of the stranger as an exceptionally relaxed burglar: but the window was secure, and so too the man's expression – he was quite at home, and apparently untroubled at being surprised in his shirt and breeches.

'What am I doing? Sleeping, or was,' he said, scratching his chest vigorously and reaching for a pair of much scuffed and muddied hessian boots. 'Would you be so good as to pour me a glass, then? It's unlucky to drink alone. You're my uncle John's Miss Fortune, I take it.'

It was hard to tell whether he *intended* the pun on her name that she heard, because his was a face that nature had already designed to be satirical. He had strongly arched eyebrows, deep-set grey eyes, broad pale cheekbones, and a wide, wry, asymmetrical bow of a mouth hooked up at the left corner. A very bad face, Caroline thought, especially disfigured with stubble as it was just now, though oddly difficult to look away from; and certainly not like the prim pedant she had pictured.

'And you are Mr Milner, I take it,' she answered, trying to pour a glass of wine with a mixture of dignity, displeasure, and insouciance – which was not easy: it was a lot to get into pouring. Really she wanted to run out of the room, except that that would complete the already ruinous impression she had made. 'I had thought you staying at the Bear Inn.'

'Was. Came away,' he said, tugging at his boot. 'Heard a din in the yard before dawn, stuck my head out of the window, saw a brute of an ostler thrashing blood out of a horse that wouldn't go in the shafts. So, swore I wouldn't stay under that roof any longer, came here, found the maid just a-lighting the fire. "Don't wake anyone," says I. "Let me lie here and finish my sleep."' He tugged fiercely at his boot, then looked up at her brightly. 'Ah, would you give me a shove?'

Stiff with surprise, Caroline found she was going over and doing as he asked, kneeling and pushing at the sole while he pulled at the loops. 'Capital,' he grunted. 'Now t'other.' Booted at last, he stood, a big bony longshanks of seven or eight and twenty, and gave her hand a shake. 'And so how d'ye do? I say, you're not some fanatic sportswoman, I hope, always in the saddle and view-halloo and all that?'

'Do I look like one?'

'Well, no,' he said, after a judicious moment. 'They usually have apple-cheeks and rumps like Herefords – only I wondered, as you looked a little doubtful at me about the ostler and the horse, and I feared you might be about to read me a lecture on animals liking a touch of the whip and foxes enjoying the chase and what-naught. Beg pardon. Is that my wine?'

'If you were to put me in a saddle, Mr Milner, I should fall straight off.'

'Dear!' he said, gulping his wine and shaking his tousled head. 'And yet you're coming to live at Wythorpe – do I have my uncle aright in what he wrote me?'

'Aunt Selina and Uncle John have been kind enough to offer me a home with them, yes,' she said, in a voice that even to her own ears came out distressingly niminy-piminy. Really he had very much put her out. 'Well,' she went on, as he shrugged on his short waist-coat. 'I should leave you to your dressing, sir.'

'Why, I'm putting things on, not taking 'em off. It's lucky you woke me, in truth, else I might have slept through breakfast, and I'm prodigious hungry. Hungry as the devil, as you might say.' Again it was difficult to tell whether that lopsided smile expressed satire: she thought it probably did. 'Mind you, I have had a most unorthodox appetizer,' he added, squinting at her through his empty wine-glass.

'I should tell you,' Caroline said, immediately suspecting that she shouldn't, 'that I am not in the habit of this.'

'Habit of what?'

'The habit of—' She frowned at him as he blandly brushed out his coat. 'Of taking wine at—'

'Five past nine,' he added helpfully, consulting a silver pocket-watch.

'At an early hour. The fact of the matter is—'

'Deuced early.'

'The fact is I have a slight indisposition. A sore throat. And I find a little canary helps.'

Stephen Milner made a noise in his own throat that, whatever its precise meaning, was decidedly not agreeable. He put on the coat, a dark cloth cutaway much past the days of its glory. 'As long as it wasn't to nerve yourself for meeting me,' he grunted.

'Good gracious, why on earth should I do that?'

'Why the devil, in fact.'

Irritated, she made a move to the door, then stopped and

demanded: 'Why should my being no horsewoman prevent me living at Wythorpe?'

'Oh, it won't *prevent* you.' He ruffled his hair, which seemed to fall into at least three partings: grimaced at himself for a cursory moment in front of the pier-glass, then turned back to her. 'Only it does limit your conversational possibilities.'

'Well, you live there – and you, I collect, don't like horsy conversation.'

'I don't have conversations.'

'Why, what are you and I doing?'

'Taking the measure of each other,' he said, with his most enigmatic, lynx-like look, and went carelessly past her to the door.

'Is everyone at Wythorpe as rude as you?' she said to his back; but got only a bare chuckle in return.

Her uncle and aunt were delighted, and not in the least surprised, when Stephen Milner walked in on them at breakfast in the back parlour; and Caroline was glad of the opportunity to sit down to coffee and fade into the background while they plied their visitor with greetings and enquiries, and he made his explanations. There could hardly, she thought, as she bit savagely into a hot roll, have been a worse beginning. When Aunt Selina turned to her, and began to make a formal introduction, Caroline fully expected Mr Milner to seize the opportunity for capricious humour. But he only said: 'We bumped into each other in the hall – but I'm glad, Miss Fortune, to meet you properly,' and shook her hand with great correctness.

'So, Stephen, when do you return to Wythorpe?' his uncle asked him.

'Don't know, sir. I've a fancy, while I'm in this part of the world, to go on to have a look at Silbury Hill. Fabulous tumulus, built, according to folklore, by the devil.' Caroline felt, or felt she felt, his eye light momentarily on her. 'That, or go home directly. I see you're packing up. I might travel back with you, if you've no objection.'

'Oh, an excellent notion,' Uncle John said. 'Best to be moving before the autumn rain – it makes such slow going even on the turnpikes. And then, you know, you will surely be wanted at Wythorpe

Manor. After quarter day there are all the matters of winter hiring, and stock-keeping, and then Isabella and Fanny will be looking to their winter season – gowns and dancing-shoes, eh?' he added, with a sly snuffle at Caroline. 'And all these things, you know, require the presence of the master of the house.'

'Lord, so they do,' Stephen Milner said, in the middle of one of his jaw-cracking yawns – but one that, Caroline thought, was a little affected, as if to cover something up.

'Isabella and Fanny,' Aunt Selina explained, 'are Stephen's sisters, my dear. Isabella is about your age – Fanny rather younger – both charming girls. I'm sure, when you join us at Wythorpe, they will make you thoroughly welcome, and be good friends to you.'

Caroline, picturing female versions of Stephen, could not quite share her aunt's confidence.

'True – true – that's a blessing,' enthused her uncle, 'for you know, of course, what we intend with our niece, Stephen – and so what d'you think of her, hey? What think you of these quaint old bodies having a young girl about the Rectory, hey? Won't it be a new lease of life for us?'

'I hope so, sir,' Stephen said, helping himself to ham. 'As for company of her own age at Wythorpe, you forget there's Lady Milner too.'

'To be sure,' cried Dr Langland, after a long moment, with tremendous awkwardness; and then, with even more unconvincing volume, 'To be sure!'

'My stepmother,' Stephen informed Caroline calmly, eating away. 'And actually a year or two younger than myself. Curious situation.'

'Augusta too is an excellent creature,' quickly put in Aunt Selina, seeming to leave quantities of things unsaid. 'We look forward to introducing you all round, my dear. Now, Stephen, what did you do with your luggage? And will you stay with us tonight, and dine?'

'I'll gladly stay, Aunt, but if you'll forgive me I'm engaged to dine with a fellow I ran into at the Bear. Name of Beauregard. We were at Cambridge together. You might recall his name from the scandal-papers.' As the Langlands only looked blank, he went on: 'Well, perhaps not. I dare say you've more sense than to read 'em—'

'Beauregard,' Caroline burst out, remembering a piece of gossip that Mrs Catling had chewed on with relish. 'Not the gentleman who ran off with the actress disguised as a page?'

'And disobliged his father, who is a Treasury minister and had him set up to marry the Earl of Melrose's daughter, to their great mutual benefit. Most shocking of all, he has married his actress, instead of treating her as a discardable mistress in the acceptable fashion. Apparently the lady herself delivered the letter announcing the happy matrimonial news to old Beauregard, dressed in her page costume, and in spite of his shock he retained enough self-possession to tip her a shilling.'

'But surely,' spluttered Dr Langland, whose mobile eyebrows had been disappearing further up his fringe throughout Stephen's narration, 'surely – I cannot conceive – however could a lady pass as a youth?'

'Oh, she was accustomed to it,' Caroline put in, 'for she was well known on the stage for breeches-parts.'

Her uncle looked helplessly from her to Aunt Selina as if one or all of them were going mad.

'Roles in which the actress dresses in male clothes,' Caroline supplied.

'I see,' her uncle said doubtfully. 'There are one or two such in Shakespeare, of course – though I had not thought the popular stage much enamoured of the Bard in these times.'

'Oh, the play doesn't really signify,' Caroline told him. 'The whole point of it is so that the actress shows her legs. I've even seen them work a breeches-part into *Julius Caesar* – I remember she finished up doing a jig round the Forum.'

'Well, all I can say, my dear girl,' her uncle concluded, after some further gapings, throwing up his hands, 'and I'm sure you'll agree, is *eheu fugaces!*'

As *bless you*! was the only response Caroline could think of making, she held her peace – especially as she felt that Stephen Milner, even when not looking at her, even when pouring cream into his cup, was somehow watching her very carefully.

'Surely this Mr Beauregard must have quite cut himself off from society,' wondered Aunt Selina.

'Absolutely so – he went down to the Lower Rooms for the ball the other night and the Master of Ceremonies refused even to look at him. Fine thing, ain't it?' said Stephen with a sharp, metallic laugh. 'So – though dining out is the greatest bore in the world – I said I'd dine with 'em – see if the corruption rubs off on me. You're a lover of the stage, Miss Fortune?'

Taken by surprise, Caroline said, hesitating: 'I – am fond of a play. My father was in the theatre once, so in a way I am bred to it.'

'We were saying how very different she will find our country ways,' Uncle John said, benevolently patting her arm, 'but she will take to them, I'm sure. The glitter of the great world, you know, is only so much froth and spume: you may look in vain for happiness there.'

Stephen Milner inclined his head respectfully, but said: 'We're all made different, mind, Uncle. You can't feed a cat on carrots.'

'Nor a pig,' said Caroline, 'on cream.'

'Just so,' Stephen said, with a fiendishly delighted look, 'though they both like canary wine.'

'Ah, is this the new slang?' Uncle John said, beaming and wrinkling. 'I do try to keep up with it. A sedan-chairman informed me last week in Queen's Square that I was niffy-naffy. I found this entrancing – such onomatopoeic gusto – that, as I told him, I almost didn't care what it meant precisely.' His face fell a very little. 'He called me something else then, which was just as peculiar, but not quite so pleasant-sounding . . . Oh, Stephen, where are you going?'

'To reclaim my luggage from the clutches of the Bear. I will take up your kind offer, Aunt, thank you.' He kissed her cheek. 'You're *too* kind – and I'm afraid that's your trouble.'

'An odd creature?' Aunt Selina said a little later, as she and Caroline took their usual walk. 'I suppose he is, my dear, in some ways. Stephen is perhaps not easy to pin down. He is much addicted to travels – he will think nothing of taking himself off quite alone to tramp about the Western Isles, say, in the very worst of weathers – and so he can be a little other-worldly, as it were, in company.'

Well, if Caroline did not quite wish him in the Outer Hebrides now, still she could not be easy with Stephen Milner about the place. She could not have said why. She came in for a few more gnarled and cryptic remarks back at Gay Street, and was treated to some abrupt and disconcerting silences, but mostly he seemed to take little notice of her for the rest of the day, until the time came for him to dress for his dinner engagement.

Or rather, not dress.

'My dear Stephen,' Aunt Selina cried, 'you're surely not going like that?'

'Oh, it doesn't signify,' he said, with a negligent glance down at his coat, which was the same he had shrugged on that morning. 'Beauregard don't stand on ceremony.' He turned suddenly to Caroline. 'What think you, Miss Fortune? Would you have me at your dinner-table?'

She felt that he was laughing at her, and she did not care for it. 'I would make allowances for you, Mr Milner,' she answered, coolly picking up a book. Unfortunately it was one of her uncle's impenetrable theological treatises, in which she was then obliged to pretend an absorbing interest while Stephen spent an unlikely time patting his pockets, picking up his gloves, and – she was sure – laughing at her some more.

The household had gone to bed before his return that night – not that this made it so *very* late, for the Langlands were always yawning by ten, and Caroline, try as she might, could not get accustomed to a retirement so early that she could only lie rigidly blinking like a child sent to afternoon bed as a punishment. He was late down to breakfast too the next morning, and looking profoundly seedy: Aunt Selina, quite alarmed, hoped he was not sickening.

'Only with a self-inflicted malady,' he grunted, abandoning an attempt at coffee, 'and curable, if one could but find the cure. The wines at Mr Beauregard's table were very choice.'

'Oh, dear.'

'You should try hock-and-soda,' Caroline offered. 'Or a raw egg beaten up with pepper-sauce – you swallow it down quick.' She performed an expressive mime, then noticing her aunt and uncle's startled looks went on hurriedly: 'You had a pleasant evening, Mr Milner?'

'From what I can remember of it, Miss Fortune. Certainly Beauregard is very happy with his bride, and she makes a much better hostess than she ever was an actress. So he has lost very little, and she has gained a lot from catching him.'

'It is curious how women are always supposed to be making these lucky catches, and never the other way about,' Caroline said. 'One would imagine we have nothing better to do than sit on the social bank, as it were, forever angling after a man.'

'Precisely what many women do,' he said, with a most irritating, secret, satisfied smile.

'How dreadful it must be to be a male, forever besieged by these husband-hunting females! I wonder you can bear it. Or were you drawing a general rather than a particular illustration, Mr Milner – for *you* cannot be the object of such pursuit, surely?'

'No,' he said, unmoved, 'women know I don't care for them, I suppose, or rather ain't taken in by them, and so I'm safe.'

'My dear nephew, such cynicism,' Uncle John reproved him. 'This is only as much to say, you have not met the right woman yet – which is what I heartily wish for you, my greatest wish indeed!'

'I take the wish kindly, Uncle, and fervently hope it will not be fulfilled. To marry is to narrow one's possibilities horribly. As no couple can agree so long, they must yawn or fight. You and my aunt are the one baffling exception.' The maid coming in at that moment, he turned to ask her: 'Jane, do you think I might have a raw egg beaten up with pepper-sauce?'

Caroline's prescription – reluctant as Jane was to serve something so unwholesome and even, her stony look suggested, positively indecent – seemed to do the trick. He was soon much restored: but she hardly knew whether to be pleased with her success, since a part of her did not particularly want Stephen Milner to be well at all. Mixed feelings was the scarcely adequate term for this vexing, perplexing consciousness when he was about; but perhaps at root was to be found the very simple human desire to know what he thought of her.

Caroline found out, later that day. Not from his telling her – which was, after all, hardly to be expected from the cryptic Mr Milner – but from that reliably mortifying practice, eavesdropping. She had started up the stairs to change out of her walking-dress, when she realized she had left a glove on the hall-table; and returning, overheard her name spoken in the front parlour, where Stephen was talking with the Langlands. Not being a saint, Caroline could not stop herself approaching the parlour door; indeed she was so far from being a saint that she hardly even tried, and was soon devoutly listening with her ear at the panel.

'And she has had to bear up against such a sudden loss,' her aunt was saying.

'Certainly,' came Stephen Milner's voice, 'it's a grief I know myself, and I'm sorry for her. But I'm also sorry for you.'

'Us?' cried Uncle John. 'My dear boy, why?'

'Because I fear you may come to regret this decision to take her in.'

'You alarm me. Do you mean you suspect some delinquency in Caroline's character that has escaped our observation? I cannot believe it—'

'Nor can I,' said Aunt Selina firmly, 'and I have got to know my niece pretty well, I think, Stephen.'

'I do not mean that at all,' Stephen said, quite cool. 'Except that you are, as I said before, too kind. I would trust to your judgement of character above anyone's. I am talking about the vast difference that must exist between her experience of the world, and the new life she is to lead. She has been chiefly raised by a rake, and it shows: she knows about the ways of actresses, and how to cure the liver after a drinking-bout, and a deal of other things that are very well in their way, but suggest altogether too much sophistication. Place her in sleepy old Wythorpe, and it would be like putting some brightly plumed exotic in a cage of sparrows.'

'Oh, come,' said Uncle John, chuckling, 'there may be a few ruffled feathers – no more than ruffled feathers, my dear boy.'

'It's true that her bringing-up has been very different,' came Aunt Selina's voice, more serious than ever, 'and sometimes she quite surprises me. But then that's not difficult, as I have lived so very retired.'

'Surprises – aye, that's what I'm afraid of, from that bold little piece,' Stephen said. 'But I'll say no more: I see you are both set upon this course, and you are such excellent people I would never oppose my opinion to yours.'

'But you don't – you don't dislike her, Stephen?' said her aunt.

There came a grunt, so sharp and expressive it made the suspensefully listening Caroline flinch. 'Oh,' he said, in a yawning voice, 'I can tolerate her, for your sakes. Well, I think I'll walk to the top of Beechen Cliff.'

'Now? But the weather – look at the window – it's raining, really quite hard,' Aunt Selina objected.

'So it is: never mind: I want to walk now.' His voice was at its most decided, and was perceptibly getting nearer to the door. Caroline sprang away, and managed to reach the top of the stairs before he came out.

A small satisfaction, to set beside much mortification. It would have been less if he had described her in terms she could absolutely reject; but Stephen Milner had actually echoed her own secret anxieties, and even amplified them. It would have been less if she had cared nothing for his good opinion; but though she found it very easy to be irritated by Stephen Milner, she found it impossible to be indifferent to him. It was all the more difficult to dismiss his strictures, because he was plainly not motivated by such interested considerations as, for example, had determined Mr Leabrook's behaviour towards her. In his every word and gesture, Mr Leabrook had had an end in view. Mr Milner obviously did not much care one way or another.

And that, Caroline told herself, with a sort of mental shake, was exactly the attitude she must adopt. Her aunt and uncle had placed their trust in her, and to *them* she would justify it, come what may – but anyone else, any long-jawed, awkward, satirical-looking Stephen Milners, could go and boil their head.

While her aunt and uncle were still occupied that day with their painstaking packing, Caroline's was very soon completed. Wrapping the miniature of her mother, in which she could now trace a fascinating resemblance to Aunt Selina, set in train some wistful thoughts. Sitting alone in the front parlour, with the rain strumming at the window, she dwelt on her father with a sorrow softened now yet still profound. She was jolted out of it by the sudden appearance of Stephen Milner at the door – jolted into wild, unexpected laughter.

'It is coming on to rain,' he pronounced solemnly, while water dripped and pooled around him. The impossible hair hung like seaweed.

'Oh, Mr Milner, I'm mistook, I thought you going for a walk, not a swim.'

'Quite refreshing really. In a wretched, dismal, uncomfortable sort of way, I mean. Best change before my aunt sees me – she'll scold.'

'And rightly. You know, you may catch the most shocking cold. But there, you would insist on going.'

'Aye, so I did,' he said, squinting at her through his sodden hair. 'A little hint, by the by, Miss Fortune: when eavesdropping, always bear in mind your shadow.' He pointed to the bottom of the door, then offered her a bland smile. 'Even under a closed door, it can be clearly visible.'

How long she stared at him with her mouth open she couldn't tell – probably long enough to add extra relish to his triumph; and when she did close it, it was with an unfortunate, resounding, even crocodilian snap.

'Well,' she said at last, 'and so now you must think me dreadfully underhand.'

Mr Milner gave only a tremendous sniff in reply.

'I will own to the failing,' she went on, 'but must add that I can conceive something much *more* underhand, and that is speaking disobligingly of someone behind their back, instead of to their face.'

'Was I only disobliging?' he mused. 'I thought I was ruder than that. Well, never mind, Miss Fortune: I have a lowish opinion of people generally, and I really think no worse of you than of the common run – except that, as I shall now candidly state to your face, you do look like trouble.'

It was her turn to sniff. 'I won't say, Mr Milner, what *you* look like.'

'Oh, why not?'

'Because I am too much of a lady.'

'Oh, I don't think so, you know,' he said cheerily, 'not at all. But yes, I really should go and change –' he bowed '– else I shall indeed be rather ill. And I'm sure you would not want that.'

'Certainly not. *Very* ill – horribly ill – distressingly ill – these I would much prefer.'

'Ah!' he cried, as if appreciating some delicate perfume. 'Would you nurse me?'

'Devotedly,' she said, clutching at her heart. 'But that is, of course, if you could *tolerate* me about, Mr Milner.'

He squelched away laughing, leaving Caroline to conduct until dinner a sharp inward debate as to whether she had scored a victory or suffered a defeat. Going down to the dining room after dressing, she was still undecided, and put aside the question to greet the gentleman who was obviously joining them for dinner – and how odd of her aunt not to have mentioned it . . .

'Oh!' she gasped, as the gentleman, turning round, turned into Stephen Milner. He looked down with amusement at her outstretched hand.

'A peace offering?'

'No – well, yes, if you like . . . Why on earth are you dressed like that?'

He shrugged. 'I'm dressed for dinner.'

'You know what I mean. Yesterday you went out to dine like a scarecrow, and now . . .' Now, she had to admit to herself, he looked rather well in the swallow-tailed cutaway coat, white silk waistcoat, and starched cravat that had made her mistake him for someone else entirely. 'Why are we so honoured?'

'Well, because yesterday you suspected me of making an affectation of casualness.'

'Did I say that?'

'No, you thought it.'

'You can read minds, can you, Mr Milner?'

'No, only yours. Ah, Uncle John – I should tell you I've decided against travelling down to Huntingdon with you. I've a fancy, while I'm down this way, to visit the old White Horse at Uffington.'

'My dear boy – down this way? That's a good forty miles, surely.'

'Yes, really, Mr Milner,' Caroline said, seating herself, 'all that way just for an inn.'

'The White Horse I mean is a great ancient figure cut into the chalk of the Downs,' Stephen began on a note of stern information: then saw Caroline's ironically raised eyebrow, realized, coughed, and actually – to her infinite satisfaction – blushed. 'As of course you know. Anglo-Saxon perhaps, or perhaps not.'

'I preferred the inn,' she said, with composure, picking up her soup spoon.

'Yes, yes,' said Uncle John, smiling at them both with benign incomprehension. 'Popularly supposed to be the spot where St George slew the dragon . . . But, my dear Stephen, I do wish we might prevail on you not to postpone your return any longer – considering how much you must be needed at the Manor—'

'Considering, Uncle, considering – but considering is what I never do, you know, and I shall return to the fold soon enough, and now where's that champagne I sent for?' Stephen said breezily, beckoning Jane forward with the wine.

He drank off two swift glasses. Caroline, observing curiously, wondered what it was about his home that he was so reluctant to face: and came across the curious reflection also, that where previously she had dreaded the prospect of a long coach journey in Stephen Milner's company, now the loss of that prospect did not afford the expected delight. Indeed she might almost have supposed – if it were not too curious altogether – that what she was feeling was disappointment.

Chapter X

Caroline's first sight of her new home was an indistinct one, for they arrived at Wythorpe late on a rainy night after a long journey from Bath that even the conveniences of travelling post could not prevent from being exhausting. Aunt Selina, from a mixture of solicitude for the horses and anxiety lest the chaise be overturned, had continually restrained their pace, so that their progress had been stately to the point of inertia. Only at the end of the second day did she let the postilion have his head, from a desire to see home before nightfall: at which point the rain came down, the roads of lowland Huntingdonshire turned bad, and the last lap became a jolting, straining nightmare of mud and wind-whipped darkness.

Through this appeared, at last, lights: Caroline's bleared eyes beheld roofs through trees, a porched door opening to reveal warm welcome radiance, servants with umbrellas. Then, more asleep than awake, she was being ushered on her uncle's arm into a parlour where candle-light, a blazing fire, and a hot, strong posset handed to her by a politely curious housekeeper all conspired to lull her into absolute numbness. Aunt Selina was all cheerful bustle, greeting the servants, enquiring after their health, and superintending the unpacking: the journey had gone to her entire satisfaction, in spite of the fact that the dreaded tip into a ditch could not have made them more late, wet, and bruised than they were. Nowhere is taste more peculiar than in what counts as an inconvenience. Soon, however, she caught sight of her niece's drooping look, and declared, to Caroline's secret joy, that for her there must be no thought of anything but bed.

The same courteously peering housekeeper lit her upstairs, and left her in a bedroom to which she tried to pay the tribute of attention before toppling into bed. Such details as she could take in were exactly like her imaginings. There was the olive-striped wallpaper: it was decidedly odd, giving her the feeling that while she was still awake she was dreaming, and that when she fell asleep she would be waking up.

Ten hours later, all the confusion was resolved by her sitting up in bed refreshed, quite well aware of where she was, and noticing that despite the wallpaper, not everything was as she had envisaged it. For some reason a rectory in a Huntingdonshire village had suggested to her mind creaking, dark-beamed, diamond-paned, even cobwebby age. But neat new sash windows threw the milky light of a clearing day on a whitewashed ceiling. She realized as she dressed on smooth, silent floorboards that the house was quite new.

'My first mistake about the place,' she said genially to herself, as she looked out at a pleasant plashy view of a broad village street winding peacefully by beyond the box and holly. For some reason then the thought of Stephen Milner recurred to her, with something troublous about it; and she hurried down.

The Rectory of Wythorpe was, as she soon found, a commodious house of whitewashed brick and red tiles, with two large parlours downstairs as well as a study for Dr Langland and the usual offices, and a stable and coach-house adjoining. At the back, on the south side, a shrubbery of laurels and evergreens divided the kitchen-garden and poultry-yard from a pleasant walled garden of lawns and honeysuckle and espaliered fruit-trees, carefully nurtured against the strong winds that blew across the flat meadows from the east. Within, while there was no extravagance, there was some elegance and much comfort, attesting to the fortune that Aunt Selina had brought to her marriage – and which Caroline's mother had forfeited – as well as to the worth of the living. Dr Langland, besides being conscientious about his duties at the little church, whose grey knobbly tower could be seen beyond the stable roof, also farmed his own glebe land; and altogether the Langlands, busy, easy, rooted, well liked, gave off an *at home* feeling such as Caroline, with her nomadic past, had never experienced.

She relished it. Aunt Selina, going over the house and explaining their daily habits and routines, remarked again more than once on how very different – restricted perhaps – Caroline would find this new life. Caroline did not fear that; and only loyalty to her father's memory dissuaded her from mentioning that, as for restriction, she could at least step out of the door here without the fear of a bailiff pouncing on her for a debt.

She was, indeed, eager to explore her new scene, and she had the promise of her aunt's company on a long walk, as soon as the many domestic matters arising from the mistress's long absence should be settled. Opportunity came sooner, however, with their first caller.

This was Miss Milner – none other than Stephen's sister Isabella; though Caroline would not have guessed it of the slight, trim young woman, luminous in a white chemise gown, who stepped sedately into the front parlour, and who put out a tentative hand, as if through a delicate mesh of shyness, when Dr Langland made the introductions. Beneath that neat buttery-fair hair was a grave, well-shaped face wholly unlike the wry Mr Milner's – quite a beauty indeed, Caroline decided, after the sidelong scrutiny appropriate to the occasion; though in a more solemn style than was usual in a girl of twenty summers. Likewise with the low, fluty voice in which she expressed a hope that Miss Fortune had not taken cold from her wetting last night.

'Oh, no, I am perfectly well, thank you,' Caroline answered, before it occurred to her to wonder how Miss Milner knew about that.

But Uncle John, quite unsurprised, said: 'Ah, you know it was past ten when we got back, then, Bella?' and it soon became clear, from Miss Milner's comprehensive replies, that in Wythorpe everything about everybody was very soon known by everybody else.

Which, Caroline thought doubtfully, one no doubt got used to.

'Well, Uncle John, my nonsensical brother wrote me that he had seen you in Bath,' Miss Milner said, after some further friendly exchanges, 'and so I could not forbear calling on you to discover if you had any intelligence of him. I had some hopes that he might have returned with you—'

'Our hopes also!' cried Dr Langland. 'I told him, "Stephen: you have been away too long." Those were my exact words to him, were they not, my dear?'

'You did tell him so, my dear, indeed, if not in those exact words,' said Aunt Selina, agreeably, and unwisely.

'Were they not the exact words? I was convinced they were. Now you mention it – and yet I'm sure I did use them – unless they were in my mind, and I chose some other expression – which I think is an occurrence we are all familiar with – yet the question remains then what exact words *did* I use?'

'The question,' Aunt Selina said, with infinite, greyly smiling patience, 'is perhaps not greatly important, my dear: as you spoke very rightly whatever the words. But Stephen elected to pursue his travels a little further. He spoke of coming home soon: that's all I can tell you, Isabella, I fear.'

'I did try, Bella, believe me,' Uncle John said, working his hair up into wildness. 'I impressed upon him – indeed I wish I could recollect my exact words—'

'Thank you, Uncle, Aunt,' Miss Milner said, 'and never mind. There are things to do with the wedding that I must consult him about: but Stephen will be Stephen.'

'Oh, you are to be married, Miss Milner?' Caroline said.

'At Christmas, I had hoped,' Miss Milner said, with a faint smile and flush, 'or if not in the new year.'

'Oh, I wish you happy – many congratulations. That is, if you *want* to be married, of course. Only, you know, there are plenty of marriages for which commiserations might be more appropriate.'

It was the kind of remark that – as she was still having to remind herself – caused Aunt Selina to look anxious, and Uncle John bewildered; but to her relief a wrinkle and lift at the corner of Miss Milner's lips showed that she did not share the Langlands' lovable obtuseness. And also that she did resemble her brother a little after all.

'I'm very happy in my choice, and very lucky,' Miss Milner said, 'thank you, Miss Fortune. And I hope I shall have the pleasure of introducing my fiancé to you presently, as you are – well, you are to make your home here: which I really think the nicest thing. As for unfortunate marriages, I know about those, and their unhappy consequences.'

A momentary constraint was lifted by Uncle John's breezily enquiring: 'Well, and where is your excellent young man, my dear? Is he at Hethersett?'

'Not yet. He is still away visiting relatives—'

'And acquainting them with his coming good fortune, no doubt!'

'Perhaps,' Miss Milner said, smiling, with a most fascinating blush that began at the back of her neck. 'But we may expect him back soon – within the month. And his word is much more to be relied on than my unconscionable brother's. Well, Uncle, I hope you find yourself improved by Bath?'

'I do believe the waters have braced my system, and purged the dropsical humours, my dear. But it would not do for me for long – too much hurry and bustle. I could never think of retiring there. I hope that won't disappoint *you*, my dear,' he added with a benevolent pat on Caroline's arm, 'for you are not averse to bustle, I collect, having lived in the great world.'

'Oh, I have had quite enough of bustle, thank you, Uncle John,' Caroline said. And now she will hate me, she thought resignedly, as Miss Milner turned her beautiful, rather short-sighted eyes upon her. Here come I from nowhere, calling her uncle Uncle, and making oh-so-light of my worldly sophistication. *Quite enough of bustle* – what *do* I mean? I think *I* hate me.

But Miss Milner only said pleasantly: 'I have been at Bath once, when I was thirteen. A fat man trod quite hard on my toes in the Pump Room, and did not say sorry. I remember his face very well, and live in hopes that I may see him again one day. Then I shall stamp on his foot; and I hope it is gouty.'

The effect of this, in Miss Milner's quiet, proper tones, was irresistible to Caroline. Her uncle, though he smiled too, began to speak about the Christian duty of forgiveness; and Miss Milner gave him a polite attention. But Caroline was sure there was a little flinty core of independence under that mild surface, which she very much liked, Indeed, something quite different began to displace her belief that Isabella Milner must hate her: something opposite.

It is this.

You know Isabella Milner. Oh, the incidental details may vary. This living instance is a young lady with a soft, purposeful step, a habit of murmuring reproachfully to herself when she feels she has acted wrongly, a liking for helpings of potatoes and mutton that may make her plump in ten years' time, an inability to deceive. Any or all of these qualities may differ: the essence of the figure is unchanged, and you know her or him.

Isabella is the person with whom, in a room full of silly, boastful people, you will exchange a silent, speaking glance that becomes a smile: the person to whom you never need to explain yourself laboriously: the person you will not compete with.

Isabella is that person you realize, deep down and at once, will be your friend.

And ten minutes later Caroline found herself putting on her bonnet and preparing to go on a walk with her new acquaintance. Conversation having reverted to local matters, Aunt Selina had mentioned that she was going to show Caroline something of the village: Miss Milner had promptly said she would be delighted to be her guide. 'Though it is a little wet still in places, Miss Fortune – I don't know whether you will want overshoes.'

'Well – you have none, I see, Miss Milner.'

'Oh, I like to jump over the puddles,' Miss Milner explained seriously.

'Then we shall jump together.'

It was now a fine fresh autumn day: the pools of water from last night's downpour made a glittering dapple all about the broad main road of the village, on either side of which clustered the cottages, distinguished by low roofs and peculiarly long, sloping dormer windows, giving Caroline the fancy that their inhabitants must go about bent double. She had conceived this as a flat, bare sort of country, but Wythorpe she found enfolded by a soft swell of hills to the west, and there were venerable trees aplenty, including at the main turning a clump of great horse-chestnuts. Two boys were pelting them with sticks for conkers; and Caroline, watching, hearing the satisfying slither and thump of the spiky green cases in their descent, was filled with an absurd happiness, which was not at all diminished by Miss Milner's next words.

'Miss Fortune, I want to say how sorry I am for your loss. I didn't like to say with Uncle and Aunt by, because I know it is awkward, and other people make it feel awkwarder. And I won't allude to it further, except to say I do know what it is like to lose a father.'

'Thank you,' Caroline said, pressing the arm which, she found, she had taken quite spontaneously. 'When . . . ?'

'Last December. He was the best of fathers – though of course one always thinks that.'

'Well, I'm not sure mine was the *best* – but I wouldn't have changed him on any account.'

'No, indeed. I *have* heard that he was troubled with – with practical difficulties – that is, Aunt Selina wrote me—'

'Lord, it's no secret,' Caroline said, smiling, as Miss Milner's colour rose again. 'Poor Papa was forever in Queer Street, and even when he wasn't, the blunt just slipped through his fingers. Money,' she added hastily, at her companion's blank look. 'Mind you, I collect that this is not a place to keep secrets in any case – judging by the thorough inspection I am getting from those men by the gate.'

'Oh, that is Mr Beeny, the smith; and on the left Mr Cubitt, one of my father's tenants, over at Hangland Farm. That is, he was my father's tenant – it still comes so natural – now, of course, he is my brother's tenant. Which does not seem at all natural. Yes, everyone will be shockingly curious about you, I'm afraid, and watch your every walk and remark your every sneeze.'

'Hm, and discuss my every purchase at the shop, no doubt.'

'I'm sure they would, if we had a shop in Wythorpe,' Miss Milner said, nimbly eluding a puddle, 'but we have none.'

Caroline could not help revealing herself a little staggered at this intelligence.

'Well, there is the Seven Stars – the inn, which we will come to presently, at the corner of Splash Lane – which is the letter-office, and takes a daily newspaper. And then I believe Mr Miles, the seedsman, deals in a few market articles – sacking and tallow and such, and will fetch them if you ask him. But generally one must go for shopping to Huntingdon – not above seven miles off. Stephen will often walk it, though of course he is a creature of odd notions. Has that hideous blush of mine faded yet?'

Caroline hardly knew how to answer. 'It – well, I do not think it hideous—'

'Thank you,' Miss Milner said, in her gravest tone. 'I have tried to think in that way myself, but it's no use, I still loathe it. If one must blush, at least let it begin in the cheeks, like a normal Christian, and not at the back of the neck. Which I know it does. I did something complicated with mirrors once and watched it. It's as if my head is on back to front. Well,' she added, looking shyly at Caroline's amused face, 'you are very forgiving.'

'Am I? I must be, for I cannot even think where the offence lies.'

'Oh, but you must know – that remark I made, at the Rectory. So very unthinking. I can only ask you to believe I truly did not mean it.'

'Now I feel as if *my* head is on back to front. Miss Milner, what *do* you mean?'

'I spoke of the unhappy consequences of unfortunate marriages,' her companion said in a rush, 'and I must suppose you would detect a personal reference. For Aunt Selina has written me, briefly, of her late sister's history – the family quarrel with your poor mother and father, I mean – and as soon as the words were out, I realized it must sound—'

'Oh! my dear Miss Milner, is that it? Upon my word I never detected anything of the sort. If my parents' marriage was unfortunate, it was so only in the financial sense; and the chief consequence was me, and I am not unhappy.'

Miss Milner gazed long at her. (What a family they are for *looking*, Caroline thought.) 'You are very wise,' she sighed at last. 'Still, Miss Fortune, I do hope I didn't offend. I truly was not thinking of that, but of something much closer to home. Though I should not say so,' she added, with a look of alarm, as if afraid Caroline would somehow seize on this. 'Indeed I should be glad if you would forget I said it.'

'I'm still getting over being called wise,' said Caroline, who had plenty of ideas of her own about what Miss Milner was referring to. 'And if I may be candid for a moment, Miss Milner, I may as well say I thought you must surely hate me.'

'Did you?' It added to Caroline's favourable estimation of Miss Milner's character that she did not go into a schoolgirl squeal of denial at this, but gave the question a sober consideration. 'You fear it being a newcomer, perhaps. I can see I would have similar fears in such a situation. Also, and at the risk of being disloyal to the sex, I have observed that women are often severest in judgement upon each other.'

'True: perhaps because we know deep down what we are like. And men are lenient to each other, on the same principle. Indeed, Miss Milner, I wonder if we have hit on it – I wonder if this is why men have the beating of us, and have gained the mastery of the world – and now that we have the secret we can rise up, and storm the Bastille of masculinity. *Vive la révolution!*'

Miss Milner looking alarmed again, it occurred to Caroline that such words were perhaps not even to be pronounced in jest in a place like Wythorpe, and she could not suppress a grimly facetious image of outraged countrymen leaping from the next hedgerow brandishing a scold's bridle. However, her companion recovered herself, and after a moment said decidedly, 'No, I don't think I would wish to lead. It simply wouldn't suit me, I fear: I hope you don't think me a mouse.'

'Not at all – but consider, you would not have to depend on your nonsensical brother, for example, to proceed with the arrangements for your wedding.'

'True – too true – though all I really wish is that he would stop gadding about, and come home long enough to set things in train. Then he might do as he pleased again – though I always do miss him, exasperating as he is. I believe he has got worse since—' Miss Milner caught herself up, and in a reactive flurry asked: 'What did *you* think of him, Miss Fortune?'

Caroline, accustomed to her tongue being quick even when her mind was not, was surprised to find herself struck into silence for a few moments. 'I found I wanted to quarrel with him,' she said finally.

'Oh, I do know what you mean,' Miss Milner said, which was more than Caroline did. 'He will not take anything seriously. And for all I love him, I am afraid that is a grave failing, is it not?'

Caroline, in truth, could think of many that were graver, and was some distance from thinking it a failing at all. So, avoiding a reply, she said: 'He is not opposed to your marriage, I hope?'

'No – that is, no more than to marriage in general, which he calls a fool's game. But he says I am too precipitate, and should wait a while. When I would gladly be married next week – tomorrow.'

'You are very eager!' Caroline said, with a smile.

'I am,' Miss Milner said, without one: which left Caroline with the problem of what to do with hers, as it felt so inappropriate: so she plumped for a quick diversion, crying out: 'Ah, now, I wonder, can you tell me the name of that flower? It is so very pretty.'

'That is a daisy,' Miss Milner said, after a moment in which politeness overcame disbelief.

Even town-bred as she was, Caroline had that much botany: this, she thought, was not one of my better diversions; and then at that thought she was lost, and began laughing like an idiot. It was the sort of moment at which a friendship is either formed, or becomes an impossibility. A frozen stare would have signalled the latter. But Miss Milner began laughing too, quite as helplessly: and when they came out of it their relation had changed.

'I can see I shall have to instruct you in these rural matters, for your own safety,' Miss Milner said. 'I would not have you walking into a pasture not knowing a cow from a bull.'

'That, you may rest assured, I *do* know.'

'Oh, you – there goes my wretched blush again!'

'Truly, though, I do wish I knew the names of flowers and things like that. Am I too late to learn? You are already well up in all that sort of thing, I'll wager.'

'Yes,' Miss Milner said simply, 'I am: I suppose it has always seemed natural to me. At the Manor we have a quantity of gardens, and they have always been my delight – oh, especially my herb garden: I hope I can show it to you some day.' She darted a doubtful look at Caroline. 'Though I realize that may not be a *very* thrilling prospect for you.'

'I should greatly like it – and I do wonder what conception people must have of me. Am I popularly supposed to have spent my life amongst fleshpots? Whatever they are. Pots of flesh. They don't sound appealing.'

'Of course it is presumptuous to draw conclusions about a person from what one has heard,' Miss Milner said earnestly, 'and I am very wrong to do it.'

'It is the most natural thing in the world, and I do it all the time. Only I am afraid I shall disappoint people's expectations dreadfully, as I'm really not at all scandalous, or stylish, or wicked.'

'Oh, but you are,' cried Miss Milner, adding hastily, 'stylish, I mean – that is, you have a look – well, I'm sure that's what they are all wearing in Town just now.'

'If they are, they are very secretive about it.' Caroline laughed. 'But I'm flattered – and I can return the compliment, and much more truthfully, by telling you that what *you* are wearing is quite the elegant thing: not that many can wear it in the way you do. Lord, such mutual cordiality – we must surely begin savaging each other soon, else what's to become of human nature?'

'Oh, but we won't do that,' Miss Milner said, her face seeming all luminous blue eyes. 'I know you are funning, but still . . . I beg your pardon, I'm very serious, an't I? I know it, Stephen is always reproving me for it. In truth, I did have this gown from London – my last visit there. When my father was alive we would all spend a month in Town nearly every year. Now, though – well, Stephen says he is sick of London, he prefers ruins and those hillocks with bones in. There is a word for them, but I don't much care to think of it.'

'He is sick of London? Then *he* has had his share of it?'

'Oh, he was there a good deal, after Cambridge: he was quite the town-buck for a time.'

'This is fine indeed. This is your true pig-headed male – he will deny you the pleasures of Town, but of course he has enjoyed his fill of them. Oh, no, I'm sorry, but the revolution it must be.'

'Well,' Miss Milner said, with a shy look, 'not all men are like Stephen.'

'Ah – you mean your future husband? I approve him already. But wait, do you mean he will be taking you off to live in Town? Am I going to lose my first friend here so soon?'

'Oh, no, we shall live at Hethersett – his place, you know. Well, of course, you don't know. It is only six miles off. But we shall spend a part of each season in Town, I think. That is – we have agreed so. Now, there is the inn I was telling you about, and that's Mrs Vine who keeps it.'

There was a reticence in speaking of her fiancé that Caroline found refreshing in Miss Milner: infinitely preferable to the gush and twitter she had observed in some young women about to be married, with their flourishing of rings and calculated indiscretions about what he whispered to her last night; and it seemed to her earnest of a true attachment, of which she was honestly glad for her companion's sake, and honestly envious.

'And this is Splash Lane,' Miss Milner went on, 'so called because right at the bottom there is a ford.'

'And when you go through it, you splash.'

'Just so. And down there at the turning is the Old Grange, lately occupied by a new-married couple named Hampson. He is a lawyer, and she is a Bristol heiress with more money than –' Miss Milner caught herself up with an abashed look '– than many people. They are very fond of entertaining – you are sure to be at a Hampson carpet-dance before long. That is – I do beg your pardon, Miss Fortune, I don't know whether you are accepting invitations yet – under the circumstances.'

'Well, I know my father would want me to, that's all I can say: just as he always loathed mourning weeds, and would hate to see me in them. And while we are about the business of flouting convention, let me entreat you to call me Caroline. I know it is reckoned a great vulgarity to be on first-name terms after short acquaintance, but I may say candidly I *feel* as if I have known you longer: also we are in a way, in a sort of way, related: also I am not so very afraid of a little vulgarity: also we can go back to Miss-ing each other when we are in company, if you like. And now, after all that, if you *don't* wish to call me Caroline, I shall be in rather an awkward position, and I shall have to go and throw myself in the splash.'

'That I could not allow – Caroline.'

Isabella, as Caroline was to call her companion, proceeded to be her guide about the village: the tour was soon accomplished, for Wythorpe was not extensive, but neither was it mean; it had an appearance of quietly thriving, and Caroline's eye fell with appreciation on the cottage gardens, still bright even at this late season with their unknown flowers, on the beehives, the venerable benches worn glassy smooth, the stone walls that bowed out with the convexity of a baby's cheek, the broad-wheeled wagons that went just a very little faster than walking pace. Still her chief satisfaction, on returning to the Rectory, was the friendship she had discovered with Isabella. And it was with the tender perception of friendship that she noticed how comparatively little Isabella spoke of Wythorpe's chief landmark – her own home, the Manor, which was visible as a cluster of chimneys on the high ground to the west, at the end of an avenue of oaks – and how little eager she seemed to go back there.

That the regard was mutual was evinced over the next few days not only by the ready confidence Isabella extended to her – and this from a nature that, it was plain, tended rather to reserve – but by Aunt Selina's benignly remarking, as Isabella's neat figure passed the front parlour window again, that they had never seen so much of their niece before. The two young women spent much time together, exchanging life-histories: there did remain patches of marked reticence about Isabella, and these included her feelings about her home life; but quiet hints there were, and Caroline was soon in any case acquainted with the facts relating to the Milners of Wythorpe Manor, these being the common property of the neighbourhood in which they were first in consequence.

The family had long been prosperously settled in Huntingdonshire. If they were notable at all, it was for a habit of not distinguishing themselves; and as no firmer warrant for respectability could be imagined, they continued to enjoy the widespread esteem of their acquaintance, to be buried with due formality in the vault at Wythorpe church when they died, and to be absolutely forgotten straight afterwards. But Isabella's late father had been of a different stamp. He had sought to be a public man. He made no less than two whole speeches in Parliament: the first, much admired for its freshness of thought and force of expression, asserting that British liberty was a good thing, and French despotism a bad thing: the second, reaffirming these trenchant points. Having further benefited his country by raising and equipping a force of Volunteers (blue jackets, white buttons, yellow facings) to repel Bonaparte if he should ever reach Huntingdon, he was duly rewarded with a knighthood, and as Sir Henry Milner retired to his estate to nurse indifferent health, and to reminisce – sometimes to the less than total captivation of his hearers – about what Mr Pitt had said to him in the lobby back in '99.

In his private capacity Sir Henry had met with no less success. He was married early to a lady of good sense and firm principle – the sister of the Rector, Dr Langland; and she had borne him three children, who grew up creditably, influenced above all by Lady Milner's desire that they should be well educated; for it was her strong if eccentric belief that for country gentlefolk to be chuckleheads and boobies was not a necessity: it only looked that way. The loss of this lady to a consumption, some five years since, was universally mourned, and nowhere more so, it seemed, than in the heart of the widower; yet as time passed, and mourning was doffed, Sir Henry revealed an impetuosity and suggestibility of temperament that it had often been his late lady's part to restrain, and that now went unchecked. He contracted a violent affection for a woman thirty years his junior: none other than the governess appointed to the instruction of his younger daughter; and to the consternation of his friends, would settle for nothing less than marrying her.

This second Lady Milner, being the choice of the first as governess to young Fanny, was naturally lacking nothing in attainments, and was of a respectable family: still, the injudiciousness of the match was felt. To the usual awkwardness of a young stepmother – actually younger than the eldest offspring and heir, and not much senior to the others – was added that of the dependant and employee suddenly transformed into mistress of house and family. Nor could she escape censure for the ready promptness with which she had accepted a proposal so materially advantageous. Sir Henry was good-looking for a man in his fifties, and had warmth and geniality to recommend him: still, even the most charitable observer could not have supposed that his suit would have been successful if he had had only his heart to lay at her feet, and not a knightly name, a mansion and park, and nine hundred acres. Not that there was much belief in a suit on the gentleman's part: it being generally assumed that the young lady had gone all out to land him.

However, Sir Henry seemed happy with his new bride: but this felicity was fated soon to end, and not by the common matrimonial decline into indifference. A twelvemonth after his marriage, he was felled by a heart-stroke, and followed his first wife to the churchyard, leaving the former governess mistress of Wythorpe Manor, and all manner of complications in the bereft family.

'Ah, Sir Henry should have thought of this,' was the general remark: for there is nothing we so reprehend as lack of foresight in others, unless it be the detection of it in ourselves. It was not that he had encumbered the next generation with legal difficulties. He had settled a comfortable jointure on his widow, whilst the estate passed naturally to his son: nor were his daughters dowerless. But he had insufficiently considered that much more unstable currency, the feelings. Lady Milner must continue to live at the Manor, but in a very singular relation to her stepchildren, one of whom was the master of the house, whilst over the two girls she bore a sort of authority, surely very awkward for all parties in its ill-definition. Had there been friendship, or even cordiality, between the young step-mother and her late husband's family, all such difficulties might have been swept aside; but this was emphatically not the case, and one hardly needed further evidence than the continual absences of Mr Stephen Milner, who seemed unable to bear being in the house.

Such at least was the general impression of what went on at Wythorpe Manor – but Caroline was eager to see for herself. It was proof of the recovery of her own spirits after the loss of her father, that her habitual curiosity was reviving – partly on behalf of her new friend, in whose situation she had a sympathetic interest; but also from sheer inquisitiveness. That she might learn something to the disadvantage of clever-stick Stephen Milner was, perhaps, a further incentive, and quickened her pulses when at last the Langlands readied themselves to call at the Manor and introduce her.

'We had better, my dear,' Uncle John confided to his wife, in what he considered a whisper, and what an auctioneer would have considered a good carrying voice for a busy market day, 'we had better, for I don't think Lady Milner is going to wait upon us, though that would be more the correct thing – much more. And I think poor Bella knows it. Dear me!'

Chapter XI

Isabella was the first to welcome them at the Manor. Indeed she came running down the oak avenue to meet them, explaining a little bashfully that she had seen their approach from her window.

'And I thought I should tell you, before you come in, that Captain Brunton is here again.'

'Is he? It seems he has only just gone away,' Aunt Selina said.

'Who? Who? Oh, to be sure, Brunton. I remember him. He is a captain,' Dr Langland explained. 'But, my dear Bella, why must you warn us? Is the Captain in bellicose mood, perhaps, standing by to repel all boarders?' His snort of amusement sent a magpie flapping from the copper beech leaves overhead. 'Or training his pistols on us from the porch-hood?'

'I think Isabella meant to spare us the awkwardness of surprise,' Aunt Selina said, 'especially as – well, I had certainly concluded his visit to be over.'

'It was, and now here is a new one begun, I suppose,' said Isabella, lightly, but with a look that on any less gentle face would have appeared like dark discontent.

'Well, and who is this Captain Brunton?' Caroline asked, slipping her arm through Isabella's.

'A kinsman of my stepmother – Lady Milner.'

'I believe he is a second cousin,' Aunt Selina added.

'Ah? One might suppose it a nearer relation,' said Dr Langland, jovially, 'they are so very thick with one another, are they not?'

'Yes, Uncle,' Isabella said, 'they are.'

Wythorpe Manor revealed itself at a nearer view as a substantial Dutch-gabled house built of mellow limestone, not more than two hundred years old, with two projecting wings either side of a central porch. There were signs of formal grounds having once surrounded it, but now a lawn of luxuriant and decidedly uneven turf ran right up to the steps, which Caroline thought much pleasanter. Within, she was enfolded at once by a smell of old varnish, woodsmoke and beeswax, and was amused, on gazing round the lofty panelled hall, to fancy Mrs Catling being forced to live here, and suffering the agony of being unable to check it all for dust.

A comfortable morning room, steeped in autumn sun, was where they were received by their hostess. Such at least they must call her: but there was not much that was hospitable about the young lady who stiffly dabbed her fingers into Caroline's palm and then swiftly reclaimed her seat by the fire. She was remarkably handsome – to the surprise of Caroline, who had uncharitably supposed that to enslave an old man of fifty, not much was required beyond the bloom of youth, and obligingness; but it was in a tall, high-chinned, black-browed style, more impressive than appealing: and she asked how Caroline did, and how she liked the country, and how she was settling in at the Rectory, in such an absent and mechanical way as suggested she was mentally ticking off a list of the requisite civilities. She was richly dressed, but seemed to have a finicking consciousness of it, and would suddenly turn her attention, when Caroline or her aunt was speaking, to rearranging the embroidered shawl over her shoulder, in a manner that made Caroline want fairly to slap her. Yet at the same time Lady Milner seemed always on the watch, observing every shuffle, interrogating every smile, with the result that her visitors became as unnatural as she was.

With her was a knotty, muscular, light-eyed man of thirty whose weathered complexion would have proclaimed the naval officer, even without the blue tail-coat and white waistcoat, and who sat stoically nursing a stocky leg and blinking as if on a long night-watch. Lady Milner introduced him with the words, 'My cousin, Captain Brunton, late of the *Northam*,' and with the first hint of warmth or animation she had shown. He only blinked harder, and muttered a gruff greeting.

'Well, well, Captain Brunton, had you no luck with their lordships at the Admiralty, hey?' Dr Langland accosted him. 'I recall, when you were last here, you were going to wait upon them in hopes of a commission.'

'No luck – as you say, sir,' the Captain answered. 'But I am still – as you say – in hopes.'

'Dear, dear – I dare swear it is the worst of all times for a man like yourself, what with the peace, and more officers being turned ashore than given ships,' Dr Langland pursued cheerfully. 'Must be dozens of half-pay captains lingering about the Admiralty corridors every day, hey?'

'Dozens – as you say, sir,' said Captain Brunton: prompting Caroline to wonder whether being at sea so long had turned the sailor into the semblance of one of his own parrots, able only to echo what had just been said to him.

'What about the merchant service? That's the other side of the peace, you know – there'll be more trade upon the seas now. Of course, it must be odd to shake down to carrying cargoes of herrings after fighting the Frenchies so magnificently. I can see that. Well, at any rate, Captain, you have a comfortable safe harbour here, hey?'

Dr Langland innocently beamed, but Captain Brunton only bowed shortly, whilst Lady Milner stirred and with a conscious look pronounced: 'I am very happy to have my cousin stay, and my late husband would, I am sure, have felt the same – that is, that any connections of mine would always be welcome at Wythorpe, without reservation.'

'I do not think Uncle John intended any such reflection,' Isabella spoke up, 'indeed I am sure of it, knowing him: for he is after all a true connection of the family.'

'Ah, to be sure,' Dr Langland said, looking about him with amiable incomprehension, 'I've known Isabella here, and the others, since they were half the height of my stick – nay, babes in arms – and yet the curious thing is it all seems to have passed in a mere twinkling. Why, I remember little Bella making a tea-party on the rug with thimbles, and scolding Stephen because he lolled about and would not sit neatly. Such a messy boy he was, and would not submit to have his hair combed, do you recall, Selina? Of course, that was before your time, my dear Lady Milner,' the Rector concluded, with another unwitting, beaming look all about, whilst Captain Brunton blinked away at his watch, and Lady Milner, who apparently never blinked at all, seemed to freeze where she sat.

'That reminds me,' said Aunt Selina, 'Stephen – do you hear anything from him? When can we expect him back at Wythorpe?'

'I hear nothing,' Lady Milner said. 'I should be glad to, indeed: there is a deal of business that the steward cannot manage without the master's approval, and he is forever troubling me with it.'

'Ah, yes, I think Isabella would be glad of his return likewise,' Aunt Selina said, 'so she can proceed with her marriage plans, isn't it so, my dear? You must both of you take this sad fellow to task when he comes home.'

It was a game attempt, Caroline thought – trying to make stepmother and stepdaughter feel they were in the same boat; but it was met with two different kinds of silence, and it would surely take a lot more than Aunt Selina's gentle persuasion to heal the disaffection in this room. Isabella was quite altered in the presence of Lady Milner and her cousin: subdued and yet soured, like a bright candle overtaken by daylight; and Caroline could understand why. There was no ease about Lady Milner – only a stiff civility, a cold straining after correctness. Something about her unrestful glance suggested that her awkwardness had unhappy roots; but still one was discouraged from sympathy, and Caroline was just wondering how the visit was to be got through when a newcomer burst into the room, pursued by a yipping spaniel, and bringing with her a new atmosphere, like a gust through a door flung cheerfully open.

'Uncle John – Aunt Selina, how long have you been here? You're not about to go away, are you? Only I didn't know – I was rambling round the garden and I quite forgot the time—'

'And without your shawl, I think,' Lady Milner said reprovingly to the young girl, who had gone bouncing over to kiss Dr Langland's cheek.

'Oh, pooh, Augusta, it's absolutely mild out, as you would know if you came away from that fire for a change. Ain't it, Bella?'

'I don't know about *absolutely* mild,' Isabella said, with a smile. 'Something might be absolutely freezing or boiling, but mild suggests a relative term.'

'Old Grave-Airs, how you talk!' the girl cried, planting a boisterous kiss on Isabella's cheek also. 'And now *you* must be Caroline!'

'I have told you before, Fanny,' Lady Milner droned, 'it is not proper to address me in that way.'

'Why, I can't call you Miss Howell any more, because you ain't,' said Fanny robustly. 'And to say Stepmother or Stepmama would be just too fantastical, when you're hardly older than Bella. Now then, how do you do –' Caroline's hand was seized '– and I'm Fanny, and I don't mind *what* you call me, only I must say I was never so glad to meet anyone – no, go down, Leo! – because I have heard so much about you, which is a dreadful old stale thing to say but in this case *true*, and I have absolutely hundreds of questions to ask you.'

'Dear me, I'm delighted, but I think you must have the wrong person – you must be thinking of Princess Caroline, or Lady Caroline Lamb.'

'Oh, pooh to them – thought I *should* like to read this book Lady Caroline has written about Lord Byron, though they pretend it isn't about him.'

'Pray don't waste your time – it is sadly dull and absurd.'

'Oh, you have read it? But of course you would – you have moved in the world – and here we are dreadfully out of things, and have to go to Huntingdon even to get to a circulating-library, and then it is half stocked with sermons. And it's bad enough having to listen to those, without absolutely sitting down and *reading* them as well. Oh, I do beg your pardon, Uncle John! Don't take that amiss – *some* of yours are actually quite interesting!'

Fanny Milner, who had plumped herself down beside Caroline on the sofa, was everything her stepmother was not, in terms of naturalness and animation. She was all in a glow from her exercise, her chestnut hair coming down in wild spirals, her skirts stained with mud: white-skinned, buxom, with a short nose and a determined chin, and a charmingly evident belief that her seventeen years had taught her all she would ever need to know.

'The way Aunt Selina found you, and brought you here – I vow it is the most romantic thing. And then your father was actually in the Peninsula, and wounded! How surpassingly glorious! Papa had a godson at St Ives who was in the militia and made a great thing of it, but all he ever did was drill round the market-place, and then go and drink himself silly with loyal toasts.'

'It is not right to speak so slightingly of the militia, Fanny,' put in her stepmother. 'They were embodied to very good purpose.'

'Pooh, I'll bet Bonaparte would have made mincemeat of them. Well, he would – I don't mean I *approve* him,' Fanny said, turning to Caroline with a roll of her eyes. 'And now is it true your father was absolutely an actor on the stage once as well? How perfect!'

'Well, opinions might differ as to the perfection of that,' Caroline said, with a glance at Aunt Selina. 'In the eyes of some people – who had eminently good reasons for thinking so – it was not at all respectable.'

'I wouldn't care for that,' Fanny said decidedly. 'I have an absolute scorn for stuffy conventions – and, Lord, we are imprisoned by them in *this* place.'

'Some conventions may appear stuffy,' said Aunt Selina, 'but there is usually a good reason for them. It is a convention, after a dull party, to say you have enjoyed it; but that is an act of consideration for your hosts.'

'And so you get invited again, to another dull party,' Fanny returned. 'No, not for me: I shall just speak my mind.'

'What if you hurt your hosts' feelings by doing so?' Isabella gently suggested.

'Oh, well, when everyone is used to being open and honest, then no one will get hurt by such things.'

'Ah, you imagine an ideal world, my dear,' Dr Langland said.

'Of course, Uncle: what other kind is worth imagining? But do you not agree, Captain Brunton? About the dull parties?'

'Parties? Oh – as to that, Miss Fanny, I am a dull fellow for parties in any event,' Captain Brunton said; occasioning in Caroline a brief mental review, to see if there were any news that had ever surprised her less.

'And I suppose you have been behind the scenes at theatres too,' Fanny went on, her tireless eyes shining at Caroline. 'What is it like? Are the actresses ever so – you know?'

'You should not badger Miss Fortune so, Fanny,' her stepmother said.

'No, no, Lady Milner, I am not badgered – only a little perplexed how to answer without disappointing. Most of the actresses I saw were married ladies, who went home after the performance to exemplary domesticity.'

'What a pity! Oh, but I'll wager they *weren't*,' Fanny said, with a poke in Caroline's ribs, 'only you can't say. Well, what about the Peninsula? Did your mother not follow the drum? I would have.'

'It is a hard life, for an army wife,' said Aunt Selina, giving a momentary impression of being about to break into poetry.

'Oh, la, I can bear any sort of discomfort.'

'I am glad to hear it, Fanny,' observed Isabella, with her old quiet smile, 'and shall keep it in mind, next time there is no chocolate left for your breakfast.'

'Boo to you, Miss Grave-Airs,' Fanny said, jumping up to slap Isabella's knees with a true sisterly affection that made Caroline smile, and made Lady Milner, she could not help but notice, draw herself in and up in still deadlier fashion.

A preliminary barrage of coughs alerted her to the fact that Captain Brunton was about to speak to her.

'Miss – er – Miss Fortune,' he said, planting his hands on his thighs, 'your father – in the Peninsula. I am all admiration. Might I ask what regiment?'

'The Twenty-ninth.'

'The Twenty-ninth, ah. And his wound? Where did he receive it?'

'Just above his right kneecap,' was what Caroline was tempted to say – but Captain Brunton's heavy manner was not propitious. 'At

Talavera, sir; and before that he was at Corunna,' she answered, dearly hoping that he would not repeat the last word.

'Corunna?' The Captain took a firmer grip of his thighs. 'Ah. It was gallantly fought. A retreat, to be sure, but gallant.'

She fancied some condescension in this, and could not help replying: 'At sea, of course, sir, you never have retreats – owing to the impossibility, I imagine, of the ships going backwards.'

'I think, Miss Fortune, you do not quite comprehend naval manoeuvres,' he began: then coughed and ran a hand through his stiff thick hair. 'Ah. You are amusing yourself.'

It was on her lips to say she had to amuse herself, as the present company was not likely to do it for her, but she relented. 'We both know there was much gallantry both on land and at sea, Captain Brunton, in defeat and victory: there, that was a very proper little English speech, and now we may nod and tuck our chins in and murmur agreement in the true English fashion.'

'Just so – just so,' he said, actually doing it: then his scalp lifted and a smile, quite a boyish smile, slowly dawned. 'Our famous reserve. It puts me in mind of when I was made Captain. I was on the Mediterranean station when the glad news came – news indeed that was the summit of all my hopes – and I confided it to a Spanish acquaintance. He remarked that my demeanour suggested I had heard no greater piece of news than an old aunt leaving me a tea-set in her will.'

It was pleasant to feel she had drawn him out, though he huffed and coloured and seemed about to go back in again, so Caroline laughed obligingly; and at once Lady Milner cut in with: 'What's that? Edward, what are you talking of?'

'Only the tale of when I was made Captain, Augusta – and Miss Fortune was just saying—'

'It was late, much later than your deserts,' Lady Milner said, in an aggrieved tone. 'You were most shockingly passed over, Edward, I shall always maintain it.'

'Well, I think it was above my deserts, Augusta, in truth: there were better men than I still stuck at Commander.'

'You should not denigrate yourself, Edward,' Lady Milner said, with her steeliest look. 'There are always people aplenty to do *that* for you, I find.'

'Oh, I have only gratitude for the service: it has been the means of my rising in the world, in a way I could never have hoped otherwise.'

Lady Milner's compressed lips revealed how little she liked the obscure origins of their family being discussed; but before she could speak Fanny interposed: 'Is it not a terrible consideration, though, that you can only rise by other men getting their heads blown off?'

'Fanny!' hissed Lady Milner; but her kinsman only huffed his inward laugh and answered, 'It is a terrible consideration, indeed. It is not the *only* way, for officers are promoted upwards as well as – as—'

'Being promoted heavenwards,' Caroline suggested.

'It is a nice ethical question,' Dr Langland said, 'for likewise, when the sun shines on me, is someone else not left in darkness? When I eat a loaf of bread, do I not take that bread out of another's mouth? What do you think, Bella?'

'I cannot imagine *you* taking bread out of anyone's mouth, Uncle John,' Isabella answered.

'That is not what Dr Langland meant, Isabella,' Lady Milner said freezingly. 'He meant the hypothetical case.'

'Lord, Augusta, we're not in the schoolroom now!' cried Fanny; and oblivious to the icy silence emanating from her stepmother, turned back to Caroline. 'You see how dreadfully dull we are here – so dreary and provincial – really you must enliven us, Caroline. I count on you – you must show us all the new modes, and spread lots of shocking scandal, and make all the men fall in love with you. Oh! and you have been lately at Brighton, I know – tell me, is it as fast as they say?'

'There are some – fast characters to be met with there, certainly,' Caroline said, thinking of Mr Leabrook. 'But for my part I prefer slow and honest.'

'Oh, I know you have to say that,' Fanny said, giving her an expressive wink. 'And what about the Prince's Pavilion – is it as fantastical as they say?'

'It looks rather like a grand birdcage crowned with onions.'

'The Pavilion is built in the Oriental style. That is why it looks odd to you, Miss Fortune,' Lady Milner informed her.

As there was no reply more civil than 'I know' to be made to this paralysing remark, Caroline contented herself with a polite nod. It was Isabella who came to her defence, saying: 'Of course Caroline knows that, ma'am, she was trying to give us a picture of it. Rather than being hypothetical.'

'Quite a vivid one indeed,' said Captain Brunton, 'though to be sure, Oriental is the correct term. Something to be said for both sides, I think, Miss Milner.'

'I thank you for the instruction, sir,' Isabella said, very coldly; and Caroline saw, with mingled sympathy and amusement, that the neck-blush was called forth by anger as well as modesty.

The amusement was possible to her, of course, because she could come away from that house: as the Rectory party very soon did, with Dr Langland blissfully remarking on what a pleasant chat they had had, and Lady Milner, in spite of having given them an indifferent welcome, contriving to make it seem they were leaving very soon, and even appearing offended by a departure she had herself hastened. But for poor Isabella there was no such escape – except by the early marriage for which Caroline could now see some very persuasive reasons.

'Not an easy woman by any means,' Caroline said later, when Aunt Selina tentatively asked her opinion of Lady Milner. 'But I dare say that, like everyone, she improves upon acquaintance.'

Aunt Selina replied, 'Ye-es,' in such a dubious tone as suggested that in this regard Lady Milner was the exception that proved the rule. 'I think they are settling a little better as a family . . . But it is so very awkward for Fanny, who was used to her as a governess, and now finds her a stepmother.'

Privately Caroline thought the irrepressible Fanny much more at ease with the situation than her quieter sister, and was only concerned at the young girl's propensity to make a heroine of herself: even on leaving the Manor, she had tugged Caroline aside and whispered: 'You shall tell me some *real* stories when Augusta's not by.' Caroline was not at all averse to being admired, but what she was being admired *for* in Fanny's case – a racy past, sophistication, the sulphurous whiff of the town and the taste of forbidden fruit – made her feel rather a fraud. Nor could she suppose Lady Milner would approve such a species of admiration; and she dreaded to think what Stephen Milner would make of it – though on second thoughts, why his opinion of her should be a matter of dread was a curious question, and one she felt disinclined to pursue.

But when Isabella made her usual call at the Rectory next morning, it was with Fanny alongside her; and during their usual walk, it was Fanny who plied Caroline with numerous questions about London, about Bath and Brighton, about actresses and demireps, dandies and Corinthians, ladies' boarding-schools and nocturnal elopements from the same (which she seemed to think so frequent they were virtually part of the curriculum), and other worldly excitements, whilst Isabella remained relatively quiet. Fortunately for Caroline's peace, Fanny was devoted to her dogs, and would suffer no one but herself to feed and exercise them, and accordingly she had to hurry back to the Manor for that purpose, leaving Caroline and Isabella free at last for confidence.

It was not long in coming. Caroline slipped her arm through her friend's, observed that she seemed a little hipped, and was rewarded with a sigh that came from a full heart.

'It is very stupid. I feel very ashamed,' Isabella said. Caroline guessed she was not the sort of person who readily wept, and there was confirmation in her expression – a look that might have been taken for grim ferocity, if you did not realize she was suppressing a flood of tears. 'I am stupid and ashamed – stupidly ashamed.'

'But so very grammatical. My dear girl, what can you have done? I see no constables in pursuit.'

'You are quite right, it *is* trivial, and I should not be such a fool about it.'

'Now I know it cannot be trivial, because it has put you out of temper, and that is not like you.'

'I declare you are quite clairvoyant sometimes!' her friend returned wonderingly, gazing up at Caroline with beautiful myopia. 'That is precisely why I hate this horrible business – because it makes me a stranger to myself. Well, it is simple enough, and you have probably guessed it, now you have seen our blissful domicile for yourself. There was another dreadful quarrel this morning – no, I should not put it so. *I* had the quarrel, with my stepmother. We are always doing it. Isn't that dreadful?'

'For you it is, I can tell. Though there are some people who like nothing better than a good, regular quarrel, like a dose of rhubarb. It is quite a refreshment to them.'

'I cannot understand it. I'm sure it must be my fault, but we just cannot get along. I thought it would be simply a matter of time – that one would adjust. Stephen said we would eventually settle down like two cats in a basket.'

Did you now? thought Caroline. You superior creature!

'But we get cross over the slightest things. This morning it was about breakfast. She has got into the habit of coming down to breakfast very late—'

'My dear Isabella, as a confirmed slug-a-bed myself, I must confess I may not be able to take your part here.'

'Oh, no, I don't mind that – it was simply that this morning she had engaged to breakfast earlier, because of Mrs Cooper, our cook. Mrs Cooper has a sister at Huntingdon very ill, and this is the day she was going to visit her, so she wanted to be off early. So, no having to cook a second breakfast at eleven – well, that was the agreement; but my stepmother forgot it, or did not trouble about it, and came down late as ever. And with no apology to poor Mrs Cooper at all. And when I spoke up about it – which perhaps I should not have – my stepmother informed me that she was the mistress of the house and the welfare of the servants was her concern and not mine. Well, I was very unwise, and said she did not seem to concern herself very much at all – and so it went on. The worst thing is – well, what I thought but did not say, thank heaven – that *she* of all people should understand their position.' Isabella grimaced. 'There. Does that not make me the vilest of wretches?'

'No,' laughed Caroline, 'not even if you had said it, instead of just thinking it.'

'I don't like myself even for thinking it,' Isabella said, shaking her head. 'That's what I mean about the change in myself. Oh, I wish I could be like Fanny: she either ignores Augusta, or laughs her off. But then she hasn't got Captain Brunton to deal with as well.'

'Dear, dear, you quarrel with the Captain too?'

'It isn't that. He is constantly intervening. I fancy he has taken it on himself to convert me to my stepmother's side. And so I forever hear his apologetic cough and his ahem, presuming to suggest . . . Well, I am being perfectly horrible today, so I may as well go on and say I do not like him being always about the house and I do not trust his association with my stepmother.'

'Lord! Do you mean you suspect them . . . ?'

Isabella shrugged. 'I should say no more. Because when we dislike someone we are always very ready to believe any ill of them. But they are so very thick together: and when I walk into the room, and they are deep in one of their talks, and break it off so that we can all be uncomfortable together – well, I feel rather like an intruder in my own home. And that, I'm sure you'll agree, is quite enough complaining from me. Now tell me how *you* do, my dear.'

'I would do much better if I could think of something to help you. But I can only come up with that most unsatisfying of counsels; patience. This is very disagreeable for you, but it will end – as one might say to a man having a tooth slowly pulled.'

'It will end. You are right, of course. I must keep that in mind – once I am married, there will be an end to all this.' Isabella fixed her gaze on a skein of geese arrowing across the cold blue sky, as rapturously as if they were leading her to that blessed future; and it occurred to Caroline, just for a moment, that a very great burden was placed on a marriage that represented an escape from misery, as well as an admittance to happiness. But then, she supposed, she knew nothing of these things; and she was distracted by Isabella's bursting out, with a shy squeeze of her hand: 'And – and how lucky I am to have someone like you to unburden myself to! There, I dread to think what colour my neck is now.'

'Between pink and lobster. And when you are a bride, you know, you may leave Lady Milner and her salty suitor to do what they will. Unless you do not like the thought of leaving Fanny in their company?'

'I would not, if Fanny were not so very well able to take care of herself. Besides, you know, she will have her heroine near at hand, to watch over her.'

'Oh, Lord – Isabella, if this is truly the case, then I beg you to be so good as to disillusion that poor girl about me.'

'Too late – you are already her model of all that is daring, dashing, and unconventional. You will have gathered she is of a romantic spirit: she has long deplored the tameness of our society here; and to know someone who has lived in the world as you have has quite put her into transports.'

'Well, I am glad to have made someone happy; but I fear she will suffer a great disappointment, when she comes to realize that I have never had an oyster supper with Lord Byron, and that my favourite excitement is a little plain-sewing in the evening, followed by a quiet hand of penny whist.'

Isabella took this last no more seriously than Caroline meant it: yet it had some relation to the truth, in that Caroline greatly valued the harmony, peace, and mutual consideration that prevailed at the Rectory, and was pleased to find herself fitting into its tranquil routines; and she was all the more solidly appreciative after the contrast exhibited by the domestic atmosphere of the Manor. Indeed that very evening she looked up to find Aunt Selina's tired pretty eyes resting smilingly on her, and to hear the heart-piercing words: 'Do you know? I can't remember when you weren't here with us.'

Still, she was not ready for decorating tea-caddies and distributing baby-clothes just yet; in sociability, company, activity lay Caroline's chief enjoyment: and so she was gratified when they were invited to dine at the Manor, a few days later, and all the more so because the invitation proceeded from the master of the house.

Mr Stephen Milner was back. He had given no hint of his imminent return to Wythorpe – all of a sudden his muddy boots were in the hall, as Isabella told her afterwards; and when he called at the Rectory, Caroline missed him, having gone that day with Aunt Selina on a shopping trip to Huntingdon. Her aunt and uncle expressed their satisfaction that he was home; and Caroline discovered in herself a strong wish to encounter Mr Milner again, a wish comparable perhaps only to that impulse which makes us prod at a bruise, for in their short association they seemed to have done nothing but vex one another.

Now, though, Caroline reflected, she had a cause with which to tax him – her friend and his sister, Isabella, who was unhappy and surely might be made less so, if he would only exert himself. And there was a certain remark about cats and baskets, which made her feel so satirical she could hardly wait for the appointed evening to arrive.

Chapter XII

Caroline dressed with care for the occasion – an evening gown of dove-grey poplin with pearl buttons gathering the sleeves: it had been finished by Aunt Selina's Bath dressmaker, just before their departure, and now came out of its tissue-paper to her mingled admiration and dubiety. It was very handsome: but was it too handsome for her? However, once inside it, and with her hair dressed and curled by Aunt Selina's exceedingly skilful maid – who had been longing to try her hand at something more elegant than her mistress's perennial topknot – Caroline recovered her confidence. She felt that she looked rather well; 'and besides,' she considered, 'I need to be dressed to advantage tonight, for *he* will soon find something to remark on if not.'

He was Mr Stephen Milner; and his disobliging words about her, overheard at Bath, were much in Caroline's mind as they rode up to the Manor – Aunt Selina having initially expressed strong doubts about using the carriage for a journey of three-quarters of a mile, but being persuaded at last by the coachman, who solemnly informed her that the horses were suffering a depression of the spirits from being in the stable so long. The representation of her as *trouble* struck Caroline as more and more unjust; and she was all the more determined to demonstrate to Mr Milner – a man altogether too sure of being always right – that his prognostications were wrong: that she had not set the neighbourhood by the ears, destroyed its bucolic peace, or corrupted its youth.

'And so,' she told herself, 'he may wipe that provoking smile from his face': yet she had the curious experience, just then, of being unable to recollect Stephen Milner's face at all. It was most odd: the image would not be summoned, try as she might throughout the drive; and this was only terminated by an even more curious experience, when on arrival at the Manor they were greeted by Mr Milner himself on the steps, and Caroline beholding him thought: But of course: I have known that face all the time.

'Uncle John, how d'you do, sir? Aunt, give me a kiss, you look well – ah, and Miss Fortune.'

'Mr Milner.'

He shook her hand, scrutinized her very briefly – with the look, she thought, of a man tendered a spurious banknote – and then turned aside to give some directions to the coachman on the stabling of the horses. He is no more civil than before, thought Caroline – but with a serene absence of rancour: for as she intended her own conduct to be beyond reproach, he might do as he pleased.

In the drawing room, though it was a mild evening, Lady Milner clung close again to the fire; but if this was with some notion of thawing herself out, it was not working, judging by the bare, stiff courtesies she extended to the guests from her hearthside station: nor was there any more ease in the manner of Captain Brunton, who stood over her like a benign warder, not knowing what to do with his hands. Joining them, besides the family, were the youngish couple by the name of Hampson, whom Isabella had described to her: he very handsome in a fat way, she very plain likewise, and both unremitting in their attention to one another, with an armoury of secret smiles, nods, and glances, that proclaimed their marriage to be of recent date as surely as if they had still had rice in their hair.

The real surprise for Caroline, however, was the change in the feeling of the house, which struck her as forcibly as if it had all been new-painted since her last visit. Isabella was in cheerful looks, Fanny's animation was more genial and less noisy: the servants were more amenable: even the spaniel's yap seemed mellower in tone. Caroline was forced to conclude that Mr Milner had wrought this change, simply by his return. She was reluctant to allow him this credit, as it must be increasing a propensity to be pleased with himself already, in her opinion, too much developed. But no, let it stand: for if his presence could be so beneficial in its effect, then he was all the more to be reproached for his absence.

This was the subject of Dr Langland's first remarks: the Rector clapping his great hands together, smiling upon the company, and pronouncing: 'Now this, my dear Stephen, is what I joy to see. The master of the house in residence, and all as it should be. You were missed, Nephew, greatly missed.'

'I thank you, Uncle, I greatly thank you,' Mr Milner said, 'and I'm glad to be back. I always am, right up to the moment when I go away again.'

'Dear, dear – what will settle you, I wonder?' cried Dr Langland. 'Perhaps a pretty young wife, like our friend here?'

There being no pretty young wives in the room, attention fastened, after a momentary bewilderment, on Mrs Hampson, who coloured appropriately. 'Ah,' said her husband, with a rapt gaze into his consort's eyes, or at least into the one that was directed towards him, 'how true, sir, how true. I can honestly say, that I never knew felicity till I knew Felicity!'

This compliment to Mr Hampson's bride, with its delicate pun on her name, was loudly admired by the Rector: although Caroline intercepted a suffering look from Isabella, which suggested she had heard the sally too many times for it to retain its entire freshness.

'Ha, I see Caroline smiles,' Dr Langland went on, 'which means, I think, that she approves my prescription.'

'I doubt whether Miss Fortune approves matrimony any more than I do,' Stephen Milner said, with a foxy smile, and a decided air.

'I'm flattered, sir,' was Caroline's calm rejoinder.

'*Are* you? Good God. Why?'

'Oh, wait, this is revealing, Mr Milner – that you are surprised at having said something nice to a woman.'

'You are wrong, Miss Fortune,' he said collectedly. 'I am not surprised, I am astonished.'

'No more astonished than I at hearing anything like a compliment from *your* lips: but so I have: and the highest compliment of all, perhaps. You have suggested that I think as you do.' Caroline made a bow of mock reverence. 'Surely no greater praise could be bestowed.'

'Absolutely so,' said Mr Milner, with a look of keen enjoyment. 'For is this not how we all proceed? "I met a very pleasant woman at the coach-stand this morning." In what way was she a pleasant woman? "Why, she agreed with everything I said."'

'Oh, Stephen, for shame,' Aunt Selina put in, smiling, but serious. 'People may be friends without agreeing on every subject.'

'So they may, Aunt: and secretly each will be hoping to convert the other to their belief. But that is only the common run of friendship. I cannot conceive true friends who are not absolutely candid with one another, including where they differ.'

As this was Caroline's own view, and she hoped a fair description of her relation with Isabella, she let it pass, observing only: 'And what about your despised matrimony – should the same prescription not apply?'

'Oh, I don't actually despise it. I only know it would not do for me.'

'True friends may be married also,' Aunt Selina said. 'Your uncle John has been my best friend for nearly thirty years.'

'Lord! Thirty years!' cried Mrs Hampson, appealing to her spouse. 'Only think of it, my love! Shall you still be as fond of me then, do you think?'

'I would say fonder,' Mr Hampson ardently replied, reaching for her hand, 'if it were not an impossibility to be fonder than I am now!'

Some caresses and simperings concluded this exchange, observed by Mr Milner with an ironical look in which Caroline also detected triumph, as if his point were being proved.

'Oh! Caroline – you will never guess what Stephen has brought me,' burst out Fanny. 'It is *Glenarvon* and, you know, I do not find it dull as you said – perhaps a little absurd in places but such passion too – and Glenarvon himself is so darkly fascinating, really I would be quite ready to throw away my reputation for him.'

'Tut, Fanny, this is not proper in a girl your age,' Lady Milner said, rousing herself from an assiduous session of shawl-smoothing.

'Isn't it? Oh, Augusta, do tell me at what age it *will* become proper to throw away my reputation,' Fanny responded, with a wicked smile, 'so that I may mark it in my calendar.'

'This is hardly a fit subject for jest,' her stepmother said repressively.

Fanny turned, still glinting with mischief, to Caroline. 'What do you say? You have seen something of the world. Isn't it possible for a woman to *fall*, and still keep cheerful?'

Caroline was careful. 'I dare say it is possible, though society is so very severe upon such a woman that she may not find cheerfulness easy to come by. It is easiest if she is like Lady Caroline Lamb: wealth and title may cushion the fall, at least.'

'Oh, society – it can only hurt you if you care for its opinion,' Fanny said airily, stretching herself out on the sofa, 'which I do not.'

'Dear, dear, I begin to repent of bringing you that book, Fanny,' her brother said. 'To think of such sensational stuff sullying poor Father's library.'

'Well, it isn't – I don't go in there to read any more. It's too deuced cold.'

'Fanny, please, that word,' intoned Lady Milner.

'But you don't like it when I say damned,' Fanny said reasonably.

Stifling a smile, Mr Milner asked: 'Why is it so cold in the library? Is there a window-pane gone? Those frames are rather ancient.'

'It's cold because there's no fire lit in the mornings now.'

'Isn't there?' Mr Milner frowned a little. 'Well, then, ask for one.'

'I've done that, but apparently it's mistress's orders,' yawned Fanny.

'I decided to discontinue the practice, at least until it is true winter, since it seems rather wasteful,' said Lady Milner, drawing herself up. 'I have not told you of this, Stephen, as I understood that these domestic matters were to be my province: though if that is no longer the case, please inform me, and I will observe the alteration accordingly.'

I must try to be charitable, Caroline thought: probably she doesn't mean to sound as if she is continually translating from Latin.

'No, no,' Stephen Milner said, 'of course not: only I hope if my sister wants something in her own home, she may have it.'

'Certainly: I have only to be asked.' Lady Milner's glance fell on Isabella, who had risen and moved away with an unsettled look. 'I feel that these things should be in the power of one member of the household only, simply to avoid confusion.'

'Confusion can be creative, I think,' Mr Milner said, on his feet likewise, ruffling his impossible hair, and jingling the change in his pockets. 'But have it as you will: so long as I am not plagued with it. Uncle John, how was your barley this year?'

This was a clear enough hint to drop the subject – clear to everyone except Lady Milner. 'Such other innovations as I have made,' she went on purposefully, 'are not, I think, numerous or considerable. There is one which I believe Isabella disapproves, and that is the servants' bedchamber candles. I consider wax a needless extravagance, and have ordered tallow instead.'

'Yes,' said Isabella, her eyes shadowy: there had been another quarrel, Caroline guessed. 'I don't think it is fair on them.'

'But it is what I use in my own bedchamber,' her stepmother said. 'I do not ask them to make any sacrifice that I am not making likewise.'

'Sacrifice, forsooth,' groaned Mr Milner, pacing, 'what is this business about sacrifices? Are we poor all of a sudden, Augusta, that you must go burning tallow in your boudoir? Surely you must dream of cattle-markets all night, sleeping in the smell of that. No, no more of it. I hereby reinstate wax. It is like me, bright and sweet-smelling.'

'Your late father never had occasion, I think, to find fault with my domestic economy.'

'Well, Father was an odd fish in many ways,' Mr Milner said, still pacing. 'Believed that cabbage-water was good for the digestion. Dosed himself with a pint of it every day.' His eye fell on Caroline, not without a spark. '"Ah, my boy," says he when I protested, "you should imagine what I would be like without it."'

'I think you exaggerate, Stephen,' Lady Milner said dourly. 'It was not half a pint.'

Scrubbing violently at his hair, and seeming, as an amused Caroline saw it, to close his eyes in momentary exasperation, Mr Milner paced harder. 'You are not about to go off again, I hope, Stephen,' said Aunt Selina, lightly, but shrewdly.

Just then Mrs Hampson gave a little startled squeal at what seemed to be the growling of a large dog behind her, but which resolved itself into Captain Brunton, clearing his throat before a broadside.

'You know, Miss Milner,' he said, bending his muscle-bound attention on Isabella, 'it is remarkable – that is, it has been my observation so – how very little light a person may contrive to see by, once they are accustomed to it. I well remember when I was midshipman on the *Persephone*: ill-provisioned, not a candle-end to be had, and the most shocking dark, crabbed ward-room you ever saw, and yet I made shift to read by the mere glow of a taper, stuck into the boards.'

'Indeed, sir?' responded Isabella politely. 'Well, if the Ouse should ever burst its banks so disastrously that Wythorpe Manor actually floats out to sea, I shall know where to come for advice.'

'I shall be honoured,' Captain Brunton said punctiliously. Then the consciousness that he had made a very silly reply crept visibly over him, and he took refuge in a torrent of coughs so loud that Fanny's spaniel began joining in for company.

'Isabella is jesting at your expense, Cousin,' Lady Milner said, with pained and distant disapproval.

'Oh, all jests seem to be at someone's expense, but usually they are just expressions of good humour,' cried Caroline, intervening on behalf of Isabella, who looked as if she had been smacked. 'I remember being in company with a gentleman who had a wooden leg: it was remarkable how every turn the conversation took ended with me making some remark about not having a leg to stand on, or about some tale having a lame conclusion, or—'

'Was the name of the gentleman Clarke?' suddenly interrupted Lady Milner.

'No.'

'Oh – then that cannot have been the same gentleman I was

thinking of. I knew a gentleman named Clarke who had a wooden leg, you see. I thought it must be the same.'

'Unless there is a sort of Masonic society, by which all men with wooden legs must bear the same name, I cannot see how it could be,' said Caroline, irritated – and, perhaps, imprudent: Lady Milner rewarded her with such a stare as she might have accorded an ex-servant suspected of purloining the spoons. Certainly Caroline felt that her wits had betrayed her into discourtesy. She flung about desperately – but found Stephen Milner coming to her rescue.

'Augusta, you take everything much too seriously,' he said with decision. 'And to show I am quite even-handed, I may say that you do too, Bella. So does the whole world, come to that. Now one of the few things that *is* worth taking seriously is a good dinner, and my nose tells me ours is ready, and so I think we should go in.'

Lady Milner sprang up with surprising alacrity – for her wand-like figure by no means suggested the gourmand: but Caroline realized after a moment that it was only a hunger for importance that impelled her. She must be seen absolutely to take precedence here, and so glided her stiff-backed way to the dining-parlour before everyone else. Caroline rather thought that Mrs Hampson, as a bride, should have had first place in the company; but in any case, Lady Milner was put into difficulty by her own haste. Stephen Milner in his restless prowlings had fetched up closest to Caroline, and so he offered her his arm: Dr Langland, with many compliments and jests to Mr Hampson about stealing the lady away, took Mrs Hampson's, while Mr Hampson, with many jests likewise – more perhaps than could be heard with entire patience – escorted Aunt Selina. Only now did it occur to Lady Milner that she was unaccompanied: she stopped, and turned to look for Captain Brunton. He was at that moment offering his arm to Isabella, but at his cousin's significant look he paused: hesitated: coughed deeply; and appeared as if he might have remained helplessly fixed to that spot for ever more, had not Isabella settled the matter for him.

'Sir, you are wanted, I think: please escort Lady Milner,' she said coolly. 'My sister will be glad to walk in with me – won't you, Fanny?'

'To be sure!' cried Fanny, seizing her arm. 'I have never understood why a woman must have a man to take her into dinner. Is male conversation supposed to be better for the digestion? Most of the men in this benighted neighbourhood can only talk of hunting and horseflesh, so that can hardly be the case.'

'Probably because of our barbaric ancestors,' her brother opined, 'all hacking away at one roast boar, and devil take the hindmost. A man's assistance would at least assure you of a decent thighbone to gnaw on.'

'And yet, you know, women can be quite as grasping and overbearing as men,' Isabella gently suggested.

'Well, now,' said Uncle John, all smiles, 'isn't this pleasant?'

Probably no one but the blissfully obtuse Dr Langland could have found it so, but it was certainly, Caroline thought, mightily interesting. She felt the moment had come for a direct attack on her partner's defences; and so, as he was seating her at table, she quietly observed to Mr Milner: 'Your cats are not settling in the basket.'

'Eh?' She had him off-guard: but he quickly recovered. 'Oh, that.' He chuckled reminiscently, then shrugged. 'Hey, well, devil knows what's to be done with them.'

'Does it not occur to you that perhaps grown women are beings of a good deal more complexity than cats?'

Mr Milner gave this a perplexed attention, as to some outlandish though intriguing theory. 'Well,' he said at last, 'cats can be very temperamental creatures too, you know. Bella had a pretty tortoiseshell once that was all good nature during the week, but spat and scratched on Sundays. We thought it must have been due to the sound of church bells. Will you take some wine, Miss Fortune?' He presented to her a face of infuriating bland puzzlement. 'What? Have you turned Methodist, perhaps, and take only water? I confess I find it hard to believe, but I'll try my best—'

'Yes, I will have some wine, thank you, Mr Milner,' she rapped at him, fighting down a smile, 'and you will not divert me from my question.'

'Does it not occur to *you*, Miss Fortune, that questioning a man you hardly know at his own dinner-table makes you a thoroughly forward little piece?'

'Does it? Well, I'm progressing anyhow. At Bath you called me a bold little piece: "forward" is just slightly less insulting. And I did get to know you tolerably well there, sir.'

'I see: and now you have added to your knowledge by talking about me with my family.'

'Oh, there are many other more interesting things to talk about, believe me – but you do come up, Mr Milner, from time to time.'

'You come up *all* the time. Fanny has made you her touchstone in her perpetual war against the conventions; and I know what a favourite you are with Isabella already.'

'She is a great favourite with me: I never knew anyone more amiable, more truly gentle-hearted, than your sister.'

'Which you find surprising, having met me first.'

'To adopt your own figure, sir, I am not surprised, I am astonished. But come: considering I am bold, forward, and – what was your other elegant expression? ah, yes – *trouble*—'

'You remember everything I say!' Mr Milner said, in a tone that mixed wonderment with approval. 'Do you write it all down – or just engrave it on your heart?'

'Considering I am all these things,' she went on, ignoring this, 'you must confess I have not yet had the baleful influence on Wythorpe you predicted. For you see, here are no earthquakes or revolutions – not even, I would go so far as to say, any ruffled feathers.'

'I am willing to concur with all you say, Miss Fortune, because of that one significant word in the middle of it: not *yet*. You have not been here long, after all.'

'Long enough,' she said, refusing to be provoked even by his satisfied smile of triumph, 'to have grown greatly attached to Isabella, and to wish – well, to wish to help her: except that that does not lie in *my* power.'

'Oh, I understand you,' he said nodding, 'indeed I do: but I fancy you overestimate the ability of a mere male to settle the inevitable differences of two women under one roof.'

'From what I see, they are eased, if not settled, simply by your presence under that roof. There, that is the first compliment I have paid you, and probably will be the last.'

'No, it isn't, it is a reproach,' he said collectedly, helping her to soup, 'and a just one as far as it goes. I certainly am disinclined to botheration, and follow the natural impulse to fly from it whenever I can. But the fact is –' he took care to lower his voice, though Lady Milner was at the other end of the long rosewood table – 'Father did leave us rather awkwardly placed by that unexpected decision of his autumn years, and there's no denying it. No reflection on the persons involved: only the situation. I'm sure I need say no more – have probably said too much: I'll only add that as you may imagine, it has confirmed my opinion of marriage as a fool's game.'

He turned then, to do the duties of the tureen for Aunt Selina, who was on his left, leaving Caroline to ponder on what he said. She suffered a momentary misgiving: had she been meddlesome? But her eye falling on Isabella, who was presenting a face of civil attention to Captain Brunton, apparently becalmed in the midst of a very slow anecdote, she dismissed it. Friendship was a new sensation to her, and precious – a gift for which she wanted to make some recompense: she could not do much, but she could be Isabella's advocate. Her glance turned next to Lady Milner, prompted perhaps by another misgiving, that her partiality for her friend made her unjust to the stepmother: but a moment's reflection and observation convinced her it was not so. She felt no malice towards Lady Milner: indeed much in her conduct was thoroughly understandable. As she sat at the foot of the table, her inability to play the hostess was sadly conspicuous: for instead of gently marshalling the conversation, and making sure that everyone was comfortable, included, and well supplied, she could only dart her unquiet glances at every separate colloquy, as if suspecting she was talked about, or seek whisperingly to engross the attention of Captain Brunton on her left, the one person with whom she seemed at ease. In sum, she was uncomfortable in her position: but to sympathize with this was not to excuse its harmful effects.

Fortunately Lady Milner's economies had not extended to the table. Plentifully came the haddock, the ham and tongue, the boiled fowls and batter-pudding and roasted saddle of mutton. Taken together with this lofty dining-parlour, with its shining sonorous boards, capacious fireplace, and monumental buffet, it afforded Caroline a glimpse of an old country style of entertaining, very different from what she was used to.

As if divining her thoughts, Mr Milner said: 'Plain roast-and-boiled, you see, Miss Fortune. For my part I hanker after ragouts and fricassees sometimes, but our cook does not enjoy them, nor, as a rule, our guests. An unspoken suspicion hovers that sauces will turn you into a Frenchie.'

'I own I am fond of a little spice, sir – though this is very fine fare, to be sure. Perhaps you could venture to serve macaroni: that at least has not the reproach of being French.'

'With Bologna sausage, Parmesan-cheese, and garlic,' he said dreamily. 'Ah! And then my neighbours would have me taken away in a strait-waistcoat. So, how *are* you settling in?' As she hesitated he went on: 'I realize that is a fiendishly difficult question. Take time to think it out. I could ask you the square root of two hundred and twenty-five in the meanwhile—'

'It is because it is a simple question, and it comes from *you*, that I mistrust it. You must mean something teasy and ironical.'

'Must I? Probably I do, deep down: but let us pretend me capable of sincerity, and of recognizing that, troublesome as you surely are, you have lost a parent, been transplanted to a new world, and had to make a deal of adjustments, none of which can have been easy.'

Now she was at a loss: it was delicately said, it seemed truly meant, and it was felt by her with a tenderness all the more plangent because it was unexpected, and which only self-command could keep from drawing a tear to her eye. So all she could do was reply honestly, and without defences: 'I'm settling in very well, I thank you. Indeed it feels as if I have known you all for years.'

He gave a shout of laughter. 'Why, that, Miss Fortune, is because you have already heard everything we have to say – have plumbed our country dullness to the depths – and have experienced a true Wythorpe evening, in which the hands of the clock do not seem to move at all, and a whole age drags by before they indicate blessed bedtime.'

'I would call this unfair, if I thought you meant it, which surely shows that I am a loyal Wythorpe native already. As for dullness – well, you are not dull, Mr Milner, I will say that for you. Though I might say many other things, much less obliging.'

'Pray,' came Lady Milner's carrying voice, 'tell us what the jest is, Stephen, Miss Fortune – do not leave us out.'

'Oh, I was shamefully abusing our quiet old neighbourhood, and Miss Fortune was defending it.'

'I see. Ah, I see – and the joke is, it is Miss Fortune who is the outsider.'

'Oh, newcomer, surely, rather than outsider,' cried Isabella warmly.

'That is what I meant, Isabella. Of course that is what I meant.'

'But what *can* you find to say in favour of this deadly place?' demanded Fanny. 'There – listen to that rain at the window. That has set in now, I warrant you, till next spring – with the interruption only of hail, ice, snow, and other delightful diversions. There is an end of any walks or drives or picnics – though to be sure there are the winter assemblies and balls, which would be some consolation if there were more of them – but one miserable mustering a month is about all our dismal district affords. Oh, but I make an exception for you, my dear hospitable sir,' she said, turning to Mr Hampson, '*you* and Mrs Hampson have made a very appreciable difference to our entertainments, and I thank you for it – no, more, I vow I would have gone stark mad without it.'

'I am glad to hear it, Miss Fanny – do you hear, my love? Here is a compliment to you, for you are the sweet inspiration behind all such things. Indeed I would say, Miss Fanny, that I never knew felicity, until . . .' A cloud passing across Mr Hampson's brow, suggested that even he began to detect a certain staleness in the figure: but he turned it smartly, going on: 'Until I knew matrimony. And on the subject of entertainments, Miss Fanny, I may add that we intend a supper and carpet-dance at the Grange on Friday next, to which we would be very glad to welcome you, and all the present company.'

'Do you suppose, my love . . . ?' Mrs Hampson made some girlish mouthings and chuckles at her husband. 'Do you suppose . . . ? That our picture will be ready by then?'

'My sweet girl, it is hardly begun! But I know what you mean – I do share your impatience to see it – to see *us*, immortalized, impregnated – do I mean impregnated? I fancy not – to see us fixed, at any rate, in paint. We are having a bridal portrait painted,' he pursued, smiling on Aunt Selina. 'And no doubt, ma'am, you are ready to call us monstrous vain for it!'

'Not at all – a charming notion, Mr Hampson. You have been sitting to the artist already?'

'Aye, aye – a remarkable young fellow, comes to us for the sittings. He has been engaged upon some views at Hinchingbrooke, but is turning his hand to domestic portraiture also, for select clients. I have studied his samples: they are very good, very lifelike: still, you know, I am a little anxious for the outcome: I am anxious that he should do *justice* to my Felicity.'

As it was difficult to conceive of an artist being actually unflattering to Mrs Hampson, short of painting her with a horse-collar and tusks, there was not much that even Aunt Selina's politeness could find to reply to this beyond a smile and a murmured agreement. Fanny, however, had not done with her own subject.

'You must promise, Bella, that when you are married you will be regularly giving parties, and keeping more company than anyone in the county – indeed you must, you are our only hope – and is there not at Hethersett a room quite large enough to accommodate a creditable private ball? I went there only once, and did not see all over the house, but I'm sure I remember Richard speaking of such a room.'

'It is not proper to speak of your sister's fiancé so,' Lady Milner said relentlessly.

'Oh, well, he is *nearly* my brother-in-law – isn't he?' Fanny went on, unperturbed. 'And when he is, I may call him by his first name, so it is only anticipating a little. Indeed, Stephen, how long *are* we to be anticipating? When is this wedding to be?'

'My dear Fanny, why ask me? I'm not marrying him.'

'You know perfectly well what I mean. Here have we been waiting for you to come home and get matters settled with Isabella, and you remain so provokingly indifferent.'

'What matters?'

Caroline could not keep silent. 'A woman going to be married likes to have such things as the date of the wedding fixed, Mr Milner – and so, accordingly, orders made for trousseaus and lace and such, and preparations for removal – matters very trifling to the male mind, I know.'

Mr Milner raised his eyebrows, drank his wine, and looked over at Isabella. 'Well, what say you, Bella? Are you all for getting these matters settled?'

'As I have mentioned to you, Stephen,' she answered, her voice quiet, but her eyes shining, 'I really would like to be married before Christmas, if it were possible: and you know Richard is now on his way home, and writes me that he is in perfect agreement.'

'Well, I don't know,' Mr Milner said, after studying her for a moment. 'It doesn't leave a great deal of time for the arrangements; and I really don't see the need for haste. Consider: you have not been properly acquainted above eight months, nor engaged above four. This is not much. People in romances, you know, wait for each other for years. And if it is a true, sound attachment, as I am assured it is, then it must be a hardy plant, and will not wilt and wither for a little delay.'

'But if it is a true, sound attachment, then it needs no delay,' Caroline said to him. 'And besides, Mr Milner, how can you, who are so avowed an enemy of matrimony, presume to this expertise on the subject?'

'Oh, very easily,' he replied with energy. 'A man who stands aloof on a high hill looking down on a landscape, sees it much more clearly than one grubbing about down there in the boggy lowlands.'

'The elegance of your language is overpowering.'

'I've always thought so,' he said, with a comfortable smile, then, turning: 'But be it as you will, Bella. As soon as Richard is back at Hethersett, let us meet and make our plans, and talk deeply of lace. I still think there is no need for hurry – and you might at least credit me, you know, with a generous motive, that I don't want to lose my dear sister.'

'I might, but I won't,' said Isabella, cheerfully. 'You'll hardly notice I'm gone, knowing you, Stephen; and besides, I am not moving far away, certainly not far enough to talk of losing.'

'Ah, Hethersett is all very well, and not far as the crow flies,' he said, gravely shaking his head, 'but it is, after all, over the border – over into Northamptonshire: where folk are queer, so I hear. They butter their bread before slicing it, and no good can come of *that*, Miss Fortune, you'll be the first to agree.'

'I didn't know we were so close to Northamptonshire,' Caroline said, again tempted to smile, yet troubled also by some fugitive memory.

'Very close,' he said solemnly, patting her hand, 'but don't fear: if they try to invade us, we shall hurl them back across the Ouse; and then we can always retreat to the fortress of St Neots, and wait for our allies of Cambridgeshire to arrive, with their fierce eels-of-war, and the army of Norfolk firing dumplings into the sky—'

'Mr Milner – I make one simple remark, and you turn madman!'

'Yes, Stephen,' Lady Milner said precisely, cutting across Caroline's laughter. 'Miss Fortune did not mean anything of that kind, only that she is unacquainted with the local geography. Here we are at the meeting of the eastern and midland counties, Miss Fortune,' she went on instructively, 'and when Isabella becomes Mrs Richard Leabrook of Hethersett, she will become a resident of Northamptonshire, though only six miles away.'

'Yes,' Caroline said, faintly and mechanically. 'Yes, I see.'

Something – some kind, tutelary spirit – had prevented her crying out at that name, but it had been a close-run thing; and now, while Lady Milner continued with some dusty remarks about county boundaries, she must somehow contain her shock and dismay, and try to make sense of this critical information.

Her reeling mind snatched at one desperate chance, only to relinquish it after a moment. It could not be a different Richard Leabrook. There might conceivably be two John Smiths with estates in Northamptonshire: but this name was not common. No: Isabella's intended husband could be none other than the same Mr Leabrook whom Caroline had met at Brighton. The same Mr Leabrook who – while engaged to that gentle, trusting young woman at the other end of the table – had coolly attempted Caroline's seduction.

Caroline blinked down at her plate. There was roast duck upon it. She could not imagine how it had got there. She did not even like roast duck. She reached for her wine-glass: that, alas, was empty, though she could not recall draining it.

Was there any other possible explanation? Caroline prided herself on an inventive mind: probably this was an inheritance from her father, who could persuade himself of the most elaborate impossibilities; but here there was no sidestepping the plain, solid facts. She had encountered Isabella's fiancé before, and from that encounter knew him to be, beneath an apparently amiable exterior, a callous and unprincipled libertine.

Her mind grasped desperately again at a passing hope – only to drop it as a disgusting absurdity: the suggestion that Isabella might already *know* this about her fiancé's propensities, and not mind. A greater nonsense could not be conceived. Far more probable, far more sadly probable, was the reverse: that Isabella was deceived, as Caroline had been at first, in her estimate of Mr Leabrook's character.

All at once she found her glass being refilled: by Stephen Milner himself, who had taken the wine from the manservant's hands. She was grateful, but his eyes were dwelling curiously on her, and she hardly knew how she would manage speech.

'You are very silent, Miss Fortune.'

'Oh – I'm sorry.'

'Don't be: I consider it a promising development.'

'Indeed: perhaps you can consider something else while you are about it, and that is how it is possible to be *very* silent, when silence is an absolute. You would not say that I was *very* perfect, would you?'

'No,' he said gravely, 'I certainly would not say that.'

There was after all a certain relief, for the moment, in quibbling as usual with Mr Milner; and it reassured her at least that she could present a normal appearance: but it could not long divert her thoughts from her disturbing discovery. She found herself gazing so fixedly at Isabella that at last her friend showed signs of discomfort, and began wiping her lips and adjusting her fichu, as if afraid there must be something amiss with her appearance.

'Now tell us, Caroline, what do you think of long engagements?' came Fanny's voice – not, just then, a welcome sound.

'I think there is something to be said for them,' she answered after a moment, 'because in an engagement, at least, one has a choice of duration: whereas in marriage itself there is no choice: all marriages are long – life-long.'

Aunt Selina smiled, and Mr Milner laughed, though in fact there were serious and even foreboding thoughts behind Caroline's words.

'Life-long – ah, thank the stars for it!' sighed Mr Hampson, gazing with renewed uxoriousness on his well-feeding bride. 'Thank heaven, I should say.'

'That's where the stars are, Mr Hampson,' Fanny informed him.

'So they are, Miss Fanny,' Mr Hampson serenely agreed, 'and that is where I am, and have been, every day since I became united to one in whom the brilliance of the stars themselves is united with such other qualities, too many to enumerate, as can only make a man hope to deserve the good fortune which placed in his way such a prize that . . .' Mr Hampson, running out of breath and grammar, paused to blow a kiss at Mrs Hampson, and then concluded more succinctly: 'Miss Milner, I wish you the same joy as I have found!'

So do I, thought Caroline, finding she had drained her glass again: so do I, and yet I fear, I do fear, that with Richard Leabrook you won't find it.

These anxious reflections were still occupying her when the ladies moved to the drawing room, and she could almost have wished to stay with the gentlemen and the port: for now any quietness or abstraction on her part must be more conspicuous; and moreover Isabella, all in a glow, moved in for a *tête-à-tête* as soon as the tea was poured. Her brother's acquiescence had transformed her: and now, indeed, the reserve with which she had been accustomed to speak of her forthcoming marriage began to break down – now she must be talking of Mr Leabrook; though characteristically she was apologetic about it.

'I know it must be a great bore for other people to have to listen to such things, which is why I try not to keep harping on it – but now that the wedding is fixed, or nearly, I cannot help but be excited.'

'My dear girl, other people? I'm not one of those, I'm your friend, and there is nothing I would like better than to hear all about it.' Such must be her reply, out of very affection for Isabella: even though there was no more uncomfortable subject imaginable than Mr Richard Leabrook. 'So do tell, when did you first meet the – the gentleman?'

'Well, we have been acquainted with the Leabrooks for some time – that is, Papa knew Richard's late father, and things like that. But I was first introduced to Richard at the spring assize ball in Huntingdon. We talked, and danced – he is very elegant dancer.'

I know, thought Caroline, smiling, and in agony.

'And the next morning he called, and – well, I'm afraid this will sound monstrously giddy and girlish, but that was it: I knew all: my fate was most happily sealed. Or my goose was cooked, if you prefer – that would be Stephen's language. Oh, there goes my neck.'

'It sounds delightful,' Caroline said. 'All that one could wish.' She was sure this must come out grotesquely stiff; but Isabella smiled and thanked her with a squeeze of the hand. 'And – and where do you suppose you will be married?'

'Oh, at Wythorpe, to be sure. My hope is that Uncle John will perform the service – that would be perfection; but all these things can be discussed and planned properly now – now that Stephen is acting like a rational creature at last, and Richard is on his way home. Oh, and I shall be able to introduce him to you, Caroline: that will make me so pleased and proud on both sides. I know you will like him. Well, in truth I hate it when people say things like that – when someone says to me, "You'll love this book," I am immediately prejudiced against it – but you know what I mean. Which is another expression I deplore, incidentally. Isabella, you are talking too much. I know. Well, stop it then.'

It was impossible not to be pleased at this access of spirits in her friend, or the happiness that obviously produced them; and yet so troubling was her secret knowledge, so subversive of the very foundations of that happiness, that Caroline was hard put to it to maintain her composure until the arrival of the gentlemen established a general conversation. Before then, however, Isabella made a confidence that further disturbed her peace of mind: for, with an expressive roll of her eyes towards Lady Milner – who was giving Aunt Selina a full account, in a depressingly fretful tone, of the continual headaches, megrims, and nervous disorders to which she was subject, and to which medical science had proved itself utterly unequal – she murmured to Caroline: 'I'm ashamed to say it, because brides should be sorry to leave home, but I shall be so glad – so relieved and thankful – to be taken away from this house.'

Talk turned to other subjects until the close of the evening: even so Caroline was so preoccupied she was unable to contribute much beyond commonplaces, and she fancied that Stephen Milner noticed, and observed her with a speculative eye. But it was Aunt Selina, in the carriage home, who showed that she had remarked it too, though with a misinterpretation of her niece's silence that left Caroline hardly knowing whether to laugh or cry. Patting her hand, Aunt Selina said: 'Dear me, all this talk of weddings. If I were a young woman, I dare say it might make me quite wistful, and wonder whether there was anyone for me like the splendid Mr Leabrook. But there will be, my dear: there will be.'

Chapter XIII

Now: let me see.

Caroline, wakeful, unrefreshed, and dressed, after a night of dragging torment interrupted only by a doze in which the same harrying thoughts visited her as dreams: Caroline, sitting at her window, solaced only by the novelty of watching the sun rise (for she is such an habitual late sleeper that the dawn to her is a sort of exotic phenomenon like an erupting volcano): Caroline, aching, strives to extract some conclusions from the night's long inward debate.

Memory, revived memory, is the unhappiest part. She has forced herself to go over every moment of her association with Richard Leabrook in order to make sure – to make doubly sure – that her own conduct was not at fault in that dismal episode. Of course she has long settled this in her mind; but the new light in which she must see the man – the loved, trusted, and respected fiancé of Isabella – has caused her to review it. But painful as the process of recollection was, it has not modified her first assessment, not at all.

Yes: I flirted with him and was flattered by him. But I can confidently say that I was *not* such a wily, irresistible siren and temptress that I provoked a virtuous man into a completely uncharacteristic lapse of morals.

Nor can she accept that her own judgement in this is hopelessly naïve. Caroline has not lived in her father's rakish world without learning all about the ways of men and maids. She knows what gentlemen feel quite free to get up to, before marriage, and even after: things that would destroy a woman's reputation utterly, but which, if discreetly managed, are regarded as little more than a natural consequence of masculinity. Still the fact is not altered. The adventure Mr Leabrook proposed to her in Brighton cannot be excused as a youthful folly, when he is a mature man who plainly knew what he was doing. Nor can it be argued that he might suppose himself free to stray, according to the tenets of a worldly society: for the girl he is engaged to is Isabella, and she is not worldly, and it is a love-match; and she could only think of her fiancé behaving in such a manner with bewilderment, dismay, and wretchedness.

Still, what troubles Caroline the most is what angered her the most, that night at the Brighton ball: the fact that Mr Leabrook so little valued her as to treat her like a piece of disposable goods. Philandering is regrettable, but that cold and calculating unconcern was detestable. And that, she realizes, is why she cannot rest with the idea of Isabella marrying Richard Leabrook. A man so insensible to the feelings of others must, as a husband, be the dealer of misery at last.

Of course, not all her uneasiness is for Isabella. She is not saint enough to disregard her own plight – the awkwardness and unpleasantness of meeting Mr Leabrook again, the difficulties in which it may place her, and indeed the not knowing just how *he* will react in turn. Should she say, 'Ah, yes, we met briefly at Brighton,' and attempt to carry it off so? But then this is begging the question – the one unavoidable question that has kept her from sleep.

Should I tell?

It would be simple enough; and here there are no alternatives to fret her. If she does tell what happened at Brighton, it must be to Isabella, plain and direct. During the night her mind has hovered longingly about Aunt Selina. The notion of confiding the secret to *her*, and letting her decide what to do with it, is tempting – too tempting. It is the worst sort of chicken-hearted half measure, palming the responsibility off on Aunt Selina, who has been infinitely too kind to her to merit such treatment. No, if I am to make the disclosure, it must be to the person it concerns.

And then – then what?

Imagination shrinks from the consequences, but they must surely be profound. Isabella's view of her fiancé must be transformed – perhaps to the point of destruction: bitter thought! Isabella, in all the joy and pride of her approaching nuptials, to be so knocked down! And what must be the effect on their friendship? Caroline might say, and mean, that it was because of that friendship that she spoke: still it is hard to see their relation emerging uninjured, even if not spoiled entirely.

Caroline again: However, I must not let that be my first consideration. I must think what's best for Isabella.

Yet even now, with the sun almost above the trees and the first stirrings audible in the kitchen downstairs, she is no nearer to deciding what that is. She only knows she cannot bear being imprisoned with her thoughts any longer.

Snatching up her bonnet and pelisse, Caroline ran out of the house, and was soon striking out across the field-paths with the dew still spangling the turf, and actually before breakfast – a revolution that, she reflected wryly, would be all round the village before the grass had dried. She had no thought of a destination as she plunged on: nor was she sure, when she lifted her head, exactly where she was, except that these dark-ribbed fields belonged to the home farm of the Manor. But exercise itself gave her a feeling of purpose, and all at once the thought of the Manor completed it.

She would go there, now. She would go and see Isabella, and – well, at the sight of Isabella's face, surely the decision would be made for her. She thought it likely that she would just pour it all out: then it would be done. Whatever the consequences, there must be virtue in a plan of such directness.

She orientated herself, after some trouble, by fixing on the church tower, and followed a cart-track that must lead to the north side of the Manor park. Yes, here was the park fence: and here, to her mild annoyance, was a stile. She had a poor opinion of stiles, and never felt her town upbringing more than when trying to get over them gracefully. But at least no one was here to witness her wobbles, she thought, springing up; and then the extraordinary thing happened. With her right leg already over the stile, she found the skirt of her petticoat had somehow caught fast around the lower step on the other side, as neatly and tightly as the upholstery on a chair-seat. After some ungainly and even excruciating manoeuvres, Caroline found to her horror that she could not move. The straddling posture meant she could not go backwards and down without actual dislocation; and the petticoat was one of her new ones, good Irish linen, and sturdily resistant to her fiercest tugs. 'Oh, for the days of poverty,' she muttered, 'when my petticoats would tear at a touch!' And indeed she was inclined at first to laughter at her predicament: but as the discomfort overcame the absurdity, and as a thick raincloud began to creep across the sun, her mirth gave way to vexation and even panic. She was assailed by a vision of her being stuck on top of this stile, and no one coming to look for her or chancing by, and rain and darkness falling – but this was ridiculous. She was on a well-used track on the Manor estate: even if she could not contrive to get free, someone must come by. Just as she was clearing her throat to shout for help, the truth of this was proved in unwelcome fashion. Striding across the park towards her was Stephen Milner.

He was the very last person she wished to see her in such a nonsensical distress, and she could have cursed the heavens, which were now scattering cold rain. As he came up she actually thought of trying to pass off her awkward perch as a comfortable rest in the middle of a stroll: but her flush of pain, and his grin of recognition, had already told the tale.

'Mr Milner,' she said, with as much dignity as she could muster, 'I cannot move.'

'Yes, I shouldn't wonder if you can't,' he said, walking slowly all round her, and examining her judiciously like a farmer at a cattle-market.

'I would be obliged if you would help me to get down.'

'Eh?' he said rubbing his chin. 'Oh! to be sure. Only – I was just wondering whether I might make some puns about your living in high style – or, is this what's meant by stylish dressing? Or, whether you consider this a step in the right direction – or, I had never thought you one to sit on the fence . . .'

She regarded him flatly. 'Have you done?'

He thought for a moment. 'Yes, thank you. So, it looks as if your nether garment is caught – absolutely pinned. How *did* you manage that?'

'Yes, an interesting technical question, isn't it, but perhaps we might discuss it when I am safely on the ground?'

'Hmm. I shall have to hoist you right up while you disentangle yourself.'

'Very well, whatever it takes,' she said crossly: he was enjoying this just as much as she had feared, and now there was the embarrassment of having literally to put herself in his hands. However, he lifted and held her up with a surprising deftness and grace; and once she was safely unhooked, set her down with no more satirical a remark than: 'The trick, I imagine, is to gather all your skirts up as you step over: though never having worn skirts myself, I can only guess.'

'I'm obliged to you, sir,' she said, trying for composure, whilst conscious of being draggled, out of breath, and red in the face. 'You are an early riser this morning.'

'A good thing for you I am – except I'm not. I haven't been to bed. I went for a ramble down to the Ellington brook.'

'Why?'

'To see the herons, of course. Now for your explanation – though I suggest we proceed to the shelter of that tree, while this shower passes.'

'Explanation?'

'Of *your* early rising.'

She moved towards the tree. 'I don't have to explain myself to you, sir.'

'Of course you don't. How long had you been caught on that stile, by the way?'

'Not long, not long . . . Mr Milner, do you think we might be serious for a moment?'

This came out almost without her volition; and once she had said it, she did not know how to go on. The impulse had been to ask him something about Isabella and Mr Leabrook, something that would help anchor her decision: something like, what did he really think of his sister's husband-to-be? But there was no making any such approach natural and innocent: it surely invited the counter-question, why she was asking.

'I can bear it for a moment, certainly.' He offered her his handkerchief. She looked at it in suspicion and surprise: was he expecting her to begin crying? And indeed, was he clairvoyant? – for she did feel like it, for no definable reason. 'Your face is wet,' he added in explanation.

So it was, from the rain: beads were falling from her brows and eyelashes. Caroline mopped her face, feeling oddly comforted.

'Actually it looked very nice. Like dewdrops on a flower or something. Yes, a compliment. Never fear, I'm going to undo it. I can tell you haven't been sleeping either, because you look rather drawn. I hope the Wythorpe mutton didn't disagree with you.'

Again she hesitated. There was a sudden and profound dread upon her, of Stephen Milner's knowing what she had to tell. Even though she had not been at fault, Caroline found she could not bear to think of that Brighton episode being exposed to his eyes. Swiftly she imagined a train of consequences: she revealing it to Isabella, Isabella heartbroken, the engagement off, tears and trouble – *trouble*, above all. And Mr Milner's direst predictions, of course, coming true. She could almost see the superior shake of his head.

And she did not want that. It did not weigh more heavily with her than Isabella's happiness, but it did weigh heavily – enough to plunge her into deeper confusion. Nor could she say precisely why she cared so much for Stephen Milner's opinion of her, especially given his infuriating habit of claiming to know all about her beforehand: but there it was.

'The mutton – the mutton was very good,' she said. 'It was a most enjoyable evening altogether, Mr Milner, thank you.'

'Thank *you*. This is us being serious, is it? Well, it's not so very bad. A little dull, but not so bad. Let's see, we should talk about the weather too, and wonder when the rain will stop, and remark that it was quite a wet summer. In truth, and in all seriousness, I'm in no hurry to get back to the Manor, because Isabella will be plaguing me about the wedding.'

'Well – I dare say she will,' Caroline said, suppressing a start. 'You agreed last evening to make the arrangements.'

'I did, didn't I?' He sighed. 'Must have been the wine.'

'You don't mean you have changed your mind?'

'Oh, I can't do that to Bella. But I still think she is in too much of a hurry.'

'Really?' Here at any rate was an unlooked-for opportunity. 'Do you entertain some doubt of the gentleman's suitability?'

'Leabrook? Oh, he's thoroughly eligible. Has a good name and a comfortable property, which suggest he ain't after Isabella's fifteen thousand, and all his teeth. Isabella adores him. I dare say they stand as fair a chance as anyone else of surviving matrimony.'

'Why then do you regret the hurry?'

'You are quite forensic today. Why – because, as I said last night, there's no need for it. Only she looks about her at the Manor, and she thinks there is. This is a frankness too far, perhaps: I am trusting to your discretion, Miss Fortune.'

'You may do so.'

He grunted, as if he doubted it. 'But come, you said you wanted to be serious: what was it you wanted to speak of?'

She looked up at the dripping canopy of leaves. 'This tree – I wish I knew the name of this tree.'

'William. Will to his friends. I do not think that is what you wanted to ask at all.' He looked narrowly at her. 'But I shall accord you the prerogative of a woman to be mysterious. It's an alder, by the by. I see the rain is clearing: are you coming on to the Manor, to call on Bella?'

This time her hesitation was only momentary: for though she was no nearer to a final decision, one negative decision was made for her now: she was not going to see Isabella and pour it all out.

'Thank you, I had better go home: there will be breakfast, and Aunt Selina will be wondering where I am.'

He raised his eyebrows. 'But why were you climbing the stile into the park, if not to call at the Manor?'

'You are quite forensic today,' she said, shrugging and half turning.

'Ah, you were coming to call on *me*.'

'No, I was coming to poach your pheasants, Mr Milner.'

'Lucky I don't keep any, then. You could have poached a hen, perhaps. There's probably a pun there about poaching eggs, but I won't pursue it. Oh, but, Miss Fortune –' he gave her a stricken look '– will you be able to get home without mishap? I seem to recall quite a large stone, almost as large as an apple, in the middle of Rectory Lane, and if you were to fall over it—'

'I know the one, sir, I picked it up and carry it in my pocket in case I need to brain any annoying gentlemen,' she rapped out, turning away.

'An unlikely eventuality, but one never knows.' She could hear, if not see, his grin. 'Good day, Miss Fortune.'

At the Rectory Aunt Selina was surprised to see her coming in from a walk at such an early hour; and she had further occasion for surprise that day, as Caroline actively sought all the dullest housekeeping tasks, and when she had done all that could be done with storerooms, preserves, hemming, and silver-polishing, was actually to be discovered in the parlour busily quilting: a sight so surprising that even Dr Langland was startled out of obtuseness, and asked if she were quite well.

What she sought in industry, of course, was distraction from the ceaseless turning of her mind. Fortunately there was no visit from Isabella today, which spared her the difficulty of keeping her countenance through the inevitable talk of Mr Leabrook. On the other hand, her absence must mean she was busy with wedding plans, as Stephen had said . . . Relief came at last with oblivion: the disturbed night and the busy day sending her drooping to bed even earlier than the Langlands' custom.

Of course, there must be a waking, and so a return to her dilemma.

But she found that, like a fever, this burden of indecision could be borne, simply because it had to be. She was even able to go on her usual walk with Isabella, and endure the discussion of the wedding: though in fact there was comparatively little of that, for Isabella's habitual reserve had returned in some degree, besides her well-mannered aversion to being a bore; and altogether there was less torment here than there might have been. Still, the most difficult day of all was coming towards her, and could not be held off by any efforts of resolve or patience: the day of Richard Leabrook's return.

First, however, there came a welcome distraction in the shape of the Hampsons' evening-party. Aunt Selina and Uncle John, feeling that the dinner at the Manor made them sufficient gadabouts for this month, chose not to go, but only on the assurance that this would not prevent Caroline, who was already invited to accompany the Manor party. The Milners' carriage stopped accordingly at the Rectory gate, on the appointed evening, and Stephen Milner stepped out to make room for her, declaring that he would walk the rest of the way to the Old Grange. At this Captain Brunton got down too, saying he could easily do likewise, much to the consternation of Lady Milner.

'Edward, what are you doing? There is no need for this, there is room enough.'

'Room enough, but only just room,' the Captain said, with justice, for the four women – Lady Milner, Isabella, Fanny, and Caroline – filled it comfortably, without the danger of crushed gowns.

'But I do not think this is proper,' Lady Milner said fretfully. 'You leave us unprotected.'

At this Captain Brunton hesitated: but Stephen breezily declared: 'Never fear, Augusta, we shall be walking at a good pace behind you, and if the last living highwayman in Huntingdonshire should pop out from behind the village pump, we shall wrestle the doddering greybeard to the ground,' and shut the carriage door.

They moved off: Lady Milner had no choice but to submit; but she kept up a murmur of complaint, to the effect that Sir Henry would never have approved it.

'Oh, nonsense, Augusta, Papa was never one to make a great fuss about such things,' Fanny said roundly. 'Caroline, I do love the dressing of your hair – what is it called? Is it French?'

'I beg your pardon, Fanny, I think I may claim to know best the ways of my own husband,' Lady Milner said.

'As he was our father for a good many years more than he was your husband,' Isabella said uncontrollably, 'the claim of knowing *best* might be more plausibly maintained by us.'

'For most of those years, Isabella, you were a child,' Lady Milner retorted, very pale.

'As were you, ma'am,' said Isabella, 'and a child living a long way away from Wythorpe Manor.' Fanny smothered a snort.

'When you are a married woman, you will better understand these things,' Lady Milner said, drawing herself up with a great display of cheekbones. 'Until that time, Isabella, I would counsel you to discretion.'

'I thank you for your counsel, ma'am, and you may be assured that *that time* cannot come soon enough for me.'

'A Grecian coque,' Caroline said; and as three round-eyed faces turned to her, added with a pacific smile: 'That's what it is called – the dressing of my hair.'

The Old Grange was, as its name suggested, a venerable building of grey stone, in which it was possible to imagine a substantial farmer feasting his work-folk at a long oak table: until you got inside, when it became impossible to imagine anything of the kind. Mrs Hampson's fortune had gone towards a thorough refurbishing in the most modern style, and on the apparent principle that one could not have too much of a good thing. The eye was assaulted by a profusion of Chinese wallpapers, japan-ware, silk screens, flower-stands, Turkey rugs, filigree-work, chaise-longues, cameos, and cheval-glasses. But neither was there any stinting in the welcome extended by their smiling hosts, who had gathered most of the sociable neighbourhood into their large drawing room, where the ladies did their best not to loll on the backless sofas, and the gentlemen not to topple the knick-knacks with their coat-tails. There was a great fire, there was choice wine, there was a highly polished new pianoforte and an angular female relation to play it; and once the carpet was rolled back and the occasional tables shifted, there was room for six couple to dance as many country-dances as they liked, while a similarly generous supper awaited in an adjoining parlour. Even those who came to sneer went away well entertained and well fed, and could report to their friends that the Hampsons were a very good sort of people, and that one could not refuse them the favour of a visit now and then.

Caroline, being civilly handed by Mr Hampson to the sort of sofa on which she could picture a Roman of the decadent sort eating grapes upside-down, enquired how the bridal portrait was coming on; and was rewarded not only with a full account of its progress, but with an introduction to the artist. This was a slightly built young man whose long crop of dark curling hair and large, brown, intense eyes gave him a little of a gypsy look; though he was well dressed in a style Caroline thought of as elegant negligence, or negligent elegance, and his manners were pleasing. Mr Hampson, like a resourceful host, managed to recollect something about Caroline – that she came from London – and announcing the happy coincidence that Mr Charles Carraway had trained in London, left them to converse on the strength of it. But this was easy enough, Mr Carraway having a quick, frank way about him.

'For as long as I could,' he answered, when she asked him if he had studied at the Royal Academy schools. 'I was brought up by an uncle – the kindest of guardians, but of limited means, who could sponsor me only so long. Then I spent some time in the studio of Signor Almansi – a sort of apprenticeship: painting foliage in the background of his vast canvases. In truth none of this quite suited me – it was simply too academic: I have an odd jumble of a brain that will not be ordered – and I longed to paint from nature. So, I have struck out alone.'

'I know those paintings you mean. Everybody's draperies are always blowing about in a complicated manner. So you have returned to native ground in Huntingdonshire, sir?'

'I have connections here,' he said, with the vaguely smiling, dreaming look that seemed to descend periodically over him. 'And a commission for topographical views at Hinchingbrooke was offered which, in my position, I could scarcely refuse. But what I have found so entrancing in this part of the world is the skies. They are incomparable.'

'Skies, sir?' put in Fanny Milner, who had been changing her shoes, and now came briskly up with her usual lack of ceremony. 'We have *those* in this country, to be sure: but the pity is, that there is so little beneath them that is worth noticing.'

'Do you really find it so?' Mr Carraway answered, not with mere politeness, but great energy. 'Tell me how.'

'Well.' Fanny for once was a little taken aback. 'Well, there is nothing very grand, or exciting, or even terrible, to be met with in a district like this: it is all just narrow provincial dullness.'

Mr Carraway, with his dreamy smile, waved a hand. 'Dullness I abhor – aye, dullness is the true enemy of the soul – not wickedness. Dullness it is that perverts and corrupts the spirit – but you know it is always possible, it always *must* be possible, to look past the dullness, and see the bright, shining heart of things.'

'It may be so for you, sir,' Fanny said, with a look part doubtful, part interested. 'But how I—'

'Please,' Mr Carraway said, leaping up from the sofa, and gracefully whisking Fanny down on to it. 'I'm not sure how to explain. I express myself poorly in words – poorly enough with the brush in truth, but no matter—'

'Oh, you are the painter!' exclaimed Fanny. 'The one who is doing the Hampsons' portrait. Well, I am glad, very glad to see you here.'

'Are you?' he said quizzically.

'Yes, because it is very liberal of the Hampsons, for at most of the parties one goes to there is no one of an artistic sort to be found, because they are not drearily respectable enough – is that offensive? I assure you it isn't meant to be – quite the reverse!'

'Oh, the respectable world and I are on easy terms. I ignore it when I choose, and it does likewise with me. Life is shockingly short to trouble about such things. Warmth – frankness – generosity of spirit – if I find these amongst respectability, I love them: if amongst unrespectability, likewise. I don't know if there is such a word as unrespectability,' he said, with an engaging laugh, 'but there should be. If not, I hereby create it.'

'I like the word. I like the thing, at any rate,' Fanny said, her eyes shining. 'There, but you have the artist's eye—'

'Everyone does. At least, everyone has something of the spirit that animates the artist. This is what I wanted to convey to you – let me see, what can I set before you . . . My lodging. It is in Huntingdon. It is above a stationer's, and the chimney smokes, and the view is of a rooftop adorned only with a dead starling. Here is your dullness, if you like. But what transforms it for me – the stationer has two little children. They play on the landing – wonderfully inventive games, dramas indeed, with numerous characters and hair's-breadth escapes and sometimes – why not? – a return from the dead, or a transformation from evil to good. I can refresh myself by hearkening to this outside my door at any time when I feel stale and dull.'

'It is an enchanting picture,' Fanny said wistfully. 'But then, you know, one cannot think like a child *now*.'

'That is because you have forgotten how,' Mr Carraway said. 'We all do – I think because we lose that spontaneity children possess. We unlearn it. There is another new word. You see, what a child *thinks*, a child *says*. And that is delightful – is it not?'

There was an uncommon vivacity in Mr Carraway's tone and expression, which made him very persuasive: though, for Caroline, not persuasive enough; for she did not believe there was any particular in which adults could be improved by resembling children, except perhaps in the matter of hair growing out of the ears. Fanny's glowing looks, however, showed that she was much enthused by these ideas; and it occurred to Caroline that she ought to make it known to Mr Carraway who his eager listener was. 'Well, Mr Carraway, this is Miss Fanny Milner, by the by,' she put in. 'Mr Charles Carraway. There. Now you have been *introduced*, you may begin talking – as if you have not been doing so for the last ten minutes.'

This was just the sort of jest to appeal to Fanny – not indeed that she saw it entirely as a jest. 'Exactly!' she cried. 'And there is that absurdity of dullness: that two human creatures cannot talk together without society first putting them on ceremony together, and making them uncomfortable. Oh, I mean no disrespect to you, Caroline – or the Hampsons' party – I have the greatest regard for the Hampsons, you know, because they have that rare virtue – sincerity. Tell me, Mr Carraway, do you need to *know* your subjects before you paint their portrait? That is, are you trying to capture their characters as well as their appearance?'

'If it is a matter of mere face-painting, Miss Fanny, which, alas, too often portraiture is, then only the likeness signifies. What I try for – I know I fail – is the essence of the person. But for that, acquaintance is not actually needed. One sees the face – one lets the strangeness of it, the beauty, the uniqueness, imprint itself on the eye – and then, sometimes – I do not say always – one *knows*.' He gazed from Fanny to Caroline, and back again, then smiled deprecatingly. 'Again, I explain it poorly.'

But Fanny plainly did not think so; and Caroline felt free to leave her with an interlocutor so much to her taste, and go in search of claret-cup. Finding it, she found also Isabella, just emerged from a long talk with her stepmother.

'There – I have made my apologies, and now, my dear Caro, I shall do the same to you,' she said, slipping her arm through Caroline's. 'For that abominable behaviour in the carriage.'

'My dear Bella, you did nothing but reply very smartly to a stupidity. More natural than abominable.' Caroline now had a peculiar divided feeling when she was alone with Isabella. She knew she ought to feel dreadfully uncomfortable – and indeed she did: yet alongside this the old ease and affection remained unchanged.

'That's what Fanny says. But I can never quite see it that way. And I ought to be in a good temper today of all days, because – well, a note came from Hethersett this afternoon. Richard was just arrived home. Yes! I shall see him tomorrow.'

'Oh, you must be very happy.' Somehow Caroline's lips had

spoken the words, and with a fair degree of conviction, while her heart drummed and her mind thrashed. She had known this must come, of course: but when did such knowledge ever soften the blow of a dreaded eventuality? She wondered if now was the time to say she had met him: she wondered if Isabella would talk to him of her new friend, and if so what name she would say – Miss Fortune? Or Caroline? Or Caroline Fortune? If the last, then he would be placed in a similar position to herself. Oh, but it was an impossible situation . . .

'I am very happy. And very warm – do you suppose there will be ice at the supper-table? Working my fan only seems to make me hotter – do you find that? Oh, they are beginning the dancing. What a splendid instrument that is – from Broadwood's, I think. My dear, are *you* feeling the heat? You look a little flushed.'

'Not at all,' Caroline said. 'Well, a little.'

'I have some aromatic vinegar, if that would help.'

'No, no. A drop more claret-cup will set me right. And now you, I think, are to be dancing.'

It was Captain Brunton who had come up and, with a civil if ungainly bow, invited Isabella to the dance. Unwelcome as the invitation might be, Caroline saw that Isabella was determined now not to be churlish, and so with equal civility her friend accepted, and walked on to the floor with the Captain. But there was another party present, Caroline noticed, who evinced absolutely no satisfaction at this development. Lady Milner watched with her most pale and peevish look: though whether her displeasure came from feeling her consequence slighted by Isabella's being preferred for the opening dance, or had its roots in a tenderer emotion, Caroline could not tell. But she had troubles of her own to dwell on just now; and seeing a stout, smiling beau preparing to put his tight pantaloons to the test of walking over to her, she withdrew to an adjoining room, where a couple of card-tables were set out for the sedentary. Here she lingered in oppressive thought for some time, until she became aware of Stephen Milner, restlessly prowling about with a book in his hand.

'Ah,' he said. 'You don't happen to have a knife about you, by any chance?'

'Come, surely it's not that unbearable. Besides, it's very bad manners to bleed on your host's carpet.'

'Oh, I don't usually reach the point of suicidal despair until the ladies start singing. I want a knife for this.' He held up the book: the pages were uncut.

'You can't come to Mr Hampson's party, and then settle down to reading his books.'

'No, I can't, because they are all like this.' He sighed. 'Which leaves me quite at a loss.'

'You do not dance, Mr Milner?'

'I do – once in an evening, twice if in thoroughly madcap mood. When I dance, though, I must talk all the time. Otherwise I begin thinking about dancing, and how absurd it is, and what prize boobies we would look if you took away the music. Well, I suppose it will pass the time: do you want to go through the ghastly motions with me, Miss Fortune?'

'How can I refuse such a charming invitation?'

Caroline found that Stephen Milner danced quite creditably for a long-limbed, absent-minded man who hated dancing. She, on the other hand, loved it: but her spirits were still damped by Isabella's news, which she could not help alluding to.

'So the famous Mr Leabrook is home, I hear.'

'Aye, for a mercy: we may as well get the precious pair spliced, and then perhaps I can take off again.'

'Again? You have only just come back.'

'Oho, I don't imagine you'd weep for my absence,' he said, with a narrow look. 'The fact is, a correspondent in Chichester writes me of some delicious Roman remains, and I'm sorely tempted.'

'Delicious Roman remains. If it were anyone else, I would think I must have misheard that, Mr Milner.'

'Well, perhaps I won't go just yet. I should miss our fights; and besides, I do want to be here to see my prophecy fulfilled.'

'Prophecy?'

'About you, Miss Fortune – about you being trouble.'

Her response to this was a disdainful look, which she intended following up with some acerbic comparisons of Mr Milner with *Old Moore's Almanack*; but then the shadow of, yes, real trouble fell across her again, and drove her back into anxious thought.

'Now, this won't do – you must keep talking to me – I'm starting to be aware of the fact that I'm dancing, and in a moment it will all look ridiculous. Oh, by the by, who *is* that young fellow arguing with Fanny?'

'That is Mr Carraway, the artist, and I doubt they are arguing: she seemed very much struck with him.'

'Ah, that explains it: Fanny always seems to be arguing when she's excited. Intense, you know. Dear, dear, and he does look as if he finds the world endlessly fascinating: what a bore. I shall have to play the stern elder brother and be introduced to him later. And what *is* the matter with Augusta?'

Lady Milner was not dancing; she was seated, as ever, by the fire, and Captain Brunton was standing, or lingering, by her chair: he high-shouldered and discomfited, she grimly silent. If there really was a lover-like relation between them, Caroline thought, then she was certainly an exacting mistress.

'What a damned plaguey set we are,' Stephen continued. 'You know, Miss Fortune, you needn't fear that Isabella will drop you now that her beau is back.'

'What makes you say that?'

'Why, it's the way girls are, isn't it? They swear eternal friendship on the strength of using the same circulating-library and liking the same shade of ribbon, and then as soon as a man's in the case it's all forgotten. But Isabella is different: she takes things to heart: very deep is Bella, very loyal and steadfast in her feelings.'

All too convincing as this was as a portrait of Isabella, it certainly did not make Caroline feel better. 'Every time I am deluded into thinking you human, Mr Milner,' she told him sweetly, 'you come out and say something to confirm my earlier opinion. "The way girls are", indeed: I never heard anything so arrogant and conceited.'

'Didn't you? Not even from me? Mind, I notice you didn't say it's not true.'

'Some of the sex are as you describe – not all: just as not *all* men are insensitive boors who are too pleased with themselves.'

His enjoyment of this remark was so great that it seemed to last him till the end of the dance, which came more quickly than Caroline had supposed; at which he made his bow, and took himself off, as he had suggested, to meet Mr Carraway. It was like him to ignore the convention of handing his partner back to her seat – she could well imagine him declaring that anyone not actually half-witted could find herself a chair; but she was surprised to find Captain Brunton suddenly at her elbow, and performing the office. She thanked him, and hinted that she must not detain him: her glance straying to Lady Milner, whom she could not suppose happy at being deserted; but he, after a polite request for permission, sat down by her as if disposed to conversation – perhaps, she guessed, in that spirit of independence which quarrelling lovers liked to show to each other. However, as he seemed more ready to cough and frown than talk, she made a beginning, asking him if he saw any prospect of going to sea again.

'As a Navy man, Miss Fortune, no – candidly, no, though it goes hard with me to say it. There are not half the ships of the line in commission as there were during the war: it is a simple matter of arithmetic. Of course one may hope. There are still ships, and men to crew them: there is map-making, convict transports, expeditions against the slave trade. But he who lives upon hope dies fasting, they say.'

'They say some very gloomy things, don't they?'

'They do,' he said, with a clenched, though not disagreeable, smile. 'They do indeed – folk wisdom – never rains but it pours – cheerless stuff.'

'I should be more inclined to trust folk wisdom if those wise old folk had not been so prone to dying when they were thirty, and setting light to each other for saying the wrong sort of prayers.'

'Indeed, I am no friend to superstition. Quite the rationalist. It made me an odd fish among sailors, who are superstitious beyond anything. But rationally – yes, rationally, I know I must abandon this hope and look elsewhere. I was not fortunate enough in prize money from the war to purchase complete independence, and the sea is all I know. I think to apply to the East Coast Revenue Service, as soon as I – well, as soon as may be.' All at once he squared his shoulders, and addressed her in his gruffest manner. 'You think badly of me.'

'Do I? I cannot think why I should.'

'Because you must surely suppose – but this is rudeness. I beg your pardon. I have no excuse – only that I have been little accustomed to society – still that is no excuse. I was going to say, you must surely suppose me a dilatory fellow. But it is wrong to attribute to you thoughts you may not possess. Wrong indeed.'

Captain Brunton, breathing hard and shaking his large fair head, was so painfully caught up in the toils of apology she was not sure how to get him out again: she could only say: 'I do not think badly of you, sir, nor hold you to be a dilatory fellow. And if I did, I should like to know what right I had to make such a judgement.'

'You are very good. It's – it's odd: I can talk with you.'

Privately Caroline thought that if this was Captain Brunton's articulacy, she would hate to see him tongue-tied: but she said she was glad of it.

'The thing is this. When I say I mean to apply to the Revenue Service, I do mean it. But the fact that I have not done so yet is not due to reluctance. I would willingly be gone in a moment. But one hesitates to open a new chapter, as it were—'

'When the old one is not resolved?'

'Exactly so.' He smiled again, with the effect of a tight knot being slightly loosened. 'Curious creatures we mortals are – how we do not know what we want, or how to get it if we do.'

'There is probably some wonderful folk wisdom on that subject.'

'To be sure. Never – never tread upon a weasel on a Thursday, or something like that.'

Though his delivery of this joke was almost obstetric in its effort, Caroline could not help but laugh. Her opinion of Captain Brunton was altered: alongside that stiffness she detected sincerity and warmth; and she was satisfied also that she understood his cryptic confidences about what kept him at Wythorpe – indeed, that they only confirmed what she already believed.

'But I have wearied you, talking about myself. What do you think of the Grange – a handsome old building, is it not?'

Caroline agreed that it was, in some surprise: for in the first place, she had asked him about himself, and in the second, most men could talk about themselves continuously for several hours before it occurred to them that the subject might lack variety. Besides, she thought, he had not really been talking about himself: he had been talking about Lady Milner.

Well, there could only be two results. Either Lady Milner sought only the consolation of a tame suitor forever dancing attendance, or else Captain Brunton would win her. Neither would be greatly appealing to Isabella – but then that, Caroline reminded herself ruefully as she stepped into the Milners' carriage that night and looked at her friend's rapt moon-gazing profile, did not matter now: because Richard Leabrook was returned, to make everything right. She was not to be spared further reflections on the dreaded event, for Fanny was full of Mr Charles Carraway and his art, and was soon urging her sister to do something to advance them.

'Bella, you must recommend him to Richard. He is a man of taste, isn't he, and would always seek to patronize the arts? Well, then – all those expensive improvements he has made to the estate at Hethersett, surely they should be recorded in a set of landscape views, say: oh, and then a wedding portrait, why not that also? You and Richard would paint beautifully!'

'But what you have not considered, Fanny, is whether Mr Carraway can paint beautifully, for you have not seen any of his work,' Lady Milner said, with her customary severity – though not, Caroline admitted to herself, without justice. 'The Hampsons may be pleased with his work, but for all their qualities, I would not judge them connoisseurs of art.'

'I can tell Mr Carraway's art, from his character,' said Fanny, loftily, 'and that is spirited, natural, forceful, and earnest. And before, Augusta, you fall into any suppositions about my having a *taking* for him, or any such vulgarly conventional nonsense, I will say I admire his intellect and his sensibility, and we find much to talk about – and I hope two rational creatures may do that, even in Wythorpe, without petty minds fancying an engagement.'

'Then that is very well,' returned Lady Milner, 'for an engagement to a travelling painter, without family or prospects, is not something that could be seriously considered for the daughter of Sir Henry Milner, even if she were of an age to be talking of such things.'

Fanny's mind must have reeled with so many stinging replies that selection was impossible, for she was uncharacteristically silent; while a pensive Caroline was occupied in gazing back out of the window to make sure the gentlemen were following on foot. It was not that she feared the superannuated highwayman of Mr Milner's jest – but she did feel a curious need to know that Mr Milner was, at least for now, near.

Chapter XIV

Caroline's first thought on waking the next morning was that Mr Richard Leabrook would be at the Manor today: her second, that she would not go anywhere near it. The encounter must come – why rush to meet it? But she had reckoned without Aunt Selina, who denied her the comfort of procrastination by declaring after breakfast that she would walk over to the Manor, to give Lady Milner the recipe for orange wine she had been asking about, and who naturally anticipated that Caroline would go with her. There was no excuse Caroline could make that would not appear altogether strange: so she must perforce put on her bonnet and set out with her aunt, clinging only to a morsel of hope that Mr Leabrook would be tardy in his visit, and they could get away before he arrived.

Turning out of Rectory Lane into the High Street, Caroline did experience a moment of pure curiosity – about what it would be like to see Mr Leabrook again, and how he would react, and what would happen – almost as if this were happening to someone else; in which case she would find the whole thing rather interesting. However, a moment later her heart sank again under the renewed knowledge that this *was* happening to her; and a few moments after that, every thought and feeling was thrown into disarray by the sound of a horse's hoofs, and by her turning to behold Mr Richard Leabrook, coming up behind them, mounted on a fine bay.

Aunt Selina, turning too, called out a cordial greeting. Mr Leabrook reined in, doffed his hat – and saw Caroline's face.

'Mr Leabrook, how do you do? We heard you were returned to us. Will you allow me to introduce my niece, Miss Caroline Fortune?

She has come to live with us at the Rectory. My dear, Mr Leabrook, of whom you have heard tell.'

For an instant, as he gazed upon Caroline, Mr Leabrook's handsome face wore the look of a man who had been mortally offended. It was followed by a fleeting expression that might have been fear; and then, with the self-command that she remembered, he gathered himself, and turned his face into a mask of absolute indifference.

'How do you do?' he said, and then: 'I trust, ma'am, I find you and Dr Langland well.'

So, he was not to acknowledge her. While Aunt Selina replied, all Caroline's anxieties and misgivings were swept aside by a sudden wave of anger. She had a vivid memory of the last time he had come to Mrs Catling's house, when he had coolly contrived to treat Caroline as if she did not exist. Now here he was, aloof and sleek as his thoroughbred mount, doing the same again. It was this anger, rather than any other consideration, that brought her to decision.

'In fact, Aunt, Mr Leabrook and I have met before,' she said.

Aunt Selina looked her surprise.

'At Brighton,' Caroline pursued. 'Do you recall, sir?'

'Ah. I believe so, yes.' He inclined his head a very little: he would not lose his composure again, but she had the sense of a victory, especially when, responding to a very slight shake of the bridle, he said in a regretful tone: 'This horse of mine never will wait. You are going on to the Manor, I take it? I shall have the honour of seeing you there anon: pray excuse me going ahead. Mrs Langland: Miss Fortune.'

Horse and rider went elegantly on their way; and Aunt Selina remarked, with a slight smile of approbation: 'He is in a hurry to see Isabella, no doubt. But, my dear, fancy you knowing Mr Leabrook after all! From Brighton, you said?'

'Knowing only slightly. Mrs Catling kept so much company there – one met everybody.'

Her aunt appeared satisfied with this; but Caroline could find no equivalent satisfaction in their meeting, beyond that small pleasure of having taken him off guard. Seeing him in the flesh had reminded her yet more forcibly of how much reason she had to dislike and mistrust him; and he, while giving little away, had given enough to show that those feelings were certainly mutual. She could anticipate nothing good from their relation: at best, there must be awkwardness and discomfort: at worst – well, there she did not like to let her imagination trespass; and she could not even feel the relief of having got the meeting over with, as it must in a sense be gone through again when they arrived at the house.

There they found all the family gathered in the drawing room: Mr Leabrook attentively seated next to Isabella, who was pink, bright-eyed, and embarrassed with pleasure. She put out her hand warmly to Caroline, crying: 'Oh, Caro, I have looked forward to this moment – now I can introduce you—'

'Ah, I was going to say, my dear,' Mr Leabrook put in smiling, 'Miss Fortune and I were reacquainted in the lane just now. Reacquainted, yes: we happened to meet when I was down at Brighton in the summer.'

'Really? How curious! My dear Caro, fancy not saying you already knew Mr Leabrook.'

'Oh, I have absolutely no memory for names,' Caroline said, with a wave of her hand, 'that was why. But when I saw Mr Leabrook's face – why, *then* I remembered.'

A short bow was all the response he gave to this: his expression was absolutely unrevealing, even if, to Caroline, his silence was not; and soon he was being loaded with enquiries about the relations in the north whom he had been visiting, about his mother's health, about the state of the harvest at Hethersett, and so on. Fanny also was not slow in telling him of Mr Carraway, and pressing the painter's talents on his attention. To all of this Mr Leabrook was apparently as calm, easy, and gracious in reply as Caroline remembered him from Brighton, before her disillusion: but in a man of such polished manner, it was hard to tell whether or not there were really perturbation beneath the surface.

At length, however, the claims of engagement were acknowledged, and Mr Leabrook and Isabella went out to walk together in the gardens. Caroline struggled to compose her own feelings, which were more agitated than she had foreseen by the sight of the trusting Isabella on the arm of a man whom she knew to be so duplicitous; and, feeling unequal to conversation, was grateful for the talkative Fanny, who readily took up the burden.

'There – I knew there was something else – I was going to scold Richard about giving a ball at Hethersett. We *must* have one soon, else I shall perish.'

'My dear Fanny, surely the winter assemblies at Huntingdon begin in a month's time,' Aunt Selina said.

'So they do, Aunt: and perhaps when I am as old as – that is, when I am serene and full of years, a month will not seem a long time, but I assure you just now it does. Besides, Hethersett is very much a place worth seeing, and Caroline, you know, has not seen it yet – and so, what more pretext is needed?'

'Greater pretext,' Lady Milner corrected her.

'Caroline, you must back me up,' Fanny insisted. 'He cannot resist us both.'

'Miss Fortune does not seem to share your eagerness, Fanny,' said Stephen Milner, infuriatingly, as Caroline hesitated. 'You needn't fear, I shall be quite happy to favour you again with my one dance, Miss Fortune, even though I have already done so once. I'm generous like that.'

'I'm overpowered by your liberality, Mr Milner, but I must insist that you grant the favour to some other fortunate girl next time. The unforgettable experience of performing a cotillion with a dancing bear is not one I would wish to arrogate entirely to myself.'

She had meant only to answer him in kind, but it came out, to her own ears at least, quite acid; Lady Milner forgot to primp long enough to look surprised, and Stephen's eye fell on her more ironically than ever. I am betraying myself, she thought: I must be natural; but it was hard, especially when she had just caught a glimpse, through the window, of Isabella and Mr Leabrook walking arm-in-arm across the sunlit lawn, with Isabella's gold-fair head inclined confidingly towards his shoulder. In fact vexation was now the first among Caroline's contending emotions, for it seemed miserably unfair that she alone was in this position. If only those danglers, Matthew and Maria, had not fallen in with Mr Leabrook on the road to Brighton, she would now be in a state of pleasant insensibility – looking forward to the prospect of a ball, wondering whether there would be white satin worn at Isabella's wedding, but able to think of other things just as easily, and with no great consequence depending on any of them. Instead there was this torment: and though she was soon granted the relief of the visit coming to an end, worse was to follow, for Stephen himself invited the Rectory family to come back and dine with them later.

Again there was no possibility of escape without drawing to herself exactly the kind of attention she sought to evade: and Caroline actually wished she could have been the sort of vaporous irritating girl who was forever having headaches, for then she could have pleaded one without undue comment, and stayed home. Instead she found herself that evening seated, perforce, at the same dining-table with Mr Richard Leabrook – only two places away from him, indeed: so that he was able, early on, to turn to her and say: 'Miss Fortune, I am informed you have suffered a signal loss: pray accept my commiserations: and also my sincere hope that you find yourself happily settled with your aunt.'

It was said with perfect correctness, and indeed delicacy: obviously Isabella had talked to him, freely and innocently, of her friend's history, and he was making the appropriate response; and only the absolute blankness of his eyes, while his lips pronounced these words, revealed his true feeling. Caroline thanked him in the same mechanical way. Here was the summit of awkwardness and unreality: she felt it acutely, and was sure he must too; and though they exchanged few remarks after this opening, somehow she felt his eyes often on her, like a chill draught from an unknown source.

Fanny soon returned to the attack about a ball at Hethersett, in spite of her stepmother's reproofs; but Mr Leabrook was in any case quite amenable. 'An excellent notion,' he said. 'I have some company coming up from London at the end of next week, and I was a little concerned for their entertainment. I dare say we could muster twenty couple, if the weather remains tolerable: and the Hethersett road has lately been mended. I wonder when the moon will be at the full—'

'Thursday sennight, sir,' put in Captain Brunton, who had been more than usually quiet.

'Ah? I'm obliged to you – then Thursday sennight it shall be. Does that meet with your approval, Miss Fanny?'

'That is just the sort of decisiveness I like,' Fanny said, 'and now all that remains is to badger you about Mr Carraway again.'

'No need: Mr Carraway may certainly come to the ball: I shall be happy to meet him. Beyond that, Miss Fanny, I make no promises, not even to oblige my future sister-in-law.'

'Hey, well, brother-in-law, that's good enough – at least you have no qualms about inviting a mere painter to a reception. Augusta thinks he must be quite below the salt, you know.'

'Fanny, you misrepresent me,' her stepmother intoned. 'I remarked only that, without independent means, the young man's place in society must be an insecure one.'

'Pooh, genius can disregard society.'

'That is exactly what it cannot do,' said Lady Milner. 'Mr Leabrook, do you not agree?'

'I do not underestimate the power of society – but I am rather inclined to Miss Fanny's belief, if it be that talents are as much to be valued as birth or fortune.'

'*More* to be valued!' cried Fanny.

'This may be very well as a principle – but what you, Fanny, would call dreary practicalities must be considered, else they may lead to far drearier practicalities,' Lady Milner said. 'In the choices of life, prudence is not necessarily a denial of happiness: it may be the very means to that end.'

'Lord, Augusta, you are marrying me off again – when I told you that Mr Carraway *interests* me, no more nor less: because he does not tell me how many birds he bagged this morning, and chuckle at everything I say.'

'I am misrepresented again – you see how it is, Mr Leabrook!' Lady

Milner sighed. 'If I am over-cautious, it is because I must act, you know, *in loco parentis*; and one would see the young – that is, those who are on the threshold of life – well advised. Mr Leabrook, now: you would not wish to see your sister throw herself away, would you?'

'Of course not, madam: yet I still believe that inclination, not calculation, is the soundest basis for matrimony. I must believe it, you know, simply because it is what I have followed,' Mr Leabrook said, with a smile and a bow of his head to his fiancée. He only showed so much deference to Lady Milner, Caroline observed; and that, of course, would please Isabella.

'And how is your sister – Georgiana, isn't it? Is she still at school?' asked Aunt Selina.

'She does very well, Mrs Langland, I thank you – knows her own mind wonderfully, and will be directed by no one, and thinks all her elders fools, which no doubt we are. She continues at school for another year, if they will have her.'

'The school is at Brighton, is it not?' Aunt Selina went on. 'Where you and Caroline met, of course.'

'At Brighton,' Mr Leabrook said. 'Just so.'

'And then she came to us,' Aunt Selina said brightly and fondly. 'It's almost like fate, is it not? If one believed in such pagan notions, of course,' she added, with a glance at her husband.

Stephen, who had been gazing gloomily into his wine-glass, suddenly stirred and said: 'Talking of pagan notions, and matrimonial choices, there are many places in the world now, just as in antiquity, where bride and groom never set eyes on each other before the wedding day. And yet they go along famously.'

'I do not see how they can,' cried Fanny. 'It is monstrous.'

'Oh, it is because, since they bring no expectations to the match, there is no risk of disappointment.'

'Come, Milner, you are cynical,' Mr Leabrook said, laughing. 'Where there is a true and sincere attachment, there can be no question of disappointment – that suggests neither party is serious.'

'Unless things should come to light about either party,' Caroline suggested, 'that were not known before the marriage.'

'It is hard to see what they could be,' Mr Leabrook said, slightly smiling, and addressing a spot just a few inches to the left of Caroline's face, 'where there has been frankness and confidence, which I take as the mark of the true attachment. Unless you mean mere idle gossip and tale-telling, from which no one is secure. But I suppose there is always the legendary sailor with a wife in every port – eh, Captain?'

'Legendary, as you say, sir, for I never met with such a case in my life,' returned Captain Brunton, with some sharpness.

'Well, Milner, if you would have us adopt barbarian customs,' Mr Leabrook went on, unruffled, 'there's a prime one for you: what say you to polygamous practices – multiple wives, like your Turk with his harem?'

'A deplorable custom,' Dr Langland said heatedly, 'treating women as mere possessions.'

'And a custom, Uncle John, that would be eagerly embraced by the average Englishman,' Caroline said, to a general murmur. 'Oh, I think it would, you know – for there are so many who do not appreciate what they have and, like greedy little boys, would grab another sweetmeat even while they clutch one in their hands.'

Isabella, laughing, appealed to her fiancé: 'Oh, this is shocking – come, Richard, you must defend your sex, else all the men will be quite beaten down.'

Mr Leabrook shook his head. 'To do so would be to contradict a lady,' he said, in his softest accents, 'who must, I presume, have grounds for this peculiar knowledge.'

'Ask Stephen,' Fanny said. 'He could find a defence for the devil himself.'

'Thank you, Fanny, but this time I must disappoint you, because I happen to believe that what Miss Fortune says is entirely true.'

'About men with many wives?' cried Isabella. 'But, Stephen, you don't even want one!'

'True: but that is because I admit that what I *would* want from a wife is an impossibility. This fantastical creature would not mind any of my follies and inconsistencies – she would be my warmest friend – she would drink too much wine with me – laugh at society instead of courting it – never talk in the morning until at least half past ten – happily stay indoors for days at a time not seeing a soul, and then on a whim go a journey of twenty miles – and all this time remain naturally elegant, clever, and good-tempered.'

'My dear nephew,' Aunt Selina said, smiling, 'I think you would as soon find a mermaid.'

'Precisely – and yet most men, if they are honest, are quite as unreasonable in their requirements of a wife: and that is why I say that three or four wives, all different, would be most men's secret ideal.'

'I think this subject is rather improper,' Lady Milner notified them.

'If I did not know you better, Milner, I would think you one of those men who seek to win the favour of the other sex by denigrating their own,' Mr Leabrook said.

'But, as you say, sir, one knows Mr Milner better than that,' Caroline put in. 'Because the one thing I will say for you, Mr Milner, is that you do not have the art of dissembling to flatter your present company.' I must be careful, she thought: but she could not help noticing with pleasure that Mr Leabrook's hand, reaching for his wine-glass, was not quite steady.

'Do you mean I'm generally rude?' Stephen enquired earnestly.

'Yes, of course.'

'Oh! good – I wanted to make sure.'

'Stephen makes a great deal of being awkward and hard to please,' Isabella said, with teasing affection, 'and yet when it comes to the tenants, and the servants, and that poor young girl who came to the door and said she was the sister of our old nurse, even though she very oddly could not remember her name, why then he is all liberality and indulgence.'

'Quite plausible,' Stephen retorted, 'forgetting your sister's name. I forget yours all the time, Anastasia.'

'Well, Milner, having found my own mermaid, I can only wish you the same luck in your fishing as I have had,' Mr Leabrook said.

'Thank you, Leabrook – that is, if I ever should decide to *go* fishing, which is highly unlikely.'

'What is this?' cried Dr Langland, in bewilderment. 'Never go fishing? But I have seen you do so, Stephen, down at the Staunch, on more than one occasion – I could swear to it . . .'

Aunt Selina having patiently explained that the fishing was metaphorical, a proceeding that lasted through the taking away of the first course and the laying of the second, Dr Langland at last gave a hoot of understanding. 'Ah. You are using a metaphor, you see. The subject of the metaphor is courtship. But come! This determination against matrimony will never do. We must throw temptation in your way. Now if some creditable person were to hold a ball, with a good deal of company – I beg your pardon? You are, Mr Leabrook? Lord, bless my soul, I had no idea. Well, then there is our opportunity. I was like you, my boy, until I first laid eyes on Mrs Langland at a firework-party for the victory of Ushant: not that she was Mrs Langland then, you understand, that would have been most peculiar—'

'Uncle John, if you absolutely insist on matchmaking for me, then I cannot prevent you,' Stephen pronounced firmly, 'but I would urge you to take up some easier pursuit, such as catching moonbeams in a net.'

There was more talk of the ball, a subject on which Caroline became increasingly uneasy as it developed: for Mr Leabrook was soon proposing further entertainments, such as a picnic expedition the day after, if fine enough, or billiards and cards indoors – making, indeed, a regular house-party of it. She was sure to be included in these invitations, as whatever might be Mr Leabrook's private feelings about her, he could scarcely afford to betray himself by so pointed an omission; but she would gladly have escaped such pleasures, which must be extending the discomfort of *this* occasion to the point of excruciation. The retirement of the ladies brought other subjects of conversation, to her relief; and on the gentlemen's rejoining them, Mr Leabrook, not at all altered by the port, begged Isabella to go to the pianoforte. Isabella played and sang with taste and purity, if little of the flourishing manner that was generally interpreted as brilliance in the performance of young ladies. She was warmly applauded – most loudly by Captain Brunton, who seemed in an odd prickly mood, and on whom the effects of the port were clearly visible; and at Fanny's urging, Mr Leabrook sang a duet with his fiancée which revealed him to be the possessor of an agreeable voice, in which expression made up for lack of polish.

Indeed, watching the two of them, observing the soft words and glances that passed continually between them, the reciprocity of gesture and manner, Caroline could not but conclude them to be an admirably well-matched couple. There seemed no want of warmth, affection or respect in Mr Leabrook's attentions to Isabella, and plainly these were what she was accustomed to, and not a sort of show put on by him to confound Caroline. Helped, perhaps, by Stephen Milner's good wine, Caroline found herself actually entertaining some slender hopes. Isabella seemed very happy with him now: who was to say she would ever be otherwise? Who could be so rash as to foretell the future? Was it not possible that Mr Leabrook felt a sincere regret and repentance for what had happened at Brighton? And was not the wisest of all courses, in any circumstance, to let sleeping dogs lie?

Slender as these hopes were – spindly, knock-kneed specimens indeed – they were the best she had; and Caroline dearly longed for some peace of mind at almost any price. They even supported her through the moments of sharp misgiving at the breaking up of the party, when Isabella drawing Mr Leabrook's arm to hers on one side and Caroline's on the other, said radiantly: 'Now this is what I wished for – all friends together!'

Chapter XV

The ball at Mr Leabrook's house was soon a settled thing. Invitations, quickly extended, were as quickly accepted in a neighbourhood not over-supplied with such entertainments at this season; and now there was nothing to do but prepare in happy anticipation – or, in Caroline's case, to dread, and wish for a way of not going to Hethersett at all.

It was nearly worse: for Mr Leabrook, in the flush of hospitality, talked of the whole Wythorpe party sleeping overnight at Hethersett as his guests, so they need not leave the ball so early to ride home; and the whole Wythorpe party must mean both Manor and Rectory families. But fortunately Lady Milner expressed some finicking doubt about the propriety of Isabella staying under the same roof as her fiancé before the marriage; and Isabella herself raised the more practical question of how so many people were to be comfortably accommodated at Hethersett, large as it was, when Mr Leabrook already had company staying for that week. So Caroline was thankful to find that idea dropped – though it did raise another idea that had been plucking at her, and which at last she had confirmed by Isabella: just who were these people from London that Mr Leabrook had to stay?

'A young couple named Downey. He invited them to come and see him a good while ago, when he was at Brighton, I believe. Oh, Caro, perhaps you know them too, then, from that time?'

'Yes – yes, I met them – they are not a couple, by the by, but brother and sister – relatives of my late employer. Well, well, how nice.'

'I almost begin to envy you that time at Brighton, my dear, for you have quite stolen a march on me – I don't know them at all – but they are very agreeable, according to Richard. Though men say that about everybody in any case – so tell me, what do *you* say?'

Caroline, still rather pained at finding herself using the phrase *how nice* – not just in response to this news, but in any context whatever – struggled a moment and said: 'Yes – certainly, they are agreeable people from what I knew of them. Now, have you decided yet what you shall wear?'

So, the company from London was none other than Matthew and Maria! The thought had hardly occurred to her when Mr Leabrook had first mentioned his expected visitors, but then everything connected with that time seemed to Caroline to lie on the other side of a great gulf; only afterwards had she begun to ponder, and to remember that invitation he had urged upon them at Brighton. It was another jolt of surprise in the placid surface of her new life – if not one that should occasion any such disquiet as the reappearance of Mr Leabrook. After all, no bitter memory attached to the Downeys: no present difficulty was presented by their past association. Still, they were in themselves reminders of that unhappy period – and what was worse, when they met her again they were likely to reminisce, in all innocence, and to talk of those evening-parties and outings with their aunt, at which both Caroline and Richard Leabrook had been present. Such talk must reveal that Caroline had known Mr Leabrook much better than her casual references to their acquaintance would suggest, which would mean more awkwardness; and thus, her best way out of the whole tangle would be to stay away from Hethersett altogether.

The difficulty was, no one would hear of such a thing. Her first tentative suggestion, to Isabella, that they might perhaps do without her, was met with such hurt surprise she hardly knew how to go on.

'I should not enjoy it half so much without you there,' Isabella said. 'That is a selfish reason, I know. And I do so want you to see the place where I shall be living – and *that* sounds as if I want to show it off – what I mean is, the place where you will always be welcome, and where we can have such pleasant times.'

'Oh, I should like to see it, indeed – in due course – but as to the ball, you know I am quite a newcomer here, and you are all old acquaintances—'

'Dear Caro, it is a ball, not a private club!' Isabella said, laughing. 'And besides, you and Richard *are* old acquaintances, as it turns out. No, truly, I will not have you feel like this – a newcomer, as you put it – and neither would Richard.'

'Has he said so?'

'Oh, no, but I know him, you see, through and through.'

Caroline found it so difficult to conjure a reply to this that the pause became noticeable; and Isabella, touching her arm, said timidly: 'I'm afraid I'm a great bore about Richard and the wedding and all. I do beg your pardon, if that is it. You are such a polite listener—'

'No, I am not, and no, you are not. I do not listen politely, but in true friendship: and you are not a bore, my dear, because, believe me, I have experience of those, and can detect them across a crowded room at fifty paces. And though I'm very sure your ball could do without me—'

'What's this?' cried Fanny, who entered the parlour at that moment with a yawning Stephen following. 'Caroline, if you do not come to my ball, I warn you I shall be deeply offended.'

'Richard will be interested to learn that it has become your ball, Fanny,' Isabella said.

'Well, there would be none if I had not plagued him into it. Now the ball cannot do without you, Caro, and I must have your reasons for thinking that it could.'

'Usually when young ladies decline to attend such an occasion,' Stephen said taking up the newspaper, 'it is through envy.'

'It is nothing of the kind!' declared Fanny, hotly, before Caroline could speak.

'I said *usually*,' Stephen said, with his sleepiest glance. 'And Miss Fortune is, Lord knows, rarely usual.'

'Absolutely,' Fanny said, with a toss of her head. 'And as for envy, I'll wager Caroline could have had a dozen matches equal to Bella's – has probably turned down a dozen such, indeed – I mean no offence to you or Richard, Bella.'

'I'm just working out whether to take any,' Isabella laughed.

'I know what it is,' Fanny pursued. 'You are afraid it will all be dreadfully dull and stuffy and provincial, compared to what you are used to –' here Caroline tried to protest, but Fanny rode over her '– and that I can quite understand, but you needn't fear, because Richard is not your average country booby. He has taste, and knows how to lay on an entertainment with style. So you see, Caro, you have no excuse.'

Caroline, with an inward sigh of resignation, smiled and said: 'Of course. I have no excuse.'

'Besides, *I* will be there, and I am a sovereign specific against boredom,' Fanny went on, 'and Mr Carraway too – now *he* is out of the common run. Do you know, when he first saw those marble sculptures Lord Elgin brought back from Greece, he fainted dead away with the ecstasy of it?'

'I did not know it, and I am surprised at you knowing it, Fanny,' Stephen said, from behind his newspaper, 'unless you have been meeting him again, perchance?'

'Certainly, once or twice, at the Hampsons',' Fanny replied airily.

'Hm. Where, of course, you talk only of Greek marbles. Of course you do,' said Stephen, and deftly dodged the cushion Fanny threw at him.

So, the ball at Hethersett must be borne. After all, Caroline told herself, it was only an evening's entertainment – nothing more terrifying than a set of dances, commonplace chat, and minced chicken patties. She was able, with a very little reflection, to pin down exactly what it was that gave her such a particular distaste for the event. First, it revived memories of that ball at the Castle in Brighton, where Richard Leabrook had tried to seduce her: second, it would mean being on his home ground, actually in his house – and *that*, as his disposable mistress, she would never have been meant to see. These were the rankling thoughts she must somehow accommodate throughout the evening, whilst maintaining the cheerful demeanour appropriate to the occasion. She reminded herself that life with her father had put her spirits to many such tests; and by degrees was able to contemplate the approach of Thursday with equanimity, if without much pleasure.

In the meantime preparations for the wedding went on apace. It was now fixed for Christmas, and everyone agreed there could not be a nicer season for it. 'Aye, nothing could be more apt,' Stephen commented, 'as Christmas is really a pagan midwinter festival, when you always sacrificed a maiden or two.' He was in his most capricious and unapproachable humour: talk of lace veils and wedding-favours was liable to make him groan aloud, and he spent much time outdoors, riding or walking about the estate, and was even to be seen in shirt sleeves helping to mend a fence or clear a pond, with an air of much greater ease than he wore in the drawing room of the Manor. As for Caroline, she was naturally much with Isabella, at the Manor and at the dressmakers' and milliners' shops of Huntingdon, talking over and choosing the trousseau – naturally, for this was the very stuff of friendship and, under other circumstances, would have been delightful: as it was, Caroline could not quite enter into the spirit without a certain strain, which she hoped her friend did not perceive.

Thursday was a fine dry evening, and so well lit by the moon that even Aunt Selina's habitual anxiety about carriage-driving was diminished, and she only clutched the straps in white-lipped alarm at every third or fourth jolt. The drive, short as it was, took them into an appreciably different sort of country, rolling, clayey, and well wooded; and Hethersett itself came splendidly into view on a ridge of high ground above a negligible village – a proper turreted Tudor mansion, much improved, but retaining such satisfactorily picturesque elements as a crenellated roof, mullioned windows, and a lodge-gate giving admittance to the park. Mr Leabrook, as Fanny had said, was wont to entertain in fine style: menservants were at once on hand to see to the stabling, maidservants whisked away their wraps in the galleried hall, and a hundred candles welcomed them to the ball-room, where a score of people were already gathered. The Manor party had followed directly after their own carriage – this as a further insurance for Aunt Selina, who could console herself that if they went into the ditch, their friends behind might effect a rescue – and it was with looks divided between bashfulness and pride that Isabella took the arm of their host, whose fine figure showed at its most elegant in narrow-waisted coat and pantaloons.

'This has been all new fitted-out, I believe,' Aunt Selina said, whispering in admiration. 'Just look at that ornamented ceiling!'

'A pretty penny it must have cost,' said Stephen, unimpressibly. 'Just worth it, I suppose, if you were to spend all your time lying flat on the floor looking up at it.' And he walked off in search of the negus, whose spicy smell wafted from an adjoining supper room.

There was no music yet from the quartet of musicians tuning up at the far end of the long, panelled room: the evening was at the standing-about stage, in which dresses were scrutinized, introductions offered, insincerities exchanged, and alliances and enmities silently plotted. Caroline, looking about at the spaciousness, the card room with tables ready, the company swiftly growing in number and noise, began to feel that the evening might not be so difficult after all: it was on such a large scale that one might easily melt unnoticed into the background, and quietly get by until it was time for the carriages to be brought round. Still nursing this pleasant hope, she turned to find her name being loudly cried across the length of the ballroom.

'Caroline Fortune! It really is you! I thought Mr Leabrook was funning when he said you were here. Lord!'

Maria Downey's tone was unusually animated, though it was with the old feline languor that she made her way across the room and took Caroline's hand bonelessly in hers.

'Miss Downey. I heard you were coming to stay. It – it is all a great surprise, is it not?'

'Great? My dear, I'm positively overpowered with it, and you know it takes a great deal to rouse me to any emotion beyond mild boredom. But pray tell, what *is* the story? Mr Leabrook is as vague as most men, and merely says you have family hereabouts.'

'So I do: my mother's family. I am living with my aunt, who is the kindest and best – but first I had better hear what story *your* aunt has told, about how we came to part.'

'Oh, an absolutely unfair one, no doubt, knowing Aunt Sophia. She informed us that her companion, having lost her father, had so shamelessly capitalized on this entirely natural event as to become quite ungovernable in temper, and so there was no choice but to dispense with her services.'

'I see,' said Caroline, unmoved, and pleased to find herself so. 'Well, Miss Downey, with no disrespect to you, I must tell you I do not at all care what Mrs Catling thinks or says about me. I feel able to say this, because I understood that was your position also.'

'So it was,' Maria said, with a pretty yawn and a distant look; and then, shaking herself, 'So it is, my dear. Though I must tell *you*, or at least I don't have to but I may as well, that my own independence of Aunt Sophia now stands upon shakier ground. You remember I told you of my rich overseas gentleman, who was going to make me what the novelists call His Own as soon as he had settled his affairs in the West Indies? Alas, a letter has reached me across those unthinkable seas – what is the *point* of all that water, I'd like to know? – which gives me to understand that he must linger longer under the tropic sun. How much longer linger? Ah, on that point he is vague, again as only a man can be – but I am not to look for his return in the near future, and indeed he suggests that I should not consider myself bound by any sort of engagement, as that would be shockingly unfair to *me*. In short, my dear, I am jilted! Is it not monstrous inconvenient?'

'Something worse than that, I would say,' Caroline answered, studying Maria's exquisitely inexcitable face. 'Though I do not know how deeply your feelings—'

'They were not deeply anything, my dear, thank heaven, but it is a great nuisance nonetheless. But what you say about Aunt Sophia is absolutely right, of course, and I certainly do not intend to begin fighting Matthew for her favour now. It would be too ghastly. No, I must look elsewhere. Truth to tell, when we came away from

Brighton I remember thinking, I doubt that poor girl will last a month – not because you didn't handle her well, my dear, you handled her better than practically everyone – but simply because there *is* no pleasing her. Well, I'm glad it has all turned out for the best anyhow, and that you are comfortably situated at last. You are in delightful looks, you odious creature. Is it the country air? I do not mean an aspersion: I am beginning to think this the best sort of life, after all. That angelic being on Mr Leabrook's arm must be his future bride, I think?'

'Isabella. Yes, she – he is a very lucky man.'

'And they smile at each other, and seem fond of each other, and everything! Really this is so much better than overseas gentlemen and their empty promises. I must look about me. Let's see, who is that very long-legged man who took himself off – the one with the provokingly sleepy eyes?'

'Oh! That's Stephen – Mr Stephen Milner, that is. Isabella's brother. Oh, no, you had better look elsewhere, believe me.'

'Why? Is he taken?'

'No, no,' said Caroline, beginning to find, for some reason, the touch of Miss Downey's silken arm through hers rather annoying. 'It is not that at all. Only that you would have to work very hard to captivate *that* gentleman. Indeed, he might as well be in the West Indies, for all the effect you will have on him.'

'Better and better – I enjoy a challenge. My dear, I must go and get my introduction to the future Mrs Leabrook, and then perhaps I can secure one with her brother. Adieu for the moment – we shall see a lot of you, shan't we? – we stay a fortnight at least. Meeting you again, you know, is quite the most . . .' A lazy laugh supplied the end of the sentence as Maria's elegant form rippled away.

Left alone, Caroline examined her own peculiar feeling of irritation. She liked Maria well enough, after all: nothing had been said that could offend. She just kept thinking of that word *danglers*, and how very true it was: for here was Maria dangling after Stephen Milner, even if only in jest, barely minutes after first setting eyes on him.

Here was Maria, and here surely must be Matthew: but she could not yet see any dark young gentleman being unnecessarily intense, and she took the opportunity of bracing herself with wine before Isabella came upon her, asked her happily if she were not glad she had come after all, and bore her off to make an introduction.

This was to a lady seated in throne-like state on a sofa before the fire – Lady Milner would be jealous of that, Caroline thought – and who seemed to be receiving a file of visitors in appropriately royal style. She was Mr Leabrook's mother, as might have been surmised from the aquiline good looks valiantly resisting the conquest of fat; and she was not at all intimidating, Isabella confided in Caroline's ear as they approached, in the way that a prospective mother-in-law was supposed to be. This Caroline found, in the course of a short interview, to be quite true: for to intimidate, one must be aware of the victim, and Mrs Leabrook would have talked on if you had fallen at her feet in a dead faint. She was a garrulous woman who had long been listened to with rather too much indulgence, and who was a little too inclined to consider herself a Character, on no greater evidence than a continual compulsion to talk about herself, and some large rings. Caroline, in a rare moment of silence occasioned by the necessity of Mrs Leabrook's sipping her tea, remarked how admirably fitted out the ballroom was.

'It is admirably fitted out. I told Richard, when we were making things ready today, I observed to him that it was admirably fitted out at last: the dining-parlour too, I am of the opinion that a dining-parlour sets the tone of the house, I remember telling my cousin so, my cousin Mrs Lilley, the Lilleys at Kesteven, it was when they were refurbishing the Great House, before that they had lived in the Dower House because of the repairs but I always said to them they would not be as drastic as they thought and, ah –' here Mrs Leabrook, with a technique a flautist would have envied, drew breath whilst still talking '– and I find this is pretty much always the case, though I can say that here at Hethersett there is very little to choose: the Dower House is rather newer than this house and in very good repair, and I don't at all mind removing there when Richard marries, it will suit me very well because for one thing it is closer at hand to my poultry-yard and my dovecotes, and I think it a very good thing that these improvements have been made before he marries: it is what I have always advocated, indeed I have been saying so to him for years and years and years and years and years, and, ah—' Here Caroline lost the thread, as she fell to wondering why the succinct expression *years and years*, which sufficiently conveyed the passage of time, was deemed inadequate by Mrs Leabrook. But she was not long in considering the mystery: the woman *would* be talking, and for someone so minded, any words would do. Caroline spent the remainder of her audience nodding and wondering, charitably, whether it was nerves that made her hostess like this; and was able to move away at last, with a polite nod and smile, in the comfortable certainty that it was not so, and that no more complex explanation was needed than that Mrs Leabrook was very talkative, very self-absorbed, and very stupid.

Still there was, as Isabella had said, nothing to fear from her: everything, indeed, appeared set fair for this marriage – with the single exception of Caroline's dark knowledge; and that began to seem more and more like some deceptive dream as the rooms filled with chattering guests, and Mr Richard Leabrook, welcoming and welcomed, moved genially among them.

'I know,' said Fanny, suddenly appearing beside Caroline, and nodding towards the figure of their host, 'I often look at him too, and think how splendid that Bella is going to be married to him. I have already introduced him to Mr Carraway – and he is most interested, as I thought, in patronizing an artist of such promise – and in short he could hardly be better, considering he is getting towards the age of thirty, when really not much is to be expected from people. At least, not in this dismal country – London I dare say is different – people are surely not so staid and fudgy there. Charles has lived in London – Mr Carraway, I should say – oh, but I needn't trouble about that with *you*, need I?'

'Well, I am not about to reprimand you for calling a young man by his first name. I know it is supposed to be very shocking, but I have never quite seen why.'

'Exactly! If only everyone thought like you. Just as the world makes a great fuss if a woman and a man who are not engaged or married write each other letters – is this not the most absurdly repressive convention?'

'I confess I do not see the harm in it,' Caroline answered honestly: though with a faint suspicion that what she was agreeing to was not a general proposition, but something rather more specific – a suspicion that deepened as she saw the burning look Fanny bestowed on the figure of Charles Carraway, who was paying his respects to his hostess.

'Do you know? I have sometimes felt I would go *mad* for the lack of someone to confide in,' Fanny said. 'Bella is dear, and sympathetic, but she so wants to believe the best of everyone, and that makes her rather conventional. Whereas you – I feel I could say anything to you, and you would understand and not judge!'

'My dear Fanny, there are limits. If you told me you had put poison in Lady Milner's tea and intended burying her under the summer-house, I should feel obliged to say something, and might even judge you with a certain degree of severity.' Caroline spoke lightly, but with purpose also – for she detected an actual confidence coming, and was anxious to deflect it. She was burdened with quite enough secrets.

And here came the donor of one of them now: Matthew Downey.

'Miss Fortune, is this not remarkable? How do you do – and who would have thought? – is it not remarkable? I am so very glad to see you again – and you know I never say these things out of mere form – really there was never anything so remarkable . . .' Matthew went on remarking on the remarkableness for so long that Fanny, who was in any case itching to rejoin Mr Carraway, made a swift escape, and left Caroline alone with him.

'And so you have actually discovered a long-lost family – quite a delightful and romantic notion: and I who have known what it is to have a family's love, Miss Fortune, can certainly rejoice for you in that. Indeed, to tell the truth when I knew you at Brighton I used to pity you for being so alone in the world.'

Caroline was about as fond of being made an object of pity as most people, but she managed to smile her gratitude for this evidence of Mr Downey's sensibility.

'Of course it is a thousand pities you were unable to continue in your service to Aunt Sophia. I really believed you suited her well, and was pleased to think of her with such a companion – yes, I truly thought you worthy of the place.'

'Thank you,' Caroline said peaceably. 'But there, I'm very happily situated now, and all is for the best. But now, how do things fare with you, Mr Downey? There was a certain lady whose name begins with P whom you used to tell me of: she is well, I hope?'

'Of course, you must often have thought of that,' he said, beaming. 'She is well – yes, I thank you, the heavens be praised, she continues well – and even bears up under the strain of this intolerable secrecy, which, to be frank with you, grows worse and worse. And yet it is more necessary than ever. I regret to tell you, Miss Fortune, that greatly as I esteem her, there is no denying that Aunt Sophia's temper has become more exacting.'

As no one was better qualified to testify to that than Caroline herself, she did not know quite how to answer: not that this greatly mattered, as Matthew was as willing as ever to dominate the conversation.

'I had allowed myself lately to hope that she and I stood on terms of better accord, without those – those misunderstandings to which we were so sadly prone,' he went on, working his hand through his hair and breathing dramatically through his nose. 'But, alas, she is in an unhappy humour again, and I hardly know how to please her. This visit to Leabrook, now – she pressed it strongly, absolutely insisted that we go, and then on our departure seemed to reproach me for going off on a jaunt when she was all alone.' Matthew sighed. 'I do wish, you know, that she had not been forced to dismiss you, Miss Fortune – it was a thousand pities for everyone!'

Caroline restrained her tongue for a moment while she made absolutely sure she had heard him right. 'Mr Downey, to say that Mrs Catling was *forced* to dismiss me is to put a very strange construction on the matter. You know – Maria has told me so – what happened: my father had died, I wished to go to his funeral, and she would have prevented me: it might be truer to say that I was *forced* to leave.'

'Ah, but she is an old lady, you know, Miss Fortune – and was, besides, very poorly at the time.'

'She had a cold, sir, such as everyone suffers once or twice in a year; and as for making allowances for her being old, I think there is an equal case to be made on the opposite side – that is, for her being old enough to know better.'

He shook his head mournfully, as if regretting this display of hard-heartedness. 'Well, I still think it a great shame – and yes, I must say it, you have made matters more difficult for *me*, though I acquit you of thinking any such thing at the time. Indeed, plainly you did *not* think of it – there's the pity!'

'Mr Downey, this is doing it a little too brown,' she said, with warmth, remembering the effort she had put into pleading his cause with his aunt. 'I freely confess I did not think of you in those circumstances. I had and have nothing but cordial feelings towards you, but I insist that you at least consider the novel notion that not everyone thinks exclusively about you all the time. Our own petty concerns, I am afraid, prevent us enjoying that luxury.'

Matthew shook his head again, more sadly: she remembered that he had, to put it lightly, never been one for irony. 'I think you are still feeling your loss, Miss Fortune, and that is why you are not yourself.'

She swallowed her irritation at the presumption of this. 'Well, Mr Downey, to lose a father, as you know—'

'Hm? Oh, that – to be sure, yes, I know that pain, indeed I think I can say no one knows it better than I – but I was thinking more particularly of the loss of your position. After all, it was one from which you might have had hopes – hopes that, if I could not approve, I could certainly understand.'

Caroline found she was thirsty: it was the consequence of doing so much gasping. 'Mr Downey,' she said, finding her breath, 'Mrs

Catling occupies, quite naturally, such a central place in your life that you assume it is the same with others. I assure you it is not. Since leaving Brighton I have had the keen pleasure of never having to give that lady a moment's thought, and it is a pleasure I would like to continue to enjoy. And if you and I are to meet without arguing – which I would much prefer – then she is a subject probably best avoided between us.'

'Very well.' Matthew gave her such a hurt, wistful, nobly forbearing, and absolutely infuriating look that if Caroline had been a rich aunt she would have cut him out of her will on the spot. 'And yet, you know, I had thought you friendly to me, Miss Fortune. I would never have entrusted you with my secret otherwise – and I am troubled to think—'

'I am friendly to you, Mr Downey!'

'And yet the way you speak of my aunt, an estimable lady for all her foibles, and who was so good to you – really I am baffled.'

Caroline gave a laugh – a short and vexed laugh, but the best she could manage. 'Clearly, Mr Downey, we are *not* avoiding the subject. Now the dancing is beginning, and I cannot suppose you would wish to partner me; so let us exit severally like they do in Shakespeare, and perhaps when we meet again we shall rub along better.'

Matthew appeared as disinclined as ever to drop a subject until he had harried it to death, so there was nothing to do but turn away from him as politely as she could. Caroline's nature was not emotionally strenuous, and she had to be much goaded before she would go to the exertion of a quarrel: still, Matthew had put her quite out of patience. 'Poor Perdita!' she said to herself. 'Is it only the secrecy you find a strain, I wonder?'

Couples were forming up. Caroline knew well that Stephen Milner had only been joking when he talked of having his one dance with her again, so it would have been sheer nonsense to look about for him, and even greater nonsense to feel anything akin to disappointment when he did not appear: so she persuaded herself that she did neither of these things. Someone who did appear very promptly, however, to ask her to dance was Captain Brunton.

He approached her with a determined air, as if this time to prove his independence of Lady Milner – though she was, in any case, being gravely squired to the floor by Dr Langland. For all his gruffness, Captain Brunton appeared such a sensible man, after the sighings of Matthew Downey, that Caroline was quite pleased to accept him. Nor was his taciturnity unwelcome just now; but as they joined the set, she began to wonder about these heavy silences and dark looks. Was he, in fact, if not actually out of love with Lady Milner, then a little in love with herself?

It was a startling thought. Not a happy one, for her regard for him, increased though it was, did not extend to reciprocation: but no sooner had she entertained it than she began to doubt it. He was more abstracted than attentive, which even in a shy man like Captain Brunton surely did not bespeak the lover; and where his grey glance did fall was on Mr Leabrook and Isabella, leading off the dance with every appearance of harmony and cheerfulness. At last Caroline made some remark about Mr Leabrook's having laid on a very splendid entertainment, and Captain Brunton burst out: 'So he might – he is secure in a felicity such as I can never aspire to. No . . . not for me,' he concluded, with a sort of growl, which gave Caroline a momentary apprehension that now *he* was going to confide in her. But he subsided into such complete, stiff-jawed silence that Caroline received a pitying look from Fanny, who was dancing spiritedly with Mr Carraway.

Caroline did not lack for partners in the succeeding dances, and one flushed young man who had drunk too much wine repeatedly informed her, with more gallantry than exactitude, that she was a magnificent Tigress. It was partly to escape the attentions of this zoological gentleman that she withdrew to the card room – in what turned out to be a mortifying mistake. For Richard Leabrook, unengaged, had just stepped in there likewise; and Dr Langland, who was seating Aunt Selina at her customary game of sixpenny piquet, looked up to see two young people not dancing; and in a moment bore down on them with all his blundering benevolence.

'This will never do – my dear Caroline, my dear Mr Leabrook, you should be on the floor – you are neither of you an old ruin like me, to be lurking about in card rooms when the sound of a country-dance calls – that is a Boulanger if I am not mistaken, and just the thing for two such elegant dancers as I know you to be. Come, do you lack an introduction? Surely not – surely you met at the Manor long since – no, no, there is no excuse for it, let us see you tread the measure . . .'

There was no help for it. Once again Caroline wished she had cultivated some missish mannerisms, so that she could have plausibly whimpered that she was tired; and Mr Leabrook, thin-lipped, seemed desperately casting about for some excuse also. But it was doubtful that anything could have prevailed against Dr Langland's overbearing conviviality; and soon they were being thrust on to the floor, where with the coldest of bows, and the briefest of curtseys, Caroline and Mr Leabrook faced each other as they had not done since that night at Brighton.

'You have seen our mutual acquaintances, the Downeys, I think,' he said at last, with colourless correctness.

'Yes.'

'They seem well.'

'They are well, I believe.'

'You know, Miss Fortune, as we have been thrown together in this unexpected way, with no help for it, I think we really ought to try at least to be civil with one another,' he said, all honeyed reason – even though he had been quite as reluctant as she to undertake this dance.

'I am being civil, sir. But if you doubt it, I can very easily be uncivil if you like – for purposes of comparison.'

'Of course I cannot deny you these pleasantries,' he said, with a bare smile, 'but I cannot think any purpose would be achieved by your continuing in them. You have formed a friendship with Isabella, I find. Surely for her sake at least you would not wish to cause unpleasantness.'

'Certainly I would not. But you chiefly want me to behave myself, Mr Leabrook, for your *own* sake, not for Isabella's. You want me to save your skin, which is a different matter.'

'If that is in the nature of a threat, Miss Fortune, I may as well say that Isabella trusts me implicitly, and is hardly likely to be moved from that trust by irresponsible gossip. My future wife does not doubt my word, and nor need she: I do not lie to her.'

'I do not mean any threat, Mr Leabrook: if I were to speak, don't you think I would have done so before now? I don't care about you: only about Isabella.'

'To whom I accord all the deep respect she deserves.'

'As opposed to another sort of girl, who deserves none at all.'

With a look that was almost bored – but which did not deceive Caroline in the slightest – Mr Leabrook said: 'I gather you are still exercised by a certain misunderstanding we had, Miss Fortune, and I am sorry for that: but all I can say is, I did have my reasons.'

'You could have had no reasons, sir, that could be anything but a dishonour to yourself, and an insult to me.'

That must have knocked him back a little, for he almost missed a step.

'My dear lady,' he resumed, 'I would in all friendliness suggest that you look about you, and consider whether it would be easy for someone like you to blacken my good reputation. Undeserved it may be – and of which of us is that not true? – but the fact is it does stand firm and solid as Hethersett itself, whereas yours . . . well, let us call it an unknown quantity.'

'My dear sir, I don't give a fig for your reputation, or my own come to that: my only concern is Isabella.'

'I must say you make very free with my fiancée's name, when you have only a few weeks' acquaintance. I would remind you that she and I have known each other much longer.'

'I query whether she has truly *known* you at all, sir.'

'I see,' he said, with a sniff of displeasure. 'So you do wish to make mischief. And to what end, I wonder – to see Isabella still trapped with her strait-laced stepmother and that Portsmouth booby who trails her about?'

'I wish to do nothing, Mr Leabrook, except to warn you that I will not see Isabella's happiness threatened. I am willing to believe you sincere in your attachment to *her*, only because that is Isabella's belief, and not because of any trust I feel able to place in you. That is all I mean to do – unless I am provoked.'

For a moment his tolerant attention was darkened, as when he had first glimpsed her in the oak avenue, by a look that might have been fear. But then he replaced it with a smile, and in his most urbane tones said: 'Miss Fortune, we don't need to talk in these dire and doomy tones, surely? You have lived in the world and so have I, and you know that a great deal of undue trouble is caused by heart-searching and agonizing and generally being too serious. At least, I had always thought you of that opinion: it's why we appeared to get along.'

'I have said all I mean to say, Mr Leabrook: and now, lest people do think we are being too serious, we had better talk about the weather till the end of the set.'

It had been an agitating exchange altogether, but something in his last remark pricked Caroline with uncommon sharpness. 'I had always thought you of that opinion' – how tired she was of what people thought of her, and the uses they made of it! For now all she wanted was the comfort of anonymity, and as she could see her tiger-man getting ready to stalk her again she withdrew from the ballroom and looked about for some retreat other than the card room, which had proved so disastrous.

Or had it? It was surely likely, in this close society, that she would have found herself alone with Richard Leabrook at some point. So, it was at least over with; and what was more, she had told him plainly enough where they stood. And yet she could take no satisfaction from the encounter. Somehow she felt as wretched and lonely as the night after the Brighton ball, when the sordid light in which he saw her had been revealed.

She opened a door at random, and found herself in a handsome library – but not, alas, alone: she could have groaned when she saw the figure moving behind a bookcase. Then he stepped out.

'Now this is a real library,' Stephen said approvingly. 'The books have plainly been read. Though I think it was Leabrook's father who was the collector. This is an original Urquhart Rabelais, marvellous thing. Also shocking, of course. You can always tell the indelicate parts of a book – where the edges of the pages are grubby from thumbs. You are unhappy, Miss Fortune.'

Caroline turned hastily away. 'Indeed I am not,' she said, in a voice so full of tears she might as well have howled it while beating her fists on the floor.

'Is it to do with the general unsatisfactoriness of life,' he asked, balancing the book on his nose, 'which it is best, by the by, to ignore, or is it something more specific?'

'Why? I mean, supposing it were – if it were in your power, Mr Milner, would you help me?'

'I might at that,' Stephen said, replacing the book on the shelf, 'because when you're low like this, there's no fun in arguing.'

Caroline was silent as she considered a whole clutch of paradoxes. For if anyone could help in her circumstances, surely it would be someone like Stephen Milner, with his absolute independence of mind, his disinclination to rush to moral judgement: she remembered the scandalous and ostracized friend he had dined with in Bath. And yet the absurd thing was, she did shrink from confiding in him of all people, and not because she feared his satire. I do care dreadfully what he thinks of me, she admitted to herself: I do not wish to be sunk in his estimation, and I don't know why, and I know it makes no sense when I did nothing wrong anyway but I simply cannot help it.

'I'm a little hot and tired, that's all,' she told him.

'Well! that's a relief, at any rate,' he said, after studying her – she had her back to him, but she could feel it – for several long moments. 'It means you have been dancing. I was rather afraid *my* absence might desolate you so much you would remain a tragic wallflower all evening.'

'Yes, I have been dancing, Mr Milner, and a good thing I did *not* wait for you, as you took yourself off so bearishly.'

'Oh, well, I knew you wouldn't lack for partners,' he said offhandedly.

'Good heavens, is that my second compliment?'

'Not necessarily. Oh, look, Byron – and Scott and Moore – these must be Leabrook's additions. As is that marble chimney-piece, I fancy. He's certainly going all out for improvements. I wish he weren't. Fanny has been plaguing me to do the same to the Manor. Stucco and a Chinese room and a grotto and Gothick arches in the cow-barn, you know.' He peered gloomily into a folio of maps. 'I always think Brazil is too big.'

'Oh, Mr Milner, don't,' she cried. He looked up in surprise. Again she didn't know why, but the thought of the Manor being remodelled in the grand Hethersett fashion distressed her. 'I mean – your house has a good deal of character as it is.'

'Do you think so?' He smiled. 'I confess I'm fond of the old place, though when I was a young pup I thought it the dullest box in creation and could hardly wait to leave it. We always think we know what we want: when in truth there is nothing we are less likely to know. There, I make you a present of that piece of wisdom, Miss Fortune.'

'Well, I certainly wouldn't pay for it.'

He grinned. 'Ah, you are looking better already. I shall vex you back into entire good humour before I'm done. Would you say we are related?'

'No – or only in the loosest sense – but I'm trying to think what this question is going to lead to.'

'Oh, don't trouble, the processes of my thoughts are so rarefied and subtle, you'll never follow them. No, I suppose we are not really relatives,' he said, rubbing his rasping chin. 'You are my aunt Selina's niece, on her side, and I am your uncle John's nephew, on his side, but it is rather tenuous, which is a pity. A true relation would allow us to be Stephen and Caroline to one another, instead of Mr Milner and Miss Fortune. Think how much more naturally, spontaneously and freely we could quarrel if we were on those terms.'

'Oh, do be serious!'

Quite gently he said: 'I am trying to be.'

But whether this were so, or whether he was merely taking his habitual irony a step further, she was not to know – as at that moment Mr Leabrook himself came in.

'Ah!' he said, his gaze just skimming over Caroline, his smile unfaltering. 'Dwellers in the abode of peace. I'm afraid I come as a destroyer, though: Isabella has commissioned me to find her scapegrace brother – sorry, Milner, her words – and make him join the dancing.'

'Oh, Lord, must I? In a minute then. Only when there are no damnable fiddling quadrilles. I always take hold of the wrong hands and it all goes to blazes. I wish we could all just wave our spears round the camp-fire like sensible heathens.'

Caroline, meanwhile, was already on her way to the door: she had had enough of Richard Leabrook's proximity for one night; and so quick was she that she hardly noticed the look, alert, hard and speculative, with which Stephen observed her rapid exit.

Chapter XVI

'Now, my dear girl, aren't you glad you came after all?' Isabella said, taking Caroline's arm as the bell was rung for supper. 'You know I simply can't be happy unless everyone else is. Though in truth that is rather selfish, isn't it? Oh, well. Now Fanny I know is happy because she is discussing the theory of the sublime with Mr Carraway. Stephen I presume is happy because he is lurking about like a dog that has had no run all day, which he seems to like best. But the person I am a little concerned for is Captain Brunton. I know I have been rather severe on him in the past – but I don't like to see him looking so mumpish. What can it be, do you suppose? Has he quarrelled with my stepmother?'

'I think it may be a love-trouble,' Caroline answered carefully, 'but I'm not sure of what sort. And then I dare say the sight of Mr Leabrook's house, and the style in which he lives, has put him in mind of his own situation – which is so very different.'

'I never thought of that,' Isabella said, with a grave look. 'Oh, but then he has been a naval captain, and they did such fine things for us in the war – he can surely hold his head up in any company.'

'Perhaps you should tell him so – in a subtle way.'

'Perhaps so. You are a thoughtful creature, Caroline Fortune.'

'Oh, Lord, not I.' Caroline laughed, feeling uncomfortable – and then feeling more so when Matthew Downey appeared, and offered her his arm to go in to supper.

'You'll forgive me, Miss Milner,' he said, 'but I know my friend Leabrook will claim his exclusive right to *your* arm – and as for me, I claim the rights of old acquaintance. Now then,' he went on cheerfully as Caroline, seeing no way of refusal, took his arm, 'is this not wonderfully reminiscent? Is this not just like the old days in Brighton, Miss Fortune?'

'Uncannily like.' She saw Stephen and Mr Leabrook approaching, and wished they had been a little quicker.

'You see, I have been thinking,' Matthew confided, 'and as you no doubt perceive, I have decided to disregard our earlier conversation. I find I can always forgive where I understand: and I understand, Miss Fortune, what made you speak with such violence. You were *hurt* by my aunt's dismissal of you – and the hurt has made you excessive. Great heavens, I should know about that! – the many times *I* have found myself angry with Aunt Sophia, when she has seemed to act slightingly. But I can assure you, the pain will pass.'

Caroline thanked him and replied, with a fixed smile, that she could almost feel it passing already.

'You know, I think it not impossible that Aunt Sophia might be brought to acknowledge you again, Miss Fortune. Not reinstate you in your old position, of course – but acknowledge you at least as an acquaintance. What do you think of that?'

As it was not possible to tell Matthew what she thought without resorting to the vocabulary of the barrack-room, Caroline only said: 'I do not look for such an honour, Mr Downey.'

'Well, I might put in a word . . . Ah, Leabrook, I was just saying to Miss Fortune how like old times this is. Do you remember when we all danced at the Castle? Maria, do you remember?'

Miss Downey, who had positioned herself adroitly at Stephen's elbow, yawned prettily and said: 'I make it a rule never to remember anything before last week. It makes life more interesting, wouldn't you say, Mr Milner?'

'Now I am supposed to ask you how,' he said, yawning back, 'so consider it done, Miss Downey.'

'You cross creature! Because, sir, it prevents the staleness of familiarity. You can greet even the dullest acquaintance with pleasure, if you have forgotten the dreary story they told you last Monday.'

'Well, you must remember, Leabrook,' Matthew pursued, 'because it was the very next day you took yourself off. I never did understand why you were in such a peculiar hurry.'

'Lord, what a memory you have, Downey,' Mr Leabrook said, laughing. 'I fear mine is more like your sister's – quite a sieve in fact. Well, shall we go in?'

'Do you know Brighton, Mr Milner?' Maria enquired, insinuating herself on to his arm.

'It's a town in Sussex, Miss Downey,' Stephen said. Caroline suppressed a smile: Maria certainly had her work cut out.

At their supper-table they were joined by Lady Milner and Captain Brunton and then, late, breathless and flushed, Fanny and Mr Carraway.

'Outside!' Fanny cried in answer to her stepmother's wishing to know, in tones of primmest interrogation, where exactly she had been. 'To look at the stars! Oh, Augusta, don't make that pursy mouth – we were not *alone*, heaven forfend. We went to the stables to consult with your head groom, Richard – old Mr Blades. He is a true countryman, you see, with a true countryman's knowledge.'

'Aye, he has certainly been telling me the error of my ways for many a year,' sighed Mr Leabrook.

'It was my idea, Lady Milner,' Mr Carraway confessed. 'We were wondering how the weather would be tomorrow, when Mr Leabrook has promised us a *fête* out of doors, and I said we must consult a man of nature, for they always know. And Mr Blades took a view of the stars, and declared that tomorrow will be fine – fine and bright.'

'Ask him who's going to win the Derby,' grunted Stephen.

'Well, if Blades is right, a picnic it shall be,' Mr Leabrook said, 'down by the pond perhaps—'

'Oh, Richard, surely it will still be too cold for sitting down outdoors,' Isabella reproached him. 'We haven't all your constitution.'

'Perhaps you're right,' Mr Leabrook said equably. 'A curse on the English climate! I was reading somewhere that it is the basis of our national greatness, because it means we can never be comfortable, and so must always be up and doing, and discovering lands and building manufactories and whatnot. For my part I would gladly exchange a few sugar islands for a little more sunshine. Well, we may certainly take a turn about the park, even if we do not eat outdoors. Mr Carraway, I shall be interested to learn what you think of the improvements. It was an associate of Repton's who did the designing. I fancy he has cleared too much timber. Lady Milner, you have an eye for such things, I judge – you will join our party tomorrow, will you not? And you, of course, Captain Brunton—'

'I beg your pardon, sir,' Captain Brunton said, in a bristling manner, sitting bolt upright, 'why do you say *of course*?'

'I meant, sir,' Mr Leabrook said temperately, after a short laugh, 'that you are of course welcome: that it goes without saying.'

Captain Brunton dabbed a stiff bow at him. 'It happens, sir, that I have other business tomorrow.'

'Edward! What can you mean?' Lady Milner cried in surprise. 'You have told *me* nothing of this.'

'It's of no account,' Captain Brunton said, 'a small matter – not worth the mentioning.'

'Then it can surely be put aside, to take up Mr Leabrook's invitation,' said Lady Milner, with a look half beseeching, half peevish.

'Of course, if you wish me to come, Augusta, then – then to be sure—'

'Oh, please, sir, don't inconvenience yourself,' Mr Leabrook said, with a negligent wave.

'Welcome to the country, Miss Downey,' Stephen said to Maria, 'where people actually argue themselves out of their pleasures. Puritan strain, you know. Cromwell was from hereabouts – the one with the warts and the Ironsides and all that.'

'Was he really?' Miss Downey said. 'How very curious! – though why it should be so I don't know, as he had to come from somewhere. The thing that fairly fags my wits is looking around and seeing so many people, and thinking that they must *all* come from somewhere – is that not the most perplexing thing?'

'In a certain sense, they all come from the same place,' Stephen remarked, his eye momentarily catching Caroline's.

'The country – the country is where I always feel most reflective,' Matthew said. 'But that would not do all the time – not for me. Now Brighton, Mr Milner, you would like it greatly – it is the liveliest of all watering-places, and for my part I always feel more *alive* where there is a great gathering of people. I don't necessarily mean *society*, for I hope I am not enslaved to that—'

'Brighton, no thank you,' Stephen said, cutting off Matthew before he could inform them about all his tastes. 'I have been there – all bright and smart and sticky like new gingerbread. Give me an old, tottering, out-of-fashion place where everyone is half mad.'

'You droll creature,' Maria said, tapping his arm, 'yet it is plain you know London pretty well.'

'To be sure he does, but he won't take *me* there,' burst out Fanny.

'Certainly not. Your head would be turned in a second,' Stephen rapped out. 'London is very well for the rich, the secure, the experienced – but for the young and unworldly, beware.'

'Oh, Caroline, wasn't it in London that your mother met your father, and ran away with him?' Fanny cried. 'The most romantic story – I was telling it to Mr Carraway. Now *that* ended happily, didn't it?'

'Well, I don't believe my mother ever regretted it,' Caroline said.

'That means only that she never *said* so in your hearing,' Stephen said, 'as any affectionate mother would not.'

'My dear Milner,' Mr Leabrook said in amazement, 'you grow moral.'

'Only to tease,' Isabella said.

'But don't you believe that people should follow their hearts, Stephen?' Fanny appealed to him.

'Loath as I am even to sully my mouth with such a locution as *following your heart*, which belongs only in the pages of a sentimental novel,' Stephen said, with tart relish, 'I will say that it is all very well if you know whither your heart is going. But I would suggest that for most of us, we can as easily follow our hearts as a blind man can follow a lantern.'

'You may say what you like,' Fanny returned, 'but I know *my* heart.'

'Pah, that's like a man with a farthing in his pocket saying he knows his wealth,' Stephen snapped.

'Fie, sir,' cried Mr Carraway, 'this is too much – is this not mere seniority scoffing at the sensibility of ardent youth? I know you are Miss Fanny's elder brother, and stand *in loco parentis*, but I must protest. I *can* protest to you, because I know you like frank speaking.'

'I don't stand *in loco* anything,' Stephen said, with an impatient look.

'Oh, you needn't leap to my defence, Mr Carraway, though I appreciate the gallantry,' Fanny said composedly. 'The fact is Stephen is always dismissive of the feelings because he is simply an awkward, contrary, impossible man.'

'Well! Brighton, you know,' put in Matthew, 'I am surprised at you, Mr Milner, for not liking it – for I like it extremely – and you, Miss Fortune, liked Brighton too, I know – is it not strange Mr Milner not liking it?'

'I like wearing flowers in my hair for a ball, Mr Downey, but I should not expect Mr Milner to finish off his breeches and tailcoat with a crown of lilies,' Caroline answered, smiling.

'I never supposed that he would,' Matthew said, with a puzzled frown.

'Gad, but I'm tempted!' breathed Stephen, in an undertone.

'Oh! wait – you are being jocular,' Matthew said, his brow clearing, 'of course – I remember that from Brighton.'

'You must all have known each other pretty well at Brighton – isn't that curious?' Isabella said.

'Not really curious,' Mr Leabrook said, 'for that's the way Brighton is – continual society. Indeed, as Milner suggests, that is all there is to it. Now, about tomorrow: I propose I send my carriage over . . .'

He did not like talk of Brighton, Caroline thought: there was something they had in common, at any rate.

Supper over, the music struck up from the ballroom again, and Maria Downey, rising effortfully from her seat, stretched her long limbs at Stephen and drowsily asked: 'Are you as averse to dancing as you are to watering-places, Mr Milner?'

'Yes – but as I *have* been to Brighton, but have *not* danced this evening, I may as well even it out. If that is what you are suggesting, Miss Downey.'

Well, Caroline thought, with a certain nibbling vexation as she watched them take the floor, she had only got him to dance with her – no great triumph; and if she thought she could induce him to seriousness, then it showed how little she knew him. Now there was a further vexation – it looked as if she herself would have to stand up with Matthew, as Isabella was being led out by her fiancé, and Mr Carraway stood ready again at Fanny's elbow. But then Lady Milner, putting by the mantle with which she had been fussing, looked up and intervened.

'Fanny, recollect yourself, please. It is not correct to show exclusive partiality to one partner all night.'

'Isn't it? Do you mean it is wrong, Augusta?'

'It is what no young woman of good breeding should do: and it will assuredly be noticed.'

'Oh! well, if that's all, I don't care,' Fanny said, springing up; but then Captain Brunton stirred and hemmed and said, with frowning looks: 'Miss Fanny, your stepmother speaks wisely, and I do wish you would heed her.'

'Do you, sir? But as you are not even my stepfather, I can hardly consider it any of your business.'

'Really, Fanny, this is shocking,' lamented Lady Milner.

'No, Augusta, it isn't,' Fanny said cheerfully, 'and only you could think it so; but I know you mean well, and so I shall have this dance with Mr Downey, if he will be so good, and redeem myself as a young woman of correctness and breeding – on condition, Mr Carraway, that you dance with Caroline. Because she at least knows there is more to life than these deadly conventions.'

As no one could object to this, or at least, as Fanny's usual self-assertion had left them speechless, Caroline took the floor with Charles Carraway: who was full of praises for his late partner.

'She has the most irrepressible spirit, has she not? Ah, spirit. Beautiful word. I shudder when I hear a man say of his horse that he is going to *break* its spirit – still more when schoolmasters and pedagogues boast the same of the children in their charge.'

'You speak from experience, Mr Carraway?'

'Yes – though only briefly. I was sent to such a schoolmaster, once. I broke his cane over my knee and ran away,' Mr Carraway said quietly, with his sidelong dreamy look. 'I told my guardian what had happened: he embraced me and said I had done right. It is so important to think for yourself, is it not? But Fanny has told me you agree on that.'

'I suppose I do: though sometimes Fanny seems to attribute ideas to me before I am even aware I have them.'

Mr Carraway laughed pleasantly. 'Ah, but I'll wager she is always right. Such is the delicacy of her perception, you know, I have more than once found her putting into words my own inmost thoughts!'

'Tut, dancing with a lady while singing the praises of another – is this your gallantry, Mr Carraway?'

'I know you don't mind it, Miss Fortune,' he said, whispery and warm, 'because you are on our side.'

Well, if it were a matter of sides, Caroline would always incline to Fanny's view of things, rather than the chill proprieties invoked by Lady Milner; but she was rather alarmed at the idea of sides being taken at all, and she might have addressed herself more seriously to this question, if her mind had not been still taken up with Richard Leabrook. She had observed a preoccupation, a silence about him since Matthew's insistent talk of Brighton: watching him at the other end of the set, she saw he looked absent from the dance, and seemed to answer Isabella's smiles with difficulty.

It is because of me: he cannot be easy with me here, thought Caroline; and though very soon after the next set of dances, Aunt Selina's retiring habits ensured that their carriage was ordered to be brought round, so putting an end to the discomforts of the Hethersett ball, there were still the discomforts of tomorrow to be managed;

and she could not stifle a fear that they must come to some sort of issue.

The next day was, as Mr Leabrook's groom had predicted, fine and bright, though with the full sharpness of autumn in the air. The party Mr Leabrook had gathered, comprising the Downeys, the Milners, Mr Carraway, Captain Brunton, and Caroline, were all young: not liable to fuss about cold, or regularity of mealtimes; and the plan was to take a tour of the grounds and park, return to the house for a collation, and amuse themselves with cards and billiards and books as they liked, or go out again, just as their fancy and the weather dictated.

A good plan; and as there was nothing missing for their enjoyment, it was all the more curious to find how heavily the day went, and what a dull and spiritless set they were on the whole.

'There is one unalterable rule of social intercourse,' Stephen Milner said to Caroline, as they set out to walk across the terrace and down to the park, 'and that is, that any group of people who say *we must do this again*, and meet up to do so, will not enjoy themselves.' He seemed so satisfied with the proof of this that he was for a time the brightest of the party; and Maria Downey, lazily flirting, declared that he was not such an ogre, brute, and savage after all. But besides this general rule there were, Caroline thought, specific reasons for their unease. There was a strained quality about their host's welcome, and his repeated professions of hospitality, that was plain at least to herself, and she guessed also to Isabella, judging by her friend's troubled looks. Captain Brunton had obviously not wanted to come, and was as gruff as was consonant with politeness. Matthew Downey had been expecting a letter from his aunt Sophia in Brighton, and could not refrain from wondering aloud why it had not come, in spite of his sister's enumerating several plausible reasons – to all of which he readily assented. 'To be sure. Of course, that must be it, absolutely . . . Still,' he would break out, after a prospect or a specimen cedar had been duly admired, 'still, I cannot help but wonder . . .' until Maria fairly groaned.

Only Fanny and Mr Carraway were really happy.

'Mr Carraway, you must run a race with me. To that summer-house. And you are not to let me win.'

'Oh, I shall not do that, Miss Fanny, never fear. But I cannot run in these . . .' his hessian boots. He sat down on the grass and began tugging at them. 'I wonder if one of you gentlemen . . . ?'

'I'll do it.' Fanny grasped and heaved, nearly went over backwards. Caroline, all on edge though she was, found their young laughter infectious: a pity that Lady Milner would surely nip it with withering disapproval; oh, the indecency of seeing a man in his stockings.

But no. There was even a look in Lady Milner's eyes, as she watched them haring off, that reflected Caroline's own feeling – that they were silly, and rather too inclined to show off their abundant spirits, and yet that there was a beauty about the two of them at that moment which sent a wistful pang to the heart.

Stranger still, when the party followed them, at a sedater pace, it was Lady Milner who attached herself to Caroline, and deliberately slowed her steps so that they walked apart from the others. If Lady Milner had any opinion of her at all, Caroline thought, it would have been that she was – like romantic novels and the pert manners of servants – generally Regrettable. And yet now—

'Miss Fortune, I wonder if I might ask you a question.'

'Certainly. Anything. Except which king came before Henry the Eighth because that I never can remember.'

She was only rattling because she was nervous; but at once it crashed in on her that Lady Milner might think this a sneering reference to her governess past. Caroline flamed with mortification, hesitated over several reparative remarks all of which seemed equally unfortunate – but Lady Milner only smiled weakly and said: 'Henry the Seventh. It would be helpful if they all went like that, would it not? No, it is rather a personal question: or at least, a question about personal matters. I suppose, Miss Fortune, you cannot fail to have observed the intimacy that has grown between Fanny and this Mr Carraway. What do you think of it?' Caroline's surprise at her opinion being sought must have shown, for Lady Milner went on, timidly touching her arm: 'You are young, yes, but older than Fanny, and I think you have had a good deal more experience of the world.'

'Well, I think – I think it is very natural. Fanny has a romantic temper, and so it seems has Mr Carraway: they both love to talk; and they have been thrown much together lately.'

Lady Milner gave her such a pained, dubious, unsatisfied look that Caroline very nearly asked if they could go back to the kings.

'Miss Fortune, I should tell you that I feel . . . a great responsibility for her. For her own sake, and for my late husband's. I promised Sir Henry faithfully that I would do my best for my stepchildren – odd though it may seem to call them such – and the one thing I can say for myself, Miss Fortune, is that I am faithful. So, I do my best. It is not always easy, for a woman alone. But that is how it must be. Certainly I shall not marry again. That is what I mean by faithfulness.'

It was difficult to take in such a sudden and strong dose of confidence. Caroline's mind made swift reappraisals while she tried, and failed, not to look over in the direction of Captain Brunton, who was striding with hands clasped seamanlike behind his back and his eyes fixed on the turf as if he were mentally measuring the distance.

'It must be a great responsibility, indeed,' Caroline said. 'And Fanny is a very – lively creature.'

'She is headstrong and wilful, and she *needs* direction. Isabella is soon to be respectably settled: I have no anxieties there. But with Fanny – I fear that she may be led into indiscretion by her – her liveliness, as you term it.' Lady Milner grimaced, as if the word were some brutal piece of coal-heaver's slang. 'This Mr Carraway seems to be respectable – as artists go –' which, Lady Milner's frown suggested, was not very far '– and Mr Leabrook has a high regard for him, which must be in his favour. Still, I feel that Fanny should be aware that this over-familiarity with the young man may compromise her reputation.'

'Fanny would say, I think, that she does not care a fig for her reputation.'

'So she would, and it is dangerous nonsense. We do not live in a state of nature: we live in society; and society has great power.' There was something behind Lady Milner's tightening voice – remembered struggles of her own, perhaps. Then she sighed and waved a hand. 'But I have said all this to her, and not been heeded. That is why I wanted to ask you, Miss Fortune, if you will speak to Fanny about this matter.'

'Me? But I – well, really, I cannot think how I can pretend to any sort of authority over Fanny.'

'No: but she listens to you.'

Caroline, about to deny it, stopped. For it was true. She was, heaven help her, Fanny Milner's oracle. She blinked away low autumn sun-dazzle, seeing between its sequined flashes Fanny and Mr Carraway falling laughing to the ground outside the summer-house, Isabella's gold-limned head inclined towards Richard Leabrook's shoulder, Stephen moodily swiping at weed-heads with his stick. She tried to sweep her scattered thoughts together.

'Fanny will not like to listen to that, I'm afraid,' she answered at last. 'That is, if I am to caution her about her behaviour with Mr Carraway – and really, Lady Milner, I'm not sure that I see anything very reprehensible in it. I'm flattered that you think my influence so great, but in truth—'

'I don't mean to flatter, Miss Fortune. I would rather Fanny heeded my advice, but as she will not, I must perforce turn to someone to whom she does listen – for whatever peculiar reasons.'

Something had captivated Sir Henry, Caroline thought with a strong awareness of her own teeth, but it surely wasn't charm.

'I will do what I can,' she said.

And suddenly there was warmth. 'Thank you – a thousand thank-yous,' Lady Milner said, turning on Caroline a brilliant, anxious smile – the first real smile she had ever seen on that sombre face.

More reappraisals. She is young after all, Caroline thought – the *gravitas* made one forget – and the responsibility must weigh heavy. And now the thought occurred to her for the first time: was Lady Milner the person to speak to about her secret knowledge? She was concerned about Fanny flirting mildly with a young man: what must she think of her other stepdaughter's prospects, if she knew about Brighton?

It was a thought – but still, no more than a thought. If you were going to speak out, Caroline nagged herself, the time to do it was right at the beginning. Lady Milner would think – *anyone* would think – why now?

Isabella would think it.

Dear God, look – we are chess-pieces, Caroline thought, as she cast her eye over the party. The fitful autumn sunlight made chequered patterns on the grass, across which the scattered figures moved in purposive clusters. Matthew talking about his aunt Sophia and the missing letter to Captain Brunton, who was divided between courteous attention and looking back for Lady Milner: Isabella being tugged away from Mr Leabrook's arm by a laughing Fanny, urging her to run a race: Maria trying to tease a response from Stephen, stalking saturnine ahead. In this game, Caroline reflected gloomily, there is no doubt that I am only a pawn, whilst Richard Leabrook of course is a king – king of all this lush domain. Yet a pawn could checkmate a king; and she felt he knew this. Even the back of his dark, elegant head – which was all he tended to present to her – seemed to say it.

The summer-house, very new, was meant to look very old. It was a Gothick summer-house. 'Ah, yes,' Stephen muttered, 'where the knights of old would unbutton their hauberks and sit down to a nice dish of tea.'

'Ignore him, Richard, he's being an absolute bear today,' Isabella said, giving her brother a mock slap.

'I plead innocence,' Mr Leabrook said smiling, 'as far as the design goes: my improver would insist on it. Echoes the character of the landscape, or something. He made it sound very fine.'

'I think it's delightful,' Isabella said; and turning to Caroline, 'Just think, Caro, when it *is* summer, what pleasant afternoons we can laze away here—'

'My dear, surely you are disposing of Miss Fortune's time quite unwarrantably,' Mr Leabrook said: the smile still in place, but with no light behind it.

'Oho, that is because you fear we shall gossip about you,' Isabella said laughingly, 'and to be sure, my dear Richard, we shall: I shall tell Caroline all about your shocking vices that you hid till after your marriage, and we shall sigh and shake our heads over you.'

There was a suffocating constraint: Isabella looked perplexed again; and when a scream rang out, Caroline thought for a moment that she had done it herself, for there was certainly one building up inside her. But it was Lady Milner – a large spider had run over her foot.

'Look, madam, there's really no harm in them,' Mr Carraway said, gently picking it up in cupped hands. 'They are actually rather pretty creatures—'

'I do not find them so, sir, and I do not wish to look,' Lady Milner said, in her most repressive tone. 'Do you think we might return to the house now, Mr Leabrook? I grow a little chilled.'

They went back to eat, drink, and not be merry; and after the meal Caroline found herself appropriated by Mrs Leabrook, who took her to view her dovecotes and poultry-houses, for she had heard how interested Miss Fortune was in all matters of husbandry. As Caroline could only with difficulty and effort tell a sheep from a haystack, it was hard to see where Mrs Leabrook could have heard any such thing; not that *hearing* was the lady's style. Caroline might as well have said what she was thinking – 'Your hen-houses, ma'am, are the most supremely dull thing I have ever been shown in my life' – for all the attention Mrs Leabrook paid to her comments. Poking for eggs, stroking wattles, she talked mercilessly. It was like someone reading out loud from an endless bad book. A series of swift transitions took her from the diseases of fowls to pride in her children.

'I can say, as so few can say in these times, that they have never brought me a grey hair. Richard's first concern, on his becoming engaged to Miss Milner, was for my comfort and security – new carpets and fireplaces to be ordered at once for the Dower House – though I said to him, "My dear, you know I don't feel the cold," which is true, I'm peculiarly hardy in that way, as was my mother, it's in the blood I dare say and, ah –' gasping in air '– that has always been his way, the thoughtfulness and regard, and one sees it too in Georgiana – that's his sister, you won't have met her, she's away at school in Brighton – the tenderest-hearted creature, and I'm glad to say none of that hard smartness one sees in girls these days, indeed when she was to go away to school I was anxious that she should not come back with a set of nasty affectations, the more so as one hears there is a rakish tone to Brighton, not that I have been there myself, because I adore the country and never like to leave it, but Richard was quite as concerned as I, for he has the most scrupulous regard for his sister's delicacy, and he personally made sure that the establishment was of the strictest principles with respect to the morals of the pupils – made thorough enquiries into the character of such males as are permitted to cross the threshold – drawing-masters and the like – in short not even a father could have done more . . .'

Having to listen to encomiums on Richard Leabrook's chivalrous attitude to the fair sex was, perhaps, a little too much after a morning that had left Caroline feeling like an overwound clock. Certainly something caused her, when she escaped from pullets and pouters and returned to the drawing room, to lose her temper in the most uncharacteristic and unfortunate fashion.

There, Matthew was holding forth about Brighton – something about its being a mere fishing-village fifty years ago, and now it was a handsomer town than Bath, or he thought so at any rate, and – 'Is it not? Miss Fortune, you know Brighton well, would you not agree? We are talking about Brighton, you know, and—'

'Brighton is a place I never think of without sorrow and vexation, Mr Downey,' Caroline burst out uncontrollably, 'and I wish you would be good enough to bore us with some other subject.'

A double regret – for the rudeness, and for the dangerous hint of revelation – occupied Caroline during the suspended silence that followed. It was Matthew himself who broke it with a gust of high, thin laughter.

'Oh! you are joking – of course you are – it is only her way of joking, you know. I remember it from Brighton. It is a sort of joking I have never quite understood myself – you seemed to get on better with it, Leabrook, as I recall – but there, I dare say it is my fault, I am rather serious by nature. Not that I dislike a joke by any means. I do believe I have rather a sly sense of humour – I remember making my father laugh uncommonly once with a remark about opera-singers . . .'

Matthew's invincible egotism came to her rescue: an undeserved rescue, she felt remorsefully, for there were worse sins than being a bore – but it had been that sort of day, and she could have yelled with thankfulness when Stephen, who had long been broodingly silent, said with his abrupt decisiveness that they should be going, and had the carriage bespoke before anyone could protest.

Not that anyone seemed likely to do so: even Mr Leabrook was half-hearted in his pleas that they would stay a little longer. Caroline had no doubt that he was glad to see *her* leave; and the bow, the look, the chill emanation she got from him in the drive at parting suggested that he wished she were going somewhere a good deal further off, and hotter, than Wythorpe Rectory.

Chapter XVII

'Oh, Caro! You too?' Fanny said. 'But I have already had the lecture from *him* – old Jack Tar within – and you may be sure I took it *very* amiss.'

It had not been easy to contrive this meeting alone with Fanny: Caroline had been forced to the expedient of calling at the Manor, waiting for Fanny to take her dogs to exercise, and then jumping up to go with her – which Isabella, settled in for a confidential chat, plainly found most odd. Now, with Fanny firing up as soon as she had tentatively mentioned the subject of Mr Carraway, Caroline inwardly cursed Lady Milner for this commission she had laid upon her. Also she outwardly cursed Fanny's spaniel, which had scrabbled its muddy forepaws on her best sprig muslin.

'Leo, go down. Well, I wonder who will address me on the subject next,' Fanny said, with asperity. 'I declare I shall have to start making an appointments book.'

'My dear Fanny, I don't intend a lecture. I care for your welfare, and I know that Lady Milner—'

'Oh, Caro, I don't mean anything against *you*, and I know perfectly well what has happened: Augusta has put you up to it, hasn't she? She cornered you yesterday, and browbeat you into a promise, and so here you are.' Fanny squeezed her arm. 'I wouldn't even mind if you did give me the lecture, because I'd know you wouldn't mean a word of it and were only trying to oblige my Pharisee of a step-mother. Now with *him* it's a different matter. He came hemming and hawing to me last night after dinner and just when I wondered whether I was under sentence of court-martial or something he began to talk about Mr Carraway – about Charles. At least so one gathered through all the coughing and circumlocuting – is that a word? Heavy hints about the danger of too great an intimacy after too short an acquaintance and so on. "Captain Brunton," said I, "I am in full agreement: I have not known you very long, and you really have very little connection with me or my family, and so it is quite inappropriate for you to address me on these intimate terms, on a matter that is really none of your business." I turned that rather neatly, did I not?'

'What did he say to that?' Caroline said, part amused, but inclining also to feel sorry for the Captain, facing the utter ruthlessness of youth: cannon-shot was nothing to it.

'Oh, he harrumphed and havered, and at last he grumbled that I should think about what he said, not merely for my stepmother's sake but for my own. Now, tell me, were *your* instructions pretty much the same?'

'I am, I know, all too easily persuaded, but the last time I took *instructions* was when I was at school,' Caroline said, as temperately as she could.

'I have offended you,' cried Fanny, almost with excitement, 'and you tell me so, instead of going all stiff and brooding! That is what I like about you, Caro. Oh, I don't mind what you say to me. I will even admit that one *must* be careful in these matters, yes, and that there are many silly young girls who have come to grief through not being so. Leo, don't roll in that. But the fact is I am not silly. My head is not easily turned.'

'I suppose we none of us like to think we are silly. But all must acknowledge that they are capable of silliness, from time to time: Lord knows, I am.'

'And what a dreary world, if it were not so! Imagine a world without folly and excess! It would be death! But I hardly need say this to you. *You* have never voluntarily worn the shackles of convention. You do not subscribe, I'm sure, to the belief that grown people with rational minds somehow do not know what is best for them.'

'No, I don't believe that,' Caroline answered honestly. 'But . . .'

'But me no buts,' Fanny laughed, taking her arm, 'for you know what I say is true.'

Caroline sighed. As so often with Fanny, one felt disarmingly helpless, as if bound with a multitude of tiny threads.

Well, Lady Milner, I tried, she thought, as she walked home; and was pursued all the way through the village by Lady Milner's imagined stare expressing Lady Milner's imagined thought: *You did not try very hard, Miss Fortune!* She was quite sick of it when she turned in at the Rectory gate, and found loosely tethered there a horse she did not recognize, a horse steaming as from a hard ride.

'Mr Downey!'

Matthew it was who stood beneath the porch, the riding-crop raised in his hand to rap. Arrested, he swung round upon her staring, his face scarlet up to the stormy hairline, his nostrils as wide as the horse's.

Intense, even for Matthew.

'Mr Downey, this is an unexpected pleasure. Please, won't you bring your horse round to the stable, where—'

'It's not my horse. It belongs to Leabrook,' he said hollowly, still staring.

'Oh. Yes, of course, it would be. Well, let me tell Jackie, and he—'

'The horse will do very well where it is. I do not intend a long stay. What I do require –' Matthew mopped his brow with his gloves '– is a private interview with you, Miss Fortune.'

'With me? How odd – I cannot conceive what . . .' She waited, nervously smiling; but though she had no notion of what it could mean, she feared it was not good. Short of vaulting over the hedge and running away, however, she could see no help for it. Matthew looked dramatically determined.

Uncle John was in his study, steeped in the Early Fathers, and Aunt Selina was on a sick visit: it was simple enough to take Matthew into the winter parlour, close the door, and brace herself. Was it her rudeness yesterday? Perhaps he had thought of something tremendously rude to say in return. Perhaps he was going to challenge her to a duel. She had never heard of that happening to a lady – but suppose it did? Should one accept? And who chose weapons? The one receiving the challenge, surely. In that case she would choose something, like spoons, that could not do much damage. Her eyes strayed longingly to the sideboard.

'Mr Downey, you must be thirsty – let me—'

'Miss Fortune, I must speak first, and ask you only to hear me. It is far from my habit to dictate the conversation in this way, but the circumstances . . .' Giving her a long, bleak look, he drew a paper from his pocket. 'This,' he intoned, as if she were unlikely ever to have heard of such a thing before, 'is a letter.'

'Ah? Oh – you have heard from your aunt at last?'

'Oh, Miss Fortune, this – this parade of yours is pitiable,' he groaned, shaking his head. 'The letter is not from my aunt. You may as well hear its contents, though you must know very well its import. It is from my aunt's lawyer in London. At Symond's Inn. He is a Mr Coker. "Dear Sir"—'

'Mr Downey, please, I must ask you to desist. I do not want to hear a letter from your aunt's lawyer – I do not see why on earth I should – these are surely private matters with which I have nothing to do.'

Matthew laughed shrilly. 'Oh, excellent! Oh, you surpass yourself, Miss Fortune – this is your famous joking, I take it, and there was never a better . . .' He staggered about, laughing without mirth.

'If you do not begin behaving like a man in his senses, Mr Downey, I shall be obliged to ring.' Obliged to ring: how stagey I sound, she thought; but the whole scene had a feeling of unreality, as if the Rectory's solid walls would wobble at any moment.

'Very well.' He straightened, glanced over the letter with glazed eyes. 'I will play your charade, Miss Fortune, and tell you what this letter is about. Then you can see if it answers your hopes – your expectations. Mr Coker informs me – on Aunt Sophia's behalf, as she does not choose to have any further communication with me directly . . .' He gathered himself, jaw convulsively working. 'Informs me that I am finished. He does not use that word, to be sure. I know too well that the law does not talk in such terms. Still, that is what has happened. I am forever excluded from Aunt Sophia's favour. My allowance is stopped forthwith, and I am to consider all future prospects, of settlements, conveyance of property, inheritance – all my expectations, in a word – at an end. There you have the bones of it, Miss Fortune. Are you satisfied?'

'Why? I mean – yes, I mean why should this be a satisfaction to me, Mr Downey? But really I don't understand any of it. Why would Mrs Catling do such a thing?'

'Oh, you keep it up finely, Miss Fortune, I'll say that for you – brilliantly done! Thus, you will make me rehearse my humiliation before you, as well as having caused it in the first place.'

'Caused it?' Caroline shook her head and went to the sideboard. 'All I can think, Mr Downey, is that you have been given the run of Mr Leabrook's wine-cellar; and all I can suggest is that you take another glass. Because often that is the one that brings you full circle back to sobriety, I find. As for this letter – well, is it not perhaps merely a threat? Mrs Catling always did like to keep you –' she nearly said dangling '– in suspense.'

'I hardly think Aunt Sophia would employ her solicitor to make an empty threat. Besides, I have a communication from my banker also. The allowance is indeed stopped, and she has ordered my advance on next month's to be repaid. No, Miss Fortune, it is all real, I assure you: you are to be congratulated: if this was your ultimate aim, you may be easy, for it is all achieved.' He ignored the glass of canary she offered him and paced and prowled. 'Your malice towards me I can in a sense comprehend – for one need look no further than motives of interest – but to betray a sacred confidence – and worst of all to betray Perdita—'

'Perdita? Your – the lady in London? Now I am convinced that one or other of us is going mad. I know nothing of Perdita, Mr Downey, but what you chose to tell me.'

'Precisely! And that is precisely what Aunt Sophia now knows!' He brandished the letter aloft, his head back, as if he were reading it in bed. 'Listen. "It has come to my client's knowledge that a clandestine engagement of a most disreputable character has long subsisted between yourself and a Miss Perdita Lockwood, of Snow Hill, London. The wilful deceit practised upon my client, who supplied the above-mentioned funds on the express understanding that nothing of this kind would be entertained, is such as to render it impossible there should be any further communication, in correspondence or in person, between my client and yourself. The funds already advanced, my client is inclined to regard as money gained under false pretences . . ." There follow certain veiled threats that any approach from me to my aunt will be viewed as intrusion and molestation – oh, but you have the flavour now, I'm sure, Miss Fortune. Is it piquant enough for you? Do you relish it?'

Caroline sat down, moving through the slow mist of realization.

'You think – Mr Downey, you think I told Mrs Catling about your secret engagement.'

'I beg your pardon, it is not a *secret* any more. It was a *secret* that I entrusted to only one person, Miss Fortune: yourself.'

'Mr Downey, you are mistaken,' Caroline said, meeting his wild glare as calmly as she could. 'I am sorry indeed for what has happened – it must be a prodigious shock to you; but this shock has made you jump to a wrong, an entirely wrong conclusion, sir. You must think in what other ways this information could have come to Mrs Catling's ears—'

'There are none! Upon my soul, Miss Fortune, you have a curious notion of what a man means when he says he is entrusting you with an exclusive confidence – as if it were the trivial secret of a silly schoolgirl which she shares with a dozen of her playfellows! No one knows – or rather no one *knew* about Perdita but yourself. And to be sure, I do not *want* to believe you could have done this. It was because I liked you – trusted you – that I let the secret out in the first place. And yet I fear there are horribly good grounds for believing it, Miss Fortune – I have been putting two and two together, and they most assuredly make four! Indeed I do believe I must have something of the clairvoyant about me – for I was only remarking to you the other day, was I not, that it might be possible for you to be reinstated among my aunt's acquaintance? And meanwhile you already had your little plan in hand, to reinstate yourself *much* more fully!'

'Good God. If I have you right, sir, I hardly know which to marvel at most – your impudence or your absurdity. Mr Downey, I am most happily reconciled with a kind and loving family: I can want nothing more: and you actually suppose that I spend my time in making mischief between you and your aunt, in hopes that the old crocodile might leave me something after all?'

'It is not what I wish to believe of you, Miss Fortune,' said Matthew, who remained Matthew enough to make a pious wince at the word *crocodile*. 'But then neither was the betrayal of my confidence. And, in truth, perhaps the signs were there to see, for you have behaved very disobligingly to me lately. My habitual fault is thinking the best of people; but now I can only draw the worst of conclusions, and hope that you can sleep at night, knowing that you have wrecked the happiness of two people – one of them an innocent, artless, trusting creature, not framed for such ills—'

'Mr Downey, I say again there must be some other explanation. I suggest you ignore those threats and apply to Mrs Catling herself, to discover where she heard this intelligence – if she will reveal it, of course – but really, that is your concern and not mine.' She rose. 'And if you have nothing else to say to me beyond baseless accusation—'

'I came,' he said, drooping like a mournful marionette, 'hoping – hoping at least that you would acknowledge the truth. That's all. I am no faint-heart when it comes to unpleasant truth, you know – indeed I have always taken a bracing sort of pleasure in facing it, just as I enjoy a cold, a really cold bath . . .' For a moment, being interested in himself again made Matthew almost cheerful; but then his brow puckered, and he snatched up his hat and riding-crop as if he had caught her stealing them. 'I shall apply to her – I shall do what I can – but I know there is no recovering from such a position. So, what do you intend doing to Maria, Miss Fortune? She will surely come before you in my aunt's will.'

'I have a plan to push her off a cliff, of course, though I must overcome the trifling obstacle of our being fifty miles inland. Really, Mr Downey, you are ridiculous.'

'Still brazening it out, eh? I suppose you have to. The mask must not slip. And to think I welcomed you!' Emotion made him alliterative: 'It was a black day that brought you to Brighton!'

'No, it was not, it was a sunny day, I recall it perfectly,' Caroline snapped, feeling tears of vexation and hysterical laughter pulling her both ways. She turned from him, drank off the canary wine herself, and was presently informed by the sound of stamping boots and slamming doors that Mr Downey had left.

I swear he slammed one of them twice, she said to herself, and then the laughter won – silent overcharged spasms of laughter, not very far from the tears; she was as sorry for Matthew as the situation allowed, but she could not like being accused and traduced in this fashion. After a while, and a little more canary, she sat down to consider how it was that Mrs Catling had found out about the engagement, but soon dismissed the question as no great mystery. For all his denials, she thought, a man who liked talking about himself as much as Matthew did was bound to let it slip in any number of places; whilst a woman as morbidly suspicious as Mrs Catling was surely not above having her nephew informally spied upon. No, the more pressing question was what he would do now. Fly to Brighton, of course: but before he did, would he keep his suppositions to himself?

Knowing Matthew, she rather doubted it. Confirmation of a sort arrived little more than an hour later. The maid, and a piercing whistle of 'Sally In Our Alley', announced the arrival of Stephen Milner.

'Miss Fortune, how d'you do?' he asked, sauntering in with his hands in his pockets. 'Would you like me to stir that sulky fire for you? And, more importantly, what the devil have you done to Mr Downey?'

Caroline groaned. 'Not very well, yes, please, and nothing at all, are the answers to those questions, Mr Milner.'

'You do look rather dreadful,' Stephen observed sympathetically, wielding the poker. 'Well, I hope it is something deliciously wicked: it will make such a refreshing contrast with damnable wedding-clothes and bride-cake. Oh, I forgot.' He reached into the breast of his coat and drew out an indiscriminate ball of fluff, which resolved itself into a tortoiseshell kitten that yawned a display of needle teeth. 'I've found homes for all of Sukey's litter: this is the last. Will you have her? She's a good sort. Well bred and civil. Rather an Evangelical in her opinions, but then they're everywhere nowadays.'

'Oh, Mr Milner, thank you – she's beautiful – I must ring for a saucer of milk . . .' Caroline hugged the mewling weightlessness to her breast. She did not need to feign delight: just now it was wonderful to embrace a creature that was entirely without opinions about her. The prickling of the tiny claws through the thin muslin of her gown, a sensation that was simultaneously tantalizing, pleasant, and nearly unbearable, somehow reminded her of something. 'What shall I call her? I seem to see Matilda in that face, but I'm not sure. Oh, d'you know, Mr Milner? I never had a dog or cat before.'

'I do know, or guessed. The effect should be to domesticate you, though we'll have to see about *that*. Also, having a cat is good preparation in case you end up an old maid.'

'I always wonder, Matilda, whether Mr Milner's charm comes naturally, or whether he works at it.'

'A little of both. Now pray tell what Mr Downey meant by his extraordinary descent on the Manor this morning. He came in with his hair looking worse than mine – refused Augusta's tea as if it were hemlock – strode about making none of the idiotic remarks about the weather and his neighbours' business that the morning caller is most strictly obliged to make – at last announced, with a lot of dramatic breathing through his nose, that this was a sort of farewell call, as he had to leave as soon as possible. I'm not sure, but I do believe he said he was forced to go and confront his unlucky and undeserved fate – four syllables in undeserved, if you please – does that sound like something Mr Downey would say? I don't know him very well.'

'You have made him live,' confirmed Caroline, glumly.

'Well. Isabella asked, in that plain, innocent way of hers, whether he had had bad news – and off he went into this desperate cracked laugh. Yes, says he, if bad news be the wilful destruction of his credit with the one person in the world upon whose goodwill he depended. I quote again, by the way. He cannot talk about it, he goes on, except to say he has been monstrously used, and if we would know more, ask *her*. With a gesture hither. So.' Stephen sat down, stretching and crossing his long, booted legs with a flex of anticipation. 'I insist upon hearing *everything*. Except the dull parts. I say, it wasn't a proposal of marriage, was it?'

'To me? Good Lord, no.'

'Well, I didn't think it could be,' he agreed, with a vigorous nod. 'That would be altogether too absurd.'

'Certainly, it would,' she said, giving him a sour look. 'No, Mr Downey is not so lost to all sense and reason as *that*, to be sure. But really, it can be of no use to anyone if I do tell you – and as I'm sure you will hear sooner or later—'

'Oh, there's no fun in that. Besides, I'm impatient. And besides besides, I'm more inclined to believe even you than Mr Downey, who for all his qualities seems to me to have a strong touch of the Gascon about him. So, not a proposal – what then? Can it be something worse, and indeed *is* there anything worse?'

'Mr Milner, I can't tell you, because – well, no, that's nonsense, because it isn't a secret any more. Oh, dear.' She gave the kitten her forefinger to bite, studying the cunning patterns of its coat. 'You have heard that I met the Downeys when I was living at Brighton. They are the only relatives of Mrs Catling, who was my employer—'

'And an old dragon.'

'Have I said that?'

'Not in so many words. Hints and suggestions.'

'Well – certainly Mrs Catling is a difficult and capricious woman. Not just to someone like me, but to her relatives also—'

'Prune-faced, flint-hearted old dragon, in fact.' He shrugged, squinted knowingly. 'Hints again. I'm sorry, do go on.'

'The Downeys came on a visit—'

'Ah, this was when you met Leabrook. Sorry again.'

'We were a good deal together,' Caroline resumed, giving him a glare, 'and got along very well, and presently Mr Downey favoured me with his confidence. He was almost entirely dependent for his present comfort and future prospects on Mrs Catling, and was accordingly anxious not to forfeit her favour. And one crucial element in this was that he should not marry, or undertake to marry, at least before he was thirty.'

'Hm, the dragon improves on acquaintance,' Stephen said approvingly. 'By the by, when you say he favoured you with his confidence, I take that to mean burdened, cursed, and afflicted you with it.'

'I'm glad someone understands that,' she said, with a reluctant smile, 'even if it is you.'

'Spoken like my old adversary. Go on.'

'Well, Mr Downey confided to me that he had contracted an engagement – a *secret* engagement.'

'Quite right too: a man should always conceal his vices.'

Ignoring that, Caroline went on: 'He knew that Mrs Catling would fiercely disapprove, indeed that she might cut him out of her will if she knew, which was always the warning she held up before him. But he was, it seemed, very much in love. She – the lady was, is, certainly not eligible. She is poor. Her father lives at Snow Hill and is an apothecary. But a good one, that is to say a virtuous one – Mr Milner, I cannot tell this if you keep laughing.'

'Forgive me – it's just the virtuous apothecary. I feel as if I have stepped into a sentimental comedy. And what can an unvirtuous one be like? Poisons his patients, perhaps. Charges them double for a bottle of coloured water with a fancy name. Oh, wait, that's an ordinary apothecary.' He put up surrendering arms. 'Yes, I have done.'

'Well, so have I in a way – for that was really all that happened. I listened, and sympathized, and promised very sincerely to keep Mr Downey's secret, as it was certainly likely to do him a great deal of harm with Mrs Catling if it were known—'

'The prune-faced dragon wouldn't want to be allied with a saintly apothecary,' said Stephen, nodding: then, wonderingly: 'Who could imagine I would ever say *that* sentence?'

'I wish he hadn't told me; but it always seemed to be a relief to him to talk about it.'

'Well, well. It appears a lot more went on at Brighton than one might have supposed.'

Caroline intently regarded the toe of her shoe. 'Yes. No. Oh, damn and blast and set fire to it all – and especially bloody Brighton – I swear if I hear that word once more I shall scream the rafters down.'

'Brighton,' Stephen said, and listened carefully to the result. 'Only a moderate scream – I knew you were exaggerating.'

'Is everything all right, my dear?' Uncle John's bespectacled face peered round the door. 'Oh! hello, Stephen.'

'Hello, Uncle John – didn't mean to disturb you – Miss Fortune was just singing me an air from the new opera of Signor Buffoni.'

'Ah! I am an old Handel man myself,' Dr Langland remarked benignly, and went off humming something not by Handel.

'Well, I can guess the rest,' Stephen said, with his boots up on the fender. 'The dragon has now found out about the engagement.'

'Yes – and disinherited him for it.'

Stephen whistled. 'Decisive in her. That was good juicy swearing just now, by the by. So, there remains just the one question – did you do it?'

'Mr Downey thinks so. He marched in here and accused me of betraying him and there was nothing I could say that would convince him otherwise, and now I'm feeling thoroughly mumpish and now *you* don't believe me—'

'Oh, but I didn't say that,' Stephen said, grinning. 'I merely posed the question, as it's sure to be in the air with Mr Downey storming about in that way of his.'

This seemed to Caroline's irritated nerves to be refining a little too much. 'Well, now that you have posed it, how do you answer it?'

'Surely there's another question first, and that is, why should you care what I think?'

'I don't,' she said, through tight lips, 'but I do care if people generally are inclined to believe this tale, and you will do, Mr Milner, as a representative sample.'

'Oh, I wouldn't say I am very representative . . .' He grinned again, yawned, relented. 'No, I don't believe it. It rather goes against the grain to say so, because as I remarked when we first met, you look like trouble, and I believe you are trouble and, lo, here is trouble amongst us. But no . . . Now what does Downey suppose was your motive? Mere malignity? Or the hope of gain from the old dragon? Well, there you are, you see: there is a kind of sneaking pettiness about this business that I just don't associate with you. If you were going to make mischief, I imagine it on a much grander scale.'

'Thank you – I think. What did Isabella say?'

'Oh, Bella adores you,' he said, shaking his head as at some pitiful aberration, 'and you know she'll go to any lengths rather than think the worst of someone.' He unfolded or ungangled himself and stood. 'Well, no doubt we shall hear more. Quite the most enjoyable fuss we have had in Wythorpe since Farmer Stride's bull got in the wheelyard.'

'I wish I could share your enjoyment, Mr Milner,' Caroline said – and then, hearing how pathetic she sounded, laughed wearily. 'Dear me, now I'm being as dramatic as Mr Downey.'

'Put it from your mind. Nine days' wonder. Ah, look, Matilda has made you her first offering. Come and dine with us tomorrow.' He was gone: somehow, unseen and in passing, briefly pressing her hand.

She could not quite put it from her mind: it was always there, like a rough place on a tooth to which the tongue keeps returning. The evening at the Rectory passed with typical pleasantness: an early dinner, backgammon with her uncle, some chapters from *Evelina*, a long session of play with Matilda and a ball of wool, chat with Aunt Selina who, unobtrusively, asked if all was well with her and did not press when she said yes, a good supper with tartlets and cheese and wine; and throughout Caroline kept thinking indignantly: And this is what Matthew Downey supposes I do not value in the slightest, compared to fawning on his wretched aunt!

Then the anger would turn inside out, and she would feel sorry for him, considering how hard he had worked to please Mrs Catling; and before bed she even contemplated writing a letter to that lady herself. First she would ask Mrs Catling to confirm that it was not she who had communicated the information – that was for her own peace; and then put in a word for Matthew. She even took a sheet of paper and mended a pen – but it would not do. Any kind of ingratiation with Mrs Catling was beyond her. She wanted to demand why getting engaged to a girl of low birth was so shocking, and why she couldn't just divide her money between Matthew and Maria, and make everyone happy. She wanted to call Mrs Catling a prune-faced, flint-hearted old dragon. Instead she screwed up the sheet of paper into a ball and amused Matilda with it until the kitten curled up to sleep inside her shoe.

The same sapped and instant tiredness toppled Caroline into bed, though for some reason she turned restless a little later, and woke to find herself amorously, inexplicably embracing the bolster.

Chapter XVIII

Frost chalked the Rectory roofs and crisped the lawns the next morning. It was as if winter, like an invading army breaking through defences, had stolen nearer overnight: it was a day of gunmetal skies, dead leaves in black heaps, stark air smelling of woodsmoke: a day that touched the instincts and prodded you to go outdoors, because soon you would not be able to. Caroline took a long cheek-tingling walk that turned into a call on the Hampsons and then – although she was to dine there later – a call at the Manor too. In spite of Stephen's assurances, she wanted to know that she still had Isabella's good opinion.

The door was answered by a maid, but it was Fanny who appeared breathlessly in the doorway a moment later and hustled her aside. 'Go, go, Jane, I'll see to this. Caro! Oh, my dear Caro – will you allow me . . . ?'

To her intense surprise Caroline found herself being tightly embraced by Fanny, who then glanced over her shoulder at the empty hall and whispered: 'Now, before you go any further, I want you to know: I do not believe a word of it.'

'Oh! Oh, you mean what Mr Downey said. Well, I thank you, Fanny, very kindly for saying so – I did hope—'

'Oh, not that! Though that too – but you know there is more, much more. Of course you wouldn't know – but you soon will. Lord, such uproar as we have been in! But as long as you bear in mind that *I* do not believe it. Come, I shall take your arm as we go in.'

'Fanny, you alarm me – what more? What has happened?'

Fanny fixed her with a solemn look, though her cheeks bloomed with excitement. 'Mr Downey was here again early this morning. Mr Leabrook was with him. Mr Downey was going to Brighton to see his aunt, and so Mr Leabrook was driving him in his gig to the coach-office at Huntingdon – but they stopped off here. To talk to Isabella. Oh, Lord, such uproar! – but we had better go in.'

Had her bewildered mind been in a state to judge, Caroline would have classified the scene in the drawing room as peculiar confusion rather than uproar. One of Fanny's dogs had knocked down the tea-tray, but no one seemed to have noticed: Isabella was rapidly and strenuously walking up and down – *ploughing* up and down, as if through mud: whilst Lady Milner, who had plainly been in tears, was making a perspiring Captain Brunton search her reticule for sal-volatile, an exercise to which his large hands were wholly unsuited.

Then they all saw Caroline, and everything stopped.

'Yes, she is here, you see,' said Fanny, at her side, 'and I have told her that *I* do not believe a word of it.'

'Whatever is the matter? Bella?' All at once Caroline felt as if she were breathing gauze. 'Won't someone please tell me what's going on?'

'Miss Fortune, it is all very shocking, and I am not sure – I am not at all sure we should be receiving you here,' Lady Milner said, regarding her as if she were an unpleasantly bright light. 'It is all so very unprecedented, I hardly know what to do for the best – but probably you had better go away—'

'Nonsense, Augusta,' said – to general surprise – Captain Brunton. 'Miss Fortune is the very person who should be here, to settle this matter once and for all. But as it chiefly concerns Miss Milner, I think we should leave her and Miss Fortune to talk alone.' He put his hand firmly under Lady Milner's elbow. 'And you, Miss Fanny, I'm sure are wholly in agreement.'

'Oh! yes – to be sure,' said a staring Fanny, allowing herself to be piloted out.

'But, Edward – what about Stephen?' Lady Milner protested. 'He really should be consulted.'

'And will be, as soon as he can be found, and as he must be somewhere about the estate, I'm sure your man will bring him back soon,' Captain Brunton said, with renewed firmness; and presently the door was closed, and Caroline faced Isabella, who was still restlessly ploughing.

'My dear Isabella, if you want to polish the floorboards, there are easier ways,' Caroline said with a tentative smile.

'Captain Brunton,' Isabella said, as if she had not spoken, 'surprising – a crisis brings out the best in him. I think it is only ordinary life that makes him awkward.'

'I don't like the sound of that *crisis*. Bella, please stop walking up and down.'

'I can't. If I do, I think I shall faint.'

'Well, then sit down. Here.' Caroline drew up a chair. The sight of her friend's stricken white face turned her sick. 'I think I must sit down too. What *is* this about? Is it what Mr Downey said? I wanted to come and see you about that. It is—'

'Mr Downey,' Isabella repeated blankly, as if trying to place the name. She sat down and looked at her hands. 'Yes, I suppose it begins with Mr Downey. Began. Oh, Caroline, I wish I could suddenly wake up.'

'Fanny said he had been here. With – your fiancé.'

Isabella nodded. With her gaze still dully fixed on her hands, as if the words were written there, she said: 'We had heard about Mr Downey's aunt disinheriting him. And how he blamed you. Surely not true, we all thought. But Richard – Richard had different ideas. He confessed to Mr Downey that he was not at all surprised – that he was sorry to say that he *could* believe it of you. Mr Downey wanted to know why – and so Richard came out with it. And once it was out, he thought I had better know at last, and he stopped here this morning to talk to me about it. What happened when you were together at Brighton.'

'Good God,' breathed Caroline, 'he *told* you?' And then: Oh, no. Stupid, stupid Caroline. No, no.

With great effort Isabella met her eyes. 'He said he was sorry that he had not spoken before – but he knew I was fond of you, and thought it best to leave it – but now with what had happened to his poor friend Mr Downey, he could not keep silent. He was willing to believe you had changed, but this showed otherwise.'

Caroline experienced the odd sensation of simultaneously feeling the heat of the fire at her side whilst being cold, absolutely cold from toe to crown.

'What did he say happened in Brighton?'

Isabella's eyes went to her hands again. 'He said you threw yourself at him most shamelessly. That you several times put him in an embarrassing position, even though he made it clear he was engaged to be married. That at last, one night at the Castle, you actually offered yourself to him, which was why he felt he ought to leave Brighton at once. He said he could understand it,' Isabella hurried on, as Caroline launched herself from her chair, 'for you were plainly unhappy with your situation, and longed to escape it – at any cost. And he felt that instead of just rebuffing you, he ought to have warned you about the likely consequences of your conduct. When he learned that you had lost your position, he suspected some such behaviour had driven Mrs Catling to your dismissal, though again he did not like to say so, because of our friendship. It has been a great difficulty to him—'

'And, oh, Bella,' Caroline cried, unable to contain herself any longer, 'do you believe him? Do you believe that what Mr Leabrook has just told you is the truth?'

'Richard is the man I love and am to marry,' Isabella said slowly, 'and so in that sense I must believe him. But, Caro, there is nothing I would rather not believe than this. I'm lucky, I have never been in a dependent position such as you were at Brighton, so I don't know what the discomfort of it can drive you to – and I do not want to judge you harshly – but to think of you knowing he was engaged to be married – and how you have said nothing of this episode all this time, and been so composed . . .'

Caroline stood looking down at her friend, and all at once the anger cooled down to a leaden, ashy sorrow.

'You do believe him,' she said, and in a few moments her mind seemed to take in whole tracts of understanding. He has done this because he fears me, she thought lucidly, and the fear has been building up, and now this accusation of Matthew's has given him an opportunity: he has seen a chance to get his blow in first, and he has taken it. Just as he saw me in Brighton as a chance for a cheap *amour*: Richard Leabrook is at heart an opportunist. Also he is a worse man even than I supposed, and he will surely make Isabella miserable. And there is nothing I can do, unless . . . 'Unless you choose to believe my account, Bella, I don't see how we can go on. And I'm so very sorry for that. It's what I have most feared, and why I haven't spoken. Will you hear it?'

Isabella trembled, but she nodded. 'Yes, Caro. Of course.'

Succinctly, plainly, and as unemotionally as she could manage, Caroline told her. She had so often imagined and rehearsed this in the toils of her indecision that it felt odd, almost unimportant, to be actually saying it at last. Almost – for as Isabella listened, motionless but for the rapid rise and fall of her breast and the visible ticking, like a smothered watch, at her throat, Caroline suspected that no more important moment had ever occurred in her friend's life – and even perhaps in her own.

'I'm not going to wake up,' Isabella said dully, when she had finished. 'This is real. This is not a dream.' She got up and began walking again. The frantic swish of her skirts afflicted Caroline's ear like fingernails on slate.

'Bella, that is the truth of what happened at Brighton. I wish, I so wish it were not. But I cannot defend myself against – against what is being said about me, without telling it. And if I have appeared composed, then indeed I have not been so inside. Ever since I first heard your fiancé's name, and realized who he was, I have been desperately troubled. I have thought over and over again what was best to do. It has been a horrible burden, especially because I could see no happy resolution either way.'

'If this is true,' Isabella said, pausing with her back to her, 'then he cannot love me. But why – why would he do that? We had had no quarrel when he went to Brighton – everything was as it should be – and when he came back he was kind and affectionate as ever. Was his love gone then . . . ?'

'All I can say is with me it was not a matter of love at all. I was to be – an adventure. A conquest. Bella, I was to be his doxy.'

Isabella turned: there was an emergent look of sympathy; then she shook it off. 'This – no, I cannot believe this, not of Richard. If he were like this, I would never have – no, his character is quite otherwise.'

'It appears so. But I am afraid you are deceived.'

'Yes. One way or another, I am surely deceived.' Isabella went to the window, confronting the bleached wintry light. 'You were not going to tell me this, Caroline – were you? It seems not: for it has only been forced out of you at last.'

Caroline spread her hands. 'I did not know what to do. I saw you so much in love, so eager to marry, so full of anticipation – and was I to destroy this? I don't ask you to put yourself in my position, with all you have to think of – only it *was* difficult.' Even to her own ears, this sounded thin, impoverished stuff. 'In the end I thought I shouldn't interfere, that my best course would be to wait and – and—'

'And bide your time?' Isabella said, with a bubble of bitterness. 'Oh, I'm sorry, Caro – only – only if it is possible that I have been deceived in Richard, then is it not equally possible that I have been deceived in you? That you invent this – account, merely out of your own jealous designs, in order to destroy what Richard and I have?'

Caroline could say nothing except: 'Oh, Isabella.' It issued from her as a pure extract of sorrow.

'I know. It sounds dreadful. I want to cut out my tongue for speaking of you so. But, you see, you are asking me to make just such an adjustment in my view of Richard. And it is so hard. I don't know if I can do it.'

'I fear you would have to sooner or later. It must surely come out. He was no novice in Brighton, Bella: he knew very well what he was about. I only wish I could convince you that my one concern, all the time, has been for you not to be hurt. And yet now – now the hurt has come.'

'True,' Isabella said, gasping back tears. 'I am hurt – and confused – and –' she covered her eyes '– tired, for some curious reason. What I must do – I must see Richard. I must face him. Look into his face, yes,' she added to herself. 'And I must think.' Now she looked up at Caroline – but not quite at her; and there was something heartbreaking in that. 'And for now, Caro, I must – I'm so sorry – I must think alone.'

Blindly, somehow, Caroline got out.

Well, it could hardly have gone worse, she thought, standing in the hall in such blank perplexity that she simply did not know where to find the door. It could hardly have gone worse – and then she looked up to see Stephen enter: windblown thatch, pale eyes, outdoor smell.

Up and up she looked, because he had never seemed so tall: unreachably so. The look he gave her was rueful, speculative, not unkind – but it seemed to come from such a great distance that her heart failed at the notion of speaking across it.

'Well, well,' he said softly, 'the curse of being always right! Trouble I said, and trouble it is!'

And again not unkindly, but seeming to leave a scrupulous distance between them, he found the door for her.

'My dear, you have told me it is the truth, and I believe it is the truth,' concluded Aunt Selina staunchly that night, after Caroline had poured out the whole story to her. She had waited till an unusually strong egg-nog, mixed by her own experienced hands, had sent her uncle into a doze over his *History of the Council of Trent* (margins generously sprinkled with explosive scrawls of 'Ah!' and 'INDUBITABLY'), for she did not want the unworldly Dr Langland's mind fretted with the matter, or her own with trying to explain it to him. Aunt Selina listened solemnly, exclaimed appropriately, and responded loyally. 'And now what I want you to do is get a good night's sleep, and let it all rest until the morrow. My one concern is that your health should not suffer from all this upset: you are already quite pale.'

Thus her dependable aunt, with one of her neat, dry kisses. And yet and yet. If anyone was pale, it was Aunt Selina. Plainly the whole thing shocked her: not simply her niece being propositioned in that way, but *anyone* being so propositioned: the very ideas of seduction, duplicity, and intrigue seemed to taint the pure air of the Rectory. And Caroline, for all her aunt's assurances, could not help wondering whether now, at last, those regretful thoughts of cuckoos and nests were passing through Aunt Selina's mind.

For Caroline the next day, two short letters.

From Maria Downey:

> *Ma chère Caroline – I write you from Hethersett and thus with a certain degree of delicious secrecy – maid's brother entrusted with smuggling out missive for a bribe of sixpence no less and so on. Of course you will know that Matthew has gone post-haste to Brighton to beat at Aunt Sophia's closed door and equally closed heart. Yes – yes, I heard all about it,* and *whom he blames for the catastrophe – and my dear, I may as well say I cannot believe it of you – there is something tasteless and provincial about it which I really do not connect with you. Not that I would blame you if you had told our aunt – dear, dear – Perdita from Snow-hill forsooth – what* was *he thinking? Anyhow I declined to go jaunting off to Brighton when I am comfortably settled here with the bountiful hospitality of the Leabrooks – you know I am quite a favourite with the garrulous Mrs L for some reason – perhaps because I don't mind her endless chatter, since it saves* me *the trouble of talking – for, my dear, you know me and trouble. – So, I told Matthew I would stay till the end of the week as we first agreed – thus I hope I may be able to call and see you* BUT *(oh, those capitals have quite worn me out) but this is very much contingent – a word I have never written before in my life by the by – because now one hears even more scandalous*

tales about you! – you wicked creature! I don't know what to believe but also, my dear, do not greatly care. I am the least moral creature in existence, and all I would like is the pleasure of your company again, if it can be managed. – Perhaps when I come to pursue your provoking long-legged friend at Wythorpe Manor? (Yes, I confess I am struggling, but I will get his heart in the end – or at least a little bit of it.) In the meantime, love and whatever you like – and oh! you wicked creature –

Yrs ever M.D.

From Fanny Milner:

My dear Caro – I told you I did not believe a word of it. And now I have heard from Bella what you said – and I am vindicated. Yours, *my dear Caro, must be the true account: and what a deceitful devil is Richard! I am shocked and disgusted at him. True fidelity is so vital – once sincerity is gone, so must be that respect on which alone the affections of the feeling heart repose: I know Charles would agree: it is one of our sacred beliefs. I may as well say Isabella continues in a much confused state – wretchedly torn and distressed; and in the meantime Stephen – what can I say? I cannot tell* what *he is thinking or which account he believes: only that he is dismally out of patience with what he calls 'the whole boiling', and is insistent that it must be settled somehow. He has summoned Richard (O! I should not write his treacherous name thus) to come for a thorough talk with him and Isabella – and he (Leabrook let me call him) is expected here any moment. Do you know that Augusta, after she got over the usual vapours, has actually kept rather quiet and sensible – is much concerned for Isabella – she even surrendered her seat by the fire for her! My dear Caro, rest assured I shall do everything in my power on* your *behalf – even if that can only be to let you know what happens. Courage, my dear friend! We shall smite the Philistines! Leo has a thorn in his right front paw by the by.*

Yours most affectionately, FANNY.

* * *

Caroline took what heart she could from these messages; still she could not be easy for a moment with the thought of what must be going on beneath the Manor roof today. Her aunt, observing her restlessness, at last found a task for her. She was to go and call upon a young woman who lived in Splash Lane, and tactfully ask her if she would come and do needlework at the Rectory two days a week. The young woman was maintaining the fiction that her husband, a carter, was on a long visit to relatives, when in fact he had deserted her to chase an actress from a strolling company who had acted *She Would and She Would Not* in Farmer Chivers's barn. Having fulfilled her errand, and found the young woman to be pitifully devoted still to the contemptible weasel who had impoverished her, Caroline turned for home thinking some hard thoughts about the perfidy of the male sex in general. But it was two particular members of that fraternity whose images, like wraith courtiers, went backwards before her as she walked. Richard Leabrook: what further lies might he be telling about her at this moment? And Stephen Milner: would he believe them?

This question produced in her a deep, sounding anxiety – which in turn set off a gust of irritation. She had done nothing wrong: it was nonsense to agonize as if she had. More important, surely, was self-belief. Did she have that? Do you have that, Caroline? Yes, came the conclusion, just as the woody flutter of a ring-dove startled from a tree above alerted her to the approach of rapid hoofbeats.

For a moment, turning, she thought Richard Leabrook was actually going to ride her down, and in that moment registered a pure surprise that life should include such melodrama. But it does not, and he did not. He reined in, he touched his hat: his superb face wore little more expression than boredom; yet there was an angry jut to the cheekbones, and something seething beneath his unraised voice as he said: 'Miss Fortune. You are to be congratulated on your success.'

'I don't know what you mean.'

'That's because I haven't told you yet,' he said pleasantly, unpleasantly. 'Miss Fortune, you will be glad to know –' he quieted his restive horse with a savage jerk on the reins '– that the wedding is off. Yes: all our plans are destroyed, Isabella is in tears, and there is to be no Christmas wedding as she had hoped: instead, an indefinite postponement. Well, are you glad?'

'Yes – assuming such a rudely posed question requires an answer, yes, sir, I am glad. But I am glad as I would be at a spell of sunshine – because it is simply a good thing, not something I intended or brought about.'

'Very pretty. Very tedious. Well, you were on your way to the Manor to find out the results of your efforts, I'm sure, so I've spared you the trouble. It was Milner who insisted the wedding be put off. Hm! *Now* he chooses to be decisive!'

There was a sharp contempt in his voice that pricked her beyond self-possession. 'If you were a better man, Mr Leabrook, I would call that unworthy. Mr Milner cares for his sister's well-being. It's lucky she has such people about her.'

'You would count yourself amongst this angelic host, of course. Despite what your jealousy has done to her. Oh, come, don't give me that look: what else are we to call it? From the moment you first set eyes on me again it has been plain that you would not rest content – you must be meddling – heaven knows why. Is it regret for saying no in Brighton? I may as well say I have long repented that moment's folly: I must have been bored indeed.'

'Mr Leabrook, you cannot insult me any more than you did that night. That is what I cannot forget – the insult – and it is what you, it seems, cannot understand. Since you maintain that you sincerely love Isabella, I ask you to consider how you would feel if she were so treated by a man.'

'But, my dear Miss Fortune,' he said, with a small laugh, 'you must see the difference. Isabella is a well-bred young woman of fortune: you are a mere soldier's get, brought up one jump ahead of the streets, and accustomed to hiring yourself out one way or another.' He touched his hat again. 'I'm sorry to be the bearer of unpleasant truths.'

'Ah, now a mystery has been solved. When I first met your mother, I wondered at her vulgarity, for it was a quality that you for all your bad character seemed to lack: but now I see the family resemblance. Good day, sir – I don't imagine we shall meet again.'

'Don't be so sure of that. There is a postponement, there is a temporary separation – Isabella says she requires time to think: and if she has the sense I believe she does, those thoughts must surely turn to the attractions of a good marriage, against those of a dubious friendship. You have not won yet, Miss Fortune.'

It was of no use crying after him, as she wanted to do, that she had no thought of winning or losing: his opinion of her – if you could call outright hatred an opinion – was confirmed. What she really needed to know, and dreaded to find out, was the opinion of her prevailing at the Manor. The postponement of the wedding suggested that her story had been taken into account, if not absolutely believed; but she still could not suppose that she would be warmly welcomed there by anyone except Fanny, and it was with a heavy tread that she entered the oak avenue that used to be her favourite walk.

Not Fanny but Lady Milner came hurrying out to the hall.

'Miss Fortune, how do you do? You find us a little disturbed domestically again, I am afraid, and so your welcome may not be all that civility should dictate. I hope you are quite well? I realize,' she added, with a rare anxious tinge of humour, 'that these formalities may seem rather absurd at such a time – but really I don't know what else to do! And how to explain to you—'

'Well, I have just seen Mr Leabrook. He was . . . informative.'

'I see.' Lady Milner's eyes – surprising, inky violet eyes – shyly searched her face. 'I may as well say, Miss Fortune, that I think this postponement a good idea, no matter what the – the real facts of the matter are. Mr Leabrook emerged from his private interview with Isabella looking furious and was barely polite. It was not, between ourselves, the way I would wish to see a gentleman behave, even if he considered himself – well – wronged. He said if there were any shadow of suspicion attaching to him, then he did not see how they could go on. I do not think he quite expected Stephen to say so promptly that, in that case, the wedding should be put off. But of course by then—'

'This,' cried Stephen, flinging open the drawing-room door, 'is exactly what I loathe about the whole business. All this whispering together in corners like a set of surreptitious witches. Come in, Miss Fortune, and let us all talk openly and frankly, for this concerns you quite as much as anyone.'

'Oh, yes, Caro, you must come in, and you must know you are vindicated!' cried Fanny, abandoning an operation on her spaniel's paw. 'Bella, tell her – tell her she is absolved and shriven!'

'Fanny, stop being sensibilitous for one minute,' snapped Stephen, who was in his shirt sleeves. 'And, Bella, leave off that writing.'

'My dear Stephen,' Lady Milner said hesitatingly, 'your coat—'

'My coat? It is on the floor, ma'am, where I threw it, because I am excessively hot and bothered and in a mood to throw something.'

'I must get these letters written,' said Isabella, who was seated with a sort of stiff diligence at the writing-desk. 'There are people to be informed – things that must be cancelled . . .' Her large, clouded, unhappy eyes, having wandered everywhere else, met Caroline's for a stinging moment, then veered away.

'Oh, Bella, I don't know what to say,' Caroline said.

'You needn't say anything, Caro, because you have done the right thing and now you are vindicated!' Fanny put in.

'Be quiet, Fanny, and, no, she isn't,' Stephen growled. 'Miss Fortune, our friend Leabrook denies your story emphatically: but then he would. If it is true, he is a villain: if it is not, you are. What matters is what Isabella thinks and feels, and as it appears she cannot quite feel the same about him just now as formerly, I proposed the wedding be put off.'

'Bella?' Caroline asked, drawing tentatively closer to the writing-desk. 'Is that what you want?'

'I want,' Isabella said, examining her pen, 'I want none of this to have happened. I want it all as before – but of course that's impossible.

And so, while I cannot believe what you have told me about Richard, I cannot – cannot quite *disbelieve* it either: because I cannot believe you are . . . what he said you are.'

'Well,' Caroline said, her throat tight, 'thank you for that – but I wish it had come to no such choice, Bella, truly—'

'I'm sure, my dear,' Isabella said, with a sunken smile, 'and I wish *we* could simply go back to the way we were together, but I—' She frowned at her writing as if it were Chinese. 'Forgive me, I can't be very welcoming just now, because when I look at you I think of *him*, and so – we are perhaps not the best company for one another at present.'

'Yes,' Caroline said, miserably regarding Isabella's tense shoulder, 'yes, I see.'

'Bella, really! You should be thanking Caro—'

'Not your business, Fanny,' Stephen said firmly, 'and I wish it were not mine either, but it is, God help me.' He had perched himself on the windowsill, from which he could sweep them all with his scornful look. 'We need not be quite so apocalyptic about it. As I told Leabrook, if he is genuine, then he won't mind waiting anyhow. He has gone off in what your romance-writers call high dudgeon, but I don't suppose that will last.'

'He is a proud man, Stephen,' Lady Milner put in, with a slight shake of her head.

'Besides, surely Bella would *never* wish to be reconciled with a man who behaved so monstrously,' said Fanny hotly.

'Again that depends on what Bella thinks and feels,' Stephen said, irritably tugging at his loosened cravat as if he longed to shed and throw something else, 'and that is Bella's business only, though I would suggest that time is exactly the thing needed to put those thoughts and feelings in order. And I say again, Isabella, there will also be time enough later to write those damned letters.'

'But you must consider, Stephen, that an engagement is a public matter,' Lady Milner said, 'and society is apt to take a great interest—'

'Society! Society my – ah, I suppose so,' Stephen said, subsiding into saturnine gloom.

'I will help you, Isabella,' Lady Milner said, and then, after a moment: 'If you will allow me.'

'Thank you,' Isabella said, with a dazed look. 'I'm sure I can manage, although – although if you could go through the list of people who should be told with me . . .'

'Certainly. We shall make sure that everything is done correctly.'

'Correctness!' snorted Fanny. 'Caro, do you hear them?'

'You think it mere empty convention, Fanny,' Lady Milner reproved her, 'but it is really another word for doing what is right.'

'Oh, but right by whose standards?' Fanny scoffed, marching about. Caroline felt herself appealed to, but she was reluctant to make any alignments just now: she was all absorbed in the unhappiness of Isabella's coldly presented shoulder. Also she knew quite well why her friend was fussing about the letters: it was something to do, occupation while the pot of grief bubbled and came to the boil. Here was an extra pity: the fact that she still understood Isabella better than anyone in the room.

'I think,' Isabella said, gathering up her papers, 'if you will excuse me, I shall carry on with this upstairs.'

As she got to the door, Captain Brunton appeared – or rather, he had been there all the time: but had been so fixedly still and speechless it was as if a piece of furniture had come to life. Now, however, he was all animation: he sprang to the door, seized the handle as if he wished to open a thousand of them, and his wary grey eyes glistened as he said grindingly: 'Miss Milner – I – I – if there is anything, anything at all I can do that may be of service to you –' he fetched a great breath '– then I hope you know you have only to name it.'

Isabella looked at him, blinking: emerging, Caroline could tell, from dark and distant thoughts; and surely for an instant thinking, *What? Do for me? What on earth could you possibly do for me that would make any difference . . . ?* But then the true Isabella stepped out from her self-shadow. She smiled as best she could and said: 'Thank you, Captain Brunton. You are very kind. Really there's no need – but you are very kind.'

She passed by; and Caroline saw her go, and saw him bow, in a dazzling tableau of realization. No, no, she thought, it is not kindness: no, no, it is much more than that.

Fanny, a little irritatingly, was at her side. 'Don't pay any heed to Bella just now, Caro. She is still quite stunned, you know, and so she's hardly aware of what she's saying, but she *will* come round, and see that you have actually done her a service.'

'I would rather not have done any such service,' Caroline said bleakly. 'What will happen now?'

'We must wait and see,' Stephen said, springing off the windowsill. 'It may be that on reflection Isabella wants to end their association altogether: or he might: or time may effect a reconciliation. Again, that's Bella's choice. But they had better keep apart just now. And I'm afraid she seems to feel the same about your presence, Miss Fortune: thoroughly irrational, but then she is a woman.'

'Yes,' Caroline said rising, 'I was forgetting what an expert you are on our sex, Mr Milner. Well, I shall go—'

'Oh, but this is unfair,' Fanny cried. 'Stephen, she cannot consider herself banished!'

'I don't,' Caroline said, with a constrained laugh, 'but it's best, just now, if I leave, especially as Isabella is not comfortable with me.'

'Spoken with excellent and surprising sense,' Stephen said. 'I shall see you out.'

'There's no need.'

'It was a statement not a question.'

So she found herself returning down the oak avenue with Stephen striding at her side, in a baffling silence that at last he broke by stooping to pick up a crisp frosted oak-leaf and declaring: 'Is it possible to imagine a more beautiful shape that that? There's one question. The other one, the one that is buzzing through your mind, Miss Fortune, is: if I believe your tale about Leabrook at Brighton, why have I not horsewhipped him?'

'That question is not buzzing through my mind, Mr Milner, nor even gently humming. You do not like to horsewhip your horse, let alone a human being; which is one of your more tolerable eccentricities. Also I'm sure Mr Leabrook would promptly have the law on you.'

'Also you suspect that I *don't* believe your story.'

'I don't know,' she said; and then again, helplessly: 'I don't know. The alternative, I suppose, is to believe him; and if that were so, you surely wouldn't be walking beside me like this.'

'Oh, I might,' he said, with a great shrug, crumpling the leaf up. 'I'm not particular.'

'Mr Milner, *do* you think me guilty?'

'Do I think you guilty? It depends what you mean – guilty of only this, or of every other transgression. I can easily believe you capable of them all. The curious point, Miss Fortune, is why you should care for my opinion on the matter.'

'It is a curious point, but let us put it aside while you give me a direct answer.'

'Oh, you know that is beyond me, Miss Fortune. All I can say is, I don't believe you are an out-and-out villainess: but I do wish you had spoken sooner.'

'Do you now? Well, that is all very well for you to say: you have not been through my difficulties. Indeed, I would urge you to put yourself in my position for a moment, and then consider what you would have done.'

'In your position? Well, let's see. I am asked by Leabrook to run off with him to London and abandon myself to dissipation . . .' He shook his head doubtfully. 'I don't know: he is undoubtedly a handsome fellow, but really there are laws, you know – and besides he would surely lose his respect for me after a while . . . Now, now, don't wave that bonnet at me – it might go off.'

'Well, really you are incorrigible,' she said, aiming a mock swipe, 'and really we should not be laughing. It is a sad time.'

'So it is, but it will get better. Isabella is no Lent-lily; and as soon as she shows some little sign of being herself again, I shall take myself off.'

She stopped short. 'You mean go away? Where?'

'Oh, anywhere that's interesting, and that's far away from all this infernal muddle.'

The anger that rose in her was so complete, so white-hot, that she might have wondered whether it was really not against him but the whole cumulative situation. However, it was not a situation that stood there with its hands in its pockets, regarding her with that insufferable look of self-possession. It was Stephen, and he got the anger.

'Yes, that's right, run away,' she cried. 'Whenever there's trouble, whenever life becomes complicated, then you must take to your heels and run away.'

'I was thinking of going by post-chaise,' he said imperturbably.

'It hardly matters how you go – or even *if* you go – because even when you are not running away, Mr Milner, you are running away.'

'Insofar as I can understand that, Miss Fortune, it sounds like the description of the eminently sensible man.'

'And suppose everyone was to run away from life in that fashion?'

'Well, everyone would be running in the same direction, which would be something. But really, I cannot comprehend your objection to my acting as any free man may do: certainly you may be sure that both Isabella and the Manor will do very well without me.'

'*You* are sure, because it suits you to think so. Others might say that this running away was the root of all the trouble in the first place.'

'It would be very presumptuous of those others, if so,' he said softly; and the hard glitter in his eyes showed her that now, at last, he was truly vexed. 'They might as plausibly point to the beginning of the *trouble* as your arrival in Wythorpe, Miss Fortune.'

'Oh, that has always been your belief, and there is nothing I can do to alter it. But at least when you are off poking about in tombs, Mr Milner, you will be spared having to observe the effects of my delinquencies here. Though no doubt there will be letters – and so when you hear of the church roof falling in, or Farmer Chivers losing his best milker, you will know who to blame.'

He frowned down at her: but a part of him appeared to wish to step back to good humour; awkwardly he said: 'This is not one of our best quarrels. It seems rather too meant.'

'I meant them all,' she said, crushingly, untruly; and walked away with her head held as high as only utter misery could make it.

Chapter XIX

There can be few places more conducive to the quiet, solitary contemplation of melancholy thoughts than a window-seat; and if beyond the window-panes there is a steely vignette of November murk and withered twigs, so much the better. As the Rectory possessed just such a seat in the front parlour, it was no wonder that Caroline betook herself to it much over the next few days; and she was sitting there, dully gazing, her knees drawn up and her temple against the cold glass, when the unknown horsewoman appeared.

'I know, my dear,' said the unknown horsewoman, turning into Maria Downey as she was shown into the parlour, 'I hardly recognize myself. Just like some ghastly thick-ankled countrywoman who rides to hounds and shouts "Yoicks."' She grimaced down at her tailored riding-habit. 'But there, *que voulez-vous*? I spent so much of my youth deliberately getting myself invited to country houses that I somehow learnt to ride, *malgré moi*. I do dislike people who lard their conversation with French tags. And so how do you do? A redundant question. You do rather dismally by the look of things.'

'No, I – well, yes. Dismal is the word. You'll have heard, of course, about the unpleasantness at the Manor.'

'Just barely,' Maria said, yawning and tapping her slender booted foot with her riding-crop. 'Mr Leabrook is not a man to prate much of his private affairs. Thank heaven. But yes, one has the gist. All I can say, between us, my dear, is that people out here in the wilds, full of all the virtues though they are, do tend to take things with a tremendous seriousness that we who have lived in other circles . . .' She waved a serpentine arm. 'Hey, well, I dare say they can't help it. It must be, as our tantalizing friend at the Manor says, the Cromwell strain.'

'I suppose . . . You had better hurry, by the way, if you wish to be tantalized any more by Mr Milner. He is leaving tomorrow morning for Dorset.'

'Dorset? Whyever?'

'I gather there is a place, or a thing, or a set of things, called Maumbury Rings, which he wants to look at.' It was Fanny who had told her this, last evening. She had been doing her best to find it merely amusing ever since. 'But you will find him at home today at least.'

'Oh! well, I think after all I will spare Mr Longlegs, this time. He is a monstrously tough nut to crack – and I leave myself tomorrow, for London. Yes, back to Golden Square, and the lamentations of Matthew. He has written me – not quite a letter, more a sort of howl on paper – about Aunt Sophia and how she absolutely refuses all communication with him and he is in despair and so on. It *is* a pity – but he *would* go entangling himself with shopkeepers' daughters. Caro, tell me – it's impossible for me to judge, you see, as he's my brother – would you call Matthew a good-looking man? A man, at least, not without attractions?'

'I . . . I dare say most people would reckon him not unhandsome,' Caroline said uneasily, 'and he can be agreeable—'

'Oh, don't fear, my dear, I'm not matchmaking,' Maria said, laughing. 'I'm just wondering whether he should not learn from this episode, and go seek a golden dolly. He is, as you say, not a fright, and he dresses well enough, and dances – and in short, there must be plenty of large-chinned heiresses sitting by the walls in the assembly rooms at Bath or Tunbridge, just waiting for such an acceptable fellow to come along. I think I must put it to him.'

'I confess I cannot imagine Matthew entering into any such scheme,' Caroline said. 'He is altogether too idealistic.' Curiously, in spite of the late acrimony between them, she found herself inclining to Matthew's side as she said it.

'Do you think so? Perhaps. A thousand pities. People will not see where their interest lies in this world! To tell the truth, I'm undecided whether to call at the Manor at all, even though I do want to say my goodbyes. I am conscious of coming from Hethersett, you see, and I don't know how glad or otherwise Miss Milner will be to see me, and whether it won't all be dreadfully awkward. What do you think?'

'I can't tell you,' Caroline said listlessly, 'as I don't feel welcome there myself.'

'Dear, dear! I wish I were not leaving you in these dumps. But look here, I do mean to return – that is, I think both Matthew and I will, before Christmas: Mr Leabrook insists, and old Mrs Leabrook insists, of course, a hundred times over. It is not as if, after all, there is any prospect of a Christmas season with Aunt Sophia: not for Matthew at any rate, and I certainly wouldn't face that horror alone. So, my dear, let us call it only *au revoir* – and when we do *revoir* each other, I'm sure all this storm-in-a-puddle will have blown out.'

'Do you think so?' Caroline said, with more scepticism than hope. 'And what about Mr Leabrook? What are his feelings?'

'Oh, my dear, you fish in the wrong pond if you ask *me* about *feelings*. I can no more read them than – than this page of Greek,' Maria said, chuckling, and with her riding-crop flipping open the book that lay on the table at her side.

'That's Latin.'

'Which proves my point exactly. Oh, it is a shocking lack in me, I know. I wonder if Matthew came in for my share of the feelings? That would explain a lot. Still, you know, my dear, insensibility—' rising, Maria slipped her gloved hand in and out of Caroline's '—it really is the best way to be. In terms of trouble.'

'Yes: I'm sure it is,' acknowledged Caroline. And she went about trying to be that way, after Miss Downey had departed. She adopted apathy, she invoked insouciance. It did not work. She was not made that way, even if she did not run to the other extreme of Fanny Milner, who descended on her as usual that afternoon with many embraces, gazes, hand-squeezings, and urgent avowals of solidarity against the blinkered and narrow-hearted world.

It was kind in her, it was touching, and it was very slightly irritating: Caroline did not have the crusader's spirit. Still she was not so over-supplied with friendship just now as to undervalue that which Fanny offered her. She even accompanied Fanny, the next week, to one of the Hampsons' evening-parties: but the experience was not pleasant. She could not help but sadly turn in her mind the memory of a previous occasion here, when Isabella and Stephen had been present – as they were now so glaringly absent. And though the Hampsons were as fulsome in their welcome as ever, Caroline detected a mixture of constraint and inquisitiveness in the other guests, which prickled her with a double discomfort: double, because she was torn between wanting to demand of each frozen smirk and sidelong glance exactly what it meant, and longing to fly from there wailing with her shawl over her head.

Mr Charles Carraway was, naturally, of the party; and Fanny, naturally, was much with him; and when the next morning Mr Carraway called at the Rectory to enquire after Caroline's health, and to ask with his dreamy politeness whether he might look over the drawings about which he had heard so much, it was natural likewise to suppose that Fanny had put him up to it.

'Oh, I don't deny that Fanny and I spoke of it last evening,' he said, smiling, glancing up from her sketchbook.

'And she said, "You must go and call on poor Caro, who is so shunned and scandalous, and give the neighbourhood a lead."'

'Now this drawing has spirit. The shoulders and turn of the neck – you have caught the tension of the figure admirably. Oh, Fanny did not say *poor* Caro: that implies an object of pity. She does not conceive you such, Miss Fortune. Neither do I. Rather the reverse. And I was glad to come: there was no persuasion against my will, I assure you. I do not entirely understand these controversies: all I can see is that Fanny likes you, and her judgement I trust, and as I have not witnessed you frightening children, picking pockets, or shooting squirrels, then really . . .' He concluded with a charming laugh, a shake of his dark curls, and a sharp prod at the next drawing. 'Ah – now this is not right. The spirit is gone. Some dullard of a drawing-master has been at you here, making you show every fold. Omit – always remember – omit a line if you are unsure of it. Ask yourself, does it serve you? If not, out with it.'

'I see . . . If only life were like that, Mr Carraway.'

'Oh, life.' He laughed, shrugging, as if she had mentioned something as abstruse as algebra, distant as the Pole. 'It is hopeless consulting me *there*, Miss Fortune. Now here is a well-rendered scene – there is dash, there is air – and those wonderful bent poplars: is this local?'

'Yes: just this side of Alconbury Hill.'

'Ah, I must take a turn that way, now that I have leisure. Yes, the Hampsons' portrait is finished: they are happier with it than I deserve, for it was an indifferent performance, I fear – though I always have this feeling after a picture is done. Fanny says it is a good sign: for what is a race, once it is won? She is an education.'

'Were you not engaged to draw some views of Mr Leabrook's estate?'

'There was talk of it. But the case is altered. Fanny would not have me do it; and I would rather not.' Mr Carraway bent to pick up the kitten Matilda, who was fighting his boots. 'She is a tiger in miniature!'

'Fanny?'

'She also,' he said, laughing.

And she also came knocking at the door very soon after. It was plain, from the mutual and complete unsurprise of the pair, that this had been arranged; and that to the desire of paying Caroline a tribute, Fanny had added the incidental but very practical plan of securing a meeting with Mr Carraway. They were both too mannerly to say so, or to make manifest their wish to go off walking together: it was Caroline who with a straining laugh shooed them out at last. She felt herself to be indifferent company in any case; and permitting a young man and a young woman to stroll about the village in broad daylight and cold weather did not seem to her fraught with moral danger.

'Bless you, Caroline. You always understand,' Fanny said on the doorstep, embracing her again. 'Oh! by the by, there is another change at the Manor. Would you believe we are to be free of Captain Brunton at last? He leaves for London tomorrow. Oh, I shouldn't be uncharitable, but really it is not a moment too soon – he has been so overbearing lately. Indeed, he was actually quite rude to you the other day, Charles, was he not?'

The painter shrugged and blinked his beautiful eyes. 'He is an unhappy man, I think.'

Ah, yes, thought Caroline: and he is making himself go away from the source of his unhappiness.

'Well, *I* fancy he is jealous because Augusta is not so thick with him any more. And *that*, most curiously, is because she devotes so much time to Isabella. Yes, I must confess, Augusta has been quite a boon to poor Bella since that beast of a Leabrook was unmasked. She reads to her and finds her little occupations to divert her mind, and generally – yes, she has shown herself rather sensitive and thoughtful! You simply never know, do you?' Fanny concluded with a very young laugh, the laugh of someone confident that they do know, pretty much, everything worth knowing.

The departure of Captain Brunton, whom Caroline had come to respect, seemed of a piece with this wintry and denuded time. Everybody is going, she thought, as she took a solitary walk later, like those leaves: she gazed up at the horse-chestnuts on the green, almost bare now, one especially solitary leaf clinging like a rag to the end of a skeletal bough and offering her a satisfyingly gloomy image of herself. She wished she could have said goodbye to the Captain, but she still shrank from intruding herself at the Manor: she did loiter a few moments at the entrance to the oak avenue, her heart dully thumping, but could go no further. Leaflike she drifted home, and found Captain Brunton in the parlour with her uncle.

'Ah, my dear – here is our friend Captain Brunton, you see, and he has been telling me the most remarkable stories of his time on the West Indies station – pagan sorcerers actually reputed to raise the dead – shocking – yet with a dreadful fascination – but lack-aday, here is an end of it, because Captain Brunton is off to London tomorrow! Is it not the greatest of pities? My dear girl, what *have* you done to people hereabouts? They are all taking to their heels!' Dr Langland was innocently oblivious that only he laughed at this joke. 'So, my dear sir, have you hopes of a commission at last?'

'I mean to try again at the Admiralty, sir, yes. But I have other business besides. As I cannot tell how long my absence may be, I felt I should step over and say my goodbyes, and present my compliments.' Captain Brunton inclined his head towards Caroline, his eyes seeking hers.

'Well, I wish you good fortune, my dear sir – heaven forfend that England should neglect her stout old hearts of oak!' Dr Langland cried, with a great clap of his huge hands. 'But I'll tell you what you should do besides, Captain Brunton – besides looking about you for a berth, you should look about you for a wife. You cannot do better, at your stage of life, my dear sir: it *grounds* a man most securely. I am for having everybody marry. Selina tells me that Isabella's wedding has been put off – I cannot think why. No, you must promise me you will look about you, Captain Brunton: I speak as a man who knows the inestimable contentment of matrimony.'

'That I do not doubt,' Captain Brunton said, with a tight, shadowed smile. 'And I believe the married state to be – all you say, sir; but I do not anticipate entering it myself, at least not – not soon.' He turned to Caroline. 'Miss Fortune, you have had a pleasant walk, I trust.'

'Oh, that's what all you young fellows say,' Dr Langland boomed over him, 'until the moment when a pair of pretty eyes smites you, and then – bang! Your goose is cooked! Oh, and it will come to you too, my dear, you may be sure, though of course it will not be pretty eyes that do it, it will be rather – I don't know what – handsome eyes perhaps—'

'I'm quite happy for my goose to remain uncooked, Uncle John,' Caroline told him. 'Even at the risk of becoming a tough old broiler at last. Thank you, I had a very pleasant walk,' she added to Captain Brunton, who was swallowing a harrumph of amusement.

'No, I am for having everybody marry,' Dr Langland said, with his beam of incomprehension, 'and really I must ask Bella why she is delaying. And it is a great pity, Captain Brunton, that we could not find you a bride here – perhaps next time you visit . . . Yes, Nancy? Am I wanted?'

'Yes, sir. Old Mr Powlett,' said the maid. 'About getting his wife churched after her last 'un.'

'Ah, indeed, I'll be there directly. Pray excuse me, Captain Brunton. Now there's an example for you – old Powlett – on his third marriage, and a father I think for the eleventh time now. Blessed matrimony, my dear sir!'

'Miss Fortune, I had hoped for a private word with you,' the Captain said, easing his tight cravat, when Dr Langland had gone. 'This is opportune. I . . .' The word, it seemed, would not come: after a moment he struck himself savagely on the knee. 'I wish I was one of those fellows with ready tongues!'

'There is such a thing as a too ready tongue,' she said, smiling. 'Captain Brunton, I am very sorry you are leaving.'

'So am I. Well, in some ways. Not in all. In other circumstances . . . Miss Fortune, I wish I might go knowing you were still a welcome visitor at the Manor: it would reassure me – please me – to think of you there.'

'Oh, Lord, Captain Brunton, it wouldn't please anyone else!' she burst out in an access of self-pity; then, recovering herself: 'Thank you, though, for the thought. It is what I would like myself above all things: but while matters stand so awkwardly . . . Unless you feel – do you? – that I might make the attempt?'

He winced. 'Just now – I think not. If I had to choose a word to describe Miss Milner, it would be *raw*. She seems to prefer no mention of – well, of her engagement, of Hethersett, of the whole business. My cousin tries, with some success, to keep her mind fixed on other things. But Augusta, I should add, has come firmly down on your side, Miss Fortune: between ourselves, she is your stoutest defender. Except for Miss Fanny, of course,' he said, with a faint smile. 'But as for Miss Milner – I believe that she still cannot quite let go of . . .' He peered into his hat, colouring. 'I should not speak of her so. It is not my place.'

'I know you do so out of kindness, sir. And I would like to think of *you* still at the Manor too.'

'Thank you,' he gasped out, crushing his hat now. 'Miss Fanny – I am afraid she resents my presence.'

Caroline struggled. 'She is – very young. Perhaps a little headstrong.'

'I wish she were not,' he said, frowning. 'But there, in that regard at least I can think of your looking after her: I know you do meet. I'm sorry, I must sound like a regular old mother hen.'

'Better than a cooked goose. I hope, Captain Brunton, you will find it possible to come back,' she said, holding his eyes.

'I hope so too,' he said, after a moment. He stood up as abruptly as if someone had told him his chair was on fire. 'Miss Fortune, if I should need to write to you, may I do so care of your aunt?'

'I'm sure that would be quite proper. Not that you need concern yourself about propriety, you know, when it comes to a person like *me*,' she said, with a wry laugh.

'Not at all – not at all,' Captain Brunton said, in his gruffest, sternest way; and in farewell he gripped her hand like a wrestler.

From the window she watched his upright, compact figure go smartly off; and it occurred to her, in an abstract way, that the Captain was a man with whom a woman might profitably be in love. Not she: the solemnity with which he answered her laugh was an exemplary proof of their suitability to be friends and no more; but someone of a serious turn of mind . . . Now I'm being like Uncle John, she reproached herself, marrying everyone off. It was after all none of her business, in more than one sense.

For which – the second sense, the sense in which she was content to be solitary, disengaged, heartfree, coolly observant – she was heartily grateful. Look at poor Bella: look at Matthew Downey: look at Captain Brunton. Thank heaven she stood outside that wearisome game.

'What are you looking for, my dear?' Dr Langland said, coming back into the parlour, and finding her staring raptly out of the window.

Nothing, nothing, nothing.

* * *

December came in rimey and rheumy. Freezing fog stealthily stalked the hollows about Wythorpe: the sheep breathed wet plumes in and out, chimney-smoke made smudgier columns in the misty air, in the church Dr Langland preached above a condensing cloud of rasps and wheezes. In this church, a couple of times, Caroline met an Isabella still hollow-eyed and noticeably thin, and they exchanged tentative words. A couple of times, also, she went with Aunt Selina to call at the Manor, and there were more tentative words: cordial enough; yet to Caroline it all seemed still stiff and empty. There was so much between them that was not to be spoken: they were like two people at either ends of a room in which most of the floor had collapsed.

Stephen was on his wanderings somewhere down in the south-west, and favoured them, Fanny told her, with the occasional scrawl to inform them he was alive. The idea of his writing letters awoke in Caroline a most absurd wish that she might get one. She kept thinking of their last meeting, of its sad and scratchy unsatisfactoriness; and thought that even to receive a page of nonsense, which was how she imagined Stephen's letters, would at least efface that impression of a last, bitter word.

Fanny still clove loyally to her, and confided one morning, after a little wide-eyed hesitation, that there had been a civil exchange of notes between Isabella and Mr Leabrook.

'No more than that,' Fanny said, 'and I think Bella is still very uncertain how she feels towards him, and he is still mighty proud – but who can say? Augusta counsels caution, caution. Yet I really believe Isabella simply cannot let go of love – and who can blame that? Is it not the hardest thing in the world to relinquish, once you have it?'

'I think it is,' Caroline heard herself say. 'And the hardest to grasp also. You have to seize it at once, else it may be too late.'

'I knew you'd agree,' Fanny said, her voice fading in Caroline's singing ears.

It was two days after this that the maid, bringing the letters in to the breakfast-parlour, caused Caroline's heart to do a peculiar and unaccountable leap when she said: 'Here's an odd one for you, miss.'

But no, not actually a letter: sealed, but not posted: only the direction 'Caroline', in what she recognized as Fanny's handwriting. And then a sharp misgiving turned her heart gymnastic again.

'It is my second Advent sermon this Sunday,' Dr Langland was saying, 'and I think to keep to tradition, and preach on Judgement – the second of the Four Last Things, you know, my dear. Death, Judgement, Heaven, and—'

'Hell and buggery,' Caroline cried out, jumping to her feet with the opened letter in her hand. 'Oh – forgive me – an old military expression. It's just that this news is so . . . Oh, dear.' Weak-legged, she sank down again. 'I'm afraid Fanny has run away with Mr Carraway.' And while her uncle and aunt gasped she stared again at the ensuing words: *just as you, my dear Caroline, advised me!*

Chapter XX

No time now for qualms about calling at the Manor. Caroline, her uncle and aunt were there before the breakfast things had cooled. They found Lady Milner and Isabella in a state of agitation bordering on the frantic. A similar note had been left on the chimney-piece for them: the servants had confirmed that Miss Fanny's clothes were gone, and Lady Milner, in the midst of questioning them, had allowed anxiety to get the better of her temper. The stable-boy, smarting at her remark that he must surely have heard something from where he slept over the stables, was divided between crying and giving notice. While Isabella tried to pacify him, the housekeeper announced with a certain veiled satisfaction that Miss Fanny's dogs were howling for their exercise, and there was nobody free to do it. And none of this was helped by their having to explain to Dr Langland exactly what had happened.

'No, no,' he kept saying, 'there is a mistake here, you know. The fact is she cannot have gone off alone with that gentleman, for you know Fanny is a young girl – that is, a maiden, you know: and they are not married. Do you see?'

In a kind of tight-jawed wail, Aunt Selina said: 'That is precisely the point, and that is precisely why we are so dreadfully concerned. My dear,' she added contritely.

Dr Langland's mouth fell open. 'Lord, bless my soul.' Blinking at his wife, he sat down heavily: luckily there was a chair there. 'Oh, heavens. But Fanny – Fanny will be ruined.'

'Yet this isn't certain, is it?' said Isabella. 'I mean about their intentions. Let us look at those notes again.' (Let us not, thought Caroline.)

'She says they are going to London – but could that not mean *after* they have eloped to Gretna to marry?'

Lady Milner said, shaking her head: 'My dear, she does not mention Gretna at all, and she surely would if that was part of their plan. There is no reason to omit such a vital fact.'

'Oh, Fanny,' Isabella said, drooping, 'what have you done?'

Perhaps, probably, she did not intend it: but Isabella's moist eyes did alight on Caroline as she said these words, and Caroline felt the cold touch of accusation. Colder still when Uncle John, saying they must examine the evidence, proceeded to read out the farewell notes in his strongest pulpit voice.

'"You must know that Charles and I are united by a love of the truest, profoundest and holiest kind, one which it is hardly to be expected would be comprehended or countenanced by society in its state of dismal unenlightenment – seeing as it does only my supposed youth and his supposed ineligibility – not the finer reality beyond. Least of all can such a sensitive plant flourish in the stony soil of a provincial backwater. The place for us is London. There are the most promising chances for one of Charles's avocation: there we shall be together and happy, and I do believe you will rejoice for us. Life is there to be lived – it is a crime to let convention and caution stifle it – so we are off tonight – seizing the moment, just as you, my dear Caroline, advised me!"' Dr Langland gaped mournfully. 'Oh, Caroline! Oh, my dear girl, this really was not responsible in you! Did you *know* of this scheme . . . ?'

'We must remember,' Aunt Selina put in, touching Caroline's arm, 'that what we hear in these notes is the voice of Fanny – and you know Fanny always does tend to put her own complexion on things; even perhaps believe what she wants to believe. And *I* cannot believe –' yet was there a quaver of query there? – 'that Caro would have encouraged this, nor even have had any notion of it.'

'Indeed I did not know about it,' Caroline said – while her mind teemed with recollected hints that now seemed obvious; and she grew as conscious of the eyes upon her as if the memories were breaking out like spots on her cheeks. 'That is, she did not tell me about any plan to elope with Mr Carraway. Yes, she has often been to see me lately –' a faint abashed turn of the neck from Isabella at that '– and to be sure, she was often talking of Mr Carraway, and her – her feelings generally, but – oh, well, you know that was Fanny!'

Suddenly she realized she was talking about Fanny in the past tense: as if she were dead. And of course it was not that bad . . . but, but.

Fanny, as a minor, could not marry without her parents' consent, at least not in England. That was why young girls defying parental edicts fled with their beaux over the border to Scotland, where different laws applied and where at the first stop of Gretna Green they could be united with their disapproved choice and return south as brides. It was a rebellion that could leave lasting family division: but it did allow a return to the social fold. What Fanny had apparently done was quite different. Socially it damned her. Doubtless, drunk with love and adventure as she was, Fanny would say she was very ready to be damned. But Caroline doubted that a gently bred girl from the shires like Fanny really knew what that perdition entailed.

In such a case much depended on the character of the man. Charles Carraway did not *appear* a heartless seducer who would take what he wanted and then abandon a girl: he seemed too romantic, unworldly. But Caroline knew better – she above all knew better – than to trust to seemings. And the mere fact that he had taken off with an innocent girl of seventeen showed him either blind or criminally careless.

But what about me? Was I neither of these things? If I did not encourage them, did I discourage them? Would Fanny have done it without my example, or what she sees as my example? Why do I keep hearing that sound: *cuckoo, cuckoo . . .* ?

'Miss Fortune, can you think of any suggestion – anything Fanny may have said, that would give us a clue to where precisely they have gone?' Lady Milner asked.

'I cannot, Lady Milner, because she did not tell me anything about this.' Unpleasant sensation, like dampness slowly drying on the skin, of not being believed. 'I know Mr Carraway trained in London: he may still have connections there; but I know no more than that.'

'I wish it were not London,' Isabella said. 'It's so big – a person can just disappear there.'

So it is, as your fiancé well knew, Caroline thought, tasting a pungent mixture of emotions: it was where I was to go and be his mistress, and when he had tired of me, no doubt I was to disappear – into that deep, deep pool of lost women, their reputations gone, their choices ended, their stomachs needing to be fed. The muslin sisterhood, as they were called: a euphemism, it made it sound almost pleasant. God forbid that should happen to Fanny.

These thoughts revived her anger against Richard Leabrook; and remembering what Fanny had told her about a possible reconciliation, she wanted to cry out in warning to Isabella: to reach out to her friend across that gaping floor. But no, Fanny was the main concern for now. Caroline forced herself up out of reflection, grasped at practicality. 'What about Mr Carraway's lodgings in Huntingdon? Something may be known there. There must be a landlord, neighbours.'

'An excellent notion,' Lady Milner said promptly. 'Isabella, pray ring the bell – we shall have the carriage made ready—'

'But, Stepmama, should not one of us at least be here, in case there is any word? Or in case Fanny changes her mind and comes back?'

As she spoke, Isabella's eyes met Caroline's, distantly, but not beyond the reach of a gleam of sad mutual amusement: Fanny change her mind? And it was the first time, Caroline realized with a feeling that was also shadowed-bright, that she had ever heard her call Lady Milner by the name.

'We can go,' Aunt Selina said, adding, with a glance at the rain-spattered window and a visible gathering of courage: 'I dare say the roads will be fair enough – won't they, John?'

'Oh! I dare say,' grunted Dr Langland, who was still poring over the farewell notes. 'Dear me! "The stony soil of a provincial backwater" – that is something of a mixed metaphor. Not a felicitous turn of phrase, at any rate. I shall tell Fanny –' He stopped and gave a violent rub at his boyish hair. 'That is, I would, if only I could see her! Will I ever see her again, I wonder? Oh, Caroline, Caroline –' he muttered, feeling his wife's eye on him, but Dr Langland's mutter was only a shout muffled '– it was not well done in you!'

'I do *not* know where the gentleman has gone. And if I did, I should enquire of him, if he *is* a gentleman, why he suddenly vacated my upstairs apartments without telling me, without leaving an address, and without paying me the three months' back rent that's owing.' The stationer spoke with affronted dignity, whilst running his flexible stationer's thumb, criss-crossed with paper-cuts, down the edge of a ream.

Caroline and her aunt exchanged a glance. This did not look good.

'Is it possible, sir, that he might have left word with anyone – spoken with anyone before his absconding?' Dr Langland asked.

'He didn't leave word with *me*,' the stationer said, consoling himself with another long riffle, 'and that's about all of it.'

Ah, but was it? Caroline had noticed the stationer's daughter, pale, pretty, seventeen, lurking and listening at the back of the shop. Quietly she approached her, the question on her face.

'No.' Tight-lipped, tragic-eyed, the girl shook her head. 'He never said anything about going. Oh, he never said!'

No, this did not look good.

'Perhaps *I* might ask if you are particular friends of his?' the stationer said. 'In which case, might you have come in order to settle that particular outstanding bill?'

'No, no, sir,' Uncle John cried, with a thump of his cane on the floor. 'We have come to settle his hash!'

'Oh,' said the stationer, going back to his paper.

His daughter slipped away weeping. This did not look good at all.

* * *

At Wythorpe Manor, news of a sort. Nothing, at any time of day or night, could go quite unobserved in the village; and it was reliably reported that a post-chaise had been seen, in the early hours, waiting at the turn to the oak avenue.

'Well, now, that's something, eh?' Dr Langland kept saying, exuding a terrible freshness. 'Now we know something. Yes, yes. Now we know how they left, do you see?'

'Oh, John, they are hardly likely to have walked to London,' cried Aunt Selina, uncontrollably. Twice in one day that the saint-like patience had lapsed: Caroline could see in her aunt's hollow eyes the coming tortures of guilt.

Lady Milner said: 'Well, I have written Stephen at his last address. I can only hope it reaches him. He must come home. He is needed.'

'Yes,' Caroline said aloud, before she even knew she was going to speak. 'Oh, yes, certainly – that is the best idea.'

The following two days brought no news of Fanny. Lady Milner said that she shuddered to think, without specifying what it was that she shuddered to think. Rumour flitted about the neighbourhood and brought a series of maliciously well-meaning visitors to the Manor, remarking, dear Lady Milner, how long it was since they had called, and how nice to see her and Miss Milner again and – but, goodness, where was delightful Miss Fanny?

The third day brought Stephen.

He had travelled post, setting out as soon as he received Lady Milner's letter, hardly pausing to eat or drink. 'Nor, I fear, shave – he looked quite a Robinson Crusoe,' related Aunt Selina, who had been at the Manor when he arrived.

'And how is he?' demanded Caroline. 'Annoyed, I dare say, at having to leave his precious mouldy ruins to come back and take charge of his own household?'

Aunt Selina looked as surprised as Caroline felt at this tartness.

'Well, he is, I think, most seriously concerned for Fanny,' Aunt Selina said. 'Though, characteristically, he calls her a little fool and says she deserves whatever she gets. But I'm sure he doesn't mean that.'

'Oh, who can tell, with Stephen?' Caroline said airily, and returned to her work. She was making up baskets for the traditional Rectory gifts to the poor and infirm of the parish on St Thomas's Day, and she found that she was cramming them so fiercely full with stockings and jars of preserves that the infirm, at least, would be hard put to open them.

She did not know why she was so out of sorts: which was another way of saying that she did. It was because she laboured still under the feeling that she was being blamed, at least in part, for Fanny's elopement. Oh, Lady Milner was very correct towards her, and Isabella kindness itself; yet she detected a watchful look about them. It made her feel like a reformed thief to whom everyone was determined to be fair, even as they kept surreptitiously counting the spoons. This was not helped by Dr Langland, who remained stuck in one of his blind alleys of misunderstanding, and kept sighing: 'Oh, my dear Caroline, if only you had said something!'

There is nothing like being harshly judged to make one harsh in judgement; and Caroline completed the filling, or rather stuffing, of the baskets with some further internal strictures on Stephen Milner's character. For he, who had been ready to blame her before anything had happened, when she was a mere unknown quantity newly added to the Wythorpe sum, must now be poised to descend on her with all his heaviest and most knowing scorn. Well, she thought: well, I am ready.

After nuncheon, arming herself with stout gloves and secateurs, she went out to the front garden and began cutting holly-boughs to dress the Rectory windows. There was still just room, beside the crowding anxiety and vexation, to find pleasure in this task, and hope of appropriate snow in the colour of the western sky, egg-white touched with lime.

'Miss Fortune, I wish to pick your brains.'

Stephen Milner had stolen upon her so quietly, and broken into her thoughts so abruptly, that she bit her tongue, nearly dropped the secateurs and turned round on him with a yelp. 'Mr Milner! Really, you could have made me cut off my finger!'

'Oh, the gloves look very strong. A minor incision perhaps, no more. I *am* sorry to interrupt you, because you looked so splendidly pagan.' He picked up a cut sprig of holly. 'Roman feast started this custom. Saturnalia. Guzzle, gobble, and grope. Not so very different from Christmas.' He had, she saw, shaved; but looked weary, his face all bony angles. 'Now about those brains. Ow, I've pricked myself.'

'Curious consequence of handling sharp objects. I'd say how d'you do, but I gather we are missing out the usual exchange of greetings and compliments.'

'Well, time is pressing,' he said, sucking his long finger. 'What with Fanny's reputation imperilled every moment. If it ain't gone already. I don't know why I'm being flippant, I don't feel it. I would love her still whatever happened, and so would you, but the rest of the world won't.'

Caroline did not know what to say. She felt as if she had reached out to grasp a holly-branch and found herself holding a blossom.

'God! Why did she have to be such a fool?' he burst out. 'Why couldn't she just come to me and say she wanted to marry Carraway?'

'You weren't here to ask,' Caroline said, as gently as she could. 'And what would you have said?'

'I'd have said, "No, you're too young, and besides he gazes through his curls too much." But it would have been a start. The battle-ground would have been decided, at any rate.'

'And then, I rather fear, she would have proceeded to run off with him. You said marry – do you think that's what she hopes? Or he intends? Or is she not thinking at all?'

'The last sounds more like Fanny. But these are precisely the questions I wanted to put to you. You were the one she was so thick with just lately – or so I hear.'

'Well, you cannot believe everything you hear,' Caroline said, thinking: Now I know what to have on my gravestone. 'If you had been here at home, Mr Milner, instead of gadding about—'

'Why is it when anyone makes the slightest motion we disapprove of, we call it *gadding about*? And what is this business of wanting me here?'

'I am not wanting – I am not speaking on my own behalf, but on Fanny's. I fear she has lacked guidance—'

'Ah, has she? I have caught a whiff of suggestion that she has had altogether too much guidance, in a certain direction.'

'I will say, for the last time, that I did not know of Fanny's plan or encourage her towards it. And a gentleman should beware, Mr Milner, of vexing a lady when she has an instrument like this in her hand.'

He did smile then, with a softening of the bony lines that she found she had been somehow anticipating. But she still thought she saw a sparkle of distrust as he bowed and offered her his arm.

'Where are we going?' she said, just before taking it.

'Around the garden. Perambulation aids cogitation. I am still brain-picking, you see. Because if anyone knows something, it must be you. I mean,' he said, holding up a shielding hand, 'because Fanny talked to you more than anyone. And she may have let something slip that you hardly noticed or have forgotten. What about family? Has Carraway any that you know of?'

'I remember him saying he was an orphan, brought up by an uncle,' Caroline said: then thought of the tearful betrayed face of the stationer's daughter, and coughed. 'This is to assume, of course, that we – we can believe everything Mr Carraway said.'

'Hm, that doesn't sound promising. There's nothing like a stern father with an unsigned will to make a young man decide to behave respectably. Well, they must live on something. I hear the Hampsons paid him well for the wedding-portrait, and Bella tells me Fanny's jewels are gone with her; but none of this is a fortune. One hope, a slight hope, is that Fanny will apply to us for funds, and give at least a forwarding address. Slight, because I'm sure Fanny, if anyone, believes that human beings can live on air. I know, she makes it seem charming, but still . . . So, if they are in London, they will be residing modestly at least, and not in the west-end squares. Therefore, that is one place I need not look.'

'You're going to search for them?'

'Yes. I'm only here to garner what information I can, and then

I'll be off after them.' His quizzical face angled down at hers. 'Does that count as gadding about?'

'No – no, of course it doesn't,' she said, slapping at his arm, somewhat tentatively, 'only – well, it's as Isabella said, London is so big – how many people live there, do you suppose?'

'At the census five years ago, the population was recorded as about one million and fifty thousand.'

'Do you write these things down on tablets and keep them in your pockets, Mr Milner? No, don't answer that. It's enough. I can't see – I don't mean to doubt you, but I can't see how you will find them.'

'Well, Miss Fortune, fortify your heart, brace your mind, and prepare yourself for a considerable privilege, because I am about to make a confession. When my father was dying, he addressed me in the terms that everyone must at that moment, and told me that Augusta was an irreproachable angel, which was excessive if understandable from a husband; that Isabella was sweet, sensible, and just a little stubborn – true; and as for Fanny, he wasn't sure, because she was not quite finished. Like pottery not yet fired in the kiln, I seem to remember him saying. What he was doing thinking about kilns at such a time I cannot imagine. Unless he could already feel the heat from where he was going. At any rate, he was right, alas. And so I am going to London to search for Fanny, because I don't think she was quite finished when she made the decision to run off with Carraway, and such a decision can't be trusted. He may *be* the one for her, and if so good luck to them: but I'll have to be convinced of it first. If they are truly in love, then he should marry her. If not, then . . . well, I'm not sure. I ought to make him marry her nonetheless. At least, I will make him stop using her.'

'I thought you didn't believe in marriage.'

'A man who never contradicts himself must become horribly bored with his own conversation. Oh, on the whole I don't believe in it, except when there is genuine love, which is such a compound of affection, warmth, ease, esteem, and various other spices and condiments rarer than powdered hen's teeth that one hardly expects to come across it once in a lifetime.'

She studied him. 'You know, in your way you are quite as romantic as Fanny.'

He conceded a smile. 'That's what my father said . . . However, endlessly fascinating subject though I am, we are not here to discuss me but Fanny. I was in the not very productive process of picking your brains.'

'I'm afraid there is nothing to pick – and don't burst yourself with wit on that remark, Mr Milner. I mean I cannot think of anything that may help you. There is only – well, Fanny did have an absurd veneration for my past. My life with my father – it all seemed wonderfully exciting to her, the regiment and the theatre and the gaming-clubs and the – well, I'm afraid even the debts and the flitting seemed to her a great adventure.'

'Ah!' he said, and with a sort of tactful lightness: 'I imagine the adventure would pall after a time.'

'I tried to suggest as much. Perhaps I didn't try hard enough. But if she is in London, I fancy that is the world she will be drawn to. The theatre districts – Covent Garden, Haymarket – and then all the little places along the Strand towards St Paul's where the authors and artists and fiddlers gather. Which is also where cheap lodgings are to be had, of course.'

Also the very places where the muslin sisterhood walked – as neither of them said, though their short silence did.

'Well, I thank you, Miss Fortune, that may help indeed. If I do have any news, I shall write at once to Augusta and Bella—'

'Will you write to me?' Her cheeks were stinging: the afternoon had turned so cold. 'There, you knew I was a bold-faced hussy, so that shocking request can be no surprise to you. But as you are so elusive, Mr Milner, I could at least then pin you down to a postal address.'

'Certainly I shall write, Miss Fortune, at your request,' he said, with a smothered wry look, and a short bow. 'But surely you are able to call at the Manor now without tearing of hair and gnashing of teeth?'

'In a way . . . Tell me, how *is* Bella? Yes, I've seen her – but it hasn't been the same. Even you must understand that.'

'Even I?'

'Even you as a typically blinkered insensible obtuse dunderheaded male, of course, and now do answer my question.'

'Well,' he said, suppressing a smile, 'she is still in the dismals, because she is Isabella and she takes things seriously; but she is not in a decline, and she has, I must confess, a good solid friend in Augusta, pompous and plaguey as she can be; and I have hopes she will come to the realization that she is after all pretty well placed, and be in no hurry to change. I've told her so – but when are we dunderheaded males ever listened to?'

'Hm? I beg your pardon, I was thinking of something else.'

'I gave you that one. I must go. Must eat, change, pack again, sleep, then off in the morning. Will you present my compliments to my uncle and aunt? And can I have a little sprig of your holly?'

'What for?'

'Has anyone ever told you that you ask far too many questions?'

'Why do you ask?'

He breathed and glowered at her, broke into a laugh. 'I want a sprig as a little piece of Wythorpe. I don't know how long I shall be in populous city pent.'

'Oh, I thought you wanted to keep it next to your heart to remind you of me.'

'As it would prickle and irritate, it probably would. I'm glad to see, by the by, that you're – well, in spirits. That you're still yourself. And don't ask me why.'

Yes, she thought, with a vague surprise, I am myself again now. Where did I go? In confusion she turned and blunderingly hacked off a whole bough of holly.

'I said a sprig, not a tree. Here, let me . . .' He snipped, pocketed. 'Perhaps it will make Fanny homesick, though I doubt it.'

'Perhaps it will make you homesick – though I doubt it.'

His hand on the gate, he wore an arrested, thoughtful look, as if stirred by some long-buried memory. 'You asked me once what it was like to be always right,' he said. 'And though I'm sure I replied with something characteristically brilliant, in truth it's hard to say. When you've never known anything else, you've no means of comparison: you don't know what it means to be well until you're ill. I'm working my way round to another confession. Yes: I have been wrong. Wrong about Fanny. I thought she would come to no harm, left to her own devices. I thought there was no need for fuss.' He followed the flight of a rook overhead as he spoke, though his eyes were not seeing. 'I thought I didn't have to be my father.'

A new world of Stephen was opened up to her then. Some instinct told her, even as she gazed at it, that she should respond to it only in the old style, if he were not to regret the revelation.

'Well, I'm pleased to know you have joined the rest of the fallible human race at last, Mr Milner,' she said. 'And I hope you will live to be wrong many, many times again.'

'Including about you?' he said, with his feline look.

'Fascinating subject as I am, we are not here to discuss me,' she said – lightly, yet with an inner feeling of lifting some horribly heavy weight.

'True. I must say goodbye. I suppose I should wish you a merry Christmas also, as I don't know whether I shall be back for it.'

'Goodbye, Mr Milner.' She put out her hand. 'Please – please scold Fanny for me if you find her.'

'With pleasure. Goodbye, Miss Fortune.' He looked down, with a faint smile and shake of his head, at her hand: it was still encased in the thick glove. She thought he said, 'May I?' but could not be sure, as she was overtaken by such an odd swarming sensation, as he delicately slipped off the glove and pressed her bare hand, a sensation that remained with her after he had gone and she walked slowly back into the house: it was as if he had taken off a lot more than the glove.

Chapter XXI

Seasonal migrations: to the Grange for Christmas came Mrs Hampson's mother from Bristol, a little squint parroty woman in a frizzed wig, prematurely aged by deafness, whom Caroline had the pleasure of meeting at an evening-party.

'Who? Who? Oh, is this the flighty one who steals the men?'

Caroline, unblushing, brushed away her hosts' emollient apologies: she could even laugh at such stuff now. More sobering was the wedding portrait hanging above the drawing-room mantel, with the dashing signature of *C. Carraway* visible in the corner. It was, as far as she could judge, a good painting: handled with assurance and a warm colourism, even if there was a sketchy tendency to make empty brushwork-flourishes out of lace and ribbons. But its associations were less happy.

The Hampsons were apologetic about that too. Attempts to keep the matter of Fanny secret had met with all the success that might be expected in that voraciously inquisitive neighbourhood; and as Mr Hampson said, while they deeply regretted what *seemed* to be suggested lately about Mr Carraway's character, for their part they had never found him to be anything but a gentleman, and Felicity was so very fond of the portrait . . . As well she might be, since it was outrageously flattering, a fact urbanely remarked upon by her mother, who remarked after long scrutiny: 'Well, that's never you, Lissie: you're twice as fat as that.'

'There is, I suppose, Miss Fortune, no – how shall I put it? – no word?' enquired Mr Hampson, one great awkward perspiring smile. 'No word about – how shall I put it? – the young lady from the Manor whom we, to our great regret, do not see any more?'

'No.' No: though Caroline had received a letter from Stephen Milner in London, to tell her that he was staying at Batt's Hotel in Jermyn Street, that London was foggy, murky, smoky, and muddy, but that he was not without hopes of success, as so many people had left Town for Christmas that the population must be down to only a million. Reading, she smiled as she ached.

Seasonal migrations: 'I do hear,' now said Mr Hampson, abandoning an unpromising subject, 'that there are visitors again at Hethersett for Christmas. Mr and Miss Downey – charming people – Mr Leabrook introduced them last time . . .' And then, realizing that this was also an unpromising subject with Caroline, Mr Hampson smiled and perspired himself into silence, and hailing an invisible new arrival escaped across the room.

Well: she wondered if she was to expect another visit, or rather visitation, from Matthew Downey, accusing her of fresh enormities, or whether there had been a peace treaty with his aunt. Not much caring, she only mildly wondered; and then, two days before Christmas, she greatly wondered at seeing a carriage pull up at the Rectory gate.

For she recognized this as Mr Richard Leabrook's carriage. Even without recognition, it could have been no one else's – black and sleek and shining, the horses not only well groomed but looking – somehow – well dressed and polite. Maria Downey got out; though she was, as Caroline could see from the two dark male heads within, not the only occupant of the carriage, which then drove on.

'There, my dear, you see I keep my promises.' Maria pressed a cold, fresh-smelling cheek against hers with a dry kiss, floated over to the parlour fireplace to warm her hands. She was in travelling dress: fur-trimmed pelisse, casquet bonnet, muff. 'I promised I would come and see you next time I was at Hethersett – didn't I? Perhaps I didn't. I certainly *thought* it. And so how do you do, my dear, and now are you ready? Are you ready for the most astounding piece of news? It is like the sun falling out of the sky. Though judging by this odious weather that has already happened. Well, it is like – oh, I can't think of any more comparisons, it's too exhausting.' Maria sat down, or rather ornamented the sofa with herself. 'My dear, would you believe that Aunt Sophia is no more?'

'No,' Caroline answered, simply and truthfully: because she could not imagine Mrs Catling dying. Undergoing a slow petrifaction into a graven image, perhaps, or being clawed down to hell like Don Giovanni, but not suffering the common fate. She sat down, then reminded herself of what was appropriate. 'Oh, Miss Downey, I am sorry.'

'My dear, you *sound* it!' Maria said, with a chuckle. 'Come, I'm sure we may be frank. Even I am only a little sorry, for after all she was not exactly a woman to inspire affection, and you can hardly be expected to feel anything. Except surprise, of course, because I'm sure like me you conceived her immortal. Well! Matthew and I had only just settled ourselves at Hethersett for a proper traditional Christmas season of gluttony and sloth, and then comes this letter from a solicitor in London – Mr Coker of Symond's Inn – acquainting us with what he fancifully calls the sad news. She died at Brighton last Friday – quite suddenly, it seems, of a heart-stroke. I know, an unlikely organ for Aunt Sophia. All matters pertaining to the estate are in the hands of this gentleman, who writes – well, he writes in true slippery legal fashion, but he says we may learn something to our advantage if we will be so good as to attend him et cetera. Well, you know what that means, my dear: the will. Aunt Sophia's long-anticipated will – what will it say? You may imagine how Matthew is feeling.'

'I can indeed.' Not, though, with any lively sympathy. And that was the pity of it all, she thought: little moved as she was herself by Mrs Catling's demise, the general absence of grief told a sad tale. 'I gather there was no reconciliation before . . . ?'

Maria shook her head. 'Not for want of trying on Matthew's part. But Aunt Sophia remained – oh, that word that's like obstinate.'

'Obdurate. Was that Matthew I saw in the carriage?'

'Yes. Matthew – and Mr Leabrook.' Maria's smile was a little diffident. 'The fact is, he is taking us to London directly in his carriage, which is excessively civil of him. He knows this may be a rather testing time, and so he has placed himself at our disposal – at Matthew's especially – to be a prop and stay to him as it were. And so, on our way we thought to say some goodbyes. That is – Matthew and Mr Leabrook have gone on to call at the Manor, to present their compliments. Whereas I – well, I elected to call on *you*, my dear. I do gather the unpleasantness still lingers. All I can do is apologize for my brother's rudeness, but he still has those peculiar ideas about you—'

'And Mr Leabrook, I'm sure, is always happy to back them up.'

'Now you mustn't be provoking, my dear,' Maria said, lips twitching. 'He may well have his wicked side, as which of us does not, but he has been excessively obliging to us. If I didn't know better, Caroline Fortune, I would suspect you of harbouring a little *tendresse* for him. Oh, but enough of all that. Tell me, what do you think? Aunt Sophia actually gone – am I dreaming? Selfish beast that I am, I wish it might have happened at another time, because I don't fancy the journey back to London in this weather, even in the comfort of Mr Leabrook's carriage – but of course we must go. You may imagine that Matthew was packing even before he had finished reading the letter.'

Dr Langland came in at that moment, full of hearty enquiries, and so was soon acquainted with Miss Downey's news. He was solemn. 'I hope your late aunt was offered spiritual comfort before the end, Miss Downey.'

'It's enchanting and dear of you to hope so, sir, but I'm rather afraid the only comforts Aunt Sophia cared for were a glass of port-wine and a hand of cards.'

'Sad, sad!' cried Dr Langland, with a shake of his great head.

'Isn't it?' yawned Maria. 'Ah, I think I hear the carriage. We are always parting! It's supposed to be sweet sorrow or something, isn't it? Those poets. They'll say anything. Oh, by the by, Caro, where is my beau with the long legs?'

'In London,' she answered, a little shortly.

'Oh, indeed? Perhaps we shall run into him. Where is he staying, do you know?'

'I'm afraid not. Present my compliments to the two gentlemen, won't you?'

Why did she lie? She couldn't say, except . . . 'Well, Stephen has important business on hand,' as she said afterwards to Uncle John who, for once, had been subtle enough not to take her up on it, 'and he can well do without Maria Downey flibbertigibbeting around him.'

'I'm not sure that's correct as a verb, my dear,' her uncle said: then smiled. 'Oh, I don't know, though.'

Aunt Selina had been at the Manor that morning, and on her return she confirmed that Mr Downey and Mr Leabrook had called there – to some surprise and awkwardness at first. But Mr Leabrook had been thoroughly correct: had explained the situation, said that he wished to accompany his friend to London at this difficult time, considered it was proper to call and make his formal goodbyes. By the end, Aunt Selina said, there seemed to be a certain thawing in the atmosphere, and Isabella—

'Well, Isabella did not exactly look happy – but rather as if she wanted to be happy if she could just manage it,' Aunt Selina said, with a thoughtful look. 'Not that it was a long visit. Mr Downey was anxious to be off – what a high-strung young man he is! – and besides Lady Milner could not be *very* welcoming, for it seems Stephen left strict instructions that there was to be no sort of *rapprochement* between Isabella and Mr Leabrook without his presence and consent.'

'Oh, high and mighty!' remarked Caroline: with an electric inward cry of *Good for you, Stephen.*

Later she thought of the Brighton days and strove to feel something profound for a woman who, after all, had met death, perhaps with incomprehension, fear, realization. But the way Mrs Catling had lived made it impossible to think of her in death as anything but an estate, a will and testament: one imagined her being filed rather than buried.

Far more perturbing to Caroline's spirit was Aunt Selina's account of Isabella. If her friend was yearning back towards Leabrook, there was nothing she could do about it – except feel this nagging dread and trouble, which she did her best to conceal through the festivities of Christmas. These in turn prompted wistful thoughts: compassionate comparisons. Here, the Yule log borne in and heaved to the back of the parlour fire, here the carollers from the village singing 'Remember O Thou Man' while the spiced ale steamed, here the ivy round the fire, the plum-cake, the wassail-bowl; and somewhere, unknown, far from home and friends, Fanny; and likewise, in a hotel at least but alone, Stephen. When they dined at the Manor on Christmas Day, no amount of goose and chestnut-stuffing could divert the mind from the empty chairs.

One welcome addition, though: last of the seasonal migrations. Captain Brunton had arrived late last night after a punishing journey by public coach and carrier. That, perhaps, accounted for his appearance – pale, heavy-eyed, close-mouthed, and seemingly wrapped in gloom. Unusually, he drank glass after glass of wine at dinner, though it had no visible effect on him. When the ladies withdrew, Caroline took the opportunity of quietly asking Lady Milner: was Captain Brunton not quite well?

Quite well: a little tired and shaken. 'And then, you know,' Lady Milner said, after a slight pause, 'he was dreadfully shocked to hear of Fanny's elopement. I declare it hit him quite like a blow. But Edward is a man of tender feelings, even if he does not choose to parade them.'

Caroline didn't doubt that: still, it was odd, for she knew, or thought she knew, that it wasn't Fanny who was closest to the Captain's heart.

His flush, when the men rejoined them, showed that he had made free with the port. But he drank his tea in separate silence. Caroline intercepted a few curiously baleful looks, as if somehow he felt himself accused, and needed to appeal to her: still, it was long before he sauntered over to her, picked up and examined her teaspoon with great care, then grumbled: 'Miss Fortune. I trust I find you well.'

'Thank you, Captain Brunton. I'm glad to see you. I didn't know—'

'I didn't know. That I would be coming. That is, I was invited. I had a long-standing invitation. For Christmas.' He spoke in a series of small, controlled explosions. 'I thought at first I should not come. Then I thought I should.' He put down the teaspoon as if she had offered him a fake for silver. 'Doesn't matter really.'

'I'm afraid you are not in spirits, Captain Brunton.'

'Not at all. Not at all. That is, I have had good news. An opening for a command in the packet service out of Falmouth. Cornwall. I believe I have secured it.'

'I am pleased – particularly pleased, for I believe they don't shoot at packet-boats, do they? Though to be sure Falmouth is a long way away.'

'It is,' Captain Brunton said, with a judicious tilt of his head, 'a long way from *here*.'

'I suppose everywhere is a long way from somewhere,' said Caroline, and thought: Dear God, I am saying some stupid things.

'At any rate, I will not be called upon until the new year,' Captain Brunton said, with an interrogative look at his own large brown hand. 'Miss Fortune, I wish I might speak with you. I had thought of writing, as you were good enough to permit it, but instead it seemed – well, I wish I might have the opportunity. To speak.'

'Well, sir, we are speaking now, and I think we are not overheard. Can you not . . . ?'

And that was the end of it, for just then the squeaking of a fiddle and a fugue of coughs announced the arrival of the village carollers at the door of the Manor: everyone went out to the hall to hear them, and Captain Brunton wrapped himself again in his gloomy cloak of silence, and did not remove it.

Was it, Caroline wondered when she went to bed that night, because of these signs of a reconciliation between Isabella and Mr Leabrook? Lady Milner might well have told her cousin of them, or Isabella, who had been in conspicuously brighter mood that day, might have hinted at it herself. If so, Caroline thought, then Captain Brunton ought not to torture himself any more. Falmouth, or indeed any other place, would be better. She resolved to tell him so; but sleet and ice, and the sort of muffled sniffling cold that is really, in its requirement that one rest and cosset, as much of a comfort as a convenience, kept her from the Manor for nearly a week after Christmas. The first meltings and drippings, however, saw her putting on her spencer and making the walk to the Manor through a world of steely sun-dazzle and crystalline puddles, a world not unlike her mood – which depended still on London, whence there was no news, even if no bad news: a mood mingled, unresolved.

She found all well at the Manor, and Isabella, with something of her former warmth, jumping up and urging her to the fire with kindly scoldings for coming out when she was still recovering. But Lady Milner was subdued, severe, and shook her head bleakly when Caroline asked her if she had heard anything of Fanny.

'Nothing. Nothing. And I assume the same with you.'

'Don't be downcast, Stepmama,' Isabella said, squeezing her arm. 'I know this sounds odd, but I have a feeling – a presentiment that all will be well in the end. Captain Brunton, you understand what I mean, don't you?'

'In this case, Miss Milner, no,' said Captain Brunton, who was standing at the window staring out, his hands tucked under his coat-tails.

'Now, sir, I declare you are a fibster, because just the other evening you were telling me that curious story of when you were at Minorca,' Isabella said, in a rallying tone, 'and you had a feeling all in the dead of night that someone was in danger, and sure enough in the morning the second lieutenant nearly fell from—'

'You remember?' Captain Brunton said, almost harshly, half turning from the window.

'Why, to be sure,' Isabella said, her eyes wide. 'You were first lieutenant, and he was your good friend, and he was made captain after Copenhagen. Women *do* listen, you know . . . Captain Brunton, what is it that you see out there?'

He said: 'I'm not sure. Well, it is a gig; but it has come half down the avenue, and stopped, and I thought it was about to turn and go away again. But no, here it comes at last. I do believe . . .'

The window-glass made his voice hollow. 'I recognize the lady in it.'

Isabella came and stood by him. It was the glass, perhaps, that made her voice the same as she said: 'Mrs Leabrook.'

Mrs Leabrook: the garrulous, fond, and foolish Mrs Leabrook, perpetually to be found at Hethersett clucking amongst her hens and pigeons: here she was, quite without precedent, arriving at Wythorpe Manor in a gig driven by a sullen groom who helped hand her shawled, scarfed, turbaned, unwieldy bulk down to the gravel of the drive: where again she seemed on the point of changing her mind before, at last, coming in.

'Lady Milner. Miss Milner. I felt I must come and talk to you.' This was only after a long rodomontade about the weather and how she did not mind it and how various members of her family, described in detail, had withstood drought, frost, and typhoon. 'I do appreciate this must seem rather strange – my calling thus, when it has not been our habit, and indeed it has long been my settled habit *not* to make calls on my own account, and it has been quite an undertaking to venture at last . . .'

For some time Mrs Leabrook, having set up camp on the sofa, congratulated herself on coming out, and might have gone on much longer had Lady Milner not put in: 'We are very glad to see you, Mrs Leabrook, but you must see that we are also a little puzzled – anxious even – to know what this matter is that you must talk to us about.'

With hen-like fluffings, winkings, and croonings, Mrs Leabrook turned herself towards Isabella. 'Miss Milner. The news I have to tell you is news that you – yes, I acknowledge it, you have a claim to know—'

'Good God,' Isabella cried, white-lipped, 'what is it? It must be Richard – what?'

'He is married.' Mrs Leabrook closed her eyes for a moment. 'Yes. My son writes me today –' she made a pantomime of extracting the letter from her pocket, gave it up '– no matter – the news is very simple. Yes. Very straightforward – but that's how Richard is, you know, well, of course you know . . . He was married yesterday, in London, by special licence. He bids me be happy. I *am* happy. No woman, I venture to say, who has known the goodness of a son such as Richard, a son who has always made her welfare his especial care even when there are many claims upon his attention – no woman could refuse to bestow her blessing . . .'

'I would be obliged, ma'am,' Lady Milner said, in a voice of ice, moving close to Isabella and laying a hand on her rigid arm, 'if you would spare us these reflections, and tell us who Mr Leabrook has married; and how this has come about; and how he explains himself, when he was publicly engaged to my stepdaughter—'

'Ah, now, my dear Lady Milner, there was after all a certain degree of dubiety about how precisely matters stood between my son and Miss Milner—'

'Indeed there was not, ma'am. That engagement was not broken off. There was an indefinite postponement of marriage, pending the resolution of a difficulty between the parties; but certainly my stepdaughter did not consider herself released from any engagement – as it appears your son has considered *himself*, with what I must call the grossest and most ungentlemanly callousness.' Lady Milner's glare seemed to pin the fluttering matron to her seat. Caroline's spinning mind registered a momentary wish that Fanny was here to see this. As for Isabella, Caroline could not tell how she was taking the news, because she simply could not bear to look at her face. 'Now, ma'am,' Lady Milner went on, 'be so good as to tell us the rest, *briefly*.'

Mrs Leabrook, moist-eyed, resentfully humbled, made another pantomime of searching for a handkerchief. 'Dear me. The lady – the lady is Miss Downey. That is to say, she *was*, for of course now her title is Mrs Richard Leabrook, or say Mrs Maria Leabrook, for I have always preferred, in some defiance of convention, that the woman's name—' A fresh glare from Lady Milner tugged her sharply away from this tempting digression. 'Miss Downey, yes, you know her, of course, and quite a favourite of mine she has been – I can say I have got to know her pretty well during her stays at Hethersett, and – pardon me, Miss Milner, but speaking *objectively*, as it were, I really cannot reprove his choice, even so sudden as it is – though I collect from what he writes me that there has been a – a friendship, an understanding growing for some time – and so though it is so unexpected, in all other respects it is, you know, a most eligible match—'

'Wait, ma'am,' Caroline interjected, with a creeping suspicion upon her, 'are we speaking of the same Miss Downey? For I know her well, and I know she has no portion – no money of her own. I hardly think you would call that an eligible match, unless . . .' Cold sure knowledge came like a cloud across the sun. 'What was the result of the will, ma'am? You know what I mean. Miss Downey's aunt, the late Mrs Catling. They were going to London for the reading of that will.'

Mrs Leabrook's dim pretty eyes roamed all around the room: then she seemed to make a decision, and with a hoist of her chins adopted a proud look. 'Miss Downey, as my son informs me, inherits her aunt's entire fortune. This I consider, as does he I'm sure, a tribute to her character. Mrs Catling, whom I did not have the pleasure of meeting, but whom I conceive to have been an excellent woman of sterling judgement, obviously saw her niece's worth, her beauty, elegance, taste, and accomplishment, and chose to reward it accordingly. As my son also perceived those qualities, and – and saw fit to pay them the tribute of his hand.' Mrs Leabrook's characteristic gasp of air was now like that of someone who has floundered unexpectedly and triumphantly through deep water to dry land.

So Maria got everything! thought Caroline. Poor Matthew. Poor indeed. Her thoughts skipped speedily and surely. Those expensive improvements at Hethersett. Maria's peculiar liking for country living. A friendship, an understanding – no, no, they have been intriguing for some time. And now Leabrook has made a very astute matrimonial choice: beauty and wealth. As for Maria – well, he is handsome, sophisticated, and also landed: in place of her unstable, peripheral life, she will be chatelaine of a mansion. And as for how they have behaved, there will be some talk, some censure, some discredit – but nothing they cannot weather, with riches and power.

Well, well. Except this was not so, it was ill, ill: look at Isabella. Caroline made herself look, at last. She was still, stiff, and pale – not abnormally so; but her heart was beating so high and fast it could be seen all through her, as a quiver on her breast, a pulse in her throat, a vibration in her cheeks. Isabella was not a swooner, but as she rose to her feet Caroline was convinced she was going to faint.

And then, rising, Isabella rose also to the occasion.

'Mrs Leabrook, I am obliged to you,' she said, in a steady voice. 'Thank you for coming to tell us, and I hope the journey has not inconvenienced you.'

'Oh, not in the slightest, my dear Miss Milner, and even if it had I was determined to do it, rather than that you should hear the news in some other way, which would be rather unfortunate – and besides I like to do things properly, it's how I am and always have been, I believe it is a characteristic . . .'

But Isabella could not be interested in how Mrs Leabrook was or where she had got it from, and with the help of a renewed firmness from Lady Milner, the visitor was very soon got rid of: explaining herself to the last even to the unimpressed maid holding the door.

And then Isabella looked blindly around. Caroline was never sure who instigated it, but it ceased to matter, anyhow, as she held her sobbing friend in her arms.

The short grey candle of winter afternoon was nearly spent when Caroline left the Manor. There had been talk – of course – though not too much, and not too deeply: it was early and difficult yet: silences, looks, the invisible binding mesh of sympathy did better. So many things were known and realized now. There must be a slow, sedimentary sinking in.

Some things, though, needed to be said, and were, between Caroline and Captain Brunton, who accompanied her to the front door.

'I do want, just once, to kick him,' Caroline remarked. 'And not from the rear.'

'I fear he would have to be standing up for that, Miss Fortune, and in my mind I have already thrashed him to the floor,' Captain Brunton said, with a show of fierce white teeth: then extinguished them in shame. 'But this is monstrous violent language.'

'Yes, thank heaven for it. Will you escort me home, Captain Brunton?'

'Of course.' Eyes front, the Captain took her arm as if it were a stick or umbrella. Along the oak avenue a rising wind licked at the black slush-puddles and tugged at the leafless branches like malicious fingers in hair. 'I'm afraid I can't speak, Miss Fortune.'

'Oh, I'm sure you can.'

'No, no, because if I do – if I do I must use the unconscionable word "bastard".'

'It is a very good word in the circumstances . . .' This was a day, she thought decisively, for truth. 'Captain Brunton, I'm so sorry.'

'So am I, Lord, so am I . . .' He glanced down at her with a jerk. 'D'you mean – sorry for me?'

'Yes. Because it is painful to see someone suffering what you must be suffering. That is, watching someone you love be so cruelly hurt – and be unable to say or do anything about it.'

Captain Brunton looked at her as if she were a witch. 'How – how could you tell? I have never – I have striven never to betray myself in the slightest . . .'

'Oh, I know. But one can sense these things.'

'I don't know how,' he said wonderingly, 'unless one is in love oneself.'

She shrugged that off. 'I'm sorry if this is – intrusive. I speak only from sympathy; and you may be sure I have breathed no word of it to anyone, nor will. It is only my private observation.'

'Oh, I trust you, Miss Fortune, there's no doubt of that. I'm just astonished. I never could see these things, never understood them in the slightest indeed, until . . . well, no matter. Oh, great God, it *is* a matter,' he burst out, 'what I have heard today – I hardly know how to bear it, Miss Fortune, and that's a fact. To see Miss Milner so abominably treated – to think of the deceit and insolence of that man . . . But, of course, you will not have been so taken by surprise:

you did your best to warn us of his real character – and I fear got a poor return for it.'

'I'm not sure I did do my best. Tell me, did you have no suspicions?'

'Oh, I was inclined to believe all *you* had said about him, and my own heart was ready to supply more aspersions; but that was precisely the trouble, you see: I was not, am not, impartial in this case. I could not even be sure myself how far my feelings against him were the mere result of jealousy. But then it is all such an infernal maze – this judgement of others. When can one be sure? When should one speak, and when keep silence? I have a poor, blundering sort of brain for such things.'

'You have described my late situation exactly, Captain Brunton, and believe me, I think no brain could have blundered more than mine.'

'Yours has been a fearfully difficult position. But then without wanting to sound like Mrs Leabrook, so I think has mine. Here – with my cousin's family – I have always been conscious of seeming to interfere where I had no business. Miss Fanny used to tell me that very plainly . . .' He slowed his pace, as if he had more to say before the Rectory drew near. 'There too – in that regard – I wonder whether I should have spoken.'

'About Fanny?' Caroline said in surprise.

'Not exactly . . . Again it is a matter of hearsay, of suspicion: of wondering whether to let sleeping dogs lie. But I will tell you now, and let you judge. When Miss Fanny began to be intimate with Mr Carraway, something about his name – which is not very common – taken together with his avocation, his manner, all revived a memory. It was something that occurred two years ago. My ship was refitting and I was a temporary landsman, sharing a set of rooms at Deal with a friend, a brother officer, name of Harvey. Poor fellow, he was dead of the East-India fever six months after – but that's by the by. Mrs Leabrook again. Harvey was the sole support of his sister, a gentle little creature, at a boarding-school in Chelsea. Well, there was a young visiting drawing-master at this school who – well, I regret to say he seduced her, and prevailed upon her to run away with him. I say prevailed upon her, not because I mean she had no mind of her own: only that what sixteen-year-old girl, with no experience of the world, can really know that mind? Well, Harvey was much distressed, and took off for London at once to try and trace them, and I went with him to offer such help and company as I could. He did find his sister at last: alone. The drawing-master had deserted her, having – well, having enjoyed her.' Captain Brunton's cheeks reddened, though it was his neck that flamed: just like Isabella's. 'She was living still in the lodging they had taken together – and, alas, would not leave it, from some wild hope that the man would return to her. My friend remonstrated with her in vain. She could not come back to her old life, she told him, even if she would: why not? Well, I think you may guess her condition. Saddest of all, Harvey went to this lodging one day to find she had gone. There was rent owing, and the landlord was turning ugly about it – and she had simply taken herself off, in Lord knows what mixture of despair and resolution and shame. He never heard any more of her. Poor fellow, I remember he was shockingly cut up. And I remember – well, look here, if you had asked me, I would have said the drawing-master's name was Garraway or perhaps Garrity – but I am a noodle when it comes to remembering names. But it seems he was young, talented, a dazzler, with no known connections . . . well, you may see the trend of my thought. But I had no *certainty*, none. And it was partly on account of this – as well as the need for a position – that I went to London myself last month. I knew there were fellows aplenty about the East India Dock who had been mates with Harvey, who started in East Indiamen; and so I asked around if anyone remembered his sister, and whether anyone knew what had become of her. On that last, alas, no: and though everyone remembered the story, all they could say for sure was that it was a drawing-master. So you see I was no more certain. But it has nagged at me – by God, it has nagged at me in a way you cannot conceive, Miss Fortune!'

'I think I can conceive it very well, Captain Brunton. And I can imagine your feelings also, on coming back to find that Fanny had eloped with Mr Carraway.'

'I doubt you can,' he said, with ferocious gloom. 'It seems to confirm – and yet still it is only seeming. If this *is* the same man, then I fear it is a poor outlook for Miss Fanny. I wish with all my heart I had spoken before – yet even then I wonder if I might not have been reproached for mere scurrilous hearsay.'

'By Fanny, I think you would indeed: it would have taken a great deal to alter her resolution, and I fear opposition, or warning, would be the one thing that could strengthen it,' Caroline said: a little more lightly indeed than she felt; the image of Captain Harvey's sister, disappearing alone into a wilderness of indifferent streets, was vivid to her mind. She tried to counter it with the picture of Fanny: Fanny who was all buoyancy and pluck, Fanny who would not, surely, allow herself to be easily abandoned.

'I'm afraid I am a useless fellow with my Carraways and Garritys,' Captain Brunton said gruffly, misinterpreting her silence.

'No, no. I'm just trying to think, on my own account, whether there is anything in what you have told me that may furnish us with a clue. All I can take hold of is this lodging that your friend found his poor sister in – do you recall where it was?'

'I never went there. But I know it was in the Borough, hard by Guy's Hospital, for my friend would lament on his sister ending up in such a dingy sort of place: rooms above a tallow-chandler's, if you please. But apparently they got them on easy terms, because of some past association of the fellow's. Dallying with the chandler's wife, by the sound of him.'

Caroline had another picture: the tearful face of the stationer's daughter. Again, this did not look good, none of this looked good – and yet, after all the various and bewildering emotions she had been through today (and one, yes, was vindication – Caroline was human), there was now another, faintly and unexpectedly stealing upon her from an inner distance: and it was excitement.

'It is better to know now,' Isabella said.

The weather had relented sufficiently the next morning to allow Isabella and Caroline to take a short splashy walk. Isabella had the careful, wakeful, oddly fresh look of someone emerging from a long bout of illness.

'It is far better to know now what his true character is,' she said sturdily, or with an attempted sturdiness, 'rather than if I had married him, and then found out. For that I have you to thank, Caro: if there had been no postponement, I might have been married to him now – or, Lord knows what, actually left standing at the altar by him perhaps. However, I don't imagine you particularly want those thanks just now. All I'll say is – oh, Caro, how could he?'

'I'm afraid he simply – followed his heart,' Caroline said temperately. 'And that was the direction it led him. Selfish – greedy – duplicitous – but natural. And I don't suppose you want to hear those things just now either.'

'Oh, I've said them all, believe me,' Isabella said, with a wave of her hand. 'No, what I mean is, how could he behave so to *you*? You told the truth about him, and he absolutely traduced you, would have seen you shunned and mistrusted by everyone, and all the time – well, all the time, my dear, you were right.'

'Well, I suppose that must happen once in a way,' Caroline said, with a smile, thinking of Stephen.

'I never disbelieved you about Richard: but I would not believe you either, in my heart, Caroline; because *I* was selfish. In that I was very wrong to you.'

'Oh, I shall bear up,' Caroline sighed, with a mock-suffering look. Some instinct told her that only lightness would do now: otherwise they might end up howling. She was pleased to see, at any rate, Isabella with her serious pensive look quite unconsciously jumping over a puddle.

'Well, even though I was so pig-headed, you did make all the difference.'

'Did you – did you still love him?'

Isabella thought for several, precise seconds. 'I loved what I thought was him,' she said; and then, with her face averted, but her hand tightening on Caroline's arm: 'Have I not, in fact, been rather lucky?'

'My dear Bella, of course,' Caroline said, returning the pressure, 'you met *me*: how much more lucky can a person be?'

The tallow-chandler's in the Borough, hard by Guy's Hospital: Caroline visited it in her dreams that night and the night after; she concentrated her imagination so intensely upon it that she could almost smell the tallow. And at the end of the second night, yawning but wakeful in the foredawn hush, Caroline was packing a couple of bags, her decision made.

The Borough was not a part of London she knew particularly well. Her peripatetic father had never lodged there, not indeed because of its generally drab and unlovely character – he had lived in worse places – but because the looming presence of the debtors' prisons, the King's Bench and the Marshalsea, made him deeply uncomfortable. 'Like a pig living next door to a sausage-maker's,' as he put it feelingly. But she knew she could find her way around: nor did the prospect of going to London alone trouble her in the least, as it might many young ladies. And as she sat composedly waiting for first light, when she could slip out of the house and walk to meet the early carrier who passed on the Alconbury road, she seemed to hear her father's shade remarking on this, and saying, in tones of modest self-congratulation: 'Ah, Caro, you see, that's your old papa's influence, and so I think I can say I didn't bring you up so badly after all!'

Aunt Selina, Uncle John: I love you very dearly. Indeed I love you more than I can express, or can ever hope to express in what I hope will be our long, long association; and certainly more than I could get into that rather craven little note I left you before slipping out this morning. But I had do it this way, because if I had announced my intention of going to London to find Fanny, you would surely have tried to prevent me – or, worse, you would have tried to come with me, which would have meant having to face all your fears of travelling on bad winter roads, for miles and miles – and that I could not bear for your sake – so this is better. And you must understand (pursued Caroline in thought, as the coach struggled muddily up Highgate Hill, and she got ready to kick the amorous old gentleman seated opposite, just woken from a doze and under the striking misconception that a snail-trail of drool added to the already debatable attractions of a dropsical belly and luxuriant nose-hair) – you must understand that I am very well used to going about alone and will be perfectly safe until my return which I hope will be soon—

And also – my dear aunt, I think after all you will understand this – while I feel that contrary to general opinion I have done absolutely nothing *wrong* at Wythorpe, I do have a great wish, an unconquerable wish, to do something *right.*

Chapter XXII

She had forgotten it, and she remembered it, all at once: the hurry, glare, stare, stink, and busy brilliance of London. Most striking, after the country, was the fact that all this was not a whit diminished by night-time, which was when the coach shuddered over the City cobbles into the Bull and Mouth. That was not the end of her journey, however: the Borough, south of London Bridge, was where she needed to be, and recollecting the White Hart as a notable inn of that district, Caroline paid for a hackney to take her and her bags thither. She meant to be sparing of her money, which, though she had a generous allowance from her uncle and aunt, she could not help feeling she was using without their consent; but the hackney was a necessary expense, as even Caroline did not fancy the long walk alone to Southwark at this hour. The Thames was a web of lights, tented with smoke: she felt the thrill of the city, along with a certain oppression; and she was desperately tired. The White Hart was a huge and ancient inn, galleried around its great central yard, and just a little dank and dusty compared with the prosperous hotels out west among the squares, with their sash windows and French sauces. But Caroline rather liked its creaking welcome, its superannuated bow-legged porter, who valiantly lugged her two light bags up the endless scranching stairs as if they were cannonballs. As a young woman taking a lodging alone, she was given her share of sidelong glances, but having taken the precaution of wearing her soberest clothes, along with a ring on her left hand – a brass ring from her bed-hangings at home – and of calling herself Mrs Milner (the first name that came to mind), she avoided the worst censure, and was able to retire to her gallery bedroom – wormy panelling, a faded tapestry screen showing white deer apparently leaping with joy at having arrows shot into them – free of the suspicion that she was there to entertain gentlemen on a rotational and commercial basis.

She woke to the rumble of wagons and the smell of coffee and – surprisingly – a protracted shiver of misgiving: just what *was* she doing? Tucked into a pocket of her mind was the thought of Stephen, and for a weak moment she reached for it. Stephen was here in London, Stephen was engaged in the search for Fanny: why not just call on him at Batt's Hotel, give him her information, and simply hand the business over . . .

'To his superior male brain?' she concluded. 'No, no.' He would like that too much.

Fortified by pride and breakfast, she went out into the Borough. If there was one thing this district was famed for, it was mud; and as overnight there had been a thaw, there were more than usually copious quantities of it about the old constricted streets; and as this was the main highway down to Kent, there were plenty of lurching coaches and wagons to spatter you with it, or to run you down if you preferred. It was a slow and dirty morning's work for her. The little winding streets around Guy's Hospital were represented by every noisome trade, it seemed, from tanneries to dung-farmers, but not a tallow-chandler was to be found. It was only when she emerged in Borough High Street again, baffled and back to her starting point, that she saw what had been there all the time. Directly in front of her, on the west side, was a row of tall square-bayed houses with latticed shop-fronts, and in the middle hung a signboard – peeling and faded, which was perhaps why she had missed it: *Gerrard & Son, Tallow-Chandlers*.

She was so excited that she did not stop to think how she might best approach this. She hurried across the road, burst into the dingy ill-lit shop, and only then, as she waited for the cracked bell to summon someone from the glassed-in counting-house at the back, did she reflect again on what Captain Brunton had told her. 'Some past association of the fellow's.' It might mean anything: it might mean, however, that the people here would seek to protect Mr Carraway. All she could think to do was look unthreatening and innocent. Unfortunately when she glimpsed herself preparing this look in the dark window, she found the effect positively half-witted, which muddled her for a moment.

'May I be of service to you, madam?'

A pale pretty watercolour of a woman in her worn thirties, wiping her hands on her apron and presenting a smile of habitual propitiation that suggested an awkward husband.

'Oh, good morning. You must be Mrs Gerrard.' Caroline took what she hoped would be an inspired plunge. 'Charles has told me so much about you. How is he? I was wondering if this was a convenient time to call on him.' She reinforced her own smile as that of Mrs Gerrard faded. 'Charles Carraway, you know.'

'I'm sorry, madam,' the woman said at last, in a mechanical tone, 'I don't know to whom you're referring. I rather fancy you've got the wrong house.' She began to retreat.

'Oh, surely not – Charles told me he was lodging here again. Charles Carraway the painter, you know: we are old acquaintances—'

'There's no one here of that name, madam. Now if you'll be so good—'

'Not Milner then? Miss Fanny Milner? I've come such a long way, Mrs Gerrard, just to seek out old friends, and could you not at least tell me—'

'I don't know who you mean,' Mrs Gerrard said, shaking her head, avoiding Caroline's eyes. 'It's like I said—' She stopped, tight-lipped, and smoothed her apron. 'Now I must be getting to my work, madam, and I'll bid you good-day.'

'Like you said? Pray, what do you mean? To who?' Caroline cried; but already the chandler's wife had shut herself up in the counting-house.

Whom, Caroline thought, whom, going out into the street with a peculiar acrid feeling of mixed triumph and dismay. Mrs Gerrard was not a good actress: she *did* know something, at least; but short of invading her premises like a bailiff, Caroline could not think how to get at it. Most tantalizing of all, this last inadvertent revelation: like she said . . . ? It suggested someone else had been asking after the fugitives. Again she fingered the pocket in her mind: could it be? Should she go to Batt's Hotel and find out?

Coming out of abstraction, she saw a lounger in greatcoat and pulled-down hat lean out of a doorway ahead, and readied herself for evasion. That was another trouble with this district: it was full of seedy fellows—

'Oh, my God!' she cried, as Stephen Milner lifted the hat and smiled his lopsided smile.

'It would appear we've followed the same trail,' he said, offering her his arm. 'Will you? I know I look rather disreputable, but it is a necessary disguise, because I've been watching the house, you see. And I'm not entirely sure whether Fanny and friend may have a view from the front windows, though I don't *think* so: my guess is they have the rooms at the second pair back.'

'Then they *are* there! I thought—'

'Oh, yes. That little downtrodden woman said she'd never heard of 'em, no doubt? Same with me yesterday, when I tracked them to this charming spot. But the lie was written all over her, poor creature: and I definitely glimpsed *him* this morning, slipping through an alley near Guy's. My guess is there's some tortuous back way behind those rambling old places, and they use that, but I can't find it. Well, how are you, Miss Fortune? Quite tol-lollish, I hope? I have always wanted to ask someone if they are tol-lollish, and now I have.'

'Oh, Stephen, stop it. You saw Mr Carraway – actually saw him? Oh, thank goodness.'

'Why? Never tell me *you* have a taking for him as well.'

'Stop it again. I'm relieved because – well, it means he is still here, that he hasn't abandoned her.'

'Ah, I see.' He looked into her face. 'I see more. You are serious, Miss Fortune. A bad sign. What more have you to tell? – and incidentally, how *did* you end up here, and are you all alone?'

'I am alone, Mr Milner, and quite comfortably so, and I will tell you – but I long to know how *you* found this place?'

'It was rather brilliant of me, wasn't it?' he said, with satisfaction. 'Oh, it has been a long, frustrating business, and at first I thought my case was absolutely hopeless. The key at last was thinking of Fanny's character, and putting that together with what Augusta told me, that she had taken her jewels with her.'

'I didn't know Fanny had any jewels.'

'Exactly, because she doesn't wear them, because she scorns such artificial frippery and prefers to appear in natural simplicity et cetera. Which suggests that she had a purpose in taking them, which purpose must have been to sell them to help finance the clandestine liaison, which again sounds entirely characteristic of Fanny: don't you think? Picture it. Carraway: "But these are yours, my darling, your property . . ." Fanny: "Pooh, I care naught for property, and besides all I have is yours, let us sell them at once." Carraway – not very reluctantly: "Well, if you say so, my bewitching angel . . ." Ugh,' Stephen said, with a grimace, 'I've made myself feel sick – but convincing, yes? So, it was then a simple matter of seeking out such jewellers as are unscrupulous enough to buy family jewels from an obviously deluded schoolgirl, and proceeding from there. In fact I presented myself as the vengeful father, and was believed, which is unflattering from the physical point of view, but it served its turn. The rogue who had bought them was canny enough to require an address from the vendors in case of trouble – and so, here we are.'

'You say a simple matter – but from what I know of London, there must be scores of such jewellers all over the city. How did you . . . ?'

'Aye, well: she is my sister, and I love the crazed vixen, and as has been rightly pointed out to me, I am sometimes too careless of my responsibilities.' Before she could speak – and something pressed at her heart to be spoken, though she could not tell what – he went on briskly: 'Now where are you staying? Somewhere, I presume: and can one get a good meal there? I've been haunting that dreary street for long enough.'

So: the White Hart, where with a feeling of unreality by no means unpleasant, she ate luncheon with Stephen in a private dining room

– dusty red curtains, Hogarth prints hanging askew on the panels, and an ingrained immemorial smell of gravy. Much to tell. Captain Brunton's story first, because it was germane, and because she still hesitated over the other.

'That was why I was so relieved to hear you'd seen Mr Carraway – because I was afraid of Fanny being deserted, as he did with this poor Miss Harvey.'

'I see, I see.' Stephen was thoughtful. 'There *may* be some other side to this story – even though, to be frank, it simply confirms my suspicion of soulful young men who pride themselves on their spontaneity. What a sibilant sentence. Hm, hm. The problem I anticipate is Fanny's stubbornness, or what she would call independence of mind. I still doubt we will wean her from him, even if she were to know this discreditable tale – don't you think?'

'I'm afraid so,' Caroline admitted.

'Which suggests – and I hope you don't think I'm being heartlessly practical here – that we must pin him down, if she is determined not to give him up. In other words, if there has not been a marriage ceremony, as I presume there has not, then we must remind the forgetful Mr Carraway of this little omission. Will you take a little more of this veal-and-ham pie? And will you tell me what else is troubling you?'

'How can you tell something's troubling me?' she said, rather sharply.

'Because you're drinking a lot of wine.'

'That's not a sign of trouble, Mr Milner: that is me: I like drinking a lot of wine,' she said loftily, drinking.

'I'm glad to hear it, for I do too, and we topers must stick together. Still—'

'Oh, Stephen, it's Isabella. No, no, don't be alarmed, she is quite well – but plainly you have not heard the news?'

'The last letter I had was from Augusta, last Thursday I think.' His eyes were flinty. 'Tell, tell.'

She told. At the end of the telling, he called for another bottle of wine, and they silently drank while the fire popped and new-shod hoofs chocked on the cobbles outside.

'If you wish to use a bad word,' she said at last, 'about Leabrook, I mean, then don't be shy of it. Captain Brunton used a very good one. He called him a—'

'Yes, to be sure. I am thinking of – well, I am thinking of a great many things. I am wishing Leabrook all the ill-luck in the world, of course, but also I am – well, I am surprised, and yet I am not at all surprised, and I am thanking heaven for Isabella's escape.' In absorbed agitation Stephen did wild things to his hair. 'Indeed, this may be the most amazing stroke of luck, because even with what *I've* learned about Leabrook, I wasn't confident of being able to cure Bella of him.'

'You mean you know more – worse about him?'

'Oh, yes: and that's why I left instructions that there was to be no reconciling while I was away. Yes, I found out about our friend Leabrook, when I went away from Wythorpe the first time in November – remember? How nice it is to rhyme, I must do it all the time. No, don't hit me, hearken. It was when Leabrook said that you had thrown yourself at him at Brighton, and you said that he had sought to seduce you in same.'

'Yes – and you skipped off somewhere to see your wretched ruins.'

'Quite right, and quite apposite, as one of the ruins I went to see was a lady well known to you. Sorry, one shouldn't speak ill of the lately deceased, and no, she was really, I thought, rather well preserved. I refer to your former employer and, I would guess, tormentor, Mrs Sophia Catling of Brighton. *That* was my purpose in going down to the south coast. I do hate to flatter you, Miss Fortune, which is why I never do – but the fact is, I could not believe what Leabrook had said about you, and so I resolved to go and call on this Mrs Catling, and see if I could find out the truth from her.'

'The devil you did!' Caroline sat back, open-mouthed. 'You – going to see Mrs Catling! I'm just trying to imagine it.'

'All my grace, elegance, and beauty contrasting with that crabbed monstrosity, I know. Well, as I say, she wasn't quite what I had thought her – and yet once she began speaking, she was, if you see what I mean. Really I think you did well to tolerate her at all – though I fancy this heart-stroke you tell me about was not as sudden as her lawyer made out, for she was not in health when I saw her. That was partly why she did not grant me a long interview – the other reason being that I was, let's see if I can remember her honeyed words, an insolent puppy to come quizzing her about that under-bred chit of whom she could recall only so much as to confirm in her mind that she was well rid.'

'Now I know you have seen Mrs Catling. Oh, Stephen, I am sorry.'

'Don't be, it's no fault of yours. Take another glass of this. Quite refreshing to be called a puppy: better than being taken for Fanny's father anyhow. Well, I tried servility, and that didn't answer, so – well, I had the measure of my enemy now, and I blustered about our ancient name and sprawling acres and *then* I saw her looking at me a little differently. Only a little, mind: insufficient ancientness and too few acres truly to impress. But she listened. And then she laughed. *Not* a pleasant sound,' he said wincing reminiscently. 'The said Mr Leabrook of Northamptonshire, she asserted, was a man of impeccable taste and manners, and would certainly not so demean himself; and as for you, Mrs Catling said she was too careful an employer to allow any kind of amorous goings-on. The reason she dismissed you, she said, was that you were wilful and impertinent and set upon going absent without leave – yes, that was her military phrase. And so be off with you – to me, I mean. Curious to think someone actually married her, isn't it? Did he never start up at night, silently screaming at what he had done?'

'Apparently Colonel Catling was a sort of male edition of her. Stephen, I am sorry again – that she was so rude to you.'

'Well, I thought I knew all about being rude, but, my Lord . . . Anyhow, off with me I went, more convinced by now that you were entirely in the right, and more suspicious of Leabrook on account of it. And then I had an idea, which – well, let's just call it genius and leave it at that. I bethought me of Leabrook's sister – the one at the Brighton boarding-school. I wondered what she could tell me about her brother. So I procured a Brighton trade directory, and then my heart nearly failed, as it appeared there was nothing *but* boarding-schools in that wretched town. Well, the only thing for it was to go knocking at the door of each and every one, asking for Miss Leabrook, and then blandly saying I had got the wrong address whenever I drew a blank. I must confess there was a risk here of appearing disreputable: but I dressed in my best, and generally tried to look sober and sensible.'

'That's just what I did, coming down to London alone.'

'Ah, I wondered what that odd ring was all about. It's harder for you to look respectable, of course: no disguising those rogue's eyes. Close your mouth, my dear Miss Fortune, it's not elegant. Well, I found the place at last; and as she had certainly heard of me, being brother to Leabrook's fiancée, and as this did establish a family connection, I was able to have a little interview with Miss Leabrook in the proprietress's parlour. Pleasant, quiet little creature – wouldn't say boo to a goose. I happened to have a goose with me, and so I was able to test it, and I could not prevail upon her to – yes, I'm sorry. Well, there seemed more constraint about her, when I talked of Leabrook, than was compatible with mere shyness. So I cultivated her. I got the proprietress's permission to take Miss Leabrook to tea at Dutton's, and there, after plying her with many pastries and ices, and questioning her as gently as possible – for I *can* be agreeable, you know, when I choose – I got her to talk freely. It did seem odd to me that she so seldom came home, and spent the holidays with friends: now I found out why. She and her brother were not on good terms – though she was still too much in awe of him to make it explicit. It seems that last year she had had a friend at the school: the natural daughter of somebody or other, who was discreetly paying for her education; and so a girl lacking family and protection. And a very pretty girl. Does it sound familiar? Yes, it appears that Leabrook *interested* himself in this girl, in quite an inappropriate way: laughed it off and denied all, when it came out. By which time the girl, much distressed, had got herself moved to another school – and of course Leabrook's sister had lost her friend. Hence the estrangement. But I could tell that the poor girl was not accustomed to being believed, and she was very fearful lest I relay any of this to her brother.'

'Dear God!' exploded Caroline. 'If I didn't know better, I would say that all you men are—'

'Captain Brunton's word, yes. Fortunately there are some examples of perfection around, like me, to redress the balance.'

'Well. I had a strong feeling that I was not the first he had approached in that way – but a schoolfriend of his sister's!'

'Unsavoury, isn't it? Well, that settled it for me. The trouble was, I kicked my heels a while, unsure how to proceed. I knew this man must not marry Bella, but the question was how to accomplish that. I could tell her this story at once, and risk her digging her heels in, as girls have been known to do when discouraged from unsuitable men; or hope that that temporary separation would ripen into proper indifference, and become permanent. Then, before I could come to a decision, there arrives Augusta's letter telling me of Fanny's mad escapade, and so I had to rush home, pick your brains as you remember, and then rush here. So in a way I'm glad that Leabrook has decided matters by showing his hand like this. And how is Bella? D'you think she would have had him, if Miss Downey had not supervened?'

'I don't know: I don't think she does either. But she is very thankful for her escape.'

'Well, you are too magnanimous to say that everyone should have listened to you in the first place, so I'll say it for you.'

'Thank you. But I would rather never have been right – I mean, how unfair it seems. There's he with his beauteous bride and her splendid fortune, and – and he's just going to get away with everything!'

'Men do tend to – and handsome men tend to more – and rich, well-born, handsome men tend to most of all. Would you really say Miss Downey was beauteous, by the by?'

'Most people would. And I thought you might judge that for yourself, as she was always throwing herself at your head.'

'Was she?' he said, with tremendous puzzlement. 'I never noticed. But look here, you don't really believe they'll be happy, do you? Two people who are, at the very least, habituated to deception: I don't believe that's a good foundation. I think there'll be affairs within a twelvemonth. Mark my words, I would say, if I were the kind of intolerable person who says "mark my words". Look at that, we've finished the other bottle. Shall we take a turn in the yard? I need to clear my head before we go on.'

Yes, she needed some air: a little time too, while she took in all he had told her. He let her think while they strolled about the inn-yard. An old carrier in smock and gaiters was unloading his parcels with infinite slowness and care, as if they were relics that might crumble at a touch: a maid was pretending not to notice the whistle of an ostler: a small boy was rolling on the ground in noisy ecstasies with an excited puppy.

'How precisely did you come away from Wythorpe?' Stephen asked at last. 'Did you simply tell Aunt Selina what you were going to do?'

'Not exactly. I left a note . . . saying I was coming to see you.'

'Ah! But you didn't.'

'No . . . I did think of it. But I wanted to do something for myself, something right and good and – oh, don't tease. What did you mean about going on?'

'Oh, I suppose go on to survey the chandler's house again. If you'd care to lounge alongside me, of course. I'll let you have half my doorway. I must confess that, after having been so superbly resourceful, I am now somewhat at a stand. The problem is our fugitives are plainly being very careful – and one cannot just force one's way into a private house demanding to examine the occupants. My hope is that Fanny must come out, at some point, and then – then I pounce. Feel free to find the notion of me pouncing hilarious, by the by.'

Caroline was gazing fixedly at the little boy with the puppy.

'What is it?' Stephen said. 'Did you want one of those instead of the kitten? They get huge and unmanageable, you know, and start doing unspeakable things to your leg in company—'

'Stephen, do be quiet a minute,' she told him, 'for I have an idea.'

* * *

A very young and dispirited costermonger, who was not selling any sprats on the corner of Borough High Street, supplied them with what they needed.

'I'm not sure as I can bear it myself,' he said hesitatingly, when they detailed their plan. 'I'm afraid I might break, you see.' But when they explained that the person they sought was quite as tender-hearted, and that therefore the experiment would not take long, and when Stephen offered him the equivalent of a month's sprat-sales for his trouble, he went along with them. More importantly, so did the half-grown mongrel dog he had tied to his barrow.

The dog appeared to think it was all a great game at first, when his master tied him to a bridle-post just outside the tallow-chandler's shop and then retreated with Caroline and Stephen to a passageway down the street. He yapped excitedly for a while: then lay down with his nose on his paws: then, sensing something amiss in his master's continued absence, began to howl, desultorily at first, and then with all the anguished soul of his canine being. It was desolate, and loud.

'This is what I mean,' the coster murmured in their hiding-place, gnawing his lip. 'I don't know as I can bear it. He don't understand, you see – far as he's concerned, I've gone.'

'Never fear,' Stephen assured him, 'if it doesn't answer within a minute or two, then just go untie him and we'll forget it. But – ah!'

The shop-door of *Gerrard & Son* had opened, and Fanny Milner stepped out. With a quick glance up and down the street she hurried over, as Caroline had guessed she surely must, to pat and comfort the howling dog.

She was still bent over him, rubbing his ears and crooning that his master was a brute, when she became aware of the three figures surrounding her.

'Hello, Fanny,' Stephen said amiably.

Fanny, rising and red-faced, looked from one to the other in gathering outrage.

'Oh! Oh, I am entrapped! Stephen, how could you – and, Caroline, you, above all how could *you*?' And to the coster: 'I'm afraid I don't know you—'

'No, that's so, and I ain't the brute you said I am,' the coster said, with dignity, gathering his squirming dog into his arms and walking away.

'A ruse, to be sure,' Stephen said, very tenderly and deftly securing Fanny's arm, 'but really, my dear Fanny, you are so deuced elusive you left us no choice. Why you are so determined not to have your dear brother and your dear friend call upon you I can't imagine—'

'You know very well,' Fanny said grandly. 'It is because you wish to drag me back to my dreary imprisonment. But that you will never do, unless you do drag me – which you will not . . .' She glared at her brother, as if he had confused her. 'Stephen, I am free, and I am happy. Can you not understand that? Caro – surely *you* can?'

'I would be very glad to know that you are free and happy, Fanny,' Caroline said, with a feeling of crossing stepping-stones. 'And because you are so dear to me, I really would like to be absolutely sure of it.'

'Well, you *can* be sure,' Fanny said, and then with a look half mutiny, half bravado: 'Indeed, step in – yes, step in, by all means, as you now know where we reside. I have no objection to that. I have no secrets. You will be supposing, of course, an illicit liaison. I do not accept these arbitrary prescriptions of society – neither does Charles: nevertheless I may as well say we maintain separate establishments within our set of rooms.' She looked so crimson and conscious as she said this that it was impossible to say whether it was an outright lie or the surprising truth: though Caroline did have her own ideas. 'You will not find those rooms particularly luxurious or well appointed: that is our way: I merely mention it, I do not apologize for it. So, if you do wish to—'

'Devil take it, Fanny, stop orating, you sound like the Lord Mayor's Banquet,' said Stephen, unimpressibly. 'D'you think we'll turn our noses up if there's no footman in powder? As we said, we've come to see you, that's all. Now lead the way, do. Miss Fortune's been making me drink too much wine and my tongue's like burnt paper, and I'm sure you can make us tea in your ill-appointed rooms.'

Partly mollified, yet with several suspicious glances, Fanny led the way: at the shop door she glanced significantly down at Stephen's affectionate arm. He relinquished it with a cheerful gesture, which made her look all the more perplexed. Presently they were passing through the shop, where Mrs Gerrard peeped out at them like a wondering rabbit, and climbing some narrow stairs. Here Stephen paused for a moment, and whispered urgently to Caroline over his shoulder: 'Whatever I say, no matter how absurd, agree with me.'

He had been right: the second floor, at the back, was where Fanny and Mr Carraway had their lodging; and it was not so very bad. There was a large sitting room, incompletely filled with the sort of furniture that must have been deeply loved by someone for it not to have been thrown away; and opening out of it a smaller room with a good window, which was obviously Charles Carraway's painting room, as he was to be seen there – framed – clutching palette and maul-stick, staring at the visitors with a good deal less than Fanny's self-command. As for the sleeping arrangements, Caroline extended the benefit of the doubt, as she couldn't tell. Though she still had her own ideas.

'My dear Charles, you see we are pursued,' said Fanny, in an excessive voice, 'pursued and actually caught, but apparently we needn't fear, as my brother *says* he has simply come on a visit, and is not going to drag me away.' She went and set a kettle over the fire. 'If he does, you know I shall fight – but I don't want you to, do you hear me?'

Judging by Mr Carraway's perspiring pallor, this advice was superfluous. But he cheered up a little when Stephen, advancing on him, thrust out a hand with a breezy 'Mr Carraway, glad to see you again, how d'you do?' and then flung himself into a creaking chair, amiably yawning. 'Well, you are snug here, I must say. Not the prettiest of situations, though, which is a pity.'

'Charles and I care nothing for fashion, Stephen, as you well know,' Fanny said airily. 'It is far more important that we live within our means, as we intend showing this is not a mere adventure; and as we have these rooms on easy terms, on account of Mrs Gerrard being Charles's cousin, they suit us very well for the time being.'

'Oh, a cousin!' said Stephen, still amiable, hands in pockets, and Caroline read his thought: *So that's what you call it.* She was divided between amusement and anxiety: for Fanny had committed herself so whole-heartedly to this life, and yet that curled charmer now relaxing into a smile half sheepish, half triumphant could at any moment walk out of the door and never come back. He had done it before. All that could be said was that he had not done it *yet*; and that was perhaps more a tribute to Fanny's qualities than his.

'Well, do tell me how everyone is at Wythorpe,' Fanny said. 'I have been meaning to write – but to get a reply, you know, I must give an address, and that – well . . .'

'That is an irrelevance now, of course,' said Stephen. 'It would have made things a good deal easier for us, as you have been the very devil to track down, but no matter – no reproaches,' he added quickly, as Fanny's chin went up. 'Well, Caroline can tell you better about that, I think.'

'Oh, yes – let's see, everyone is well, Uncle John and Aunt Selina, and Isabella and Lady Milner, and Captain Brunton was there for Christmas—'

'And they are looking after the dogs, aren't they?' Fanny put in, with a brimming look. 'They haven't – taken it out on them? I so wanted to bring them, but it would have been impossible—'

'My dear Fanny,' laughed Stephen, 'do you suppose we whip your dogs daily, to punish you for your elopement? They are as spoiled as ever. I call it an elopement, by the by, for want of a better term.'

'Words are only words, you know, Mr Milner,' said Mr Carraway, finding his voice. 'It is feelings that count. It is our feelings that have guided us, and they are guides that, I believe –' he gave his misty sideways look '– can never lead us wrong.'

Caroline could contain herself no longer. 'It would be interesting,' she said, as temperately as she could, 'to know if Miss Harvey still agrees with those sentiments.'

Fanny, making tea at the crowded table, froze with spoon suspended. 'Who is Miss Harvey?'

'"Who is Sylvia, what is she, that all our swains commend her"?' sang Stephen, badly. 'One for the pot, remember, Fanny.'

'Miss Harvey,' Caroline said, 'was the sister of a naval officer, a friend of Captain Brunton's. She ran away to London from Deal with – well, I believe with this gentleman.' Who had gone very pale again. Should she, Caroline wondered, add that they had taken these very same lodgings? No: that was too much.

'Yes,' Mr Carraway said, nodding earnestly, 'yes, that is correct, that was the case, indeed.'

Fanny finished making the tea with a certain vigour. 'You never told me this, Charles.'

'Not strictly,' Mr Carraway said, with a judicious frown, 'not strictly perhaps – but you know, Fanny, I did tell you I had loved before. I never made any disguise of that.'

'Yes, Charles . . . Though I did not know it was that sort of love.'

'Oh, my dear girl, what other sort is there? You know my nature: I cannot tack to the winds of convention: I am all or nothing.' Mr Carraway did some wistful blinking. 'If you would know about Miss Harvey, I can tell you. I can tell you that it was all a piece of youthful folly. I was young, she was very young, and we hardly knew what we were about. And I regret it, for it ended unhappily.'

'Particularly so for Miss Harvey, was it not?' Caroline suggested.

'What does this mean? Charles?' Fanny demanded sharply: and Caroline felt a little hope in that sharpness. This one, Mr Carraway, is made of sterner stuff than Miss Harvey.

'I do not know what story you have heard, Miss Fortune,' he sighed, with a limpid look. 'If it represents me in a bad light, I cannot help that. I can only say that our separation was a mutual affair. As I remarked, we were both young and absurd, and we fell to quarrelling over trifles. Then there was a lasting quarrel, and I took myself off, and when I returned to – to where we lodged, she had taken herself off likewise, and that was the end of it. It sounds a sad tale, but really it is not: for we were not good for one another. And there can be nothing worse than two souls yoked inharmoniously together – is that not a living death?'

'Aye, aye, there's something in what he says,' grunted Stephen, who under lowered lids had been watching the painter carefully. 'What do you think, Fanny? Ah, tea.'

Fanny glanced, perplexedly, from Stephen to Caroline to her raptly gazing lover. 'I think,' she said, 'it is a great pity. And I agree with Charles: of course I do. Though I think it was also a pity, Charles, that you could not tell me about this – did you think I wouldn't understand?'

'I would have to be an even greater fool than I know myself to be to think *that*,' he said meltingly, 'for you always do understand – always! But come,' he added more briskly, 'you do right, indeed, Mr Milner, to appeal to Fanny: for that is what the whole matter is about, is it not? Fanny's choice: Fanny's decision: that is, thank heaven, to be with me. Are we to respect and abide by that decision?'

'Quite so,' Fanny said, rallying, 'and I tell you, Stephen, you will not fence me about with your spirit-soiling prohibitions.' Proud of that one: she has lain awake thinking them up, Caroline guessed.

'No intention of any such thing,' Stephen said, standing up and roaming about as he drank his tea. 'Just wonder whether you wouldn't like to seal it – your decision, I mean – by getting married. It would be so much better in all ways, you know.'

'How?' said Fanny, scornfully.

'Well, you love each other, don't you?'

'Absolutely! How can you doubt it?'

'My dear dramatic sister, I don't. That's why I'd suppose you'd like to show that love to the world. Proclaim it. Rather than this, which is almost as if – that is, it might be misconstrued by duller spirits – as if you are ashamed of it.' Stephen finished his tea and beamed.

'Pooh, you don't understand me very well, Stephen, if you think I care for that,' Fanny said, with tense gaiety; and stole a look at Caroline. 'You understand, Caro – don't you?'

'Oh, yes,' she answered easily, 'though I do tend to agree with Stephen – about showing your love to the world, I mean.'

'And then there's your money,' Stephen went on. 'Dear conscientious Father made sure you and Bella had your fifteen kothousand apiece as a marriage portion, and it seems a pity that it should lie there a-rusting.'

'Money,' Fanny pronounced, 'is sordid stuff, and we don't care for it.'

'Not a whit,' Mr Carraway said, with – to do him justice – what seemed like complete sincerity.

'Don't you? Hey, well, it does seem a shame,' Stephen said, shrugging indifferently, 'as when two such people as you are in love, it's nice to see them properly set up. A good painting-studio, for example, and plenty of room for dogs, and spare money to help the needy, and – well, anyhow, it was just a thought. Really that's not why we're here. Aha, you are about to say, then why are you here? I'll tell you: to give you our news. Our own most happy, most delightful news.' He came over and took Caroline's arm. 'Caroline and I are getting married. Yes!' he cried loudly, covering her yelp of surprise. 'Yes, is it not the most delightful thing? You'll observe the engagement ring – best that could be got out in the wilds. And so we've come to Town to get a licence, so we can be married as soon as may be. Oh, we did think about going through the whole business of calling the banns, but it takes so long – and why delay? The fact is, as we've found, when you're in love everything is romantic – even getting a marriage licence from Doctor's Commons. Isn't that so, Caro?'

'Yes, Stephen,' she managed.

'Well, aren't you going to congratulate us?' Stephen pursued. 'I had thought, Fanny – and this is why we were so eager to find you – that you of all people would be pleased for us. I know how fond you are of Caro – and now you are going to be her sister-in-law!'

Staggered as Caroline was, she did register a small pleasure in seeing the rather too self-assured Fanny reduced to such silent astonishment; and that helped her to collect herself.

'Yes, Fanny,' she said, 'I hope you are as pleased as I am, my dear.'

'I – oh, yes, I am,' stammered Fanny, 'only it is so – so very unexpected!'

'Love is always unexpected, I believe,' Caroline said. 'As for me, I can think of nothing better than being united with the man I love for the rest of my days – openly and in the eyes of the world – and amongst those who are dear to me.' She found this both very easy and intensely difficult to say.

'Quite so,' Stephen said, with hearty approval. 'Well, that's our news, and thank goodness we found you so we could tell you it – and now, what say you dine with us on the strength of it? The four of us, tomorrow evening, at Grillon's – what d'you say? Call it a settled thing. I'm at Batt's in Jermyn Street if you need to say nay for any reason. But do come. It would give us great pleasure.'

'Then – yes, thank you, we shall be happy to join you,' said Mr Carraway, who had the dawning look of a man woken from a bad dream and realizing none of it was true. 'And – many congratulations to you. Eh, Fanny?'

'Yes,' Fanny said, in a small voice.

'When you said agree with you on everything, no matter how absurd,' Caroline said, as they turned into the yard of the White Hart, 'I didn't know you would—'

'Say something so *very* absurd? Yes, apologies for that, it must have quite shocked you. But you see my reasoning. Fanny has always taken you as her model, inexplicable as it is; and so my hope is that if she supposes you reconciled to marriage, then . . .'

'Oh, yes, I do see. But what do you think of Charles Carraway? Do you want your sister to marry him?'

'Yes, because if she doesn't, she will ruin herself for his sake; and because she does, God help her, love the man, and I think he loves her as far as it's possible for him to love anything better than his mirror. And besides, I do believe she can manage him. She might even make something of him at last. What do you think?'

'I think . . . yes, I would go along with that.'

'You're not under obligation to agree with me now, you know.'

'I know, idiot. Stephen, this deception – this pretence –' she glanced at the ring on her finger '– it will surely have to be revealed at some point.'

'Oh, we'll cross that bridge when we come to it. And with luck it will have done its work by then. You're tired, I think.'

She was: an odd, dropping, childlike tiredness of body; and an even worse one of mind, as if she had been coldly and diligently thinking for a whole week. Yet I haven't been thinking of anything really, she thought, paradoxically: and I don't feel as if I could ever think again.

'Well, I prescribe an early supper and bed. And in the morning I'll call for you. We should go shopping: find something nice for Aunt Selina, who is no doubt sick with worry. And for Bella.'

'That's a good thought . . . And, Stephen, might I pay a call tomorrow? In truth I don't know why I should care, but being in London puts me in mind of Matthew Downey. I'm sorry for him. He was so dreadfully disappointed in his expectations from Mrs Catling, and he did so try to please her.'

'Hm, and was not half so obliging to you, as I recall.'

'Well, yes, and as I said I don't know why I should care, but I would just like to see him once.'

'I know why,' Stephen said, in his cryptic way, leaving her.

Chapter XXIII

He had forgotten her. Caroline, lingering in the coffee room of the White Hart next morning, avoiding the speculative eye of a lean sporting gentleman drinking his breakfast with one grasshopper leg propped, excitingly as he thought, on the fender, looked at the Dutch clock on the wall, saw the morning was half gone and called down apocalyptic curses on the head of Stephen Milner, who had said he would come for her and had forgotten.

Why so apocalyptic? I don't know why.

She suddenly sprang up, resolved to find a hackney and go to Golden Square by herself, and found Stephen's waistcoat in front of her nose.

'Trifle late, sorry. The fact is I had a visitor at my hotel early this morning.'

Drawing in breath to say she didn't give a damn about that, she found herself saying: 'Oh, who?'

'Carraway. Come come, I've a hackney waiting for us. That gown's pretty, is it new? Yes, it was Carraway, with his curls combed and his coat brushed, and actually, I suspect, absent from Fanny without leave. He had come to return the favour of my call, he said, and was generally obliging and conversational and, oh, so wanting to say something more. Which I got out of him at last over a devilled breakfast. He had been thinking over – they had both been thinking over – what was said about marriage yesterday, and he was inclined to think it was rather a good idea. He had always believed that one should be prepared to change one's ideas, otherwise one was a mere slave of – well, I didn't really listen to that part. The end of it was that he was very ready to obtain a marriage licence, if I would be so good as to show him how it was done, as he was a mere babe and child in these matters – well, never mind that part either.' Stephen handed her into the hackney waiting at the mouth of the yard. 'So I took him straightway down to Doctors' Commons to apply for a licence, and now he has gone home to tell Fanny. Or at least, to tell her presently – after playing her on the hook for a while. He is not stupid. He is not very good, either, but then I don't think he is very bad: Fanny will always have to watch him, but I'm sure she is quite capable of that; and in short, I think we have made the best bargain in the circumstances.' Stephen rapped on the carriage roof. 'Oh, and also I hinted that if he played any of his old tricks, I would suspend him from a high place, and not by his neck.'

'Well, you might have added that while he was up there I would be throwing things at him; but beyond that, yes, Mr Milner, I think you have brought it to a satisfactory solution.'

'We, Miss Fortune, we: I fancy we work rather well together; do you think we might set up in some sort of business along these lines? Oh, by the by, what did you think of Fanny's claim about their keeping separate establishments?'

'Candidly, I did not think much of it.'

He smiled caustically. 'Neither did I. All the more reason to pin him down, before any little curly-haired, misty-eyed babies appear. We're going to Golden Square now – I don't think the Lent law term is sitting yet, so I dare say you'll find Mr Downey at home – unless you've changed your mind?'

She had not; and with the lightness of relief on her, was quite ready to shake Matthew Downey by the hand, and sincerely commiserate with him on his disappointment. The Downey house in not-very-fashionable Golden Square stood tall, shadowy, sooty, behind an ornate railing: a dowager making the best of her bone structure and a few pieces of jewellery. Their names, Mr Milner and Miss Fortune, produced a peculiar flurry at the top of the stairs in the roomy, tomby hall: the maid peered uncertainly up as if wondering whether to deny that there was anyone at home after all; but presently, with an audible hiss of 'Oh, *Mother*!' Matthew Downey himself descended out of the gloom, with a smile as warm as a carnival vizard.

'Mr Milner – Miss Fortune – this is so very unexpected, you must excuse . . .' He did not say what they must excuse, but stood irritably rubbing his neck and glancing about him. 'Hannah, is there a fire lit in the drawing room?'

'Not as I know on,' said the maid, stumping away.

'Perhaps you'll be so good as to step into the study, if my papers won't incommode you. I was studying late last night. Mother . . .' He waited until he could shut the study door behind them. 'My mother is a little flustered, and presents her apologies – that is, I do.' Matthew, unshaven and unbrushed, his collar-points wilting, looked a little seedy. There was a brandy-bottle amongst the tumble of books and papers on the desk, which he successfully drew attention to by grabbing it, trying to fumble it into a drawer, and dropping it on the carpet. 'The fact is . . . Mother was somewhat fearful on hearing your name, Mr Milner, that you had come to remonstrate with her.'

'Remonstrate? At this hour of the day, I can't even remember what the word means,' Stephen said.

'You are very good,' Matthew said, with his usual regretful frown at the introduction of humour, 'but I'm sure you take my meaning. Indeed I cannot otherwise account for this unprecedented call – welcome though it is,' he added sepulchrally.

'We came, Mr Downey, because we were in Town, and we simply wished to pay our compliments, and above all to say that we are sorry about your aunt's death – and sorry also for the sequel.'

'Exactly,' Matthew said heavily. 'And the sequel includes what my sister has done. Believe me, Maria has shocked us all – but that is no excuse. The fact remains she has married the man who was to have married Miss Milner – and that is why, sir, my mother is so embarrassed—'

'Oh! Lord, she needn't be,' said Stephen, soothingly. 'Believe me, sir, that matter is all settled, and I don't intend any remonstrance: not that you and your mother had any part in Miss Downey's action anyhow. For my part, I wish the new Mrs Leabrook well, as I'm sure you do.'

'Wish her well?' cried Matthew, with a stare and a flourish of nostrils. 'I wish her ill, Mr Milner – nothing but ill!'

'Come, I'm sure you don't mean that,' Caroline said. 'It must have been a great blow when Mrs Catling – did what she did with her fortune; for you had indeed been a devoted nephew. But that was her choice, or rather say her caprice, and Maria really can't be blamed for that.'

'I see you do not know the half of it,' Matthew intoned, slumping into a seat, and then removing a broken tobacco-pipe from under him. 'Forgive this appearance. What you see, Miss Fortune, Mr Milner, is a flattened man. I have been run over by the speeding chariot of fate, and caught up in its spiked wheels.'

'I hate it when that happens,' said Stephen.

'If it were only my late aunt's extraordinary coldness to me in the matter of testamentary dispositions – though that, by the by, I can still scarcely believe . . .'

'Mr Downey, I should say I had the honour of meeting Mrs Catling, not long before her decease,' Stephen said, 'and if it's any consolation, I would surmise she had not then quite the strength and clarity of mind for which I believe she was famed. So—'

'Do you think then I could contest the will?' Matthew burst out, his eyes kindling: then he slumped again. 'No, of course not: too late: it was watertight. She saw to that. Oh, yes . . . Miss Fortune: I am glad of this opportunity. I wish to say something to you. I owe you – an apology.' This cost him a visible effort. 'Yes, an apology. That time at Wythorpe – I fear I jumped to conclusions. Entirely erroneous conclusions, about who had betrayed the secret of my engagement to Aunt Sophia. I do have a hasty temper: but my brain is generally quick, and this I think is the reverse side of the quality . . .' But even dwelling on his idiosyncrasies could not cheer Matthew today: a thick sigh escaped his chest, and lowering his eyes he said: 'It was Maria. She was the one who told Aunt Sophia about my – about Perdita. It turns out – as I discovered only by accident, from a chance remark by the servant who takes in the post – that she has long been opening my letters. And one of them – a very tender, very private missive from Perdita – was even found among my aunt's effects, with an enclosure from Maria. So. Pray accept my apology, Miss Fortune – and consider me punished enough.'

'Oh, Mr Downey, I am so very sorry. That was a dreadful thing for Maria to do – I am disgusted, quite disgusted with her.' And Caroline meant it all, and wished she could banish the image of Mrs Catling's magisterially curling lip as she read a tender missive from Perdita of Snow Hill, because it was causing her own lips to twitch in quite another way.

'It is no matter, Miss Fortune. There is a last irony. My Perdita – is not my Perdita any more. She is false.' Matthew picked up a paper-knife, and seemed to contemplate doing something Roman and final with it. 'She has severed our connection, and turned to another. Indeed she is already affianced to him. He is a grocer and tea-merchant in the City – and not at all in a small way. Perdita informs me he has fifty yards of frontage.'

'A man stands no chance,' murmured Stephen, shaking his head in bitter agreement.

'I hardly know what to say,' Caroline said, discreetly treading on his toe, 'except again that I'm sorry, and – well, Mr Downey, it seems to me that almost everyone has acted in a deceitful and shabby and disgraceful way, except yourself. It may be difficult to see that as a satisfaction just now, but I hope that in time it may come to be so.'

'Thank you, Miss Fortune,' Matthew said, with rich despair, 'but I do not see how!' Yet there seemed to be a newly thoughtful look in his eyes as they left him amongst the folios and tobacco-fug; and Caroline was not without hope that in a few months' time he might be bowing to an amenable young woman at a carpet-dance, and talking about himself with as much interest and enjoyment as ever.

'Well, I think you were right,' Caroline said, as they took their places in the hackney once more. 'Leabrook and Maria Downey are very well matched, and I dare say will soon begin making each other as unhappy as they have made others.'

'Amen to that; and I have some moderate good news on that score. A letter from Isabella this morning, telling me the Leabrook story in her own honest fashion, assuring me she is in good spirits, and seeming – well, it's hard to be sure in a letter, but seeming quite strong and sensible. Augusta, she says, has been a great help to her – and also Captain Brunton, which is a surprise. Are they rubbing along better now?'

'They are rubbing along very much better: and besides, Captain Brunton is in love with Isabella, and has been for a long time.'

'The devil he is! Why – why did he never say?'

'Discretion, Stephen – have you no notion of discretion?'

'I suppose not. Hm. Well, she does ask in this letter, as I have been everywhere in the kingdom, what Falmouth is like.'

'That's where Captain Brunton is going: he has a post in the packet service.'

'Well, well. I wonder . . .'

'So do I: but let us just have quiet hopes. One wouldn't wish to tempt Fate, when everything has turned out so well.'

'Turned out well? I don't know about that: I don't know that I can quite echo your satisfaction, Miss Fortune. Turned upside down is the phrase I would use to describe my world since you arrived in it: truly there has never been a moment's peace. There is only one thing for it. You will have to marry me directly, as you are surely as much in love with me as I am with you: and I am the only one who can restrain you, my darling Caroline, from creating disaster wherever you go.'

'This is . . .' She looked at him. 'This is . . .' She looked everywhere but at him: out of the window at the glistening streets. 'This is Covent Garden.'

'Yes, I know a good jeweller's here, and really we must do something about that ring. May I take it off?'

Inert yet trembling, she gave him her hand. 'I don't understand,' she said.

'Insanely soft skin. What don't you understand?'

Everything: nothing: her mind was somewhere off circling in space, and could only grab at something in passing. 'When I said I didn't know why I cared about Matthew, you said you knew why. And I didn't understand.'

'Oh, yes, I knew: I knew why you cared: because that's you: because in spite of your manifest faults and weaknesses, which I have always been kind enough to point out to you, you are still, Caroline Fortune, the dearest, warmest, most generous, and good-natured, amusing, entrancing, and bewitchingly beautiful woman in creation.'

'Oh . . .' Abruptly she seized his hands in wild, absurd excitement. 'Oh, Stephen, what are we going to do?'

'After the ring, you mean? I suggest follow the prevailing fashion, and go to Doctor's Commons for a marriage licence. After that, we shall live, love, and be happy as mortals can be: we shall drink and make merry, we shall be silent and watch the herons, we shall go to the races and go to blazes, we shall talk as only you and I can talk—'

'Not all the time, though. There is a time for not talking.'

'There is assuredly a time for not talking. But now, Miss Fortune, I must ask you for a formal answer, for as this is the only proposal I ever intend making I don't want it wasted – though you must excuse my not going down on bended knee in the approved fashion – constriction and motion of the hackney-carriage makes it at the very least inadvisable, you know – risk of being pitched forward and inadvertently anticipating the intimacies of the wedding-night—'

'Oh, Stephen,' she cried, laughing and weak, 'you mustn't keep – keep *blinding* me with words!'

'It's the only thing I can do.' (With melancholy resignation.)

'Why?'

'Well, I would prefer to do the blinding with a kiss, for example: but I can't rely on my powers to do so.' (In a tone of frank explanation.)

'Understandable: but if you wish to make the experiment, I shall submit.' (Sturdily.)

'Very well: thank you, I shall try: though I have no great hopes . . .'

'Stephen?'

'Yes, my darling?'

'I can't see a bloody thing.'

G